# THE REBEL OF SEVENTH AVENUE

ANNABELLE MARX

Storm
PUBLISHING

Ebook ISBN: 978-1-80508-994-0
Paperback ISBN: 978-1-80508-996-4

Cover design: Eileen Carey
Cover images: Arcangel, iStock, Shutterstock

Published by Storm Publishing.
For further information, visit:
www.stormpublishing.co

## Also by Annabelle Marx

*The Herbalist's Secret*

*For all the garment workers, everywhere.*

'The model he imagines is, first and foremost, a beautiful object, excellently made and finely sewn; so that if, years afterwards, it were discovered at the back of some cupboard, although the fashion which inspired it has long gone out of date, it would still inspire astonishment.'

*Survey of Parisienne Couture 1956*, Celia Bertin

# Prologue

'I haven't seen this in over forty years.' My voice breaks slightly as I watch Mandy, my ever-faithful carer, minder, and friend, put the box on the table in front of me and carefully undo the faded ribbon, pulling off the lid and putting it to one side. I hold my breath as she pulls back the tissue paper and reveals a swathe of yellow chiffon.

'Shall I lay it out on the table?' Mandy asks.

I put my hand out to touch the fabric. As I nod my head, unable to speak, I catch a faint aroma of my old boarding-house room: candlewax and mould.

Cautiously, Mandy picks up the fabric, puts the box on the floor and lays it out on the table. A full-length gown, made from a pale-yellow chiffon with a yellow satin sheath under-dress. The chiffon is cut in a wrap style, swathed from the waist to the hem and then pulled upwards again at the back. There's a chiffon belt that sits on the high waist. The long, tight-fitting sleeves are finished with a deep cuff of the same yellow satin, which is pointed on the top of the hand.

'If you don't mind me saying so,' says Mandy, 'this seems

very unlike any of the other dresses and coats and skirts that we've been going through. This seems very...' She hesitates.

'Bland,' I say matter-of-factly.

'Well, I wasn't going to put it quite like that, but now you say it.' Mandy laughs nervously.

I lean forward and pick up the belt on the dress, also made from the same colour chiffon. I rub my finger along the irregular pleats and concealed fastening. 'I made this thinking it would become my wedding dress, thinking I'd make something that, on the surface, looked conventional.' I pause as my breathing becomes loud and a little erratic. I blink hard several times before continuing. 'Pale yellow was the closest I was ever going to get to wearing white for my wedding, but I also decided to make it a dress with a dual personality, because, you know me, I don't like to be predictable.'

I turn over the belt to reveal the reverse made from a burnt-orange slubbed silk and the initials M & J embroidered intricately onto the centre of the belt.

'I made a double-sided belt so that once we were married, I intended to turn it over and show off a little bit of my personality. I did the same with the cuffs.' Carefully I turn the pointed satin cuffs back on themselves to reveal the exact same embroidered initials. I run my thumb over the metallic gold and copper threads, picking at the tiny jet seed beads, pulling at the one pink crystal bead that seems a little out of place. My gaze deepens, no longer on the dress, somewhere behind it, remembering his smooth skin, the smell of his workshop, that smile, the way he so deliberately rolled his shirtsleeves up.

'And then there was the under-dress.' My heart is now racing as I pull away the chiffon to reveal the daffodil-yellow satin and pick up the side seams, showing Mandy the smaller embroidered initials, interspersed with tiny yellow daffodil heads running all the way down the sides of each seam.

'Oh, these are so sweet. They must have taken hours to sew.'

Mandy puts her glasses on and studies the embroidery. 'Why did you spend so much time on the under-dress when no one would see it?' But before I can speak, she answers her own question. 'Oh, I get it.' She smiles. 'Your husband would see it on your wedding night. He'd see all the effort you put into it.' But then she frowns and puts her head on one side, her eyes narrowing. 'But you didn't ever marry...' Her voice trails off and she looks back down at the dress.

'No, I never married.' I sigh, the memories clouding around me. Eventually I pull myself out of the reverie and say, 'If I had, I fear that I'd have ended up making bland dresses like this. As much as I loved him, it would have stifled me, I think it would have drained me of all my colour.'

## Chapter One

### The Mourning Dress

*A black suit made from Henrietta cloth comprising a long, tailored jacket and matching dress. The jacket has three sets of detachable collars and matching cuffs made from crepe, velvet and black lace respectively, so that the suit can be made to look different on each wearing.*

# Maw

## Edinburgh 1902

The day there was an urgent knock at the door was the day my life began to form, the day the first permanent stitch was cast.

Two burly men hauled our mother through the door. Her left eye was bruised, her skin sweaty and the colour of crumpled calico, her leg set in a surprisingly neat and clean splint. Before we could ask about their grim expressions and the state of our mother, a woman strode in behind them. Everything about her radiated impressive authority, from her rigidly austere posture to the cut of her silk dress that probably cost more than every item of our imposed threadbare wardrobe.

The woman surveyed the scene in front of her.

Our one-room apartment may have been spotlessly clean, but our tenement block was old and crumbling, with damp walls and cracking plaster. This was a room that housed three people who couldn't afford anything other than the necessary; we didn't have a comfy chair for our guest, there was no sofa to recline on, no pretty bedcover to brighten the atmosphere. She would have seen Maw, now lying on the only cot in the room,

Netta standing open-mouthed at the range, her wooden spoon suspended above the frying pan, me with my back to the wall holding my breath, trying to become as small as possible. She'd have noticed the sparsity, the dim corners and worn floorboards, the cupboard with the door slightly askew.

Her face was quizzical as if she was unable to understand the life that we lived, so used was she to her own cushioned world of abundant light, well-aired rooms and plentiful food.

The men retreated whilst the woman walked over to our small kitchen table, pulling out the only proper chair in the room, and sat on it.

'Children,' she said, her voice wavering between command and plea. 'Perhaps you could sit, I must discuss your mother with you.'

Netta and I glanced at each other before carefully sitting on the cot, close to Maw. She winced, her face grey and clammy, her eyes too bright and her breath shallow.

'I am Mrs Robertson, your mother's employer.' She gave us a pinched look that emphasised the dark circles under her eyes. 'And you are...?'

Netta glanced at me, gesturing with her eyes for me to speak first.

'I'm Maisie, ma'am,' I stuttered, 'and this is my sister, Netta... ma'am.'

Mrs Robertson gave us a condescending smile. 'Now, you must listen to me carefully as I won't repeat myself.' She pulled herself upright, taut, as if she was a rubber band that had been pulled to its limits, waiting to be let fly. 'Your mother has had an accident. Her left leg has been badly broken during a fall. The doctor has seen to her, put a splint on her leg and given her some laudanum. She mustn't put any weight on the leg for at least four weeks. It will be your job to see that she does just that.'

She turned to our mother. 'Now, Dorothy.' Here she hesitated, uncertainty and insecurity beginning to seep from her pores, a marked contrast to the woman we'd let into the room. 'I am sorry for all that has happened to you. The doctor tells me that you may have difficulty walking from now on.' She swallowed loudly.

Maw was quiet, her eyes narrowed in suspicion, waiting to hear what was to come next. Mrs Robertson fidgeted with the gloves in her hands, almost as if she was wringing out a wet handkerchief.

'I saw what happened; I saw what my son did to you. I saw you fall.' Her voice had dropped almost to a whisper.

My twelve-year-old mind began to gallop, I thought that my maw must have tripped over one of her son's toys. Maybe, because of Mrs Robertson's tone, maybe her son did it on purpose: a sly little boy putting a wheeled wooden toy in the way of a servant, just for fun, just to see what happened. That would be the worst of it, wouldn't it?

Maw said nothing, her hands balling up the edge of the sheet. I looked down at my lap, my legs swinging below the bed. The tension between the two women was almost a physical presence, as if there was a fifth person in the room. Eventually, Mrs Robertson broke that strain.

'I saw him push you down the stairs.'

And then she relaxed, her hands setting the gloves still onto her lap, she bowed her head slightly giving a long and slow breath out. It was as if she'd just had a tooth extracted and now she could carry on with her life, the pain removed, and the problem solved.

The room was silent, the three of us waiting for more. Only the everyday sounds of our building intruded: a crying baby, a running tap, footsteps outside our door. I couldn't look at Maw, keeping my eyes on my swinging legs, the rhythm soothing me.

'Oh, do keep still, child.' Our visitor's sharp tone made me blush, almost bringing tears to my eyes.

'My family do not know I'm here,' Mrs Robertson continued quietly.

Maw took a breath as if she was about to say something, but she was interrupted by her employer.

'And nor will they.' Now there was steeliness in her tone before she again changed to remorse. 'My family has ruined your livelihood. And for that I am sorry. Wilcox tells me that your husband left you years ago and that you rely on the income you receive from us.' As she said this, one of the men returned carrying several large packages and a dark-wooden box with a handle on top. He left these on the table and looked to his mistress.

'Thank you, Wilcox. That will do for the minute. Wait for me at the carriage.' She dismissed him with a wave of her hand and he again left the room.

Maw tried to draw herself up, a strange look on her face that I couldn't understand, before wincing from the pain of the movement. She stayed half propped up on her elbows.

'Girls, the doctor will visit regularly to make sure your mother is healing. He will keep a good eye on you, Dorothy. You have been a good worker, and a loyal servant in a time when our family is facing difficulties, when scandal could easily destroy us. I would like to repay you for your faithfulness, and also give you the best chance of a full recovery. Whilst you are recuperating, Wilcox will bring food, he will take your laundry and deliver it back the following day, he will see to it that you have enough coal to last for at least the next six weeks. On the table is a casserole from Cook, some eggs brought up from the farm this morning, two fruit cakes and a plate of Cook's best scones.'

She stood up and turned to the table. 'But you can't live off my charity forever.'

Looking at the dark-wooden box she began to unclip the fasteners at the bottom. 'I want to make sure that you have a way of supporting yourself, Dorothy, that doesn't require too much physical effort. I am worried that your leg may not heal as it should, that you might find the strains of working in a house such as ours too much. To compensate, I have bought you the latest Singer.' She lifted the coffin lid from the box to reveal a black and gold painted sewing machine. From the package beside it, she pulled out a small green booklet with a large red 'S' on the front cover. She read.

'Singer Sewing Machine No. 28. Vibrating shuttle for family use.' She began flicking through the booklet. 'Apparently, it comes with two bobbins, two shuttles plus needles of various sizes. This booklet gives you full instructions, showing you how to use it. I will be sending you a package of other items you'll need, such as pins, a pin cushion, a measuring tape, tailor's chalk, cutting scissors, and threads of various colours.' She put the book down. 'I will also send over the wherewithal to complete your first commission. I know you are a competent seamstress; my lady's maid tells me you have helped her with some of the hand sewing, so I'm sure you can master a sewing machine. Your timing is fortuitous; my dressmaker has recently had some trouble or other.' Here she batted the trouble away with her hand, as if it was no concern of hers. 'I will soon be needing new undergarments: new chemises, drawers and petti-coat-skirts. I will provide you with enough calico, cotton and lace plus the required patterns, and my necessary measure-ments. If you prove proficient at making these I may commis-sion further work, dresses and outer garments, and might even recommend you to the ladies in my circle. But let's not get ahead of ourselves.'

I turned to Maw. Her mouth was slightly open, her cheeks now flushed, and she was blinking very fast. If I hadn't known my mother so well, I would have thought she was about to cry. But my mother never cried.

'It should take about six weeks for your leg to heal if you look after it properly. As you will be unable to work during that time, I will see to it that your rent is paid. Now, girls,' – and here she looked at me – 'I expect you to nurse your mother with care. She is your breadwinner. She will be able to give you a good life if you let her rest and recover from this accident. And don't you forget that it *was* an accident.' She glared at Netta, to me and finally to Maw. 'Your mother tripped and fell down the stairs. If I hear a whisper of malicious gossip, I will know it came from you and I will simply take away my custom.

'Once the six weeks are up, I will expect my new undergarments to be delivered within two weeks. That should be plenty of time to familiarise yourself with the machine and learn what's needed. I know you are a good learner, Dorothy, I fully expect you to make the most of this opportunity.'

She stood and swiftly made her way to the door, before turning back and fixing her eye on Maw.

'You must never tell anyone who gave you this sewing machine, who paid for your doctor or provided your food. When you have finished the garments, you must never come to the house yourself; send one of your daughters. Nobody must know of this connection, not even the staff. They already know too much.'

She pulled down her veil, tugged on her gloves and left as quickly as she had come in.

The three of us were silent for what seemed like several minutes. I was struggling to understand what had just happened, but I could tell by my mother's wide eyes and her inability to speak that something important, something life-changing had just occurred.

Finally, Maw threw her head back on the bed and let out a full-throated belly laugh, a bitter, unfamiliar laugh, that frightened me.

'She would like tae repay *me* for my faithfulness.' She spat the words out. 'More like she wants tae pay me off, keep me quiet.' Her tone was sour. 'I'm not proud. I'm happy tae take what she's giving. There's plenty others who'll give up that weasel of a son.'

I shivered at her hostility, so often her reaction to the mere hint of charity, to the suggestion that we were too poor to look after ourselves.

To distract myself, I moved over to the table to look at the sewing machine. To my untrained eye, it was a thing of beauty: the intricate gold decoration and swirling text painted on the black, smooth, rounded surfaces, the highly polished hand crank, the inlaid pattern on the metal panels. I ran my hand over the top of it and peered at each individual part, so intricate, delicate, and mysterious. I had never known an object of utility to be so exquisite.

Whilst someone else did our laundry and delivered our food, Netta went to work at her new job at the North British Hotel. Fresh vegetables in abundance, newly baked bread and more meat than we'd ever eaten in our lives meant that Netta lost her pallid look, Maw healed quickly, and I learned the feeling of fullness after a meal. The plentiful food improved our mother's mood so much that she appeared to quickly forget the hostility of our encounter with Mrs Robertson and the fatigue of her life before.

'Maw, you need tae stay in bed,' I grumbled on yet another day away from school, the room shrinking in inverse proportion to the amount of time I spent there. I wanted to be at school, to learn, not entertain our mother.

'Hmph,' she muttered. 'I'm bored, I need tae do sommit. I cannae stay here just looking at you.'

I too was bored. I'd cleaned everything, several times over, the dinner was cooked, waiting for Netta to come home, there was no longer any washing to do. Already Maw had unwound two old pullovers and used the wool to knit a new cardigan for me, my doll had two new sets of clothes made from an old dress I'd grown out of and she'd re-trimmed Netta's summer hat with the remaining dress fabric. All our socks were darned, and her torn petticoat mended. She was sitting up in her bed fidgeting. If she didn't have some sewing or knitting in her hands she would always be restless. There was still one more week to go until she was allowed to put weight on her leg.

'Why don't we get the sewing machine out and see if we can make it work?' I suggested. We'd both been eyeing up that dark-wooden box, with the handle on top, sitting on the table; it had been like a warder, watching us, perhaps waiting to see if we would disobey the doctor's instructions, sneak on us, tell Mrs Robertson to take it back, its new owners not worthy of its beauty and value.

'Aye. Lemme get at it.' She wriggled to the edge of her bed.

'No, you have tae stay there.' I went over to the table and unfastened the clips before pulling up the deep coffin lid that covered the machine and putting it away behind the chair.

'Maw, you take the booklet and read it to me. I'll lay out all the pieces on the table and we'll work out which bits go where.'

I dragged the table as close to the bed as I could. I pulled out the shuttle, and the bobbin, we inspected the threads we'd been given, I found a needle and Maw haltingly read the instructions showing me how to set it into the machine correctly. I spun the hand wheel slowly and we both watched the needle bob up and down. Then we learned how to thread the machine, discovering new words as we worked, wondering at the crisp, shining parts that we were handling. Next, we had to wind the silk thread onto the bobbin, place it in the shuttle and thread it. Finally, I dropped the shuttle into the base of the machine and pulling the lower thread up we were ready to sew.

Maw read slowly, articulating each word as if she'd never heard them before. 'Place the material tae be sewn beneath the presser foot, lower the latter, and commence tae sew by turning the hand wheel over towards you.'

I did as she said, slowly turning the wheel. Gradually the cream calico scrap I was using moved towards the back of the machine. The gentle clatter of the moving parts, the eyelet jogging up and down, the jerking thread, the neat, straight stitches on the fabric. I had never seen anything like this. The continual motion of many connected pieces, the way each part of the machine worked in harmony to produce this neat line of thread became hypnotic. I felt as if I was caught in some kind of spell, the magic of the machine holding me in a strange state of suspension.

'Come on, hen, show me.' Maw squirmed with impatience. I cut the threads and handed her the scrap of fabric. I'd folded it in half before I put it through the machine, and now I pulled it open to the stitch line, showing her the neat finish: no holes, no loops of thread, all in one straight line.

Quickly she put it down. 'I dinnae care what the doctor says, it's ma turn.'


At the beginning, Maw wasn't a quick learner. There were days when knots of thread had to be cut out of the shuttle carrier, needles snapped as she forced too much material through the machine, thread broke, fabric would end up puckered. But she was a methodical learner who never gave up, so that by the time the six weeks was up, she was fully proficient in using the machine, had understood when the thread's tension needed changing, what size needle was required when. In time she would become an accomplished seamstress – she savoured mastering a skill, a skill that was beyond beating a carpet or polishing the brass.

Her first commission was delivered exactly on time and was steadily followed by more orders from Mrs Robertson and, eventually, other customers appeared on her recommendation. Nothing too showy to start with: shirts, underclothes, the occasional day skirt. Maw would take me to these women's houses to measure up; her leg never healed well enough to kneel or bend down for any length of time. So, I learned how to measure the body, understand where the tailoring was required. Then she moved on to show me how to pin and baste the pieces of garment, hand-sew a hem and how to cut pattern pieces to save the most material. Whenever I could get her away from the machine, I began to use it to make my own clothes, occasionally taking instruction from Maw, but soon I was as capable as she.

One evening, after we'd eaten our supper and Maw was finishing a pair of men's pyjamas, we received a parcel. We were used to packages of fabric being delivered, it was a regular occurrence, and this was just as we were expecting: the material, pattern and threads required for a new garment. But we'd been waiting with a little more anticipation for this one. Mrs Balfour, a new customer, was giving our mother her first commission for an evening gown.

Clearing a space on the bed, I untied the string and pulled away the paper. Inside was a cloth of a bright tomato red. I carefully drew it out and spread the fabric across the bed. It was a colour never seen in that room, so bold, too brash, like a bloody gash on a sallow skin. Holding it up to the gaslight, I was surprised by the shine of it, how there seemed to be more than one colour, a sheen of a thousand different reds all gathered together. It had a smooth, waxy feel to it, oozing elegance and luxury, despite the audacious colour.

'This won't suit Mrs Balfour,' I said, matter-of-factly.

'What d'you mean?' Maw snapped at me, accusation in her eyes.

'This would suit a woman with dark features and dark-brown hair. Mrs Balfour is pale; her face is like a white sheet. She'd look ill wearing this.'

'How can you know that?' She leaned towards me. 'How can you know? When did you last go tae the Assembly Rooms for a dance?' Her voice was mocking.

I looked at Maw and shrugged. 'I just know it. Look.' I picked up the fabric and took it over to my sister. 'Netta has dark eyes, darker skin than mine, and reddy-brown hair.' I held the fabric up against her face. 'See, this makes you look warm and healthy. But if I put it against Maw's face' – and here I did just that, against her pale skin and faded red, almost grey hair – 'it makes you look as if you havenae seen daylight for weeks.'

She stared at me. 'You cannae say that. It's all blether. And who are you tae say what would suit our customers?' She huffed in dismissal. 'Mrs Balfour wants a dress in bright red, she can have a dress in bright red. She can have it in bright orange with pink spots, for all I care. She's paying me tae make the gown she wants; she's nae paying me tae have an opinion about how she looks, and ma daughter disnae have an opinion either. You just do as you're told. Put that away and get ready for bed.'

Later, as Netta and I lay on our bedroll, waiting for sleep to come, she turned over and whispered in my ear, 'What colour would suit her?'

I thought. I envisaged Mrs Balfour: a pale, big-boned woman, who stooped to hide her height. 'A deep purple, but I'd use a velvet, not a silk.'

Netta continued working at the North British and when I left school at thirteen, I also started work with my sister: long, hard days in the steamy laundry rooms that I hated, my hands red and raw. I didn't like the girls that worked there. They spent their days gossiping and giggling; all they wanted to do was bag a man and start a family so they could get out as soon as possible. I would have rather stayed at home and helped Maw with her sewing, but there wasn't enough work, nor was there enough room, and at thirteen you aren't given a choice. You do the work you're lucky enough to find and take the money handed to you.

Now that Maw was making gowns out of more expensive fabric, she needed more space so that it could be better cared for and not get caught up in our laundry, dinner dishes and bedding. With the damp walls, rough wooden floors and mouldy plaster, we had to be careful that the fine silks and linens were not ruined.

But with three of us earning we found that we could afford to move into the next-door apartment giving us one extra room.

One additional room, when you've been used to living in one small space, felt as if we'd been given extra gravy with our dinner every day. Maw could shut herself away in the bedroom with her bed, the sewing table and her new dressmaker's dummy. Netta and I still shared our bedroll in the main living area, but we no longer had to listen to the light snores of our mother or block out the greasy gaslight when she had to stay up working late. With her door shut, the whir of the sewing machine was slightly muffled, and we didn't need to worry about the possibility of treading on precious fabric when we were getting ready for bed. Maw's room was kept religiously tidy: there was never a shoe out of place, her few clothes were neatly folded into the cupboard, and her bed was never rumpled, almost as if she never slept in it; the sewing machine was oiled and polished every week, the scissors and threads always put away; the dressmaker's dummy stood in the corner of her room, the elegance of the half-finished gowns it wore always so out of place in that shabby but immaculately clean room.

Predictably, my sister soon met her husband. Duncan Wood was a carpenter at the hotel. She misinterpreted his good manners and tender gestures – a stolen daffodil from Princes Street Gardens, a pair of socks knitted by his mother –

as creative and ambitious intentions. The truth was that Duncan was lazy in an oafish but endearing way, and had less money than we did. His family were so overcrowded in their home that he couldn't wait to move in with us, thinking two rooms for just four people was nothing but the height of luxury. And just like the other girls in the laundry, Netta thought marriage was an easy way out of a life of drudgery and found herself married at eighteen because she was pregnant.

My relationship with Netta became more complex. Her desire to have five children and a continual life of wiping snotty noses and washing her husband's dirty underwear filled me with dismay.

'Don't you think you're just swapping one laundry for another?' I said one afternoon, as we were hanging the sheets out in the yard at the back of the tenement.

Netta snorted. 'I'd rather be washing ma own sheets than those of some la-di-dah gentleman who probably had sex on them three times the night before. At least I'd know who'd had sex on ma sheets.' And here she shrieked with laughter.

I pegged the sheet with extra force. 'But...'

'Nae, Maisie, away with you and your dreams. This is our life; get on wi' it.' She picked up the tin of pegs and began walking up the stairs, back to our rooms. 'Your heid is filled wi' those lies from our cousin Aileen.' She sniffed as she pushed open our door, me running after her.

'Why would you say that? She's in New York!' I said. 'She's working in New York.' I couldn't help the wonder in my voice. 'And it's not in a laundry.'

'She's a lazy good-fer-nothin'. Aye, and that so-called husband of hers. I bet you, if you somehow' – and here she rolled her eyes – 'got yourself onto a boat to America, and went tae see her, you'd see she's full of shite.'

'No, no, no. You're wrong.' I opened the drawer of the

kitchen table and took out a small pile of letters. I picked up the top one, took it out of the envelope and unfolded it.

'Listen to what she says.' I read out the letter.

*I've started a new job in a chocolate factory. Donald is happy because whenever he kisses me, he can smell the chocolate. The girls in the factory say I'll get sick of the smell, they say they never want to eat chocolate again, but they're wrong. I wake up smelling of chocolate and I go to sleep smelling of it. My hat smells of chocolate, my petticoats and my handkerchief.*

'See,' I said, folding the letter back into its envelope.

Netta put down her pile of laundry and, for a moment, she was my sister again, not some harried mother who never had time to take a breath. 'Maisie, my wide-eyed sister, who has big dreams and high notions.' Her voice was soft, just like when we would share a bedroll, just like when we'd whisper our dreams to each other in bed at night. 'She'll be living in some run-down tenement, doing the laundry just like you an' me. Letters are for telling lies and the sooner you learn that, the sooner you'll realise that this is the life we are supposed to lead. Now, could you get on and peel those tatties like you said you would?'

Some days, after a shift at the North British I'd have to bandage my hands, they were so red and raw from the long days in the steamy laundry rooms, stirring vats of stained bedsheets and wine-splattered tablecloths, the soap not agreeing with my skin, the heat exacerbating the irritation.

'Laundry work isn't for ma Maisie's fine hands,' Maw would say as she gently rubbed Vaseline jelly into my hands. When the skin was too raw, I'd just watch Maw at her sewing machine and draw my own designs in my pocket notebook, coming up with ideas that she would scoff at. Other days, when my hands were better, I'd be allowed to work on Maw's commissions, but only under her steely, protective gaze.

'Maebe one day those fine hands will be able tae give up the laundry and make those curious designs you spend your days drawing, those strange Maisie McIntyre dresses. One day they'll be the making of you, never mind what Netta says.'

The rhythm of the needle, the treadle, the thread, these things smoothed out the rucks in my mind that a day in the laundry caused, the constant noise of Netta cooking, shouting at the girls, cajoling Duncan into helping with the chores. The softness of the material soothed the rough of my hands, the neatness of my stitches put away my resentment, giving way to a temporary calm.

Having the sewing machine meant that we could also make our own clothes. Previously we'd done this by hand, but now we could do it much quicker and, if I was clever, could make something that was a little more interesting than the traditional shirt-waist and skirt. But for Netta's two girls, Ava and Carla, Maw found the tiny armholes and collars too fiddly for her progressively arthritic fingers.

'I'll make them,' I said.

'Oh, nae you don't,' said Netta. 'I'll nae have you dressing ma girls in those fanciful clothes.'

I opened my mouth to protest but she continued.

'I'll nae have ma bairns in smocked dresses with ribbons an' bows an' all that fuss. We'll be the laughingstock of the street.'

Maw rolled her eyes at me on the sly, as Netta spoke, a complicit gesture that made me flatten my lips to suppress a smile.

'If you make anything for them, you make sure they're clothes that look exactly the same as every wee girl you see out there,' Netta continued, pointing towards the road. 'I wilna have ma girls standing out like some doll. Just because you like tae be different disnae mean that the rest of us do.'

It was at this point that I began to split into two, I became two different entities, two different people to fulfil two different roles. The first was Maisie McIntyre, the dutiful daughter who went to work at the North British, who put up with the monotonous, hot, mindless work, who came home and helped her mother with her dressmaking commissions. I was the one who went to the haberdasher's to buy the materials and fabrics, who made clothes for the family that set us in our place in society, that made sure we looked exactly as everyone expected us to. The second was the Maisie McIntyre who spent her time in the laundry designing dresses in her head, using every spare moment to watch the women of Edinburgh and how they dressed. I kept my notebook with me at all times; whenever I saw a belt, buckle or bow that was interesting I drew it, only to find myself later designing a dress that I thought it would work on. I studied women's shapes, what suited each type, and what didn't.

I learned to shift from one Maisie to the other, to switch from duty to desire, from everyday grey to vivid colours, to change from necessity to want.


'Maisie, I need you tae run a wee message down to Crawford's. I'm in' some o' thon green ribbon tae finish the cuffs on Mrs Balfour's new evening dress, some more o' this green thread and I could be doing wi' some new needles for the Singer. I've broken two already today. The tweed for Mrs Robertson's jacket is causing havoc on the machine, it's too thick.'

Maw held out a piece of paper with a pencilled list and a few coins. She wheezed at me as she spoke. 'I cannae go today. I'm no' up to scratch. This cold disnae wanna shift.'

If I'd been a good daughter, I'd have thought about my mother's health, but I only thought about the haberdasher's and how quickly I could get there. Going to Maurice Crawford's on

Cockburn Street was an errand I was always happy to run. There I could revel in the business of dressmaking; there I could discuss the merits of one fabric over another. But it wasn't even Crawford's that I wanted to see. If I could get my errand done quickly enough, I'd have a bit of time to run down the hill to...

'And none o' that disappearing off tae brood in Jenners. I've tae get Mrs Balfour's dress finished tonight and I'd like tae get it finished before dinnertime. Mind you come straight home.'

'Yes, Maw,' I shouted as I ran out of the apartment.

The fabrics hall at Jenners Department Store seemed to have an invisible thread that pulled me towards it, drawing me away from the chaos of our cramped living conditions, to a place where I could stroll amongst women who took leisure time and luxurious fabrics, warm clothes and dry shoes for granted. I could scrutinise the way they held themselves and analyse the styles of dresses being worn, I could touch the fabrics on display, feel how they would move, whether they were crisp like a taffeta or soft like a georgette. This became my library, my technical school, where I could learn about the materials required to dress a woman, their advantages and their disadvantages. I would hear snippets of conversation regarding the best way to finish a dress, which fastenings worked best for which part of a garment, when to use chiffon or organza.

Working in the laundry, I'd be in a tunnel of hot steam, harsh gossip and monotony – life seemed so narrow and constricted. But standing in the fabrics hall at Jenners, the high, glass roof spreading an optimistic light over the room, my pinched and spare world opened up as if someone had unlocked a box full of opportunities. Fashion, I came to realise, wasn't just about beautiful dresses, it was about self-respect, freedom of expression and power.

When I returned home that evening with paper bags full of ribbon, thread and needles, dinner was over, Maw in a fitful sleep, and Ava and Carla were in bed. Netta was finishing the washing up, Duncan reading the newspaper.

'Better wake our maw. She's got that gown to finish and she's nae happy wi' you.' Netta scowled. 'Yet again, Maisie McIntyre's dreams are more important than Maw's work. Do you have any idea how we'd manage wi'out the money her dressmaking brings in?'

But Netta wasn't going to ruin my afternoon of ideas. 'It's nae bother. I'll finish the dress; I know what's needed.' I put the bags on the table, removed my coat, kept my voice calm. I didn't want to antagonise my sister. 'No need tae wake Maw. And I'll package it up and deliver it on my way tae work tomorrow.'

Her mouth opened. She was brewing for a fight but held her tongue.

I wiped down the table, dried it off and then pulled out the green ribbon I had just bought. I began to lay it out, cutting it into short strips and then making it into a lattice. Velvet has a nap to it so that when it's placed in different directions, it looks almost as if it has two distinctive shades of the same colour. Quickly I made two lengths of green velvet ribbon lattice, four widths wide, long enough to create deep cuffs, looking like a discreet green checkerboard.

'What do you think you're doing?' Netta leaned over me to look at the ribbon. 'I thought Maw just needed the ribbon tae edge the cuffs she's already made?' Her voice was full of disdain. 'You're not doing another of your Maisie McIntyre trimmings are you?' She tutted. 'That'll put Maw in a flap. Tha's not what Mrs Balfour asked for.'

I closed my eyes, just for a moment. 'I know. But I saw a gown today that was finished in a similar way, and I thought it would look good on this dress. Mrs Balfour disnae mind if we do things a bit differently, she likes tae look like she can afford a more expensive seamstress.'

Netta picked up a pot from the side of the sink, dried it with the tea towel and slung it into the cupboard under the sink. The pan crashed as Netta slammed the door shut. 'Maisie McIntyre, always with a smart solution.'

The next morning, I was up early, tiptoeing around Maw, leaving her to sleep, avoiding the chaos of breakfast, not wanting to face Netta's criticism again.

That evening I came home to find a note to Maw from Mrs Balfour.

*Mrs McIntyre*

*I received your latest gown this morning. I was surprised at the changes, but I grant you, the dress is all the better for it.*

*Perhaps you could make yourself available next week. I'm in need of an outfit for my daughter's wedding and I'd appreciate your opinion.*

*Yours*
*Mrs Balfour*

'Hen, I didnae know what she was talking about, but Netta told me what you did. She thinks you're being too bold.' Maw stopped as she wheezed, putting her hand to her chest. She closed her eyes and took a few shallow breaths. 'Tell me about the ribbon. I want tae know.'

As I explained about the checker-board cuffs, the lines creased around her eyes, her chuckle interrupted by a cough.

'Ma Maisie.' She patted my hand and closed her eyes again.

'Maw? Are you well?' Our mother rarely showed affection. A nod of approval maybe, perhaps a discreet wink, occasionally a treat such as a penny bun or a piece of tablet, but almost never a spontaneous touch. No hugs, no linking arms on a walk, never a kiss goodnight.

'Aye, I'm well.' She sighed, patting my hand again. 'Never bin better.'

'Maw, should you be seeing a doctor?' I awkwardly kept my hand under hers, despite the cold emanating from it.

'I dinnae need the doctor. What I need is ma Maisie to go an' see Mrs Balfour. You take her on as your own customer; I've got too much else tae be doin'. Besides, she likes your strange Maisie McIntyre ways.' She gave me a far-off, enigmatic smile. 'I like your strange Maisie McIntyre ways too.'


Despite her protestations, Maw's so-called cold never did go away and her breathlessness increased. To make sure she could rest, I took on more of her work. I'd get the sewing machine out once everyone had gone to bed, leaving Maw to sleep on our makeshift bed, whilst I worked at the table late into the night. In that quiet time, I could be the Maisie I wanted to be. I could strip away the laundry girl, the chores and the babysitting and step into another world of colour and creativity.


Just a few weeks later, our maw died, in her sleep, aged forty-eight.

'Weak heart,' announced the undertaker in his monotone as he asked us what had happened. 'Breathlessness, tiredness, swollen legs, all classic symptoms.' It was almost as if he was pleased with his amateur diagnosis.

I watched the men take Maw's body away, remove the spirit of our home, the machine that stitched us all together. Small hands fitted into mine, warm, pudgy fingers searching for the comfort I couldn't find. I looked down at the girls.

'I have tae get tae work. I'll be late.' My voice was like some kind of automaton, mechanical and inhuman. I handed Carla to her father and gave the fidgeting Ava back to her mother. 'I need tae get dressed.' I was still in my nightgown, my hair still in its nighttime braid. I picked my way over the empty bedclothes, the crate full of dirty washing, slipped behind the kitchen table, pulled my work dress from the cupboard and shut myself in Netta and Duncan's bedroom. I pressed my forehead against the door, the walls seeming to draw closer with each breath. Outside, life crashed on – Ava knocked over her cup of water, Duncan's sharp rebuke, Carla's whine, Netta's distracted scolding. But in here, where time stood still, I was caught between what was and what could be.

I left without clearing Maw's bed, unable to touch the sheets that still held her shape. Outside on the street, the normality of life, the nonchalance of Edinburgh, felt like a hard slap. I walked fast, hoping the exercise would help untangle some of the tumult inside me, like a knotted ball of wool that becomes impossible to untie, the harder you try to ease the knot, the tighter it becomes.

The day after we buried my mother, I found myself sitting alone at Maw's sewing machine. It was a Saturday afternoon and Netta and Duncan had taken the children out to Holyrood Park to escape the gloom of the apartment, to let the girls stretch away from the silent strictures of mourning conventions.

My mother's sewing table sat in the corner of the main room, a sturdy table with thick legs and two wide drawers. The left-hand drawer held a haphazard jumble of pins, scissors, tailor's chalk, those kinds of necessary tools required for dressmaking, but the right-hand drawer was filled with spool after spool of neatly stacked thread, reels arranged on their side in rainbow order. That kind of military orderliness made me feel safe and in control. Living in such cramped conditions, I would always need to be tidy, folding my clothes, straightening the cutlery, ensuring the chairs sat exactly square to the table. When I felt out of sorts or frustrated, opening the thread drawer would give me some strange kind of comfort – I'd run my fingers along each spool, letting them spin, enjoying the shuffle of the soft wood of the spool dragging against the harder, dark wood of the drawer.

Maw would never again sit at this table, would never again thread this needle, or spin the hand wheel. My mother, who had taught me everything, who had sewn me together. Never again would I be able to watch her work – gathering, pleating, basting, stitching. Now it was me sitting at her table, knowing it was down to me to finish what she'd started.

There were three commissions, an evening dress, a mourning dress and a shirt that was almost complete. By now I knew my work was as good as my mother's, maybe better, I could easily finish those garments.

The machine had already been fully threaded by Maw, a pale-green thread matching the material of Mrs Robertson's almost-finished cotton shirt. I fingered the thread, ran my hands along the central barrel of the machine, knowing she had only been doing the same thing a few days ago. The green fabric had the faint earthy smell of my mother, that smell that still lingered on my bedsheet. It felt out of place that this shirt, handled so intimately by my maw, my dead parent, would soon be worn by someone else.

I took a deep breath and sat up straight. All I had to do was sew the collar before attaching it to the main body of the garment, a simple job. As I got to work the hypnotic sound of the machine helped the disquiet in my head, the needle and thread doing their job, the way the sewing machine parts all moved together in harmony, the needle dipping up and down, the reel of thread fitfully spinning, the smooth motion of the material – these orchestrated movements took me away from the cramped rooms and the new uncertainty of life without my mother.

I made quick work of finishing the shirt, but the two dresses would have to wait until everyone had gone to bed. With a sigh, I unthreaded the machine and put the bobbin and spool into their correct places in the right-hand drawer of the table, gave the machine a quick polish and put its lid on. I was unused to the eerie quiet; there was little noise in the building, most families out making the most of the fine weather. I didn't enjoy silence, inactivity always sending me into a melancholic downward spiral. With nothing else to do, I decided to tidy up the left-hand drawer. I pulled out the pins, needles, scissors, the thread hook, threw away some old scraps of material until I found Maw's collection of fabric samples. These were in a handmade book that she would take to customers to encourage them to buy. As I took this out, I discovered a beautiful fabric envelope lying at the bottom of the drawer. I picked it up, frowning at the yellow silk taffeta that I didn't recognise, at the red decorative frog and matching Chinese ball button. Carefully I undid the fastening and peered into the envelope. It was thick with five-pound notes.

Instinctively, I looked around to see if anyone had seen me. Of course, I was alone, nobody could see what I had found. Warily I pulled the notes out. They were crisp and unused, pristine and beautiful: blue and orange printed onto a yellow paper, intricate blue patterns on the left-hand side, the detail on the royal coat of arms breathtaking. As I admired the elaborate patterns, I slowly counted the sheaf of paper.

Thirty notes.

One hundred and fifty pounds.

I had never seen so much money, had rarely even seen paper notes, never even touched one. My heart was thumping and my hands clammy. I couldn't even imagine what this amount of money would buy. A horse? A house? Would we even be able to spend it? The shops we frequented only seemed to take coins. My fingers stroked the virgin notes, admiring the illusory quality, worrying that the sweat on my hands would make them vanish.

Where had this money come from? How did it come to be inside Maw's sewing drawer? She could never have earned that kind of money. Surely Netta knew nothing of it; she never went near the sewing table. There was no letter of explanation to help solve the mystery.

My heart was now beating so fast I could hardly breathe. I got up, just to be able to do something, to force air into my lungs, and began pacing up and down the tiny room.

This money was for our family, to make our lives better.

Turn.

Perhaps I could keep it all for myself.

Turn.

Should I tell Netta?

Turn.

But if I didn't, she'd never know. I could just leave and start my own life somewhere else.

Turn.

But if Maw had left it for us, she'd know what I'd done. Somehow, she'd know. I came to a halt. What should I do?

Standing in the middle of the room I heard footsteps on the stairs, voices: Netta and Duncan returning with the girls. Hurriedly, I gathered up the notes and, without thought, rolled them up and put them in my dress pocket, shoved the fabric envelope into the drawer and looked up to see Ava burst into the room.

'Auntie Maisie. Auntie Maisie. Look what we made.' A long daisy chain hung from her grubby index finger.

With one hand I took the daisies, crowing my delight, with the other I carefully removed Mrs Robertson's green shirt before Ava's other grimy hand could lean on it. Putting the shirt on top of the sewing machine I said, 'Well, hen, we must make a crown.' Swiftly, I turned the chain into a loop, making a hole in the end stem and hooking the daisy head from the other end into it.

'There, fit for a princess,' I said as I sat it on her golden-brown hair. Ava beamed, in that way that only very young children do, sticking out their stomachs, chins in the air, eyes alight.

Netta arrived, dark rings under her eyes, hair spilling from under her hat, face shimmering with sweat.

'Away wid you, Ava. I'm dunnin and I need some tea,' she said, dropping heavily onto the wooden chair by the table.

'I've got tae deliver this shirt tae Mrs Robertson,' I retorted, ignoring my sister's plea. The sudden claustrophobia of hot bodies in close proximity, the noise, gave me no space to think; I had to leave. Quickly I threw the sewing tools back in the drawer and folded the shirt before finding some paper to wrap it in. 'I need tae go before it's too late. Duncan can make the tea.'

'He widdnea how,' Netta said as he walked into the room.

I picked up my coat and the parcel. 'Well, now would be a good time tae teach him.'

On the street, I stopped to re-arrange myself. I tried to do up my coat buttons, but my hands were shaking. Instead, I took the coat off, it was too hot and I wasn't sure why I'd brought it.

With my coat hung over one arm, and the parcel under the other, the walk to New Town should have been soothing and distracting. Spring was having its effect on everyone: women displaying the new season's fashions, children skipping and laughing without worrying their parents, smiles on every face, brown paper parcels of Saturday afternoon shopping, flowers tentatively blooming, summer hats on their first outing of the year, trimmed with new ribbon. But I couldn't see any of it, couldn't appreciate the detail. It was as if I was enclosed in a smudged glass bubble.

In this strange haze, I made my way to Heriot Row and

delivered the parcel. But as I reluctantly began to make my way home, that invisible thread started to pull at me, pull me off course and soon I found myself standing in front of Jenners.

Without stopping to admire the window displays, I headed straight for the haberdashery department. Just looking at the lace in the glass counter gave me the sense of stability I needed. The coloured ribbons, the varying widths of elastic, the different sizes of scissors, the pinking shears, measuring tapes and tailor's chalk and the orderly way in which they were displayed started to make me feel at home, as if I was again in my own skin, in the place that I should be. I fingered a few of the buttons on display, pretending to see if they matched my coat, before stopping at the vast rainbow array of thread. Usually, I would run my finger along the display shelf that the reels lay on and breathe in the faint aroma of the colour. But something was out of place.

'Can I help you?' The officious voice made me jump.

'This spool of thread was in the wrong place; it was with the blues. I was just returning it tae its correct position.'

'I'm sure I can do that for you.' The sales girl's voice was sharp, as she pulled the green thread from my hand.

'Look,' I said, putting on my friendliest smile, 'it should go here, with its green friends.'

She looked me up and down, assessing my sweating face, my slightly rumpled shirt, the skirt, my old shoes. 'Is there anything else you'd like help with?' The chirpy question was in contrast to her look of distrust as she returned the spool to its correct home.

I shook my head and quickly walked towards the fabrics hall, annoyed at myself for being so meek, furious that a shopgirl could make me feel so small. I had no more intention of stealing the thread than she did.

But in the fabrics hall, I was quickly able to soothe the red of my cheeks and escape into the great cavern of riches, a huge room on the ground floor of the department store with a top-lit galleried saloon which rose to the full height of the building, throwing the day's sunlight over an array of colour. The room was busy with ladies poring over fabrics and patterns: a young woman with her mother, disagreeing over how much flesh could be exposed on her proposed new evening gown, an elderly woman matching buttons to a dark fabric, three girlfriends giggling over a selection of silks. The right side of the room was dedicated to an array of mundane cloth: towelling, linens, ticking, muslin and calico, the left side of the room housing the more magnificent fabric: brocaded silks and satin, wool and tweed, chiffon and crepe, organza and taffeta. Down the centre was an ever-changing display of the very finest of the materials, languorously draped to catch the light from above, to snag a passing admirer.

I'd never been in a position to afford these fine fabrics; I'd hardly ever dared look at them. Patting my pocket to check the roll of notes, my anger was quickly forgotten as my eye was caught by a bolt of decorated yellow silk. I pulled it out to look at it more closely, to check the pattern and see where the repeat came in, see how the light affected the weave, understand how the colour changed when the material moved. Standing in front of the nearby mirror, I held the silk up to my body and close to my face. Immediately I realised the colour was all wrong, but as I was putting the yellow material back on the counter, I was distracted by a bright shimmer of blue beside me, a startling colour that drew me greedily towards it.

Pulling out several yards I laid it on the countertop so I could see the true detail. It was a peacock-blue-green silk covered in an occasional repeating pattern of tiny birds, brown flecked with white and orange and some occasional metal thread, the birds' eyes red and beady, appearing to watch me. Despite the bright colour, there was a gravitas to the fabric that drew me in. The silk appeared to be faultless, not a line or slubbed knot in sight.

Quickly I pulled my notebook and pencil out of my coat pocket and started drawing, working up a design, a dress that would show the cloth to its best advantage. As I drew my heart beat faster, my drawing became hurried.

'Can I help you?' A salesgirl, probably the same age as me, interrupted my drawing trance. 'This is one of our finest silks, imported all the way from India and is hand woven.' The girl fingered it carefully, envy in her voice.

Wary of the way the previous salesgirl had treated me, I put on my best New Town accent. 'I'm considering making an evening gown.' I searched her sallow face for evidence of suspicion.

'What style?' Her eyes widened eagerly.

Relieved, I opened my notebook and showed her my sketch. 'I think I would give it short sleeves and swathe blue chiffon over the bodice. A low neckline would be edged in the same orange and brown as that of the birds. The skirt would be trained and the chiffon over the sleeves puffed. I'd add three tucks above the hem, some fabric-covered buttons to the back of the sash and make a couple of bold star flowers in the orange and brown and add one to the sash, another to the swathed chiffon.'

She wriggled with excitement. 'I've got just the right colour of organza for the edging, and we've recently had a new delivery of chiffons; I'm sure we can find the right colour to complement this blue.'

We both leaned forwards to get a better look, both carefully running our hands over the pattern. As we did this the girl became quiet, looking at my hands next door to her own, mine red and raw, slightly swollen, one of my fingernails ripped, hers pale and smooth, thin and elegant with neatly clipped nails. I felt a sudden rush of shame, that feeling when everything shrinks, your heart contracts, even your skin seems to shrivel.

'Can you afford this fabric?' she whispered to me, her face reddening.

I should have been grateful for her discretion, but the shame masked everything. My face blazed as I struggled to find the roll of money in my pocket. 'Aye, I... of course I can,' I stuttered loudly, drawing attention to myself. 'Look. I have more than enough money.' I thrust the roll of five-pound notes at her and as I did this they fell to the floor. Dropping my notebook, I scrambled to pick them up.

The girl fell to her knees to help me pick up the money, carefully piling up the notes, straightening them and then rolling them back up before handing them to me. 'Here. I'm sorry... I didn't mean...' Her blush was deeper than mine.

We both stood up to disapproving stares and whispering amongst the women close to us.

'Why don't I go to the haberdashery department and get you some half-inch buttons for covering with fabric, some blue threads for us to match to the material, and maybe some orange ribbon? And whilst I'm doing that perhaps you'd like to look at our range of chiffons,' the girl said loudly, pointing towards the rolls of fabric. Suddenly she winked at me, threw me a conspiratorial smile before trotting out of the room.

I straightened myself up and looked around. The women began turning away, back to their own business, but anger began to bubble up inside me, incomprehensible, irrational anger. The girl had tried to be discreet, had tried to help me, but the humiliation of it all, the way people stared, nudged each other, tutted, almost as if they were relishing the entertainment, made me behave in a manner I couldn't account for.

Slowly, deliberately, my hands shaking with resentment, I began to roll up the silk, making sure there were no folds in the cloth. Checking around me, I could see that all the other women and salesgirls had lost interest, no longer was I the centre of attention. Finally, closing my eyes for a second, I slipped my coat around the neatly rolled material. It was a little awkward to hold, as I was trying to make it appear as if the coat was hanging over my arm.

And then I walked out. Keeping that air of confidence and making myself breathe, I walked all the way through the fabrics hall but, just as I was being ushered out of the main entrance by one of the doormen, tipping his hat to me as I passed, just as I thought I'd made it, someone called after me.

'Miss! Miss!' My heart dropped to the floor as I turned, fully expecting some officious salesman to be chasing after the precious blue silk. I clung to my coat, awaiting my fate.

A gentleman, smartly dressed in a morning coat and top hat, held out one of my five-pound notes. He'd been running and was a little out of breath. 'You dropped this. You mustn't go without it.' He had that boyish, slightly red-cheeked look of someone who spends time outdoors. His eyes were gleaming with his good deed. 'Please, I believe this is yours.'

I searched his face for some hint of irony, some idea that he was laughing at me and was ready to show me up to the door-man, but I could see none. Confused, I took the note from him and haltingly said, 'Thank you.'

'My pleasure.' He did a little bow, tipped his hat, and then winked at me before returning to the shop.

I walked out onto the street, bewildered and occasionally checking behind me, taking a deep breath to gather my wits. Eventually I crossed Princes Street, trying to walk slowly, nonchalantly, past the Scott Monument and down into the Princes Street Gardens. It must have been about five o'clock. The shops were beginning to shut, picnicking families were thinking about going home, but there were still couples walking, caught up in each other, using the fine weather to eke out a few extra minutes together.

Sweat was pooling under my arms. My heart was racing and I couldn't bring it under control. I wanted to sit on one of the benches, to calm down, to watch the front entrance of Jenners, to see if policemen might be rushing in, rushing out, running after me, into the park, brandishing their truncheons, shouting and blowing their whistles. But I had to keep going, walking fast, urgently, fearful of someone seeing through me, recognising me for the thief that I was. Over Waverley Bridge, up Cockburn Street, not even glancing at Crawford's, wishing I could turn back and return the precious fabric. My hands became clammy and the roll of material was slipping out of its disguise. I had to stop and re-wrap it, worried my sticky hands would mark the silk.

'Watch where you're going, you fool!' a man shouted, just managing to avoid me where I'd stopped. I closed my eyes, trying to calm myself. I was sick, sick to death, of being seen as a dirty, grubby, stupid girl, who had no agency. This fabric was going to help me move on. This beautiful fabric and the implausible roll of money sitting in my pocket.

I smoothed my coat down and made myself walk slower, turned myself into just another person strolling along the street, emptying my mind of my thievery, until I reached Richmond Place. Here I willed myself into the good Maisie, the Maisie who helped her sister, who looked after her sweet girls, who didn't steal.


Just as the one hundred and fifty pounds became an oppressive weight in my pocket, the task of concealing the stolen silk became an all-consuming burden. Keeping a bolt of fabric hidden in a small tenement apartment, one that shimmers and almost irradiates colours that are rarely seen in such a place, is a task that cannot be underestimated. Colour is one of the differences in the rungs of society: grey, beige, brown, forest green, these are the colours at the bottom, the colours that sit comfort-ably with the sticky mud that the ladder sits in. As you rise up that ladder the colours become livelier and brighter: lawn green, sky blue, ruby red, sun yellow, fuchsia pink; these are colours for the privileged, these are colours that signify that you've landed in a world of extravagant dresses and comfortable beds. When those bright colours are spotted amongst the greys and the browns, they stand out, they tell the onlooker that some-thing is amiss. I had to keep that iridescent fabric well hidden, away from inquisitive nieces who would do their best to find what should not be found. I wrapped the fabric in some leftover ticking and pushed it to the back of the small cupboard close to my bedroll, hiding it amongst other leftover materials, waiting for the time when it could be used.

Keeping both money and cloth hidden had me continually on edge. When I was at the laundry, I'd spend every moment worrying that Netta would discover the fabric as she looked for a needle to darn her socks, or I'd be unnecessarily concerned that the other girls I worked with would find the roll of five-pound notes hidden in my skirt pocket. At night I'd lie, unable to sleep, going through every possible way of solving the situa-tion I found myself in: give all the money to Netta and throw away the fabric, give myself up to the police and go to prison, keep the money and fabric and leave.

After five days of little sleep and my mind caught in a never-ending whirl, the solution presented itself to me.

With supper over, I wanted to set about finishing the mourning gown that Maw had been making, the last of her commissions.

'Netta, could you not keep the bairns in the other room whilst I finish this? Is it not their bed time?'

She sighed loudly. 'Cannae we just have one night where we don't have tae tiptoe around the sewing? Cannae we just sit, maebe play a wee game o' cards and mend our clothes, just like we used tae? We'd play Snap, Maw'd darn, we'd argue, she'd tell us off. Ava and Carla, always having tae be clean and quiet. It's not the way bairns should be.' Her voice was sharp, her dark eyes narrowed in irritation.

'I have tae finish this. It's promised tae Mrs Foster tomorrow.'

'I'm sick o' that sewing machine, I'm sick o' the noise it makes, the space it takes up. I'm sick of treating those dresses better'n we treat the girls. Could you not be doing it later? When everyone's in bed?'

There was little left to do to the dress – sew the hem, add lace to the cuffs and some discreet beading on the collar – mostly hand work, but sewing black fabric by gaslight is difficult, the details disappearing in the shadows. I had good eyesight, but even this kind of work was testing to already tired eyes. It was early evening and there was still some good light to work by. I wanted to make the most of it.

But before I could argue, Netta said, 'Anyways, we have something tae tell you.' She turned to her husband. I couldn't quite work out the look on her face: pride, exhaustion, sadness, and happiness all rolled together. Duncan came over and sat down beside her.

'I'm in the family way again,' Netta announced, her chest puffed up and her chin jutting out like a proud bird who had outdone me, but there was a tone of despondency that she couldn't hide. Duncan, with his wide, helpless features, looked at the floor.

My heart sank. Another screaming baby, more washing, less space, more of my time taken entertaining the other bairns. The walls of the room again moved closer to me, the air thickening. But just as I'd recollected myself enough to be happy, exclaim my surprise and heartfelt delight, there was a knock at the door.

'A note for Miss Maisie McIntyre,' Netta taunted in a singsong voice as she shut the door, and before I could reach for it, she'd opened it and had begun to read. She shook her head, tutted, and whistled before waving it in front of me.

'Mrs Foster. Full payment for the mourning dress, but she'll nae have it. She'll not wear a dress made by a dead woman. Nae sewing to do,' she crowed with a sardonic grin on her face as she slapped the letter down on the table in front of me. 'She disnae know that Maw didnae make that dress. So what. Paid is paid.' She pocketed the coins that had come with the letter.

An unwanted mourning dress, a roll of five-pound notes, a sister who couldn't see the opportunity, another baby and a stolen bolt of luxurious silk in need of a rich client. These things were set out in front of me, and, slowly, that evening as I lay on my bedroll, the skeleton of a plan began to form in my head.

## Mrs Rex Marshall

The corridor of the first-class deck on the SS *Furnessia* was a muddle of voices, stewards directing porters, mothers shouting to their daughters. Children ran into trunks, wide-brimmed hats battled with wall lanterns. It was all very inelegant and chaotic. I'd expected first-class to be more serene. Following my steward, I kept as close to him as I could.

'Your cabin.' He put a key in the door and pushed it open with his body, directing the porter to come in after him and holding the door for me.

Ahead of me lay a narrow bed with painted railings, to ensure I didn't fall out during rough weather, and a small seating area. Between both was a piece of mahogany furniture, too large for the cabin, that held a basin, mirror, bookshelves, somewhere to place my cup of tea and many clever little storage spaces made to ensure nothing moved when the ship was at sea. My trunk and sewing machine were placed beneath a tiny porthole and next to my own bathroom.

The steward held out the key. 'Don't forget there's always a steward on call, just at the end of the corridor, if you're in need of any help.' At last, he left me in peace, shutting out the chaotic noise as he closed the door.

Leaning against the door I let out a long breath. The cabin was only a little smaller than the rooms at our Richmond Place tenement and I had it all to myself: a proper bed, with crisp clean sheets, my own bathroom with no one dirtying it for me, no one sloshing water on the floor. With childish glee I realised there was hot running water and the first thing I did was fill the bath, knowing I could stay in it as long as I liked, use as much water and soap as I wanted, and dry myself with the big, white, soft towel, unused by anyone else.

Lying in that tiny bath, knees bent, toes wriggling, hair frizzing in the heat, I considered how I'd packed my trunk, taken the train to Glasgow and bought a first-class ticket on the next liner bound for New York with a boldness I never knew I had. And now, here I was, wallowing in the height of luxury, with no children to feed, dress or entertain, no cooking, cleaning or washing to attend to, no rats and no cockroaches, no snores or noises of Duncan giving my sister his unwanted attentions late into the night.

Nobody had run after me, nobody had questioned or challenged me: no police, no angry sister.

The tension of the last few weeks soaked into the bathwater. But there was no time to idle. I had work to do.

'Seventy-seven benevolent elephants.' It was time to practise my American accent. 'Seventy-seven benevolent elephants,' I repeated again and again. My friend Laura, assistant costumier at the King's Theatre, a perfect mimic, had learned accents from watching rehearsals and had taught me New Town, English, Irish and American accents, saying they'd be the most useful in a sticky situation. We'd dress in gowns from the costume department, she'd do my hair, cover my face in powder and we'd sneak into the bar at the interval, becoming part of the scene, listening to the way people spoke, the types of conversations, the cadence, their lilts, their mannerisms. This tongue-twister was my warm-up, she'd told me. Then we'd go on to words that were very different to our usual Edinburgh everyday accent:

'Mobile, fragile, herb, water, leisure, vase. Mobile, fragile, herb, water, leisure, vase,' I repeated again and again, talking to the swirling steam in the bathroom, conjuring up potential scenarios, greeting my imagined fellow passengers, chatting over dinner, readying myself for the days ahead.

The next morning, I redressed myself in Mrs Foster's mourning dress and jacket. The suit was made of the softest black Henri-etta cloth with little embellishment. It didn't need any decoration as the fabric alone made it stand out. Cut from the finest wool it draped beautifully and I'd only had to make minor adjustments so that it fitted me. I'd added three sets of inter-changeable collars and cuffs for the jacket so that it would appear to be different every time I wore it. I kept the same cuffs from the day before, made from crepe with three discreet jet buttons, the matching crepe collar studded with tiny jet beads. I dressed carefully, attending to the required illusion: money, connections, pretty but not too pretty (mustn't outshine my peers), demure (a widow must not be brash or surrounded by any hint of scandal). This meant a fresh, healthy complexion, hair not too severe, maybe a loose curl here and there, jacket buttoned all the way to the top. Looking in the mirror I again practised my tongue twister, silently thanking my old friend for the training I never knew I'd be in need of.

I stood back to inspect the finished article.

'Good morning. What a pleasure to meet you. I'm *Mrs* McIntyre,' I said in my newly acquired American accent, putting my hand out to greet my companion in the mirror. But there was something wrong. Looking down, I realised that the illusion of quiet elegance was being ruined by my red and raw hands, hands that did not belong to a woman of society. Hurriedly, I rummaged through my bag and found the pair of black gloves Laura had given me – the final touch steadying me, letting the slight panic fade, my racing heart start to slow down.

The first-class lounge reminded me of the salon at the North British: a wide sweeping staircase leading into it, columns decorated with marble effect, sparkling chandeliers, large Persian carpets, mini palm trees and rows of tables with leather armchairs. If we weren't swaying slightly, you'd never have known we were at sea.

Breakfast onboard the SS *Furnessia* was a sumptuous affair. A large buffet table was heaving with piles of fruit, much of which I didn't recognise, bread in every shape and shade of brown that could be imagined, the smell of sausages, bacon, kidneys, smoked mackerel and black pudding, wafting around the heated serving platters. I ordered a pot of tea and, whilst I had no breakfast companions, I made the most of my time alone watching everyone take part in the serious business of breakfast.

The ladies were dressed as if ready for a day at the races: sumptuous day dresses, parasols and veils; long, three-quarter and short sleeves, lace, chiffon or cotton cuffs, velvet, taffeta and silk bows, the occasional trim two-thirds of the way down the skirt, unusual and the very height of fashion; one of the elderly women was still wearing a bustle, all black and stiff.

I was desperate to take out my notebook, but kept it in my pocket, sipping tea instead. My job was to find my perfect model, the ideal mannequin for the peacock-coloured silk. Too tall and pale was no good – that fine blue silk would be washed out. Too fat would make it difficult to create a truly flattering design. Blonde could work, but I thought that dark hair would create a better contrast. A young, fresh complexion would complement that precious, vibrant fabric. I just needed to be patient.

'Mrs McIntyre, may I introduce your table companion.' A steward turned to show me a tiny bird of a woman.

'Well, how delighted I am to meet you.' She stepped forward and held out her gloved hand as if I was to kiss it. There was something of the teenage sparrow about her, all beaky and brown, awkwardly dressed in a suit that seemed to overpower her tiny frame, making her appear almost as if she was just a dress with no person inside it. She had slightly olive colouring, her hair like dark-brown wire, backcombed into an old-fashioned bouffant that made her small face look even smaller, almost out of proportion. I couldn't guess how old she was; her manner was youthful, energetic, almost naïve but the way she dressed, the way she held herself, suggested that she was much older.

'Mrs Rex Marshall,' said the steward with a slight bow and left us.

'Oh, honey. I can't tell you how pleased I am that you're not some dusty old relic,' she said as she sat down. 'Back home in Alabama, the only McIntyres I know are ancient; I was terrified you'd be one of them. But listen to me, prattling on. I see that you're in mourning. May I ask what you're doing on this boat?'

'I'm returning home after visiting my late husband's family in Edinburgh,' I said mournfully, looking down at my plate for a moment. 'I felt I should go and pay them my respects and take them some of his favourite trinkets and photographs so that they could have some remembrances of him.'

'Oh, my darling girl, you must be devastated. I simply would not know how I would manage without my Rex. He's my absolute rock. You know we're on our honeymoon? He'll be joining us shortly. He's just been to check up on his mother.' She leaned in and dropped her voice. 'Heavens, his mother is such a grouch in the mornings. I do my best to avoid her before ten o'clock.'

'Your mother-in-law came with you on your honeymoon?' I couldn't help but ask.

'Oh, Lord, yes.' She rolled her eyes. 'One of the reasons I come down to breakfast early is I know she won't be up for a while. I can have my coffee in peace. Talking of which...' She stood up awkwardly, her dress hampering free movement. 'I'm just gasping. Shall we go over to the buffet table?'

As we began to make our way, she suddenly stopped, standing back to look at me.

'*Who* is your dressmaker? That dress has been tailored beautifully. It utterly suits you, my dear.'

'Well... I have a dressmaker in New York. I'd highly recommend her.'

'I'd say you need to introduce me to her. My mother-in-law insists I use her seamstress, she's so old-fashioned, all beiges and browns...'

She was interrupted by a small but insistent gentleman.

'Julia, darling, I'm afraid we must go.' He checked his pocket watch. 'Mother is waiting for us.' His voice had a sheen of weariness to it.

'Oh, Rex, darling, I haven't even had my coffee yet. It's not as if we're going anywhere, can she not wait two minutes?'

The gentleman stroked his beard fastidiously. 'No, it's best not.' He put the watch back into his waistcoat pocket and smoothed it down, then rubbed his fingers against his thumb, as if brushing off unseen crumbs to an unheard beat.

'Oh, honey,' Mrs Marshall said as she turned to me. 'I just *so* want to talk to you. Will you be here tomorrow? Well, heavens to Betsy, what a stupid question.' She touched my upper arm. 'You won't be going anywhere, and neither will I. I'd just love to have a proper gossip with you. Let's have breakfast tomorrow morning.'

'Julia,' the husband repeated in his tired manner.

The tiny bird pulled at the cuff of one of her sleeves, then the other, her mouth twisting to one side, looking down at her feet. 'Of course, darling.' And taking his arm she gave me a bright smile.

'Tomorrow, Mrs McIntyre.' And with that, I watched her walk away, that tiny brown bird, with diamonds in her ears and on her wedding finger.

A good figure, the right colouring, plenty of money, malleable, perhaps too talkative, but I could work with that.

I'd found my model.

As she and her husband continued towards the stairs, I was already working out the best design to suit her shape, an evening dress, perhaps with a chiffon partial overskirt but with a large opening at the front, tantalising us with the shimmer of the peacock silk.

I went up to the buffet table in a kind of trance, not really taking in the display in front of me, piling my plate with whatever food was in front of me, head filled with possible neckline shapes, types of sleeve and waistline, embroidery to embellish the skirt.

'Honey, sausages and strawberries.' A languorous English accent. 'What a fascinating combination.'

I turned to see a tall man, not much older than myself, well-dressed and with an air of comfortable confidence. The three-piece Prince of Wales check suit had been tailored to perfection, the white shirt had a silky lustre to it that made me want to touch it, the rich quietness of his silk tie, and the handmade quality of his shoes all made my heart skip a beat at the thoughtful elegance. No one else on board had such an impressive suit of clothing; there was nothing ready-made about this man.

I looked down at my plate and blushed intensely. 'It seems I wasn't looking at what I was doing.' I closed my eyes for a moment, putting my mask back on. 'A bad night's sleep, I'm afraid.'

'Your bad night's sleep has made my morning.' He clicked his heels together and gave a slight bow, an amused look on his face. 'Mr Aidan Cruickshank at your service.'

There was something about this man that seemed faintly familiar: the cut of his suit, the fresh face, the slight look of boyish glee. I glanced around me, worried about how this encounter would look. 'Mrs McIntyre,' I said, reluctantly holding out my gloved hand, just as Mrs Marshall had, but I kept my voice non-committal.

'Would you excuse me, Mr Cruickshank? I must return to my table; my breakfast will be getting cold.' And before he could answer I left him, my under-arms slightly tacky, my heart beating a little too fast.

The following morning, after another wallowing bath, the luxury of tea in my cabin and a few minutes with my sketch-book, I changed the collars and cuffs on my mourning suit (over-sized black woollen cuffs with satin piped edges, held together with large black toggle buttons, a plain woollen pointed collar with matching satin piping), and took myself back to the first-class lounge to work on my friendship with that tiny, awkward bird.

She was waiting for me at the breakfast table. 'Oh, thank God. There you are, daahling!' The familiar voice drew out the word as if she was pulling on a piece of string. 'I do hate my own company. Come, sit by me.' She patted the chair beside her. 'You and I are going to be *such* great friends; I just know it.' She scrunched up her face in delight, pulling her shoulders upwards.

Julia Marshall, or rather Mrs Rex Marshall as the newlywed liked to refer to herself, stood at a dead five foot and would never wear any kind of heeled shoe because she believed they would do her feet damage. She hardly wore any make-up; a dash of rouge and a smear of lipstick enhanced a fresh, vigorous but pinched face.

'Good morning,' I said, 'I do hope you were able to sleep.' I'd overheard the polite greetings on my way to the table and was doing my best to mimic them, taking care with my American accent.

'Well, to be perfectly honest, I didn't sleep well. I believe it's very important to take an hour's exercise every day, without it, I just feel awful. When I lived at home, in Alabama, I could run on my parents' land. I'd run forever, but, of course, I can't do that on board, and I don't think I'll be able to do that in New York, now that we're moving there. How I would love to run around Central Park, but it seems it isn't the thing, and anyway, what would I wear? Us ladies of society simply can't run the circuit of Central Park in their skirts. At home I could wear any old thing, I could run for miles and never see a soul, but in the city, I need something that's suitable for a woman of my position. But if it could be comfortable too, wouldn't that be just swell? I do hope someone will come up with something soon as I'm just dying to get out there. Running gives me so much energy.' She touched my hand and lowered her voice. 'God knows I need that vitality after the deadly tea parties my mother-in-law organises.'

'And tell me of your honeymoon.' I could see she was in the mood for talking.

'Oh, honey.' She patted my hand. 'I do love a person who wants to know all about me.' She took a deep breath. 'We've been away for three months, but honestly, it only feels like three short weeks. We have just had such a ball; I can't tell you. We've been to Paris, France, followed by a driving tour down to Nice and on to Monte Carlo. Darling, the money we lost at gambling! Rex has banned me from the casinos, it was doing his reputation no good. But I'm just fine with that.' She leaned towards me and began whispering, 'I don't really like gambling. But I'd never done it before, so I just *had* to give it a go.' She laughed so loud I almost jumped. 'It's like champagne. I'd never had it before our wedding day, but oh golly, that stuff did me in. I've sworn never to touch alcohol ever again, I just couldn't get my head off the pillow the next day.'

It was as if a dam had burst, almost as if she hadn't spoken to anyone in days and just needed to make sure she still had a voice. I looked around the room, letting the words waft over me. After a while, I realised that Mr Marshall was walking purposefully towards us. I leaned into my companion and pointed him out.

'Oh, dear Lord, I know that walk,' she whispered. 'That means his mother's on the warpath.' She clung to my arm. 'We've hardly had a moment to ourselves all honeymoon, half the reason I insisted we go to the casinos was because she wouldn't come with us. It was simply delicious to be away from her perpetual frown.' She squeezed my arm and gave an almost inaudible squeal.

Mr Marshall arrived by our side and stood to attention. 'Mrs McIntyre.' He bowed stiffly. 'Julia, Mother is awaiting our morning visit.' He twisted one end of his moustache before rubbing his thumb and fingers together as he'd done the day before, as if to a beat in his head.

Mrs Marshall blinked before carefully standing and taking her husband's arm. 'Honey.' She winked at me. 'We've still got days to catch up. Maybe you could join us for dinner tonight and then you could meet the mother who keeps us so busy.'

I watched them leave the lounge.

'No sausages and strawberries today?' That languorous English accent.

'No, sir. Not as yet.'

'May I join you? My table companions seem to never take

breakfast and I find I'm in need of company. I feel as if I've been in solitary confinement for the last twenty-four hours.'

I waved at the chair opposite me, trying to appear indifferent.

'Are you travelling with family?' Mr Cruickshank asked in a careful, polite manner as he sat, indicating to the steward that he'd like coffee sent to the table.

'No, sir. I have been visiting my late husband's family in Edinburgh.' I held my gloved hands neatly in front of me.

'My most heartfelt condolences.' His hand to his heart, his voice appearing more delighted than sorrowful. 'May I enquire as to which part of Edinburgh his family resides in?'

I couldn't help the twitch of my mouth, my attempt to suppress a smile. Was he assessing the viability of the widow? If so, he was too keen, the lack of subtlety almost shocking. 'Charlotte Square, but the family seat is in Ayrshire.' A little extra detail to tantalise. Why not have some fun?

He was slightly better at hiding his own twitch, but the glimmer in his eyes gave him away.

'And you, Mr...?' I asked, feigning forgetfulness.

'Cruickshank.' He repeated his name with a tight smile.

'Ah, yes. My apologies. Why are *you* on board?' I looked around the room as I spoke, as if I were trying to find someone.

'I'm looking to expand my horizons,' he announced pompously and then set off on a rambling explanation of a great American tour, pointedly telling me of family on Fifth Avenue, cousins in Rhode Island, a much-anticipated trip to Washington and a visit to the family's cotton plantation in Georgia.

As the coffee arrived and the steward poured for us both, I considered Mr Cruickshank and his laid-back manner that people who've grown up with money have. It makes them appear handsome, leisurely and attractive, even when they aren't blessed with natural good looks. But he'd have been striking even if he'd been born in the worst of the slums in the

Grassmarket. He seemed to ooze self-confidence, a natural self-belief that he could achieve anything he put his mind to. His chiselled features, slightly hooked nose and deep-brown eyes were complemented by a dark crop of wavy and unkempt hair, too long for the current fashion and suggesting a hint of rebellion. He exuded an irresistible sexuality and the faintest whiff of insincerity.

Was I *his* mark, *his* ideal model? Had he been watching me from across the room?

I interrupted his monologue.

'Mr Cruickshank, perhaps you would excuse me. I'm not good company just now and you may find that solitary confinement is preferable to a conversation with this rather gloomy widow.' I stood up. 'Perhaps we could continue this conversation tomorrow.'

Hurriedly getting up, I stood on the hem of my dress and wobbled slightly, knocking over my half-drunk cup of coffee and, as I tried to steady myself, I put my left hand in the pool of spilled coffee, soaking my glove.

'Ach, ye nugget!' I said and, without thinking, pulled the glove off and quickly put it between two napkins on the table to try and get the liquid off as quickly as possible.

'Are you all right? You're not burned?' My companion stood and picked up my hand, my left hand. He looked at it and then at me. Quickly I pulled it away.

'Thank you, I'm fine, it wasn't that hot. I must take your leave.' And with the soggy glove in one hand, I left the lounge as fast as I could.


I almost ran to my cabin, but before I could reach my door, I heard his voice.

'Mrs McIntyre. Perhaps you'd wait a moment.'

I made myself stop, took a deep breath and smoothed down

my hair. As I turned, he was almost upon me, picking up my
gloveless hand and standing too close to me.

'I'm concerned about your hand.' He looked down at my
red, ringless fingers. 'I wanted to make sure you get to see a
doctor.' There was amusement in his voice.

I said nothing.

'I'm a little confused. No young widow residing in first-class
would have such rough, work-scarred hands, no distraught
widow would have taken her wedding ring off.' He caressed my
hand, almost as if it soothed him. 'Such a tiny hand.' He put it to
his mouth and kissed it, before breaking into an unreadable
smile.

'So, what *are* you doing here, *Mrs* McIntyre?' He said this
slowly as if enjoying the moment.

'I'm travelling back home...'

'Oh, I don't think so. That slip of the tongue, that Edinburgh accent doesn't quite fit in with the image of the lonely,
demure widow from America, does it?'

Gently he pushed me against the wall, the handrail pushing
into my back, his body pressed into mine. He was taller than
me, his chin at my forehead, so he bent his head to whisper in
my ear.

'You and I are just like two peas in a pod... not being
truthful about who we are.' He stood back to get a better look at
me. 'I think...' he continued, assessing his mark, 'we've met
before. I couldn't work it out until just now. You're that girl in
Jenners, the one who stole the bolt of peacock-blue fabric and
boldly walked out the door.'

My stomach heaved. The man who had returned the
dropped five-pound note, who had winked at me, who knew I
was a thief and a fraud.

What to do? In those days I wasn't quite yet formed, my
boldness had yet to peak. I should have made friends, got him
on my side, but I could see there was danger – he was too confi-

dent, too attractive, just a bit too smooth. I knew that trouble would surely follow him, trouble which would jeopardise my new friendship with Mrs Marshall, my potential new client, my pathway into New York society.

Just then I heard someone whistling, footsteps coming towards us. He loosened his grip and I wriggled out of his hold.

My companion stepped away from me, smoothing down his ruffled hair. 'Let's continue this talk at dinner, where we can both play our parts, fool those around us, mock their gullibility.' He clicked his heels together, gave a quick bow and left me with my mouth open.


Mrs McIntyre was suddenly taken ill by the seasickness and found herself unable to leave her cabin for the remainder of the voyage. Mrs Marshall and Mrs McIntyre exchanged notes: Mrs Marshall professed extreme sorrow at not being able to cement their new acquaintance, happy reunions were pledged on arrival in Manhattan and Mrs Marshall was promised an introduction to Mrs McIntyre's much-admired seamstress as soon as could be arranged.


The remaining four days of the voyage were spent in self-prescribed solitude. With a locked door I could reject any advances from Mr Cruickshank, and I could hide from Mrs Marshall. I ordered food at odd times, I took three baths a day, I revelled in my own company and, thrillingly, I began designing a dress for Mrs Marshall.

I took the silk fabric from my trunk, pulled out a length of the material and spread it across my bunk before sitting on my knees to inspect it.

The peacock green-blue was sumptuous, the cloth shimmering, throwing out many different colours. I was mesmerised by its quality. The darker greens in the small repeating pattern of trees were a mixture of a shiny emerald green and something that felt more earthy, more natural. The tiny brown birds were embroidered and raised above the rest of the pattern, neat brown, white and sunny-orange stitching that was so delicate I couldn't imagine who had fingers small enough, or eyes sharp enough to sew the pattern so uniformly. The more I looked at the fabric in front of me, the more I wondered at the dyes that had been required to create it, the workmanship involved, and the patience and creativity needed to produce such a master-piece. I sketched and drew until my fingers hurt.

In Mrs Rex Marshall I had found the ideal model. Every-thing about her suited the material: her olive colouring, dark-brown hair, deep-brown eyes and petite frame. They were the perfect balance for this lavish fabric. And she would undoubt-edly have the right kind of event to wear it to. But she was too conservative, too boyish in her manner of dressing. I was going to need to persuade her to change her style, inject colour into her wardrobe, make her more confident. Somehow, I'd have to find a way to introduce myself as *Miss* Maisie McIntyre, despite my deceit, and then persuade her to give me her patronage.

But those four days of much anticipated solitude quickly became dull, the throb of the ship's engines drilling into my ears, the lack of fresh air making me feel lead-like. Then there were the continuous notes from Mrs Marshall wanting to check if I'd recovered, and the occasional insistent knock on my door from Aidan Cruickshank.

Finally, on the day before our arrival in New York, I left my cabin at midnight, dressed in my normal shirtwaist and skirt, wrapped up in my slightly shabby shawl, hoping most passen-gers would be asleep or too tired to notice me.

'Sir,' I said to my friendly steward, 'perhaps you've noticed there's a gentleman who seems a little too insistent on seeing me, knocking on my door at all hours,' I said wearily, slipping a coin into his palm. 'I need some fresh air and I'd like to make sure he won't be bothering me. Is there any chance you could sneak me down to the third-class deck, so I know I'll have some peace and quiet?' I saw that he'd noticed what I was wearing and I leaned into him. 'I'm in disguise,' I whispered. 'I thought it would be safer.' And I handed over another coin.

The fresh air was more than welcome, the cool blast on my hot cheeks reminding me of the days I would leave work after a ten-hour shift at the North British, the relief so intense I'd feel as if I was a calf who had been kept in all winter and had just been released into the spring fields. And just the same, I wanted to kick my heels and run up and down the deck to get rid of some of the pent-up energy surging around my body. Instead, I wrapped my shawl tightly against the brisk wind and began walking along the deck.

'Another one who can't sleep?' a heavily accented voice asked out of the dark.

I turned to find a short, wide-hipped, olive-skinned woman, facing me, wrapped up in an intricately patterned shawl. She had a tired smile on her face and the same slightly red-cheeked appearance of someone who has been kept indoors for days.

'Aye,' I returned. 'Too many things in my head tae sleep,' I said, happy to be back speaking with my native Scottish accent, feeling more comfortable in less grand surroundings.

'I wish that was my problem. Too many people in such a small space, children feeling sick, Nonna who can't keep down anything, my cousin already homesick for Glasgow, my husband worried we won't be allowed into America.' She drew a deep breath, closing her eyes, turning her face to the wind.

'Only a few days tae go. It'll be over soon.'

Her eyes still closed, she replied, 'I hope so. And the food. Oh, the food is just terrible. It's so...' She turned to me. 'Excuse me for saying so, but it's so boring.'

I laughed. 'Meat and potatoes?'

'My little ones need a gentle broth to settle their stomachs, some decent vegetables, soft bread.' She leaned heavily on the railings. 'But you are right. This will be over soon.' She rubbed her face with her hand.

'If you don't mind me asking. Where did you get your shawl from?'

Suddenly the tired expression was replaced with a wide smile. 'I made it myself. I love to knit and it's so easy to take with me – when I'm waiting at the doctor's, or in the queue at the bakery. It calms my mind and makes me feel like I am achieving something on those days when all I seem to have done is swept the floor and wiped away the tears of the children.'

'Can I look at it more closely?' I asked.

'Of course.' We moved to a more sheltered part of the deck where there was better light and less wind. The wool was very soft, the pattern almost like the Fair Isle pullovers I had seen, but with much brighter colours. The stitches were tiny and consistent, the pattern intricate.

'Where did you learn tae do this?' I loved how different it was.

'I taught myself. When we arrived in Glasgow, I would see these children in the park wearing such beautifully knitted hats, but they seemed to lack something, some...' she searched for the word, 'vibrancy. I managed to study a few hats in a shop one day and then went home and drew my own designs. I had lots of leftover wool, so I just used what I had. Some of the wool had belonged to my *nonna*, some to my husband's. It was passed on to me because I like to knit so much. But I found the colours of wool in Glasgow a bit dull, so I also learned how to dye to get some more exciting colours.'

I fingered the shawl revelling in the colour and the workmanship.

'You should sell these. I would bet naebody in America has seen anything like this.'

The woman laughed. 'When would I find the time? I must find work when I get to New York, we have so many mouths to feed.'

Her dark, almost black eyes matched her long hair which, although tied back in a bun, was frizzing in the sea air. She had the soft features of a woman who has given birth to several children and the dark circles of someone with never-ending chores. But nothing about her suggested bitterness or rancour as she held her hands on her hips and her eyes glittered.

'Where will you look tae find work?' I asked.

'My cousin is working at a garment factory. She says they are always looking for women who can sew. I will go there. I'm lucky that Nonna can mind the *bambini*.'

My ears pricked up at this. I was going to need to find work. I might still have the best part of the stolen money, but I wanted to hold on to it as I would need it to set myself up in business when the time was right.

'I'm useful with a sewing machine. Do you think I could get work there too?' My heart began to beat a little faster, the hairs on the back of my neck lifted.

'I am sure. But my cousin, Isabella, says they work you hard and don't pay such good money. It may be we only go there if we can't find work elsewhere.'

'Where have you come from?' I asked, not able to recognise her accent.

'Italy. A small village in the Tuscany mountains called Barga. But we have been in Glasgow for the last five years. My daughter was born there. When we arrived in Scotland, we had run out of money to get to America. We stayed until we could afford for us all to join my husband's brother in New York. I pray we will be there soon.'

As she spoke I realised that for the first time since my mother had died, since I'd made the decision to steal the blue fabric, to lie to my sister, to leave my home and start a new life, that I might have found someone I could be myself with.

'I'm Maisie. It's nice tae meet you.'

Again, the woman gave me another of those genial smiles, the kind of smile you have to earn and it reminded me of the day my mother had patted my hand, the day she'd said she liked my 'strange Maisie McIntyre ways'. That smile almost made my eyes prick.

'And I am Rosa. Rosa Bassino.' Suddenly her Italian accent became exaggerated in her excitement. 'I think that we should be friends.'

## Chapter Two

### The Peacock-Blue Evening Dress

*A full-length, sleeveless evening gown made from a peacock-blue silk with a blue chiffon over-bodice and half-length sleeves finished with dark-blue chiffon ties at the cuffs. The whole dress is brought in at the waist by a thin band of dark-blue velvet, embellished with an oversized orange organza rose.*

# Boldness

## 1910

I stood on 59th Street, across the road from the entrance to The Plaza Hotel. This imposing building was surprisingly alluring, the first three storeys enthralling me with its rusticated marble, the upper floors calming me with their cream-coloured, enamelled bricks topped by the sloping roof with ornate copper and slate dormers and gables. Its stateliness matched the grandeur that strode through its porticoed entrance, singular dresses constructed in multiple layers, furled parasols with sharp edges, tailored suits and gleaming top hats. Watching the business of this overpowering building, I began to recapture something of the optimism I'd felt on the ship's deck on the day of my arrival, a stirring enthusiasm that had begun to slip away over the previous ten days.

My cousin Aileen had grudgingly offered me space in her apartment until I could find my own lodgings. The sharp contrast between the first-class lounge and her noisy, dingy one-room tenement, filled with her sometime husband, another couple and an atmosphere of rotting food, was inevitable.

Picking my way through the mess of dirty dishes and chocolate wrappers, I had been shown a small pallet to use as my bed. I remembered Netta's warning, how I'd so easily dismissed her words of the 'good-fer-nothin' husband' and the 'pigsty', and gritted my teeth.

In need of an income, I had gone with Rosa to the garment factory on Washington Square to find a job as a seamstress. Getting the job was easy, our machine skills were more than adequate, and we'd naïvely celebrated our quick assimilation into the New York workforce. But all too soon I realised I was in yet another bad, underpaid job, I was living in similar poor, cramped conditions. What had been the point of leaving Edinburgh if I was stuck in the same life all over again? So, taking matters into my own hands, I dressed in my Sunday best, I put the bolt of blue silk in my carpet bag along with my sketchbook, and took myself to The Plaza, shuddering at the thought of meeting with Mrs Marshall and revealing my complicity. Worst-case scenario I would be sent back to Scotland branded a liar and a fraud, a failure and a disgrace.

I crossed the road and climbed the steps into the hotel with a straight back, catching the eye of the doorman as if I did this every day. To hide my shaking hands, I held my carpet bag firmly in front of me.

'Miss McIntyre to see Mrs Rex Marshall,' I announced to the concierge behind a deep mahogany desk. I spoke in a soft, understated Scottish accent. This was to be the way Maisie McIntyre, seamstress, dressmaker, perhaps one day a couturier, would speak from now on. An alluring accent, not too harsh, just enough of a lilt to make me noticeable amongst the notable women of New York.

Turning to look at the elaborate marble foyer and the immaculate rococo furnishing, I feigned disinterest. To help push down the rising terror I made myself remember the words of my friend Laura.

'It's an act, that's all it is, and if you see it simply as that then you'll be away. Hold your head high, never let your shoulders slump, don't cower in a corner. Just act in the same way the other women do. Look everyone in the eye, don't fidget, don't hesitate, don't stutter. Act full of confidence; you'll be amazed at the effect it has.'

That all sounded so easy, but standing in the spacious lobby, watching the polished and refined guests wander through into the public rooms, I felt as if the smell of Aileen's filthy tenement must be radiating from me, like the musty odour of a dead mouse.

My nervousness was temporarily replaced by sheer terror as I rode the elevator, with glass doors that revealed the mechanical pistons at work, reminding me that I was dangling over a deep shaft that I could fall into at any moment. Bile began to rise the nearer I got to the top floor.

The elevator operator rang the bell, calling the floor number, before sliding the door open and revealing a large lobby, the floor shining with black and white tiles. The space echoed with the sound of my shoes and, just as I was about to knock on the door, it was opened by a maid.

'Miss McIntyre?' she asked, surveying me carefully.

I nodded and the maid led me into a cavernous apartment, decorated unlike anything I had ever seen. Marble columns lined the hallway and wide corridor, gold and red brocaded wallpaper in between each pillar, a parquet floor with a herringbone pattern spread through the whole suite of rooms, embroidered silk curtains framed each large window overlooking Central Park, the room filled with more rococo furniture, this time in a green and yellow colourway. It seemed as if there was space to fit all the families from the garment factory, with plenty of room to spare.

'Miss McIntyre... oh!'

Julia Marshall pulled back as if she'd been bitten. Confusion covered her face as she then leaned forward to look at me more closely.

'Aren't you *Mrs* McIntyre? Aren't you supposed to be in mourning?'

'No, I am *Miss* Maisie McIntyre. Never married, never widowed.'

'But you look exactly like Mrs McIntyre. How can that be? Your face is the same, your hair is the same, your figure is the same. Are you related?'

'That's because I *am* the same person.' I made my voice as light as I could as if this confession was just an unimportant piece of information that we could dispense with as quickly as possible.

'Mrs Marshall, I lied to you,' I said, looking her square in the face. 'I made up my story, pretending to be a rich widow because I knew you wouldn't speak to me as Maisie McIntyre, a mere dressmaker from Edinburgh. I needed you to see me as someone who dressed well, someone who understood the meaning of quality workmanship, someone who wanted the same things for you.'

Mrs Marshall slowly walked around me, eyeing me up, looking at every detail of my dress, my hair, my hat and my bag before she finally said, 'You lied.' Her voice was bland as if she couldn't find the right emotion, as if she couldn't work out what her own thoughts were.

Finally, she stood still. We held each other's gaze as I tried to control my breathing. When she still hadn't moved, still had said nothing, I began considering making my excuses and leaving, cutting my losses and leaving with my dignity. But then, out of the blue, she burst out laughing, that too-loud, too-showy laugh.

'I couldn't be happier.' She thrust her arms out to me and held me by the shoulders. 'Nobody has ever admitted to lying to me before. And there have been plenty who have. Everyone thinks I'm a fly-by-night, silly little girl who only married Rex for his place in society and his access to the Four Hundred. Nobody has ever considered that I might not be quite as stupid as I look.'

She circled me again. 'Except for you, *Miss* McIntyre. And for that, I am truly grateful.'

She said my name with a hint of triumph in her southern twang, clapping her hands in glee, like a little girl at a birthday party. 'So, what have you brought me?'

The quick progression from high tension to extreme relief made me momentarily speechless. 'Well...' I gathered my wits, fumbling with my bag. 'I have a particular fabric that I want to show you. I believe your colouring will suit it perfectly. I also have some sketches that I've made, illustrating how I think we could show this fabric, and you, off to their best.'

I moved over to a sofa table close to one of the windows and pulled out a yard of the fabric so that it could be seen in the daylight. 'This peacock blue will work perfectly with your darker colouring. It will highlight the sculptured look of your face and the freshness of your skin. Come over and have a look.'

Mrs Marshall came towards me slowly, peering with uncertainty at the cloth, her hands clasped behind her back as if she were being made to inspect a dead body.

'I'm not one for bright colours.' Her voice was full of doubt. 'I prefer something more muted; I don't want to stand out. I prefer to hide behind my clothes, wear something that doesn't show up my obvious imperfections.' She pointed to her strange, fleshy-coloured dress. Her movements hinted at the restrictions caused by the corset she wore. 'But I do love it that I have the tiniest waist of all my friends, even if sometimes I have to sit down due to lack of breath.' She laughed nervously.

'Mrs Marshall. Have you not heard that restricted dresses are out of fashion?' I looked around the room and quickly spotted the latest copy of *Vogue* on a small coffee table. I walked over and picked it up. 'Have you not read this yet?' I queried, flicking through the pages.

'Oh, no. The hotel put these magazines in our suite, but I have never dared show interest. It seems to me that giving too much attention to fashion makes you appear somewhat whimsical.' She flicked her hand as if to bat away the suggestion. 'Miss McIntyre, I already know what my reputation is, I don't want to turn the myth into reality.'

The complete look of seriousness on her face made me smile. I moved over to the grand sofa, sitting and patting the space beside me.

'Mrs Marshall. Perhaps you would sit beside me?' Once she was seated I looked her straight in the face. Suddenly I felt the confidence that I'd been feigning. It seemed that Mrs Marshall and I were no different; we had both been dealing in falsehoods of one type or another.

'I can understand that many people would see the study of dress and fashion as shallow and meaningless. But those people miss something very important. As a woman of influence in society, it's imperative that you dress the part. You need to make sure that what you are wearing is appropriate and completely suited to the occasion. If you turned up at the committee meeting for a fundraiser for, say, a charity raising money to buy new hospital beds for a foundling hospital, wearing a pink chiffon tea dress, some might think you weren't taking the event seriously. But if you turned up wearing a well-cut, sombre two-piece suit, perhaps with one or two well-placed embellishments to show your personality, people would look at you very differently. You know that men of business wouldn't wear slacks to a board meeting. Just because they don't have the burden of so many changing fashions it doesn't mean that they don't also take their dress seriously. And so must you.'

A look of unqualified relief came over Mrs Marshall's face.

'Miss McIntyre. I can't believe that I've never seen it like that. My father used to get so exasperated with me when I kept talking about what new dresses I could have, that he made me think that the whole thing was a childish frivolity that I should hurriedly grow out of. What a darling you are to make me see that it's something more than that.'

She clasped her hands together on her lap and straightened up. 'Well, I think you'd better show me your sketches.'

Before she could change her mind, I took my notebook out of my bag.

'Look. Your petite figure is perfect for the new designs that are coming over from Paris. You don't need to wear corsets anymore. The waist is higher meaning that you'll be more comfortable. The skirt is loose with gathered folds going down to a narrow, ankle-length hemline. This means you can move around much more easily. You could even dance.'

'Oh, Lord. I simply can't dance. I'm so unladylike, especially in these tight dresses. I just lose all my puff. Rex is quite the dancer and gets most upset when I have to sit down for fear of passing out.' Her eyes were suddenly bright with excitement, until, abruptly, she said, 'But wouldn't that hemline be a bit racy? I'm not sure what my mother-in-law would say.'

Quickly I picked up the magazine again and flicked through the pages. I stopped at a photograph of a woman with an extraordinary tumble of curly hair.

'Look at this.' I showed her the image. 'Have you heard of Mary Pickford?'

'Oh yes. The Girl with the Golden Curls. She's quite the up-and-coming little starlet.' Her voice was a little tart as she said this.

'Look at what she's wearing. High waist, shorter hemline, loose skirt.'

'Yes, but she's an actress. Everyone knows they have questionable morals.' She put her hand on her hair as she spoke. 'I'm sure my mother-in-law would have something to say about me looking like an actress.'

I put the magazine down and again looked at the woman in front of me. 'But what do *you* say, Mrs Marshall?'

'Well...' She stumbled through her words. 'I... I just don't rightly know.' Blushing, she looked down at her feet.

I suppressed the urge to sigh. 'Look at the front cover of the magazine. The model is wearing a white dress, her waistline is just a little higher. Can you see how much easier it would be to wear? And at this time of year, in the terrible New York heat, that dress must be so much more practical.'

'Now, Miss McIntyre, when has practicality ever been a consideration in a woman's attire?' Mrs Marshall laughed, the embarrassment quickly forgotten.

'Women are driving cars, playing sports. You like to keep fit; I know that. There are people out there trying to help women find clothes that suit their lifestyle. You don't want to spend your life sitting in a hotel drawing room just looking pretty, do you?'

'Why, you seem positively angry at the idea that women are nothing but clotheshorses. Do you not like us to look good?'

I changed tack. 'I want you to look the best you possibly can. Let me take some measurements and then I'm going to go away and make you a dress. It will be unlike anything you've ever worn before, and I can guarantee that you will love it. The toile will be ready in two weeks and the first fitting for the dress will be four weeks later. If you're happy with it I'll require full payment before I go any further.'

I gave her my most persuasive smile. 'Is there somewhere we can go so I can measure up?'

The enormous, high-ceilinged room, with large windows on two sides, was filled with eight long tables, running the length of the room, each holding up to thirty-five electric sewing machines. At the beginning of the day, this light-filled room would seem impressive, but as the day wore on it would become overbearing and hot, the constant, loud, stuttering thrum of the sewing machines making everyone anxious and jittery. Concentrating on sewing for nine hours at a stretch, with hardly any breaks, was exhausting and, despite the noise, some girls would fall asleep at their tables. This was what we all dreaded; nobody wanted to be caught napping or making a mistake. But I found that I could lose myself in that oppressive noise. The machine sewing was simple enough that I could do it whilst thinking of the work I needed to do on Mrs Marshall's blue evening gown. I'd already worked up the designs, created a paper pattern and was ready to cut the calico to make the toile. I mentally listed which pieces to hand baste first, how much work I could manage each evening to get the toile finished on time.

The noise suddenly stopped, the closing bell shrieking, the power cut off and the machines were abruptly silenced.

The scraping of the wooden chairs on the floor, the chatter of the girls as we all made our way to the exit, the waiting as they unlocked the doors. As it was a Saturday, we finished a bit earlier and we had pay to collect, so we all congregated at the end of the room. I could see Rosa, dark circles under her eyes, her cheeks flushed and those usually bright, beady eyes somehow diluted, washed out by exhaustion.

'Where's Isabella?' I asked. It was unusual for Rosa to be seen without her cousin.

'She arrived five minutes late for work today.' She leaned in towards me. 'It's early days, but she's with child and she is sleeping so much just now, she overslept.' She let out a large sigh of exasperation. 'They sent her home!' She gesticulated wildly. 'They said she was late and didn't want her working, even if she said she'd make up the five minutes in her break time. I don't understand these mean-minded men. They have no idea that losing one day's pay is like losing one day's food.' Her black hair began to spring out of its bun and her cheeks became a deeper red. And then she lowered her voice as we came closer to the table where they were handing out the pay packets. 'They have no... I don't know the word... ah, yes. They have no compassion. They are unreasonable and petty.'

Already it was becoming easy to forget that excruciating poverty. I had the cushion of the stolen money, even if I wasn't spending it, and I had the anticipation of payment from Mrs Marshall in a few weeks' time. I was making sure that I didn't have to rely wholly on the poor pay packet from the factory. Isabella and Rosa and most of the girls in the factory weren't in a position to do that, and I had to remind myself of that fear of no food, that fear of having no coal for the fire that would pervade every moment of your day.

But before I had a chance to give my opinion of the men who worked on our factory floor Rosa whispered, 'What excuse do you think they will give me today? That I'm too stupid, that I'm Italian and therefore I can't count?'

Approaching the table there was a nervous silence, heads bowed as the girls picked up their pay packets.

'Maisie McIntyre,' I said, my stomach contracting.

Pointing to a line in the book, the bookkeeper passed me a pen and I signed my name. As I took the small envelope, I made a point of opening it immediately and checking how much was inside.

'Eight dollars,' I announced.

'What did you think?' the bookkeeper growled. 'Did you think I'd short-change you?'

'It's not unheard of,' I said defiantly and then flashed a sarcastic smile at him. 'I just hope you've done the same for my friend here.'

Head down, Rosa approached the table, mumbled her name and took her envelope, scurrying away.

In the corridor Rosa grabbed my arm, annoyance on her tight lips. 'Maisie, you're so bold! If I said that they'd sack me. I can't afford to lose this job,' she hissed.

'They won't let you or I go. We're too good at our jobs. There's not many out there who can make up the samples. It's those other girls who just sew one part of the shirt, they can be easily replaced, but we know what we're doing, we learn quickly. They'd find it more difficult to replace us.'

We joined the line of girls waiting to get into the freight elevator back down to the street.

Rosa shook her head. 'It's easy for you. You don't have *bambini* to feed.' And as she said this, she brought her bag out in front of her and opened it up, thrusting it at the man at the entrance of the elevator. He gave the inside of it a cursory look and then moved on to me.

'Hands up,' he barked and then, with his grubby, nail-bitten hands he patted down my waist, under my arms, brushing my left breast. I closed my eyes as he moved down to my thigh and between my legs.

I braced myself for this daily humiliation, thinking of my mother and the so-called accident that had broken her leg.

'I saw him push you down the stairs,' Mrs Robertson had said. Had my mother been rebuffing unwanted advances? Had she said 'No' once too often to a man who was used to getting his own way?

I grabbed the man's arm.

'Dinna think of it for a minute,' I growled at him, an unusually harsh Scottish accent materialising in my anger. 'Aye, I've come across the likes of you before. Next time I'll kick you where you know it'll hurt and I'll scream 'til your ears bleed.' I was looking at him directly, our noses almost touching. 'You're outnumbered here, the women would have your guts for garters.'

The Saturday night bustle of the girls stopped, the chatter

about which movie to go to, which dance hall, all dissipated as every eye landed on us.

'If I was going to steal, I'd steal sommit worthwhile, not a piece of cotton.' I threw down his arm and walked into the elevator. Leaning against the side I suddenly had to gasp for breath.

'Maisie,' Rosa said, putting a hand on my arm. 'Breathe slowly.'

She rubbed my back in her motherly way. I brushed away the threatening tears: tears of relief, tears for my dead mother, even if her touch had been rare, tears for the familiar life I had left behind.

The rest of the girls trooped into the elevator, subdued and looking away from the gates as they were closed. The noisy and faltering journey from the ninth floor was filled with the odd whispered 'thank you' or 'well done' in Russian, Italian, Polish and more. I didn't really know what they were saying, but the gist of it was obvious.

Outside, Rosa took my arm as we walked towards Little Italy.

'You need to be careful, Maisie. If you lose your job, how are you going to pay for the room in your new boarding house? I don't even know how you can afford it now.' She sighed. 'If I was your mother, I wouldn't know what to do with you. You are too fearless, and you are still a *bambina*! One day it will get you into trouble.'

She rubbed my cheek as if I was her own child. 'We must get going. Matteo will be waiting for us. Are you all packed up?'

'Yes,' I said, wiping my face, 'everything is ready to go.'

The cart drew up outside number six, Jones Street, a red-brick, five-storey house with a front door that was too narrow, dark arched windows on the first floor and the now familiar zigzag of the metal fire escape staircase on the outside.

Matteo pulled my trunk from the cart and handed me my sewing machine, giving Rosa my carpet bag. I knocked on the door. My new landlady, Mrs Majewski, her worn, brown cardigan matching the peeling paint of the door, ushered us in.

'So, Miss McIntyre,' she said curtly. 'Follow me.' Turning, she led us up three flights of stairs, leaning heavily on the banister, her substantial woollen stockings bagging at her ankles. I turned to Rosa and noticed her nose wrinkling at the smell of stale cooking.

Mrs Majewski, one of those capable but long-suffering widows, opened a low door with one of the many keys on a chain that hung around her waist and led me in to a small, narrow room containing a low metal bed, with a thin, stained mattress and bedding piled neatly on top, a small table with spindly legs and a rickety chair sitting beside a reasonably sized window, a small basin in one corner and a tiny fireplace.

She held the key out to me as if it was filthy. 'You must be in your room by ten p.m. and the electricity will be extinguished at ten thirty. I will not have anybody coming in after that, I won't have my sleep disturbed. The water closet is down the hallway on the right and the bathroom is next to it. Two baths a week for each person, you work out a rota with the other girls on this floor.' She coughed a small, ugly cough, no hand in front of her mouth. 'There is a parlour downstairs where you can sit with the others and sew or play my old piano, maybe even talk to each other. Breakfast is at seven o'clock and dinner is at half past seven in the evening. You must not be late or there will be no meal for you. No food in your room, no guests, no washing to be done in your room. Laundry will be taken once a week. Your meals and laundry are included in the rent. Five dollars a week, payable on a Sunday or I throw you out.' Her voice was a monotone, with no emotion, not a flicker of feeling passing over her face.

She dropped the key into my outstretched hand. 'I expect my girls to have morals. I will not put up with lewd behaviour and I insist your room be kept most clean and tidy. You understand me?'

I wanted to laugh but her claw-like hands made me hold back. 'Mrs Majewski, there'll be no time for bad behaviour, I promise you.'

She glared at me, grunted and left.

'Well, this is good,' said Rosa as she shuffled into the room. 'You have a table to sew at and such a big window. Plenty of light.' She put my carpet bag on the bed and looked about her. 'All this space to yourself. And so clean.' She ran her finger around the basin, along the wall. 'Yes, it's good and clean. Now, let me help you unpack.'

Matteo put the trunk on the floor, and I opened it up, the bolt of blue silk on the top.

'Is this the silk you are using to make the dress for Mrs Marshall?' Rosa asked, wonder in her voice.

'Yes. Shall I show you the design I'm working to?' I took out my sketchbook from my pocket.

Rosa inspected the drawings carefully, then bent down and felt the fabric, almost caressing it, then went back to the sketches. 'This will be beautiful, but I think you should be bolder. After all, this is a beautiful material, it should be given a beautiful setting. Do not have a chiffon overskirt, it will hide that shimmering fabric. Make the rose on the waist bigger, make it really stand out and be more playful with the sleeves, perhaps give them ties at the end to create some extra movement. It's a bit serious just now. Make people smile when they see it.'

My understanding of line and colour was improving but Rosa too easily exposed my limitations when it came to the ornamentation and embellishments; I was being too safe, perhaps even a little dull.

'Maybe you could come and look at it tomorrow. I'm going to work on this in my spare time this week – by the end of the week the bones of it will be in place. Perhaps you could help me come up with some ideas?'

'Of course! I will come. Oh... I mustn't forget.' She pulled a cloth-covered object out of her bag. 'A present to welcome you to your new home.' She placed the parcel on the table and unwrapped it. 'This is my *torta margherita*, an Italian cake that I know you will like. Sometimes we eat this for breakfast, sometimes for celebrations, so I think we should celebrate your new home.' She pulled a knife out of her coat pocket and began to cut three pieces. 'I know that grey old woman said no food in your room, but she doesn't need to know.'

She handed me the yellow sponge cake with a very light dusting of icing sugar on the top. I was starving, not having eaten for hours. Such light and fluffy sponge, a hint of lemon and deliciously sweet, such a simple flavour, a taste that temporarily took away the dreariness of my very first home, gave some extra light to that tiny room.

Five weeks after moving to the boarding house I was back at The Plaza, but this time I could greet the doorman with a confident smile, I didn't need to steady my hands, I even thanked the elevator operator as if I did that kind of thing every day. If only Maw could see me, acting as if a visit to The Plaza was commonplace, off to take a fitting with one of New York's most talked about newlyweds.

In those five weeks I had settled in to my new life, long, tedious days at the garment factory, followed by late, exhilarating nights creating the new dress for Mrs Marshall by candlelight, first the toile and then the real thing. The long hours had me in a stupor, but adrenaline, fear and bravado were keeping me alert.

The maid ushered me into Mrs Marshall's bedroom for the fitting.

'There you are, Miss McIntyre,' she said, looking at her watch as if I was late. 'Can we get this over and done with as soon as possible?'

Trying to ignore her unexpected brusque manner, I pulled the gown, wrapped carefully in tissue, out of my bag. She made no comment as I held it up, there was no excitement at the sight of the shimmering fabric. As this was the first fitting using the final fabric, the dress was only hand basted, so I had to gently coax her into it. The surprising silence, from a woman who never stopped talking, didn't bother me as I needed to concentrate, pinning Mrs Marshall into the gown and making any adjustments that were required. The pincushion on my wrist was in constant use, delivering and receiving pins whilst I persuaded the fabric into place. Once I was happy with the fit, I asked her to walk up and down the room. I wanted to see how the skirt flowed, how the light caught the metal thread on the pattern, how the peacock-blue silk came alive with movement, giving it a depth that was missing in its static state. I listened as the dress rustled, as the layers of fabric whispered to me. For the first time since I had stolen that bolt of blue cloth, I could see it as it should have been used.

I stood back to admire the result. The peacock colours, with their shimmer and luminosity, had changed Mrs Marshall from an everyday, insignificant mouse to someone that shone, to a woman that could bring brilliance into an already bright room. There was now a glow that gave her a surety I hadn't caught before. My whole body fizzed with satisfied excitement, my heart running too fast, little flickers in my stomach.

Finally, I asked her to look in the full-length mirror and tell me what she thought.

Her mouth kept twitching between a smile and a grimace, her eyes darting across the room to the door to the drawing room.

'Would you be able to hurry this up?' she asked. 'I have an appointment that I mustn't be late for.'

Was this how it would be? No comment, no pleasure in her attire, no wish to enjoy the dress. I let a beat go by, only flattened my lips, kept my hands by my sides.

'We need to get this right, I don't want to waste your time and have to re-do it later.' I tried to keep my voice level.

Her body softened a little at this and she lowered her voice, leaning towards me. 'It's only that my mother-in-law is in the next room, and I don't want her to see this yet.' She glanced back at the door.

'Do you not think she'll like it?' I asked.

She looked down at her hands. 'No. She always disapproves of my dress. She believes I have the wrong figure and that nothing will look right on me. Whenever I've loved something, she puts it down, always finds something to criticise. If she sees this now, before it's finished, she'll persuade me to change it, make the skirt bigger or lower the hem perhaps, maybe even' – and here she gazed carefully at the blue skirt of the dress, her voice quiet with uncertainty – 'change the material.'

'I think we should ask her.' I walked over to the door.

'Oh, no! I don't advise that.' Mrs Marshall's body became rigid, and she blanched. 'She'll just cause trouble,' she whispered, putting her hand up to her lips as I knocked and immediately opened the door.

In the drawing room, a tall and severe woman, probably in her early fifties, stood in front of one of the windows overlooking Central Park, holding her gloves neatly in both hands. The sunlight gave her an unnatural halo, emphasised by the shimmer in her pale-grey gown.

'Excuse me,' I interrupted. 'Mrs Marshall would like your

opinion on her new dress. It's the first fitting and she's a little unsure of its suitability. We'd be delighted if you could join us.' I held my arm out towards the door and waited.

Her eyes narrowed as she registered my appearance: my clothes, my hair, my general suitability. Wordlessly she came towards me, her movement suggesting that she was fully upholstered, that everything was kept in check, that nothing was given to chance.

'Of course,' she said. 'What a sensible idea. I take it that you've already come to understand that most clothes simply don't suit her.' She swept past me and into the bedroom.

I followed, watching the older woman move around Julia Marshall, inspecting her from all angles, saying nothing. The junior Mrs Marshall continued to stay stock-still, but I noticed her dark eyes appeared to have changed to a pale brown, her breathing seemed a little erratic and her hand was at her neck in an attempt to hide the now rising colour.

It was then that I realised that the younger Mrs Marshall had been trying to copy her mother-in-law or, more likely, had been persuaded to. The same bouffant hairstyle, the pale colouring, the out-of-fashion dress style, even down to the same type of heeled lace-up boots, so impractical for a warm September day.

'As you can see, Mrs Marshall, we've been working on a dress for your daughter-in-law's fundraiser in a few weeks. This is a design that's in keeping with the newest fashions that are coming out of Paris. You'll notice the higher waistline which suits Mrs Marshall's tiny frame, that makes her seem a little taller. I expect you've seen the likes of Mrs Hamilton Cary wearing dresses like this. The skirt is much less full and tapers in at the bottom, but we're still able to accommodate a small train at the back. See how the folds at the waistline shimmer, hinting at a liquidity that will only increase when she moves. I think you'll agree the blue-green brings out her own natural colouring, makes her look less washed out. The fabric was specially imported from India.' I kept on talking, worried she'd interrupt and throw me out. 'I'm looking to make a pale-blue chiffon over-bodice which introduces some additional discretion to the gown without it being too demure. I understand Mr Marshall loves to dance and this dress, with its freer structure, will allow your daughter-in-law to join her husband on the dance floor.'

The elder Mrs Marshall had come to a halt and was staring at me. I suspected that she was a woman who was rarely short of words, but, just now, her mouth was open in a perfect 'o', her breath held, a slight look of confusion on her face, as if she'd not been in this situation before.

Finally, she let out a deep sigh and began.

'Well, well.' Her words were almost accusatory, and my heart gave a small hiccup. 'What's your name? I didn't catch it.' She leaned towards me, looking me over myopically, as though she might find my name somewhere on my person.

'Miss McIntyre,' I said, trying my best to stay polite.

'Ah, yes. Miss McIntyre. At last, someone who's taken my advice. You've actually studied the girl in front of you. You've understood the faults in her shape, and you've been able to bring out the best, hide the many weaknesses. Thank goodness for changing fashion, where would she have been without it? Yes, this will do very nicely. She will complement Rex accordingly. This will ensure she makes the entrance required of her, will ensure people notice her and, perhaps...' Here she looked down at her junior. 'Perhaps, for once, you will no longer fade into the background.' She sniffed, her hands clasped together in front of her as if holding up her more than ample bosom. 'I believe that this may be the first dress I approve of, the one that will help you take your rightful place by your husband's side.'

Her jaw was set, and her eyes narrowed. Then she walked around her daughter-in-law again, examining every detail.

'Yes, very good. Carry on.' And with that, she left the room.

The junior Mrs Marshall had her hands on her hips as if she was ready to roar with laughter except that her inbred good manners wouldn't let her. Her now wide eyes had returned to their deep, amicable brown, the profound flush on her neck already receding.

'Well, I do declare, Miss McIntyre. You have tamed my mother-in-law! Nobody, but nobody speaks to her like that.' She turned to look at herself in the mirror and began moving her dress around, checking the back, the waist, the underneath of the arms. 'I should take that lesson from you. Just talk to her like you know it all. Yes, you are quite the mother-tamer.'

And just like that the mood of the room changed, from the earlier oppressive silence to frivolous nonstop chattiness. No longer was I the irritating seamstress pinning her into a dress she thought she didn't want; suddenly she was telling me all, as if we were the closest of friends: how inadequate her mother-in-law made her feel, the expectation of her performance at the fundraiser in a few weeks, the loneliness of New York when all her friends and family were back in Alabama. She continued, meaningless chatter the content of which I cannot remember. But it served as a strangely calming background music whilst I concentrated on my work. Finally, I was able to relax and pretend this was what I did all day long.

And then we were done, and I was again walking, trying not to run, through the foyer of The Plaza, down the steps and over the road into Central Park, relief coursing through my veins, almost making me laugh. Somehow, I'd pulled it off. Somehow, both the Mrs Marshalls thought I knew what I was talking about, they'd accepted me as someone who understood how to dress them, make them look good. And there was money in my pocket. True to her word, Mrs Marshall had paid me in full.

It was a hot Saturday lunchtime, and for the first time since my arrival in New York, I had nowhere to be.

The whole cross-section of New York society was out either to see or be seen, the jumble of costume that walked past me a welcome distraction from the profound release that was beginning to make me overheat. Women in cool summer dresses with wide-brimmed hats decorated with pastel flowers, occasional flashes of brilliance in bright-pink satin sashes or girls' yellow hair ribbons, the gentlemen sporting near-identical boater hats, street boys with ripped shirts and grubby knees weaving in and out of the crowds, no doubt pickpocketing, slow widows in their heavy black dresses with their bejewelled lap dogs, nannies pushing large prams with lace-bonneted babies. Walking the tree-lined Mall, I felt as if I was in some kind of mesmeric trance. Everyone seemed to float by me. Eventually, I reached the Lake, found an empty bench, and sat, closing my eyes, leaning back and letting the sun on my face, not caring if my skin turned a shade darker or another freckle appeared, the luminosity of my indoor white skin in need of toning down. I soaked up the heat and listened: the tap, shuffle, tap of an old man walking with a cane, a dog splashing in the water, small feet running, the repetitive creak of an ancient wheelchair, the swish of a silk skirt.

I continued to sit, my eyes still shut, my muscles beginning to relax. Five weeks of only occasional snatched hours of sleep was catching up with me and I felt as if my whole body was going to sag, the ability to hold myself upright seeping away.

My tired mind strayed to Netta and what I'd left behind: my constantly anxious sister, her sweet but hapless husband, her two innocent daughters and another child on the way, their never-ending worry about money, that damp and cold tenement. Had I made their lives easier by ensuring they had one less mouth to feed or would the loss of my earnings have made life even more difficult? The answer was obvious. But if I could make my mark here, in this city that seemed more open, that appeared to have doors with well-oiled hinges that would not so easily be slammed in my face, then maybe I could push those doors wide open. Then I would eventually be able to support them, send money home, be the good sister I should have been.

That thought brought me back to the dress, the dress folded carefully in the bag at my feet, the bag that held my future. There was much work to do and I needed to get on with it.

I got up to make my way back to my boarding room, but as soon as I stood there were black spots in my eyes, and my legs gave way. I staggered, trying to keep myself upright and fell straight into the path of a gentleman who caught me.

'Whoa! Easy does it.' He steered me back to the bench. 'I think you should sit and catch your breath.'

Gently he sat me down and then kneeled in front of me. 'Are you all right, miss?'

Uncomprehending, I stared at him. His eyes, full of concern, had a kind intelligence embedded in them. He held himself with a solid dignity. He must have noticed my hesitation because he leaned back slightly, as if remembering the social boundaries he was subject to, as if he'd just recalled that he shouldn't have touched me.

My puzzled fog began to lift. 'Thank you. I'm sorry to put you out,' I said, intrigued by this man in front of me. 'I'm afraid I forgot to eat today and...'

'Oh, that'll do it. A girl's got to eat. Well, I have an easy solution. There's a pretzel cart just over there. I'll get you one and that'll help get your strength back.'

He walked off before I could say any more and I was left watching this stranger amble towards the cart. He had a jaunty walk, as though he was on his way to the fair. He wore a white collarless shirt, with its sleeves rolled up and tucked into a pair of brown woollen trousers, and a brown flat cap that covered his crown of close-cropped curls. He chatted amiably to the vendor before digging deep into his trouser pocket and handing over a coin, then returning with two paper bags and a small paper pot.

'Here you go. New York's finest soft pretzel.' Again, he kneeled in front of me and handed me one of the bags.

I pulled out a dark brown, shiny knot with three holes. 'What is it?' I asked.

He pulled back in mock horror. 'You've never heard of a pretzel?'

'I've only recently arrived in New York,' I retorted.

'Well.' He smiled. 'It's like a bread roll. It's got a slightly chewy crust but is soft and doughy on the inside. And it's oh so beautifully salty.' He said this with a singsong lilt, pointing to the coarse grains flecked across the top of my pretzel. 'The Germans invented it and it's one of the best things about this fine city.' And suddenly there was a brilliant smile that took over his whole body and made me unable to do anything else but join in.

I buried my teeth into the pretzel, thankful for any food, but that warm, salty bread, crunchy and soft all at the same time, felt like a hearty welcome, as if New York had just opened its front door to me.

'Welcome to Manhattan!' the man crowed. He had a habitual blink that was disconcerting when he looked straight at me, as though each blink allowed him a little more access to my mind. 'There you go. There's colour returning to your face. Now don't forget the mustard.' He put the paper pot of yellow sauce beside me on the bench.

'I have to fly. An appointment, you know.' He tipped his cap and turned on his heel.

'Wait,' I called after him. 'What's your name?'

Spinning on a sixpence he took his cap off and bowed. 'Joseph. Joseph Jackson at your service.' That devastating smile, then he ran off before I could say thank you.

# Rosa

I stood across the street from the entrance to 130 MacDougal Street. For the last nine months, I'd walked past this building, on my way to and from work at the garment factory. A three-storey, red-brick townhouse with a cast-iron double porch over a shared brownstone stoop. The top floor had two unusual glass domes, with iron finials and scalloped edging on the roofs. Every day I'd wondered what those domes were for. Today there was a notice in the ground floor window:

*Top Floor Studio*
*Suitable for an artist or dressmaker*
*Enquire within*

The sign held me to the spot. Despite the exhaustion that was making my body ache, a stab of excitement compelled me to pull on the doorbell.

It was opened by a stocky man with an orange beard and thinning hair.

'Yes?' he queried, looking past me and then up and down the street.

'I'm here about the studio.'

'Just you?' Again, he checked behind me.

'Yes,' I said. 'Just me.'

He stared and then leaned forward slightly as if he was shortsighted and was trying to get a better look at me.

'I'm a dressmaker. Miss Maisie McIntyre.'

He grunted. 'I am Mr Franke. That's spelled F R A N K E.' He said this as if it was of utmost importance, before turning and leading me up the stairs. Following him up the three flights, I noticed that he kept hitching his trousers up. Every turn of the stairwell there would be another hitch, but he didn't seem to know that he was doing it, almost like a tic, a habit he didn't realise he had.

At the top of the stairs was a bright-red door, newly painted with a gleaming brass knocker. Mr Franke took a large ring of keys out of his trouser pocket, unlocked the door, and pushed it open.

'Please,' he said, gesturing towards a small vestibule with two doors and a small skylight in the ceiling. Taking the left-hand door, he led me into a large light-filled room glowing with the soft orange hue of the spring sunset. The daylight spilled through from two glass domes in the ceiling and three big sash windows overlooking the backyard of the building. The large octagonal domes had tall panes of glass on each side, the ceiling bearing an intricate white plaster rose on a background of fuchsia pink.

As I stared upwards, he continued. 'The last tenant was an artist. He insisted everything be painted white except the ceiling of each dome must be pink. Please don't be alarmed, I will paint it back to white.'

'Oh, no! We must keep it. I like the colour contrast.'

He frowned. 'Is a dressmaker an artist too?' His German accent was suddenly very pronounced as if the idea of another artist was unsettling.

I smiled. 'Yes, of course.'

'Oh.' He hitched his trousers up again, blinking.

'Do you find artists to be troublesome tenants?' I asked, enjoying his discomfort.

'Well...' He shuffled and again pulled at his trousers. 'Only that they tend to keep strange hours and I don't like my other tenants to be kept awake.'

Just as he said this there was a wail from downstairs. The landlord looked up and reddened. 'My daughter.' He shrugged. 'She is young.'

I began to walk around the room. The whitewashed floor and walls were shabby and in need of a coat of paint, but it was spotlessly clean, with little sign of the previous tenant. As I pictured exactly where I would put the cutting table, two large sewing tables, perhaps three tailor's dummies, my heart rate accelerated, butterflies somersaulting in my stomach. I could clearly see the cabinet where I'd keep all my threads, in neat rows and colour order, I'd have a large chest with small, hand-sized drawers for any embellishments and adornments needed. Beads of every colour made from ceramic, glass, wood, porcelain, or jet. There'd be sequins, spangles, rhinestones, and seed pearls. Flowers made from silk, felt, tweed, gauze, and suede, buttons crafted from Venetian glass, ivory, polished wood, and metal. Every kind of fastening from hooks and eyes, snaps and button loops, belt, and shoe buckles. I pictured ribbons in all colours made from silk and velvet, and drawers full of gold and silver braid, perhaps some cord trimming. I could see the wall at the end of the room holding a large pinboard with swatches of fabric, maybe my latest sketches, there'd be room for a cupboard to keep all the rolls of material.

'Miss McIntyre.'

I was pulled out of my reverie.

'There is a kitchen, through here.' Mr Franke opened a door at the far end of the room and showed me a tiny area with a sink and small range, a narrow cupboard to one side. 'You can make your cups of tea in here.'

All very well, but I wanted to be back in the studio, again walking around, again placing the imaginary furniture, finding a place for the scissors, needles, tailor's chalk...

'Please, Miss McIntyre.' The voice was impatient, wanting attention.

'Mr Franke.' I sighed, clasping my hands together to hide my frustration.

'You must see the other room. Come.'

The front room had three windows overlooking the street, ideal for a salon and a fitting room for my customers. I paced the room, envisaging a comfortable armchair, perhaps a sofa and a small table where I would serve my New York ladies their tea, there would be space to walk up and down in their new dresses, a few full-length mirrors placed along the walkway. No longer would I have to traipse around Manhattan, lugging precious bags filled with expensive fabrics to my small band of now loyal clients. They might complain at having to climb three flights of stairs, but I'd entice them with tea and cake and the fun of a fitting session in my own premises.

As I kept walking the floor, placing my imaginary furniture, designing soft furnishings to minimise the stark whiteness of the room, I could feel a whisper of something pulling me back to my childhood. At first I couldn't catch it until, finally, it came to me – a homely clean smell, the smell that would be in our tiny tenement just after my mother had scrubbed the floors, making me feel secure and free of chaos.

As soon as I recognised it I knew that I would take the studio. Renting the whole floor would be expensive, fitting it out even more so. But I'd been frugal, putting money aside for this very purpose.

The landlord again hauled up his trousers.

'Mr Franke, can your wife sew?' I asked.

'No.' He giggled nervously. 'Whoever heard of a wife who can't sew.'

'I wondered if you've ever tried a belt, or perhaps braces. Do you not get tired of always hitching up your trousers?'

He looked down at his waist. 'My pants? No. My wife won't have those items in the house. Some upset from her childhood.' Pulling up the offending trousers, he expanded. 'The belt buckle most specifically.'

I pushed away the rising images and circled him. As well as the black trousers, he wore a crumpled white, collarless shirt, sleeves rolled up and a shabby black waistcoat that was too short in the body so that the bottom of the shirt spilled out. 'Well, as soon as I've moved in here you must bring me all your trousers and I'll take them in for you. Then, at least, you won't lose so much time hitching them up.'

With a bewildered smile, he said, 'Perhaps I can speak to your husband about the rent.'

'There is no husband,' I said, holding my left hand up for him to see my bare fingers.

'No luck?' he asked.

'No need, Mr Franke.'

'Well.' He looked down at his boots, so large they reminded me of a clown's comedically big shoes. 'I'm not sure that dealing with a woman is correct. Perhaps this isn't a good idea.' He gave an embarrassed shrug.

'Would you deal with a woman if she gave you three months' rent upfront?'

He blinked but said nothing.

'Four months.'

Again, he blinked.

'We'll be quiet and clean and make sure the rooms are well-maintained. But mind, we'll have important ladies visiting, so I hope you'll be keeping the entrance and stairwell in good order.'

The orange-haired man scratched his head, then his beard,

before making out to hitch up his trousers, and then stopping, his face reddening slightly.

'Mr Franke, you know you won't get a better offer.'

'No, I don't believe I will.' His shoulders sagged and he put his hands in his pockets. 'But there'll be no animals and no parties. About that, I must be insistent.'

No animals I could promise, but no parties...

'I wouldn't dream of it, Mr Franke.'


I had to stop myself from flying down the three flights of stairs and onto the street. He didn't need to know that I was afraid I might vomit at any moment, my own body surprised at my audacity. I ran until I hit the corner of Bleecker Street and stopped to catch my breath.

I'd done it. I'd pushed open another door. I could forget the garment factory, now I could work for myself.

I had been earning good money on my dress commissions, more than I had ever imagined I could. Mrs Marshall had been true to her word. Following the triumph of her new blue gown, she'd commissioned three more dresses and recommended me to her friends and peers. For the first time in her life, she'd been noticed, people listened to her and no longer invited her as just a companion of her husband or mother-in-law. Now she found that she was surrounded at the theatre interval, her mantelpiece thick with invitations and I was spending every spare moment designing, sewing or visiting new customers, sometimes an hour's trolley bus ride away. Nights had been spent completing these commissions, days at the garment factory. It was no surprise I could hardly keep my eyes open.

But renting a studio, fitting it out, employing perhaps two seamstresses, and finding new clients to cover all those costs was something else. I may have opened another door, but I hadn't made it through yet and it was already threatening to slam shut on me.

I hurried along the street, aware I was late for supper, but I couldn't consider missing it – I had big news to tell, and I was glad of my friends to share it with.

The walk from MacDougal Street to West Houston Street, the move from the Village to Lower East Side was like watching a change in climate from hot to cold, from almost bohemia to certain poverty. The clothes fitted a little better on MacDougal Street, the heels a little higher. The street had discreet decorations, colourful shopfronts and artistic signs, the men wore bow ties and the children skipped. But as soon as I turned onto the great wide West Houston Street the atmosphere shifted. The noise of the street car, the hooting of car horns mingled with the smell of horse manure, the boys selling chewing gum on busy corners, the men sitting outside the bars with rolled-up sleeves, hats pushed back, a glass of beer in hand, the exotic aromas of the evening's dinners whispering around my head. The voices were louder and less comprehensible, the waistcoats more threadbare, the children's shoes more scuffed as they ran between the food carts. There was a stubborn vitality here that was in stark contrast to the one-dimensional world I'd inhabited in Edinburgh: it was noisy, vibrant and full of energy.

I arrived at the Bassinos's building, a rickety tenement where the windows were not quite square to the walls. I could already hear Rosa, her husband and two other voices, all speaking at the same time, inside their second-floor apartment. Smiling at the noise, I made my way up the stairs to the Bassinos's front door.

There were few things I missed from my life in Edinburgh, but gathering at the table for a family meal was one of them. Before Maw became ill, with her sleeves rolled up and her grey apron over her skirt, she would produce steaming tatty soup or great pots of stovies. She'd slam the pot on the table and, red in the face and her hair frizzing with the moisture, she'd serve up her plain but satisfying food with a 'Get that down yer neck,' and a strangely pleasing thump as she sat down hard on the only proper chair in the room. I could never start my food until I'd heard that whack of substantial skirt-covered rump against plain wood. When Maw was alive, mealtimes were noisy and laced with an unspoken togetherness, a restrained kind of love that smelled of foggy warmth and meaty gravy. Once she died, both mine and Netta's kitchen skills were tested to their worst. The two of us hated cooking and produced dried-up, lifeless suppers that encouraged no cheer around the table. The first time I had been part of one of Rosa's family dinners I almost cried, remembering how much sitting around a table with family, friends and good food meant to me.

'Maisie! *Ragazza mia!* Come in, come in!' Rosa threw her arms up and gave me an enveloping, motherly hug, her soft, fleshy body so comforting, her dark hair smelling of the best of her home cooking. She ushered me into the room where I was hit with the rich, sweet smell of the sauce bubbling on the stove always producing a fizz of anticipation, a little tug at my stomach. Sitting at the crowded table were Rosa's husband, Matteo, their two children, Roberto and Annina, and four others: Matteo's mother, Nonna Bassino, a tiny, shrivelled woman wearing black and an enormous smile, Isabella, Rosa's cousin, holding her recently born baby, her husband, Simondo, and another of Rosa's cousins, Irene, who we worked with.

Rosa was wearing one of her own handmade shawls, one of those beautifully knitted pieces with their tiny stitching and careful detailing that fascinated me: those striking designs that resembled the Fair Isle patterns. Rosa's shawls always matched the personality of the owner. Isabella's coordinated with her colouring perfectly and enhanced her complexion, Nonna

Bassino's shawl was, of course, black but Rosa had flecked it with tiny sprigs of yellow flowers, delicate and discreet, befitting a widow but somehow displaying the same warmth that could always be seen in Nonna's face.

The room was an overcrowded muddle of pots and pans, haphazard chipped crockery, a few glasses, enamel jugs and mugs, a smattering of tin cutlery and an enormous glass pot of dried pasta. A range stove stood to one side with steaming pans and the noise of the bubbling sauce. This was the only living area in the tiny apartment for seven people, dominated by the table and all its occupants sitting on upturned crates, wobbly stools and Nonna on the one chair.

'Maisie, sit down, please. Now.' Rosa gave me one of her maternal glares. Then she repeated the same line she said to me every Friday evening. 'You need feeding. You look so pale and too skinny. No Italian girl would be allowed to get so thin.' She pulled me towards the table, her face creased with mock concern. 'Those men, they won't want someone who doesn't have a little bit of flesh on them.' She winked at me with her usual hint of mischief and sat me down.

'*La cena sarà pronto tra poco. Bambini, lavatevi le mani!*' Her voice was suddenly sharp, her eyes now tired as she shooed her children off to the sink.

Rosa's pasta pomodoro was unlike any food I had ever eaten. The rich scent of tomatoes, the warm burst of basil flavour, they would all produce a living, breathing kind of joyfulness, a feeling that took over the whole body and gave it a sense of performance, as if everyone at the table, laughing amongst the steaming plates, was taking part in a heart-warming play with nothing but happy endings, as if nothing bad could ever happen to us.

'I have news,' I interrupted as we began piling up our empty plates.

The noise around the whole table came to an immediate

halt and all faces turned to look at me. I chewed my lip, the butterflies in my stomach churning vigorously. If I gave voice to my plan it had to become reality.

'I've decided it's time to set up my own business. I'm going to leave the factory and rent a studio so that I can become a dress designer.'

Nonna and Isabella murmured their surprise, the two children stared at me uncomprehendingly, Rosa shook her head.

'No, Maisie, how can you do this already?' She shrugged, she gestured towards me, she stood up from the table. 'This is not right. You are too young, you need a more steady head, you need to do your time and get more experience. Always, Maisie, in too much of a rush.' Her Italian accent had become more pronounced, as if she was telling me off, just as she did Roberto and Annina, just as a mother would to her child.

'Rosa, I've been sewing since I was twelve years old, I've made dresses for women of society in Edinburgh and now here in New York. I dress Mrs Marshall, Miss Milholland and Mrs Laidlaw and they pay well. I want to sew beautiful dresses for beautiful women.'

'You want to sew dresses for rich women,' Rosa retorted, a glint in her eye.

'Well, yes, that's true.' I laughed. 'But I won't be shouted at by the factory foreman for not being quick enough, I'll never again be locked in at my place of work.' I gave her a shrug, doing my best to copy the gesture she used whenever she was teasing. 'I want to sew in a place that's full of light and promise, I want to pay the women who work for me a decent wage and let them go home on time to see their families.'

Rosa sat down again, putting her hands on her lap. 'How will you do this, Maisie? How do you know how to run a business?'

'I've found a studio that will let me do all those things,' I said, avoiding the difficult question. 'It's too good to let it go. In fact, it's perfect. If I don't take it now, I know I'll regret it. It'll mean a lot of hard work, long days, and late nights, but it's going to be the work I've always wanted to do. And' – here I paused for effect, looking over to Rosa – 'if I employ you as my first seamstress, then I know I will have the right person with me to help me run that business.'

There was noise of wonderment as the understanding of what I'd just said sank in. Isabella quietly translated for Nonna Bassino. As I watched Matteo's mother open her mouth with happy shock, Rosa blanched and then she put her hand to her throat.

'You mean I can leave the factory?'

I nodded. 'I'm going back to the studio on Monday, just to see it in full daylight and double-check it's everything I thought it was. I hope to sign the paperwork as soon as I can. I'll need your help furnishing it, getting samples together and making it a place our customers want to be. If I'm lucky I can get possession of the studio sometime next week. Then we can start work.'

Rosa's eyes filled with tears. 'And you'll pay well?'

I nodded again. 'I'll pay you three dollars more than the eight you're already getting at the factory. You won't need to work at the weekends, unless perhaps we're too busy and I need some help. If you do want to earn extra money you can take some of the embroidery home at night; you're much better at it than I am. And when we need to take on more girls, perhaps you could manage their workloads, help me train them up. You could become the fitter and oversee the workroom. Perhaps one day you could be the Premier.'

The tears now fell down her face. For the first time since I'd known Rosa, she was speechless. The whole table was dumb-struck; nobody said a word.

Suddenly worried, I asked, 'Is that a problem?'

'No!' Rosa sobbed. '*Non è un problema.*' She went off in a stream of Italian, incomprehensible words at high speed.

Finally, she wiped her face, smoothed down her hair, the dark tresses escaping from her usually tight bun, and sat up. 'I am sorry I was cross at you. I'm sorry for crying.' She sniffed. Her Italian accent was again stronger, as if she had reverted to her initial days of learning English. 'I have hated that job as much as you. It's much worse than the factory in Glasgow. I've been dreaming of doing the sort of work that you've been able to do with Mrs Marshall. I couldn't be more...' she searched for the word, 'grateful. This will make our lives easier.' She put her hand on her heart and looked at me with deep gratitude.

'Mamma, Mamma.' Roberto wriggled onto Rosa's lap, even though at the age of seven he was a little big for this. 'Are youse a'right?'

Roberto's accent, a mixture of Glasgow and Italian, having been born in Barga, Italy but brought up in Glasgow, always confused me, the contrast between Rosa's loud Tuscany accent and that odd Scots Italian always making me want to do a double take.

'Oh yes my *piccolo pollo, tutto è bellissimo.*' She gave her son a sloppy kiss on the cheek and popped him down on the floor.

'But I do have a favour to ask of you,' I said, slight trepidation in my voice. 'I have to deliver Mrs Marshall's latest dress by tomorrow afternoon and I'm running a little behind. I know you planned to go and see Matteo's brother tomorrow.' I winced a little, knowing my request was asking a lot of Rosa. 'Is there any chance you could take my shift so I can finish the dress?'

A darkness flitted across her eyes and her jaw twitched, but she pushed it away, quickly replying, 'Yes, of course, Maisie. We have to finish those new samples tomorrow, so one of us must be there. If I do this shift then I will take Annina and Roberto to see Marco on Monday.' And then her eyes lit up. 'And maybe it will be my last shift ever! Think of that. Yes, I will do it and I will pick up your pay packet for you too.' Now she was speaking fast, her voice rising with excitement. 'Oh, Maisie! You will never have to step into that terrible place ever again.' She took my hands, squeezing them and then gave me a hug.

'I almost forgot. I have something to give you.' She pulled back and disappeared into the small bedroom before returning with one of her handmade shawls. 'I made this for you. You never look warm enough. And if you insist on not eating then perhaps this will help.' She thrust the shawl towards me.

Taking it from her I unfolded it and examined the pattern. It was different from her usual shawls. Normally she chose a pattern and repeated it throughout the shawl, but this one had several panels with each one having an entirely distinctive pattern and colour range. The designs were still the unique Rosa Bassino mixture of Fair Isle and floral inserts, but the colours were much brighter, unlike anything I had seen before. It was almost as if she had produced a sampler, showing off all her skills and ideas.

'Rosa, this is...' I didn't know how to describe it without it sounding insincere. 'This is the best knitting I have ever seen. The detail, the colours, the intricacy. It's...' And then I found my eyes filling with tears. Nobody had ever made anything like this for me. My mother used to make all my clothes as a child, but they were utilitarian, all made from basic cotton or rough wool, the standard dress with no embellishments. But this was a work of art, made with real love and by someone who understood me.

'Oh, no, no, no.' Rosa stood up, shaking her head and wagging her finger at me. 'No more tears. Put it on, I want to see how well it suits you.' She took it out of my hands and threw it over my shoulders.

'*Bello.* This is good. It suits you. Many colours and many patterns for the many faces of Maisie McIntyre.' She held me at arm's length and inspected me, approval on her face.

## The Fire

Just before four o'clock the next afternoon, I stood on the top step of Mrs Marshall's new grand corner mansion on Fifth Avenue, experiencing an unnerving lightness, like the end of the summer term, knowing you have weeks of light-filled summer days ahead of you, no homework, no classes, no teachers. A weightlessness that held no responsibility, only good fortune and sunshine.

I had delivered the finished dress, it had been greeted with Julia Marshall's usual screech of excitement, the promise of three more commissions and recommendations to two other friends. Any concerns that Rosa had voiced the night before had been pushed away by Mrs Marshall's strength of conviction in my abilities. But as my feet hit the street, a nagging anxiety began to pull at me. It was time to go and find my friend, so that I could make sure she never returned to the factory, that she would come with me to see the studio next week and start work as soon as possible.

Quickly I began to walk towards Washington Square. I could have taken the trolley, but Rosa and Irene didn't finish work for another hour, and I had a nervous energy that I needed to get rid of. The piercingly bright day was fading into late afternoon, the shadows now lengthening and the lights beginning to create an atmosphere of warm geniality. Horse-drawn carriages and noisy automobiles were haggling for space on the road, shoppers were dawdling on the pavement; I dodged them all as if I was dancing an instinctive reel, my steps light and involuntary. I sidestepped the countless building works where the street was being widened and the grand Fifth Avenue residences demolished, making way for more modern buildings to house big, bright shops – the kind of shop a couturier might need.

As I reached Washington Square, I slowed; I was hot, a slight film of perspiration on my forehead. There were families in the square, enjoying the very last of the evening sun, you could smell the coming of spring, that hopeful smell that urges you to be outside, to breathe the long-awaited freshness in the air. Walking through the square I could see Rosa, in my head, packing up her day's work; Rosa was always slower and more deliberate than the other girls, folding her work carefully and delivering it to the foreman with a respectful nod, no rush to leave, ignoring the girls' Saturday night chatter as she checked her pay packet carefully, counting those coins and notes meticulously, already apportioning them to the next week's food bill.

There was a brisk wind, and now that I was dawdling, I began to feel cold and buttoned up my coat. Reaching the edge of the square, at the corner of Washington Place, I walked over to the door where the girls would shortly appear. I thought of the conversation I would have with Rosa, how I would hug her for making it through her last day at the Triangle Shirtwaist Factory, how we might celebrate with a gelato on our way home, how we could look forward to more colourful work days and a safer life in my new studio. But as I was playing this out in my mind's eye, I heard a shout.

'Fire!'

I turned around. There was a man across the street looking up at the top of the building that housed the factory. I followed his gaze. A plume of smoke rose into the darkening sky, an orange lick of flames in one of the large windows on the east side of the block.

'Fire!' the man shouted again.

Then I heard bells and sirens in the distance and more shouts across the street. As I began to comprehend what was going on, the sounds around me, although getting louder, seemed to muffle, almost as if I was under water or my hearing had become damaged. The smell of burning began to permeate my dulled senses. Anxiously I watched the entrance where Rosa should be appearing, but it remained empty. Up the street I could see a few girls who must have just come down on the freight elevator, emerging from the Greene Street entrance. I rushed over to them. I recognised Yulia, one of the Russian women I'd often sat close to in the factory.

'Have you seen Rosa? And Irene?' I shouted at her. 'Where are they?'

She looked dazed, her face dark with a sooty sweat, a bruise on her forehead, her clothes dishevelled as if they'd been pulled at, and there was a rip on the shoulder of her coat. It was as if she too was struggling with her hearing, as if everything around her was moving sluggishly. Eventually she shook her head and gave me an uncomprehending shrug.

I intercepted another, Tessa, who Rosa and I would often share our lunches with, hardly recognisable with her blackened face.

'Rosa?' I grabbed her arm. 'Irene?' But she was just like Yulia, slow and incoherent, her eyes glazed, her face streaked with tears. Then another stream of women fell out of the entrance on Greene Street, and, running up to them, I shouted, 'Rosa, Rosa, Irene!' my voice cracking. But any response was smothered by sirens and bells, the thundering of horses, the clattering of the fire engines making everyone turn. The horses skidding to a halt, the men jumping out, the air becoming more acrid, the tongues of flames above us becoming longer and hotter, the plume of smoke becoming darker and more insistent. Suddenly we were surrounded by crowds of onlookers, jostling for the best position, elbowing to get to the front, crossing themselves, praying, hands over their mouths, wails of distress, wretched howls of anguish. But as the sirens quietened there came another noise, a sickening thud, a sound that seemed to go straight through me, so unfamiliar and ominous. Then another thud and another, bodies falling like apples off a tree. I looked up to see flailing arms, cries and then a shrieking as two women, hand in hand, leaped from a flaming window; then they were silenced by the double thud that felt like a punch to my stomach, as if I had been winded and was struggling to breathe.

The crowd became silent as the fire ladders sat hopelessly against the building wall, too short to reach the top floors, unable to help those women in the windows, as fire hoses shot great blasts of water but rarely hit their target, ineffective streams gushing down the side of the building. Soon the police pushed everyone back as the blood on the sidewalk, mixed in with the water, made for a slippery, dangerous mess. And then suddenly there was no noise, no more thuds, no cries, no clattering, just silent prayers as we watched the police cover the bodies in white sheets, tag their feet, as bewildered, blackened women wandered aimlessly, most of whom I couldn't recognise, none of whom were Rosa or Irene.

I stood on that street for hours, dazed and nauseous, trying to work out what had happened. But, of course, I knew what had happened. The locked doors, the doors that, once unlocked, opened inwards onto a narrow corridor, being no help if there was a surge of panicking women trying to get out. I could see it clearly, more clearly than the wet, soaking mass in front of me: the smoke, the shrieks, the clawing at the door, the turning to run and see if the door that led to Washington Place would let them out, but it too would have been locked, the fire escapes also blocked with bolts of spare fabric, spare flammable cotton fabric. The more I played out the scene in my head, the greater the rise of bile, until I had to lean over, hands on my knees and retch. Was Rosa one of those bodies or had she made it out? I watched as a firefighter carefully brought a blackened body out of the main door of the building, laying it down cautiously like a large, wet rag doll alongside the other women. This was the first of a stream of charred figures to appear, unrecognisable, blackened lumps of flesh. The line of bodies grew, waiting to be taken away by the wagons that were lumbering northwards along Greene Street, ambulances taking the bedraggled and blackened injured away. I stared at a police officer as he began picking up items from the street, a charred hair-ribbon, a small leather handbag, a half-burned envelope just like those used for our pay packets, putting them into a wicker basket which soon became full. I looked down at my feet and my eye was caught by a glint. Bending down I picked up a broken hair comb made from tortoiseshell with a tiny spangle hanging off the spine. I held it between my thumb and forefinger, just staring at it, then beyond it, before carefully putting it in my pocket.

'Miss?' The policeman was in front of me, his truncheon in one hand, the wicker basket in his other. 'Miss, you should move on. We have to clear this place.' He had weary eyes, there was blood smudged on his hands and across his forehead where he must have wiped the sweat. I felt the comb in my pocket, rubbed my thumb over the broken spine, the spiky edge giving me a strange reassurance.

'Miss?' He stepped a little closer.

I nodded, unable to speak.

With no idea where I was going, I began to walk through Washington Square, almost unable to see. But as I moved the fog in my head began to clear and I realised where I needed to be.

It was only a two-block walk but I ran. The crowds were dispersing, but I still had to weave my way through small huddles of mourners and gossipers. As I ran, every scenario went through my head. How had the fire started? Was it another cigarette in the rag bins? The more questions I asked myself, the faster I went. How many people had got out? How many had died? The piles of bodies on the sidewalk made it seem as if no one had survived, but there were those dazed, charred, walking wounded in the distance, perhaps Rosa had been one of those. I ran to each one, grabbing them by the elbow, frantic to see their faces.

'Rosa? Rosa?' I asked desperately, tears now running down my face. None of them was Rosa.

When I arrived at the West Houston Street tenement, I could see that the windows were dark, but I climbed the stairs, two steps at a time, gulping for air, tripping over my skirts, almost falling over. I knocked on the door, out of breath and not expecting an answer.

A man I didn't recognise answered the door. He had the look of Matteo but was shorter, his face less good-natured, his despondent shuffle and red eyes a forewarning of what was to come.

'Rosa? Irene?' I asked, wiping tears from my face.

A slight shake of the head and a resigned gesture to *come in* was all he could manage.

'Where are they?' My voice rising, the question asked too quickly, too impatiently.

He looked down at his worn shoes, wet with dark stains riding up his shabby trousers. 'The pier. They've taken them to the pier.'

I couldn't swallow, my throat closing. Charities Pier was where they'd taken the bodies. Turning away, unable to look at the man, I could see Nonna in the dark, sitting in her usual chair, but she seemed to have shrivelled since I saw her just a day ago, as if she had dried up, withered into a papery, frail version of herself, that would turn to dust if I touched her.

I kneeled in front of her suddenly feeling the dreadful silence in the room. The Bassinos were always talking, always doing something: cooking, sewing, cleaning, sometimes playing cards, but now there was nothing – no voices, no noises from the stove, no heated discussions, no gesticulations, no laughter, just an emptiness that was alien to me. The room was freezing, there was no fire in the grate, no coal in the stove. It was as if the business of the Bassino family had completely shut down, that their reasons for being had ceased.

I took her hand and said, 'I'm sorry.' It was the only thing I could say.

Slowly, she took my hand and put it on her heart, covering it with both of her cold, wispy hands.

That gesture created such a flood of emotion in me that the tears returned, this time in great streams, nose dripping, eyes puffing, hiccupping, as the horror of the evening played out in my head, again and again. The thud of the bodies as they hit the ground, the constant *drip drip* of the water running down the sides of the building, the occasional sob or moan from the bystanders, that terrible coppery, metallic smell that was still in my nostrils. Nonna stayed in her seat, patting my hand gently and whispering, 'My Maisie, my Maisie,' as if she was drawing out the toxic images, just like a hot poultice will draw out the poison.

Those words helped calm me, the same words my maw had once used. I leaned back, wiped my face, smoothed my hair, and sniffed back the emotion.

'I should have been there. I should have been there instead of Rosa.'

Nonna shook her head. 'No, no, no,' she said gently, and then more sharply she said something in Italian to the man.

He shook his head, his elbows on the table, head in his hands.

'Where are Roberto and Annina?' I asked, suddenly feeling that I needed to make myself useful.

The man nodded towards the closed bedroom door. 'They're asleep.' He sighed. 'We haven't told them yet. We thought it better to let them sleep, they will find out soon enough.' There was a depth of weariness in his voice that struck me, a resignation at the difficulties to come.

'Would you like me to stay and help when they wake up?'

'No,' he said curtly, too quickly, with a stiff shake of his head. 'I think you've caused enough problems already.'

It was like a sharp slap to my face, the crack slicing the eerie silence in the room. He and I stared at each other until I had to look away, shame rising up my face like a girlish blush.

'Aye,' I whispered, getting to my feet. 'I'll leave you to it.'

That fire destroyed so much. Rosa had been the captain of her family's ship, running and administering the needs of her crew. Now the sails were flapping in the wind, the ship directionless, unable to move forward. Over the next week I tried to visit to see if I could help, but Matteo was wordless, motionless, incapable of pulling himself away from his grief. The apartment was cold, the stove empty, no more of those welcoming aromas as Nonna had taken to her bed. I worried for Roberto and Annina, who stayed huddled in a corner, unwilling to take any consolation from their mother's friend.

The following Sunday I had originally planned to spend the day with Rosa, making plans for our new business, but I hadn't the heart to do it without her.

I dressed with no purpose and could settle to nothing. Out

of habit I took the lid off my sewing machine but could think of no reason to use it, this piece of machinery that had become another arm, another part of me, now seemed useless, I couldn't bear to look at it. Quickly I put the lid back on. I paced my room, the smell of Mrs Majewski's breakfast rising up the stairs making me feel queasy. Finally, unable to bear the starkness of the room any longer I put on my coat, hat and gloves and went out.

An hour later, feeling empty and a little lightheaded, I sat down on the wall opposite the entrance to The Plaza Hotel to rest. Sometimes I would find it soothing to watch the fashion walk up the entrance steps: the close-fitting, long-silhouette coats with fur collars, the tailored suits with brocaded buttons, the wide-brimmed hats with oversized feathers. But this time I couldn't so easily steady myself; I was too off-balance to be mollified by a moment of fashion-watching.

'It's designed just like those French châteaux, but with way bigger proportions. Its façade is made from marble and white terracotta and the copper mansard roof reflects the green of Central Park.'

These words, so out of context, crashed into my thoughts, confusing me, making me feel as if I was just waking up. I turned to see a man I recognised but couldn't place: the kindly eyes, the worn bowler hat, the jaunty manner. I tried not to stare as I attempted to work out where I'd seen him before. Not only was his conversation out of context, so was he. My world of the rich women of New York or the poor immigrant workers in the garment factories did not include anyone of this man's colour.

I must have frowned because he then said, 'You going to need another of those pretzels? You sure look like you're in need of some sustenance.'

Joseph Jackson, my rescuer that time I'd almost fainted in Central Park, supplier of warm pretzels and sage advice.

He was sitting on the low wall which bordered Central Park, arms crossed and leaning back to admire the building in front of him. He looked as if he was going out for tea with an elderly aunt, wearing an uncomfortably rough woollen suit, white shirt and tie, bowler hat pushed back on his head.

The thought of food, something warm, salty and doughy, suddenly felt appealing, but I didn't know this man, a complete stranger, and I wasn't ready to be friendly with him quite yet.

He must have noticed my reticence as he returned to his original subject. 'Twelve and a half million dollars. That's what it took to build this beauty. Can you imagine ever having that kind of money?'

I didn't answer, just looked up at the building across the street.

'D'you know, Mr Sterry, he's the manager of that hotel, he said, just when they opened, he said, "Building a house like this is much like making a woman's dress. Everything is specially made and specially fitted for the purpose." How about that?'

'How do you know that?' I asked, my attention caught by his analogy.

'I read about it in one of those architectural magazines. I work at an architectural practice just down on Broadway.' He pushed his hat back on the crown of his head. 'All this building work that's going on just now, it's so... exhilarating. Can you imagine? The new inventions we're constantly seeing, the tallest skyscraper, the elevators, the moving stairs.'

'I've never paid much attention to buildings,' I said as I considered the ironwork holding up the portico, patterned as if it was a dark embroidered motif on the white marble, and the raindrop-shaped lanterns that resembled individual pearl beads placed strategically on ebony-coloured embroidery.

Joseph leaned back, his eyes widening. 'Never? You don't know what you're missing. Have you not seen the Dakota Building, St Patrick's Cathedral? Surely, you've seen the new library they're building just down the road?'

I shook my head. 'No. Too busy making dresses for fine ladies.'

And quite suddenly, there was that smile, the one I hadn't quite been able to forget. 'So, you're like an architect too!' He stood up and with a grand bow, taking off his hat, he said, 'Pleased to be acquainted with you, miss. Joseph Jackson, aspiring architect, at your service.'

I got up from the wall and gave a slight inflection of the knees. 'Maisie McIntyre, aspiring couturier, at your service.'

'Say, would you like me to show you St Patrick's Cathedral? It's just round the corner.'

For those last few minutes, I'd forgotten about the fire, I'd been the Maisie I was before. All I wanted was to be her again, without the fire, with Rosa, with my friends. And because of that I went with Mr Joseph Jackson so he could show me St Patrick's Cathedral, I went so that I could have a little bit of normality back, to pretend that nothing had gone wrong.

## Chapter Three

### The Gym Suit

*A sleeveless black cotton and linen bloomer suit cinched in at the waist by a matching belt. The suit is fastened by four black buttons on the belt and four matching buttons on the shoulders. A light woollen long-sleeved slip is worn underneath for colder days.*

# Joseph

## 1911

I stood in the near-empty studio, surrounded by the few possessions that were part of my new working life – my tailor's dummy and sewing machine, a small sewing table, a bag of left-over fabric, my box of threads, a small wooden chair, and a new set of drawers – all dumped in a muddle, looking insignificant in that big, airy room. It needed to be filled with more tables, more tailor's dummies, fabric and patterns, seamstresses and ideas, but I was finding it difficult to concentrate, overwhelmed by what I had committed to. I simply couldn't decide what I should do first: arrange the little furniture I had, start work on my three new dress commissions, or measure up for new curtains in the soon-to-be salon. The only way I knew to make myself focus was to arrange my many spools of thread in their new home, the top of the new set of drawers, putting them into my obligatory rainbow pattern. I mouthed 'Richard Of York Gave Battle In Vain' as I slotted each colour into its correct place. The order settled me, calmed, and grounded me, reminding me of my mother, the haberdasher's shop, of the things that I grew up with, pushed away thoughts of Rosa, her children, what might have been.

My head clear, I sat at my sewing table and began to draw a layout for the room, putting tables in places where the work could be done as efficiently as possible, so that seamstresses didn't trip over bolts of cloth, so that embroidery could be done using the best possible light. It was just after midday and the room was flooded with cheering sunlight, so welcome after the rain and dark misery of the last couple of weeks. The two octagonal glass roof lights were letting the sharp April light spill into every corner, but the room felt stark, the walls newly painted white and smelling so strong it made me a little dizzy. I was impatient to add some colour, the pale blandness oppressing. Maybe I could make something with my leftover swatches of fabric, perhaps create some sort of collage from an assortment of embellishments and hang it on the walls.

When I'd drawn up the plan for the studio, I walked into the large room at the front of the building, my shoes giving a pleasing click on the bare wooden floor. This would be the salon, a room for my customers, which was north facing and cold and would need to be dressed with thick and colourful curtains, warm rugs on the floor, comfortable chairs for taking tea, in winter the fire would need to be roaring. It would be my showroom, a dressing room and somewhere my customers could relax, a welcoming and vibrant place, so comfortable they'd want to stay. I paced the room and sketched.

So much furniture, fabric, so many things required. The list became longer and longer until panic began to catch at the back of my throat. I sat down on the floor, my back to the wall, and closed my eyes. How I wished Rosa was here; I needed her efficiency, her sensible head. I looked at my layouts, my lists and couldn't see how I was going to pay for everything required – I had almost nothing left of the stolen money, it had been used for the four months' upfront payment of rent. I sat on that cold wooden floor, my head in my hands with tears beginning to well up.

Running my hands through my hair, I kept my eyes closed and wished myself into one of Rosa's hugs, the warmth of her cushiony body, her slightly sweet aroma, the softness of her shawl. In the nine months I'd known her she'd become my sister, my mother, my best friend. I'd come to rely on her more than I'd been aware of, the way she'd gently rein me in and be the voice of reason, always able to solve a problem. She would have known what to do. I felt the enormity of her absence as if I'd lost my mother all over again, but this time it seemed so much worse, as if I'd lost everything.

Slowly I became aware of the noise of footsteps coming up the stairs, penetrating through my fog of grief, followed by a tentative knock on my door. My first visitor. Who knew I was here? Perhaps it was the landlord, Mr Franke, checking up on me. I let out a heavy sigh before standing up, wiping the tears from my face, straightening my hair, my skirt, taking a deep breath and opening the door.

'Mr Jackson. What are you doing here?'

He stood on the threshold with a small bunch of yellow daffodils, staring at me with a nervous blink.

Without answering my question, he walked in, handing me the bouquet. 'I came to see the famous dress designer in her new studio, and, don't you know, famous dress designers must always have flowers in their studio.'

I'd never received flowers before. Eight small, vibrant blooms, with their delicate petals, tied together with brown string. Mouth open and unable to speak, I gestured towards the studio.

Once in the room, he did a three-hundred-and-sixty-degree spin, surveying the space. 'This is a grand wonder,' he said, turning the words slowly as he began knocking on the walls, picking dried up bits of putty out of the window frame, tapping his shoe on the floor and finally inspecting the open drawer of threads.

Whilst he examined every detail of the room, I brought the bouquet up to my nose, the smell, the colour, the simple decadence beginning to fill the cavernous space that had opened inside me. But those flowers also reminded me of Rosa and her little tokens of friendship: the cake when I moved into my boarding house, my shawl, the ritual of Friday night dinner. My eyes began to prick dangerously. I needed to stop this emotional torrent, so I quickly busied myself, finding my old cup nestled in the bag of fabric, going to the tiny kitchen to fill it with water and putting the flowers in it.

Wiping my eyes again, I placed the bouquet in the middle of the sewing table. I stood back, enjoying the splash of colour.

'What do you think of my studio?' My voice was practically a whisper. *My studio.* Saying those words was exhilarating, but my stomach was churning, the excitement mixed up with nervousness, worry and anticipation, an almost overpowering feeling of sadness. I touched the necklace I had recently made myself, using that broken piece of tortoiseshell comb I'd found outside the factory on the night of the fire, tied onto a leather string, now sitting around my neck.

'Well, I'd say you're going to need a bit of work from a carpenter. Those windowpanes could do with a little attention and the floorboards are telling me they'd appreciate some love.' His delicate hands stroked the wood grain as he spoke of work that I hadn't even considered. 'And as luck would have it, you find a carpenter standing right in front of you. But I'd say you've found yourself a small bit of workaday paradise.' He spoke as if he had put serious thought into every single word he uttered.

'Miss McIntyre, you've managed to find an unusual building. On the face of it, it's a typical Greek Revival style building, you can tell from the wooden bracketed cornice on the front façade, the floor-length parlour windows and their prim stone lintels; it's just like many of the homes built during the run-up to the Civil War. But do you know what makes this building so special?' His eyes were sparkling as he spoke, his whole face alight. 'It's that cast-iron double porch. The lacey filigree isn't seen in this part of town – maybe up in Gramercy Park – but not down here. And then, just look at those roof lanterns.' He pointed to the glass domes in the ceiling. 'I've not heard of those in this kind of building before, maybe in some grand hall, or some of those Quaker Meeting Rooms, but I'd sure like to know who built this house and what they intended this room for.' He turned to look at me. 'Do you think they somehow knew that the world-famous couturier Miss Maisie McIntyre was going to start her career in this very building? Did they know that some of the world's most famous dresses were going to be made here?'

How I needed that enthusiasm, that belief in me. It felt as if he was injecting life directly into my veins. As he spoke the panic began to subside, and, little by little, that old single-minded confidence began to return. The blackness of the last couple of weeks – after the fire, the mass funeral, the Bassinos, the guilt – it was starting to fade, the hurt easing marginally.

Eventually, he stopped, almost out of breath. 'Yes. It's a great wonder, Miss McIntyre. That's what it is.' Then he shot me that smile, his eyes startlingly illuminated and his whole face a mix of joy and excitement, and I almost forgot every niggling problem.

But then, all at once, the smile faded, and he clicked his heels to attention. 'Oh, Aunt Bettina!' He smacked his forehead. 'Look at me, getting all carried away. I almost forgot. You must come with me.'

'I can't, I've got things to do here, I really must get on.'

'Oh no, they can wait. I promise you; you'll want to see this.' He grabbed my coat and hat from the chair, handed them to me and frantically gestured towards the stairs.

Out on the street, he said, 'Follow me. It's just a couple of blocks away.' And at that, he turned on his heel and headed towards Sixth Avenue. I struggled to keep up with him, almost running, feeling more and more uneasy as we travelled.

'Mr Jackson, please, stop,' I said, catching my breath. 'I need to know where we're going.' I grabbed his sleeve and pulled him towards the steps of a brownstone on Leroy Street. 'Who are you? You've acted as my guide when you showed me the outside of St Patrick's Cathedral, once you rescued me from exhaustion and lack of food, and now you just show up on my doorstep. I don't know who you are. You could be taking me to some scandalous basement bar where I'm expected to drink bourbon and dance for my dinner, or maybe you're taking me to an evening church service. How am I to know?'

He blinked that nervous blink, three, four times, before looking down at his feet. He seemed to be weighing up what he should say. Finally, he looked back up, the blinking gone, replaced by an amused tip of the head, his lips pursed.

'Miss McIntyre... I am Joseph Jackson, eldest son of Mr and Mrs Gabriel Jackson, formerly of Brooklyn, sadly now presiding at Green-Wood Cemetery. I live with my sisters, Oti and Audrey, on San Juan Hill. We come from a respectable family: my mother was an elementary school teacher, my father taught junior high, Oti works in a haberdasher's in Harlem and Audrey in the store just around the corner from our basement apartment. I am hoping, one day, to become an architect. When I'm not working, I'm studying architecture and working in my little workshop making furniture – hand-crafted, hand-designed by me. I don't drink, my parents didn't drink, I've attended church every Sunday since I can remember, and I say my prayers at night.

'I am not taking you to any den of iniquity, Miss McIntyre, I am taking you somewhere to expand your mind. I am taking you to a library.'

He took me by the elbow and gently turned me around to

face the opposite side of the street where there was a flat-roofed, two-storey, red-brick building. The large ground floor windows were arched, and the green front door had the words Hudson Park Branch Library painted above it.

'Why?' I blustered.

But he didn't answer, simply said, 'When you go in you ask at the desk if you can apply for a library card. They just need the address of your boarding house. Then you ask them to show you where the periodicals are.'

I stood looking at this man, dressed in a sober manner, his hair cut tightly, his shoes gleaming. I was confused and caught off guard, hesitating and powerless to move.

'In you go,' he said as he herded me across the street, as if I was a small child. 'I'll be there in a moment.' And he gestured towards the inside of the building.

Pushing down the hysteria, I opened the door and walked across the floor cautiously, as if it was made of thin ice, in awe of the building I was going into. Ahead of me were rows and rows of dark wood bookcases, shelves filled with books. There were tables with a few people reading newspapers. There was silence. Just looking at all those books made me go cold and clammy, and I began to imagine that the people in there knew that books gave me a feeling of dread, made me shut down, worried that I was about to fail.

I'd never enjoyed reading; it had always been a chore, the letters would jump around on the page and land all jumbled up. I didn't read for pleasure, no novel, no poem, rarely more than a newspaper headline – it was exhausting. But I'd always been able to draw. Instead of writing about that tale we'd learned from the Bible that day at school, I'd draw the whole story out. Instead of copying out the sum from the blackboard, I'd draw four apples plus six apples equalling ten meticulously sketched green apples. When these things were shown to me in pictures,

I understood them immediately. When they were presented to me in words or numbers, I would always stumble.

But, out of deference to Joseph's enthusiasm, I did as I was told and was eventually shown into the main room of the library. Joseph sat at the other end of the room, nonchalantly reading a newspaper. Discreetly he pointed towards a table with a pile of magazines: *Vogue, Harper's Bazaar, The Woman's Magazine* and a few others I'd never seen before. Finally, I realised why Joseph had brought me. I could come here and look at the latest fashions for free, anytime I liked.

I sat at that table suddenly greedy for information. I became oblivious of everything or anyone else around me, staying until closing time, poring over pictures of the latest fashions from Paris and London, the most up-to-date patterns and photographs of New York's most recent newlywed in her stylish wedding dress. I took out my pocket notebook and began to draw: a cream wrap-over tea gown with a twisting rope of greenery, intricately embroidered from shoulder to hem; a lavish opera coat made from bronze silk taffeta with panels that flared to a wide knee-length hem; a summer dress made from layers of baby-blue chiffon. My sketchbook quickly became full, each illustration annotated with the type of material to be used, the colour, the cut, the buttons. Every single detail.

All too soon it was closing time and the pinched-faced librarian made to usher us out. To me she was all politeness, but to Joseph, she spoke in a dismissive tone – I almost felt that she would have pushed him if she hadn't been so worried about touching him – making my jaw clench and my lips flatten with indignation. What had he done to incur her disgust? Before I could protest, he put his finger to his lips and shook his head discreetly.

Outside it had turned dark, the temperature had dropped sharply, and I could see my breath in the shimmer of the streetlamps. As soon as my feet hit the paving I opened my mouth, angry words rising up at his quiet acceptance of such behaviour.

'Ah, now, don't you go getting all het up under the collar,' he said, palms splayed upwards, shoulders shrugged. 'She doesn't know any better. It's not her fault. She's been brought up that way, that's all.' He walked on, putting his hands in his pockets.

Again, I found myself running after him.

'But she had no right...'

'I know that, and you know that, but she doesn't know that. She'll never listen to the likes of us. No point in getting ourselves into trouble. Come on.' He beckoned for me to follow him down the street, walking me back to my studio.

And that was how we fell into a strange pattern, a routine of discovering the city that had become my home. On Sunday afternoons I'd leave my work, meet Joseph and find a new bit of Manhattan: the new Pennsylvania Railroad Station, one of the galleries in the Metropolitan Museum of Art, or he'd take me on an architectural tour of the grand Upper West Side, past the Dorilton, the Dakota and the Ansonia Hotel, and, of course, we walked every inch of Central Park. We even took a half day off the day after the New York Public Library opened to apply for library cards. But he always kept me at a respectable distance, as if he was my tour guide, making sure no unspoken line was crossed.

But I also had to work. I had rent to pay, and I needed to furnish my near-empty studio. My customers liked my new space and were happy that I was more available. Dress commissions were rolling in, but I'd had no time to find anyone to help me. Working late nights, early mornings and only ever taking a break on a Sunday afternoon meant I was hardly managing.

One Sunday, I was so caught up in my work that I forgot to meet Joseph, only remembering when I opened the door to him.

'Joseph, I'm so sorry.'

'Our theme today is the Astor family's mighty hotels,' he interrupted in his tour-guide's voice, walking into the studio. 'We'll be taking in the architecture of the elaborate and immense Astor Hotel on Times Square, followed by the Knickerbocker, the St Regis, culminating in the world-famous Waldorf Astoria. We'll be studying the Beaux Arts and German Renaissance design styles, plus I think you'll find that there'll be some fine people-watching, something I know you're particularly partial to.' He gave an elegant bow as he took his hat off.

'No. I can't. I have too much work,' I snapped. 'I have all this embroidery to do, four dresses in the next week and...' My voice broke, caught by a lack of sleep and, yet again, that now too familiar feeling of rising panic, that feeling that I wasn't in control. 'And I'm just not getting it right.'

I'd never been that good at detailed embroidery, I didn't have the patience for it, the attention to detail and the ability to sit still for long periods of time. But Rosa, she'd had the perfect temperament for it, the eye for the tiny detail – she could take each design apart and focus intently on every separate compo- nent, making sure the finished pieces fitted together perfectly. I could only see the overall design and was frustrated by the need to be slow and meticulous. As the weeks went by the finishing work was piling up. Every time I looked at it I saw Rosa, every time I tried to work on it I found myself wanting to ask her which stitch she would use, or what colour she thought would work best. Those times we'd sat embroidering, it was as if we were threaded together with friendship, our differing strands twisting together perfectly. But because of my selfishness, because of my ambition, I'd cut the companionable yarn that held us together. Whenever I thought of this my mind would go down in a spiral – I should have taken her place at work that day, I should have let her visit Matteo's brother, then there would be no Bassino orphans, no wretched and rudderless husband...

'Uh-oh.' Joseph shook his head. 'That's not the Maisie I know. When did you last eat?'

'What is it with you and the need to eat? Why do you care about when I last ate? It doesn't matter.'

'Oh yes, missy, it does. You can't concentrate if you haven't eaten. And when did you last sleep?'

I sighed. 'I had a couple of hours yesterday evening.'

'And food?'

Instinctively, I closed my hand around the needle I was holding and clenched my fist tight. The prick of the needle, the sharp pain giving some relief to the guilt that was clogging up my head, the frustration that was seeping in, letting me have a moment of clarity. I squeezed harder, the relief increasing, so I squeezed harder again.

'Oh, now, just let me take that from you.' Joseph quickly and effortlessly removed the dress from underneath my hands as a bubble of blood began to ooze down my fingers. 'You do not want that dress ruined. Now, come over to the sink and I'll clean you up.'

As Joseph ran my finger under the cold tap, found a spare scrap of calico and carefully wrapped it around the wound, he continued. 'If you don't take care of yourself, there won't be any Maisie McIntyre designs, there'll be no customers walking through that door.'

He tied off the bandage and, continuing to hold my hand, he ran his finger over my thumbnail, his soft skin contrasting against the roughness of the many pinprick scabs on the underside of my thumb. 'Fine designers should have fine hands.' As he said this he gently kissed those old wounds.

It felt like a firework had been set off in my chest as those soft lips touched my fingers, as if all my breath had been taken away, and suddenly all those unsurmountable problems were thrown aside. I studied his face, trying to calm my beating heart and noticed a small vertical scar cutting through his left eyebrow, like a chalk mark, and had to stop myself from running my finger over it.

'You should meet my sister, Oti. She can embroider like an angel. Those dresses she makes for herself, the dresses she wears when she goes out dancing, they're magical.'

'She does?' My voice was a little raspy.

'Oh yes, those dresses can light up a room. Now I know she's my sister, but you should see them, I think you'd mightily agree.'


The next morning I returned to my studio before dawn. I'd managed to finish the dress I'd being working on the day before but as the day progressed I struggled to complete the high collar of a fitted jacket that matched a grey silk evening gown I was working on: diamanté studs surrounded by embroidery in coloured and metallic threads. Yet again, the frustration was mounting as my inability to create what I had designed played out. Not only that, but the studio was a mess as I still hadn't cleared up after myself. There was fabric scattered across the cutting tables, discarded paper patterns and thread, half-drunk cups of tea and empty porridge bowls, the bin overflowing with scraps of material. The mess was making me agitated, but I didn't have time to do anything about it. The meal and a few hours' sleep had made me a little more patient, but patience couldn't hide my clumsy needlework.

'Oh, dear Lord,' came a voice from behind me. 'You sure are in *some* trouble.'

I looked up to see a tall woman stride into the studio and put her large carpet bag on the floor. 'Joseph said you'd be in need of help, but I reckon you're in need of a whole *army* of help.' She put her hands on her hips and surveyed the room, taking in every detail: the mess, the dressed tailor's dummies and the designs pinned to their sleeves, the half-open drawers, the ignored whistling kettle in the kitchenette, the bruises under my eyes.

'First of all, you need someone to clear up around here,' she said and began tidying.

I stood up and put a hand on her arm to stop her. 'I don't need a maid,' I replied softly. 'I need someone who can help me sew.'

She looked straight at me, bold eyes searching for sarcasm. Suddenly there was that smile. I was slightly dazed, my heart jumping a small loop – a feminine version of Joseph. She dropped the fabric she was holding and laughed.

'I think we're going to get on. I'm Otella, but everyone calls me Oti. Now, what do you need help with?'

I gave her the collar I'd been working on. 'I can't make this stand out, there's something missing when I work on it. I know how I want it to look – here, see the pattern I've drawn – but I'm struggling to make it... well... zing. I feel that what I've done here would only bore people.'

We sat at the table, side by side, and examined the collar. Then she gave me another of those enormous smiles, her eyes now shining. 'I've never met anyone who understands this. If I showed this to my friends, they'd all think it was just right. But you, you know it's wrong.' She touched me on the arm. 'Yes, you and I are going to get along *just* fine.' And with that, she carefully unpicked my stitching and re-worked it.

Joseph hadn't exaggerated his sister's ability. Her embroidery sang. The complexity of the stitching, the small changes in her use of colour, the addition of the occasional unexpected spangle or brilliant, all brought it to life. It gave the design a depth and character that I could only dream of when I embroidered. And whilst she worked, she'd hum, tongue between her teeth, seeming to disappear into another world, somewhere that cocooned her and gave her a magic power, the ability to turn an ordinary gown into something extraordinary. Her nose would twitch as she'd get something just right, her eyes narrow when she wasn't happy with what she'd done. Once she'd finished the collar, she completed some tricky tasks on the sewing machine, giving me the confidence that she would be able to pick up anything I might ask her to do.

As we worked, we talked. Was this as much an interview by Oti about my suitability as it was for me?

'If I'm working for you, those white women aren't going to like it.' She kept her eyes on her work as she spoke, her nose wrinkling. 'You think they'll take to me, looking as I do?' Now, she looked up, mischief in her eyes.

I blinked.

'That Mrs Marshall, she will not take to having a black girl measuring her up, touching her, even touching her dresses. How are we going to deal with that? I'd say you're going to have to keep me in the studio, not out front with your customers.'

I liked that she was saying 'we', as if I'd already employed her.

'Am I being a bit too plain-speaking for you?' she asked. ''Cos Joseph tells me you prefer someone who says it like it is.'

To that I could only laugh. 'You be as plain-speaking as you like... and so will I. But would you be happy to hide away, like the help in the kitchen?'

'Well, let me see. Either I stay working at the haberdasher's, selling cheap fabric to the women in Harlem, which is all very well, but here I'd get to do this.' She held out the embroidery she was working on. 'Something most people can't do. I'd get to do this all day long, make beautiful things: beautiful dresses made with beautiful fabrics. I'd get to make something the rest of the world gets to see, not some something that's only seen in church on Sundays.

'We've been hiding out like the help in the kitchen for years.

If I have to do it for a bit longer, to do the thing I love to do, then I'm okay with that. For the moment, anyway.'

I was appalled by this. 'Don't you want to show them your work? Let them know what you can do?'

There was a flicker of withering pity in her eyes as I said this, but quickly she softened, and simply said, 'One day.'

'Tell me about Audrey.'

As I said this, she huffed. 'Hasn't Joseph told you all this? What *do* you two talk about every Sunday afternoon?'

I stared at her. 'Well, architecture, art, design... those kinds of things.'

'Very highbrow, I must say.' Her voice was full of sarcasm, but she was smiling as she spoke. 'Perhaps you two don't talk, maybe you're getting up to other stuff...'

Just as I was starting to protest, she laughed, a deep, throaty cackle.

'I'm jesting you.' She ran her hand across her cheek. 'My baby sister works in the store just down the road from our apartment. But, that Audrey, she sure as hell does *not* take after her name; she's not noble and she's not strong; she's a lazy, good-for-nothin' girl.' I sensed she'd said this many times before. 'She thinks the sun comes up just to hear herself crow, doing nothing to help our cause. Every day I think she'll lose her job 'cos she just does the bare minimum. It drives me crazy.'

But she said all this with a smile on her face. I frowned at her, narrowing my eyes in an unsaid question.

'She's my sister so I can't always be mad at her.'

'And Joseph?' I asked tentatively.

A large intake of breath. 'I tell you, he's sweet on you. But I guess you know that already. What I want to know is, are you sweet on him? 'Cos you've got to know there's going to be a whole lot of trouble with a white girl seeing a black man. There's not going to be many people happy with that.'

Before I could say anything, she interrupted me. 'What you

need to understand about Joseph is he dreams big, but he treads too carefully, he's too willing to accept life as it is. He's the first to stand back and keep quiet when people treat him badly 'cos of the colour of his skin. Sometimes I think he's just too afraid to fight.

'Don't get me wrong, there are times I don't blame him, we've seen some bad things. But when something's handed to you on a plate...' Here she put her sewing down and whistled through her teeth, shaking her head. The skin under one eye started twitching and I wondered if she was replaying a common argument she'd had with Joseph.

Eventually she continued. 'Take that Mr Tandy he works for. There's a man who's had to fight for everything. Did you know he was one of the first black men to graduate in architecture at Columbia? That man, God bless him, he's offered to sponsor Joseph if he applied. He's got the talent, now he's got the means, he just needs to...' Her voice trailed off before she turned to me. 'He's scared to walk through an open door in case they slam it in his face.'

'And you?' I asked, wanting to lighten the darkening mood.

'What about me?'

'What do you want to do?'

'Don't you think I haven't noticed you changing the subject,' she teased before sighing and picking her sewing back up. 'Truth is I haven't let myself look too far ahead. But I know what I don't want – still living in some basement apartment in ten years' time, living with my sister and brother, still worrying about money. I don't want no more debts to pay off, no more making do.'

There was a hard conviction in her voice, in the way she clenched her jaw – something I recognised, something I could sympathise with.

Within twenty-four hours we'd finished the three dresses

and the jacket, tidied the studio, arranged the furniture and hung the curtains in the salon.

Oti and I made a complementary team. I dealt with the customers, designed the outfits, looked after the books, and made sure people heard about Maisie McIntyre's creations. Oti kept the studio, dealt with our suppliers, and, using her contacts from the haberdasher's, she found better fabric manufacturers and importers, and we both did the dressmaking. Her strength was in the finishing. I could give her a gown to embellish, and it would be returned almost as a different dress, something on a higher level. It didn't matter whether it was embroidery, beading, smocking, adding a trim of silver braid or creating a corsage of silk rose heads, Oti had learned how to bring a little bit of herself into these startling trimmings. Her work was confident, almost defiant, like its maker.

And, at last, I could begin to design, making the kind of gowns that I had been dreaming of. Finally, I had time to study the designs emerging from Paris, time to think up my own ideas, not just making copies of those Parisien dresses, time to persuade the Fifth Avenue ladies that my sketches weren't too radical and that the continuing hike in hemlines wasn't too racy. Although most of my customers were still friends of Mrs Marshall, I was beginning to get the occasional mention in the social pages and was starting to see a trickle of new customers coming in, with no affiliation to my patron.

Eighteen months after my arrival in New York I was living my life as that girl in Edinburgh had imagined it: I had a business that was beginning to make money; I had a new friend in Oti, and with her ability to sew, to talk straight and stop me from being too impulsive she reminded me a little of Rosa; I was happy; and I was too busy to consider whether I was falling in love with Joseph.

. . .

Mrs Marshall sat down on the new sofa, having changed back into her day dress.

'My mother-in-law will be just tickled pink to see my three new gowns. There isn't one of your designs that she's disapproved of. And, Miss McIntyre,' she said in a tone of mock deferential approval, 'I can't believe you've managed to persuade her out of her corsets. I could have sworn she'd go to her grave in one of those hideous things. You know, I actually believe she's a nicer person without them; it's a wonder what a bit of oxygen does to a person's temper.'

Now that Julia Marshall dressed in clothes that complemented her shape and colouring, she appeared more self-assured, even seemed a little taller than her diminutive five foot. But the severe bouffant hairstyle remained, I hadn't been able to change her mind on that front.

'It's my helmet, darling, my protection from the big, bad world out there. I've stopped being invisible now that you've taken away my beige dresses. It's a wonder what a big hairstyle can do to keep away those vultures looking for a rich patron for their charity or, can you believe it, for their family.'

'I heard you've been accepted into the Colony Club,' I said, lightly.

As I spoke her eyes widened and her face changed from that of a slightly bored young woman to one of an over-excited child.

'Oh, honey,' she exclaimed, touching my arm.' You cannot believe the thrill of saying to Rex, "I won't be joining you for dinner tonight, darling, I'll be dining at my club." Who'd have thought I'd ever be able to say that?

'Did you know they also have lectures in the club every Tuesday evening, on literature, politics, art, and music? I don't believe I've ever had so much to think about. Mind you, I'll give the politics a miss, a bit too dreary for me – I'm terrified I might fall asleep – and what would that do for my reputation?' She gave one of her too-loud laughs, her hand over her mouth.

'I heard they have a running track. Is it really suspended from the ceiling?' I asked.

In 1912 women rarely exercised. It was seen as unladylike, dangerous even. Perhaps a genteel game of tennis was acceptable, or a stroll in the countryside, but not a vigorous run, a run where you'd break a sweat, where your heart rate would treble, where your calves might be seen. No, polite society didn't like the sight of an energetic woman – maybe one of those varsity girls, all gung-ho and jolly-hockey-sticks, but not a woman of influence, not a well-bred woman of the Four Hundred. The Colony Club on Madison Avenue was breaking all these rules, a women-only private club with high dues and an intimidating list of members such as Daisy Harriman, Gertrude Vanderbilt Whitney and Anne Morgan.

'I had a go on it yesterday.' She was almost breathless as she spoke, her cheeks reddening, her pupils dilating. 'What an adventure! And there's a gymnasium too.' But then her face fell, a little pout appearing. 'There was just one thing that ruined it a bit. The running wasn't nearly as fun as I remember. Exercising in a long skirt, even if it does have those drawstring ribbons that pull up the hem slightly, is so clumsy. I felt like I was running in my bedclothes.'

'Well, I've been thinking about that. Since you can now be away from the prying eyes of disapproving gentlemen, I thought that perhaps you might want to consider wearing something that wasn't a skirt, that would give you some free movement, not be so restricting or hot.'

Mrs Marshall stared at me. 'Whatever made you think of that? You're here to make silk dresses, not gym slips for refined women. You really should think about your place, you know. If this got out, they'll have you making undergarments if you're not careful. Don't worry about me, stick to the couture, darling, not sports outfits.' Her voice was a little vinegary.

I stood up. 'Let me get it for you. Then see what you think.'

I left the salon and walked into the studio, making sure I shut the door behind me.

'Have you got the gym suit for Mrs Marshall?' I asked. 'I need to give it to her now whilst she's in a good mood.'

'Oh, that thing,' Oti muttered, contempt in her voice. 'I don't understand why you even made that garment, encouraging that woman to run around like some child at school, showing so much flesh.'

'When did you get so prudish?' I asked, amused by her disapproval. 'Anyhow, she won't be seen in this, she'll be hidden away in that club where only women can see her.'

Oti handed me two folded garments. 'No, it just isn't right. A woman of her position.'

'One day, there'll be women playing basketball in outfits shorter than this, I guarantee you.'

Oti snorted. 'Now you're just playing with me.'

I left her with a smile on my face and brought the gym suit to Mrs Marshall.

'This is what I made you.' I held up a black cotton and linen one-piece sleeveless gym suit. 'It's a bit like those bloomer suits girls wear at college, but I've made it from lighter material, to let the air in. I've also made you a cotton sweater to wear underneath if you'd like to cover up a bit more. All the other gym suits I could find were all made from wool and must get very hot. Would you like to try it on?'

For once, Julia Marshall was speechless. To fill in the awkward silence I continued, 'You'll find you can move your arms more freely, and without petticoats you'll feel less restricted. Perhaps running could be more... fun in this.'

She stood up silently, intrigue written all over her, and came to inspect the costume. She rubbed the material between her fingers, she held it up against her, even put it up to her nose and smelled it. But all too quickly the interest fell away, replaced by a look of resignation.

'What would Rex say? Even worse, what would my mother-in-law say?'

My mouth twitched. 'Are they members of the Colony Club?'

'Oh, honey, don't be silly. Men can't join, and Rex's mother wouldn't be seen dead in there, she thinks it's full of deviants like that Bessie Marbury. I don't dare tell her I'm a member.'

'Well, then, what are you worrying about?'

She looked down at the gym suit, held it back up against her, considered the cotton undershirt. A little shiver of exhilaration seemed to run over her. 'All right. But here's what we'll do. I'll show this to the board at the Colony Club and suggest that they ask you to make enough of these suits so that each member can buy one. That way I won't be the odd one out and you get a large amount of business. Does that work?'


Now I was living two parallel lives: increasingly busy dressmaker to the rich, white women of New York; Sunday afternoon almost sweetheart, to my black, architecturally minded admirer.

To manage this I had to dress the part: simple but stylish when in my studio, never wishing to outshine my customers; subdued and unobtrusive whenever I was out with Joseph, not wishing to draw attention to either of us. I was weaving my own blanket of mixed yarn, thinking I could combine every new strand I spun. But not every length of yarn I spun was as strong. Of course, at least one was going to break under the strain.

. . .

Somehow five months flew by. The Colony Club order nearly broke us, virtually every member required at least one gym suit, but it paid for completing the fitting out of the studio and a pay rise for Oti. And then we were back into summer dressmaking – lace and chiffon, day dresses, tea dresses, evening dresses, the two of us spending every hour struggling to fulfil our customers' requests, badly in need of more seamstresses and hand embroiderers. But I was ignoring the problem, using the excuse that I was too busy to find any new staff.

'When the summer rush is over, I promise I'll spend some time looking for the right people to come and work for us,' I kept assuring Oti. She was beginning to get that haggard, no sleep look from being in early, staying late and taking embroidery home. She was just as dedicated to the work as I was, revelling in the freedom to do what she was good at. But Sundays, our only full day off, were important to both of us: Oti needed her time at home, her Sunday worship, her time to make sure Audrey was kept in line, I needed my few hours with Joseph.

Joseph was the very definition of conservative, a man of convention – always dressed as if he was going to work or off to tea with an ancient aunt, always walking on the roadside of the pavement, going ahead to open doors, paying for every cup of tea or meal we ate together, and, in public, he never touched me. When we were out, we'd walk slightly away from each other, we'd look at different pictures in the galleries of the Metropolitan Museum, we'd sit a yard apart on the benches of Central Park. We learned the tea rooms that accepted a mixed-race couple – even in a city that had no law against miscegenation there were very few places that welcomed us.

But our relationship couldn't continue on tea and talk. I wanted more. Those few snatched hours on a Sunday were no longer enough. I wanted to be able to touch him, feel the warmth of his skin, the thrill of his breath on me. I wanted him to kiss my hand just as he'd done nearly ten months ago. Why had he not done that again?

One Sunday in early April, we were out on our usual afternoon walk, Joseph playing the tour guide. We'd been to see the Clark Mansion on Fifth and 77th, an enormous house in the style of a French chateau, a rich man's folly that made me laugh out loud and then we were walking back downtown and found ourselves outside the St Regis Hotel.

'Do you think that one day we'll be able to walk in there, arm in arm, without hotel management taking notice?' I asked.

My question seemed unanswerable. I had no doubt that, one day, I'd be accepted through those doors, but I was uncertain that the two of us could ever stroll in without being hastily evicted.

'Could we go back now? My hands are freezing.' I'd forgotten my gloves and, despite the brisk walk warming me up, my fingers had turned white at the tips.

And then, just as if we were standing in an empty field, with no one to notice us except the field mice, he picked up both my hands, the touch making me feel as if I'd been hit by a jolt of lightning. He balled my hands together and covered them with his own warm, soft hands, just as my mother had when I was a child, and then brought them up to his mouth and began to blow gently, through the gap between his thumbs.

This small act of kindness made me ache, made me close my eyes, made my middle burn with a long held-back desire, a lightning bolt of sexual charge, ten months in the making. Something loosened in me.

I leaned forward and whispered into his ear, 'Let's go back to my studio.'

The wisp of his breath on my cheek heightened that sense of intoxication; I caught the smell of him, always so clean and well-scrubbed.

'I have a better idea,' he said, pulling back to look at me. 'My place is closer. Why don't you come and see my workshop? I've been talking about my furniture for so long, it's time I showed you.'

I could hardly hear him for the slamming of my heart in my chest, the persistent background noises of the city pushed aside. But I was certain of what he'd said and before he could change his mind, I replied, 'I'd like that.'


Joseph, Oti and Audrey lived in the basement of a rowhouse on West 58th Street and Amsterdam Avenue. As it was a Sunday, despite the cold, people were out on the street: children were playing on the stoop, mothers in their church clothes, the men's ties loosened, waistcoats unbuttoned, sleeves rolled up. Joseph waved me towards the steps down to the apartment, all eyes watching us.

'Seems like you're a Sunday afternoon marvel. I'm afraid you'll be the subject of a lot of gossip for the next few days,' he said, winking at the child hanging over the stoop banister whilst he opened the door.

Inside was a small, four-roomed apartment that smelled of furniture polish and scrubbed floors. It was neat but sparse.

'Audrey and Oti are out visiting this afternoon. I was hoping they'd be back by now, then I could tell those busybody women upstairs that you were visiting for them. Seems like I just turned you into a hussy. But don't you worry, I'll get Oti to set them straight. Come on this way.' We walked through the sitting area, into the galley kitchen and out into a tiny backyard.

The yard was mostly taken up by a lean-to, leaving only a bit of space for some scrubby grass and an old wooden chair. 'Gets about two hours of sun on a good day. Audrey loves to sit out and catch those sun rays.' He opened the door of the lean-to.

'Welcome to the workshop of the soon-to-be renowned carpenter Mr Joseph Jackson.' He ushered me in with a flourish.

Inside was cramped but meticulously tidy – a heavy wooden bench sat against the wall of the house, every inch of the wall covered in carpenter's tools: two different-sized saws, two hammers, three chisels, a long wooden ruler hanging beside its shorter companion, a hand plane and a set of wooden callipers. On the bench were old food tins filled with nails and screws, clips and drill pieces, a few paintbrushes and cloths. All the tools were well worn but spotlessly clean, everything was hanging neatly or sat on the bench in sharp, military fashion, no sawdust, no wood curls on the floor.

'This here is my thread drawer. Being here calms me, makes me feel safe. This is where I can forget about everyone else, about those fools that stared at you on the street and get on with the fine business of creating something.' He looked just how I would feel when I was with my threads, lighter, as if anything was possible.

Running my hand along the workbench with its snicks and cuts I could imagine him in a larger studio, one where he could afford all the tools he required, using the finest of woods, working for the best of society.

On the bench was a wooden stool. I ran my hand over the top, savouring the warmth of the smooth wood, the slight curve in the seat, appreciating the pattern of the grain.

'I've just about finished this. Only need to varnish it. Had to borrow a wood-turning tool, don't have one of those myself. Took me a while to learn how it works. Had to borrow it off the shop down the road; luckily he's sweet on Oti and was happy to lend it if it meant he could come by and pick it up, hoping to get a glimpse of my big sister.' He rubbed his hand over the barrel of one of the legs, talking too fast, his face becoming a little shiny.

'I've got a present for you,' I interrupted, wanting to again feel the wisp of his breath on my cheek.

He stopped, confused. 'Say what? A present? Why would you get me a present? It's not my birthday.'

'I can get you a present if I want to,' I said playfully, opening my bag and pulling out a folded piece of material. 'I made you a shirt.'

Holding it up against his chest I said, 'It's made to measure, I had Oti measure you.'

'Oh, now, that's not fair. She said she was making me a new jacket, which now I come to think of it, I haven't seen any evidence of. You and she are as sly as each other.'

'Come on. Off with your jacket, off with the shirt. I want to see that it fits.'

'Why, Miss McIntyre. I do declare,' he said in a high, coy voice. 'You are being mighty forward today.' He backed away a little, onto the side of the workbench.

Having none of it, I approached him and went to pull his jacket off. He flinched.

I stepped back. 'Why are you so hesitant with me? I know you want to be with me, I know you don't want to spend your life walking two steps behind me. Don't you want to touch me? Don't you want to hold my hand? Don't you want me dressing you in your new handmade shirt when nobody's looking?'

He sagged as if I'd just punched him in the stomach. 'I do. I truly do, but I'm scared. I'm scared what those people out on our street will say about us, I'm scared that someone will punish me—'

'Punish you?' I interrupted. 'Perhaps I'm naïve, but there's no law against us being together.'

'That may be true but, I'm sorry to say this, you are being *mighty* naïve.' He let out a great sigh.

'You see...' – he played with the button on his jacket – 'my friend Jacob, he and I grew up together, he did just what you and I are doing. He walked out with the kindest, sweetest white girl. One day, they were walking down the street and she'd got upset about him being late. She raised her voice, and suddenly, from nowhere, they were surrounded by three white men. They said they were sure Jacob was hitting on Sarah, that she was frightened. So, they went on into him.' He bit his lip and looked up at me. There were tears in his eyes. 'They beat him until he couldn't move no more. Died two days later. Didn't matter what Sarah said to the cops. There was no telling them that Jacob was anything other than a rapist. Those three men were seen as heroes. Darn near broke her.' He looked down at his hands. 'Maybe I'm just worried that's going to happen to us.' His voice was a whisper.

'So, you don't want to see me anymore? Is that what you're saying?' It felt as if the walls in the workshop had just fallen away and a cold wind was now whipping across my face.

'I don't know what I'm saying,' he croaked, before clearing his throat. 'I just wish it wasn't so.'

All I wanted to do was take him in my arms and erase those memories. I'd become so used to hanging back when I was with Joseph, but now there was no one watching, no one to disapprove. With my heart thudding in my ears, I began to unbutton his shirt, slid my hand under the material and pushed it off his shoulder, pushing the other until the shirt fell off his back. There was a shock of electricity and we both jumped. With a nervous giggle I tried to keep my breathing under control, picked up the new shirt, keeping my eyes on Joseph's and pulled an arm on, going around his back and pulling on the other arm, then drew the front of the shirt together so that the placket met the buttons and began to do them up, but Joseph caught my hand. We held each other's gaze, the rest of the world suspended, the only sound the rustle of his new shirt against his skin.

'You sure about this?' he whispered, bringing himself closer to me, that fresh smell so intoxicating to me.

. . .

I couldn't concentrate on my work, despite deadlines that we had to meet: dresses required for upcoming soirees, parties, and theatre openings.

'You've got ants in your pants, girl,' Oti commented. 'What's up with you? I've never seen you so distracted. Don't tell me Joseph has finally made a move on you?' She rolled her eyes. 'That boy, he's got the slick moves of a snail.'

I laughed. 'Well, maybe I made a move on him,' I said, coyly. 'I made him that shirt and I had to make sure it fitted properly.'

'Oh, I see how it is.' She grinned. 'Thank the Lord! I thought you'd be doing nothing but talk for the rest of your lives.' But a cloud crossed her face. She looked down at her left hand, rubbed a sore spot on the heel of her thumb.

'You know I'm a plain speaker, so I'm just going to say what's on my mind.' She let out a heavy sigh. 'That boy always takes the path of least resistance. He's used to doing as he's told, without much thinking. Most people tell us not to do things: don't mix with white people, don't walk through the same door, can't eat in the same restaurant, don't breathe the same air. And here you are suggesting the very thing we're told we shouldn't do. Now don't think I'm against what you're after. I'm not, I see how happy you make each other, but...' She stopped and sighed, now looking at me directly.

'You and Joseph do things too differently,' she said carefully. 'Where you push straight through those brick walls, he finds ways around them, keeping his head down, staying safe. Did he tell you what happened to his friend Jacob?' She held my gaze.

I nodded, putting my sewing down.

'Well now you know why he is like he is.' She'd softened her voice, looking down at her own sewing, inspecting her work before she put it down again abruptly.

'And what were you doing trying to take his shirt off?' Her eyes were wide, irritation in her voice. 'What were you thinking? You don't want anything interrupting that great Maisie

McIntyre ambition of yours. No coffee-coloured baby to get in the way of your plans.'

In my family, this kind of candid conversation would never have happened, or if it had it would have been excruciating, stomach-twistingly embarrassing. Maw would have gone red in the face, harrumphed and quickly found an important chore that could no longer be put off, Netta would have shooed the children out of the room, Duncan would have picked up the newspaper to hide behind. But here, Oti's dark eyes were now full of concern, she was leaning forward, looking for my reaction, wanting to help.

'I know that brother of mine, not considering the consequences. He's more worried about what people think of him, not what's going on in his heart.

'I know you're both capable of making your own choices, but I'm just pointing out that he'll need keeping on the road you want to travel – I don't believe that boy has ever made up his own mind.' Here she rubbed the bridge of her nose. 'What I'm wondering is, how much Maisie McIntyre wants to be with someone who doesn't have the same mind as you, who flinches from any kind of conflict. Where's that going to leave you when he's still working as a clerk and you're dressing the First Lady?'

The following Sunday, instead of dressing in my usual neutral outfit, ready to blend into the New York crowds, I wore a new dress I'd made for myself, dark bronze with a midnight-blue underskirt and lace trimming.

When Joseph appeared at his usual time, he bowed, he gave me his elbow and then he flashed me that irresistible Joseph Jackson smile. 'Miss McIntyre. Would you accompany me to the park? I wondered if you'd like to walk down the Mall today, it's such a beautiful day – a day to be seen.'

I blinked. He picked my hand up and kissed it. All that

confusion erased with one kiss, that one tiny movement. Arm in arm we walked down the stairs.

We walked all the way from MacDougal Street to Central Park, side by side, not seeing anyone around us. And we talked, finally being open about our misunderstandings, about what we wanted to do and how we'd go about it, about how we could possibly make our lives work. I clung to his arm, cherishing the warmth of his body, the harmony I felt when our shoulders touched, the way he blinked at me when he was nervous. Arriving in Central Park, I felt lighter than I had for months, I could feel that optimism that I'd had when I first arrived in Manhattan. The sun was out, a welcome interlude after days of rain. Walking down the Mall we began to notice our surroundings, the crowds beside us, the bright orange and red of the autumnal leaves, the children weaving in and out of the obstacle course of women's skirts, the smell of pipe smoke cutting through the cold afternoon air. The sun was beginning to go down, it was cooling off and we should have been thinking of turning around to go back to my studio, but we were still talking, still cocooned in our personal bubble, taut and ready to burst. It was then that I noticed Mrs Marshall walking towards us on the arm of her rarely seen husband. Rex Marshall spent many weeks away, usually on business in the South. His family wealth had been accumulated through the railroads, a wealth that only seemed to increase, however hard his wife tried to spend it. Julia Marshall was making the most of the unusual opportunity to promenade with her husband, stopping to chat with those they passed, waving at others further away. She wore a burnt-orange military-style winter coat that I had made, with matching fur hat, cuffs and muff. They made a striking couple: well dressed, happy and with an air of rich contentment.

I was just about to approach her when she noticed me. Unlike when she had recognised others she knew, this time she just blinked, her face became pale and a look of discomfort crossed her face, as if she had indigestion. And then she turned her face towards her husband and carried on walking past us, with no acknowledgement, no nod of the head, not even half a smile.

'What is it?' Joseph asked.

I had turned to watch the Marshalls walk on behind us. The colour had risen in my face and I felt the prick of humiliation.

'Nothing,' I said. 'I thought I recognised someone, but it was a mistake.'

The next day Mrs Marshall had an appointment where I was to show her some new designs for her summer wardrobe: three evening gowns, three day dresses and a travelling suit. I had laid out my drawings, along with snippets of my chosen fabrics, samples of embroidery and other suggested embellishments such as flowers and covered buttons to be sewn onto a sash. A tray with tea and cake was waiting. Normally she looked forward to these sessions, where she could be herself, instead of the person her mother-in-law thought she should be. She'd be chatty, gossipy, take time over the details of her new outfits and discuss what event each one was needed for, she'd always be appreciative of the designs, always happy that they were just that little bit different. But this time she was unusually fussy, finding problems where there were none and becoming even more irate when I tried to correct her.

'No, these just won't do,' she finally said, pulling away from me, where we'd been huddled over the drawings. 'I don't know what's got into you, Miss McIntyre. These outfits are just plain old boring. These are the kind of dresses I might have worn before I met you, when my mother-in-law was in charge of my dressing. Since when did you start using brown fabric in your repertoire? When did a simple design of beige polka-dots on a white chiffon become something you'd recommend? What has become of you?'

I felt as if I'd been kicked. Her words couldn't have hit me harder if they'd tried. When had I ever designed anything that could be considered boring? Unwittingly, she was simply echoing what Oti had told me the day before. These two women knew my work the best, these two were most familiar with my love of bright colour and the interesting little details. I knew that they weren't wrong.

I sat up straight. 'Why don't I take these away and, if you can come back next week at the same time, I'll show you something else I've been working on. Something much more striking. I was just concerned that you would find it too outlandish, that you'd stand out a bit too much. I was worried that your mother-in-law might not take to my new ideas.' Here I was ad-libbing. I had no new designs in my back pocket, I had nothing else to fall back on.

'Miss McIntyre. Since when did you care what my mother-in-law thought?' There was a tart mocking tone to her voice that grated with me.

She stood up. 'I know exactly what your trouble is, Miss McIntyre. You're seeing that man, that...' She couldn't bring herself to say the words. And then her whole demeanour changed, she became serious, her voice turned to a growl, her eyes to steel, her mouth rigid.

'Being seen with... someone like that' – Mrs Marshall's voice dropped to a hiss – 'will destroy everything you've built. My friends won't have their dresses made by a woman who...' She had her hands clasped in front of her, her knuckles white, the skin so taut on her bony hands they seemed claw-like, ready to pounce. 'I'll be forced to take my business away and when others find out why, they will most certainly follow.'

Slowly I put my hands on my lap, fingers splayed out on my skirt, forcing myself to stay silent, pushing the anger down.

'Do you hear me?' Her voice was sharp now, her colour rising.

The air in the room was thick with her words. I thought of Oti in the next room, who had made so many of Mrs Marshall's dresses, whose clever, quirky ideas had made them so much better, whose fierce pride and professionalism had produced works of art. I thought of Joseph and the way he used his workshop to calm him from the kind of words I was listening to.

'Do you understand what that would mean? Your business would be in ruins. There would be no more recommendations. I know my influence and just one word would take away the regard that some hold you in.' She bent down, putting her face right in front of mine, her words making her seem ugly. But as she stared directly into my eyes, she softened, her voice lowering. 'Now, I have no wish to lose you. You have made me into a woman of note.' She couldn't keep my gaze, turning away as if the truth was too difficult to meet face on. 'Your ideas and your understanding of what suits me, what makes me stand out have made people take me seriously. You have given me a confidence I didn't think I possessed. Even my mother-in-law treats me with more respect. I'm no longer the silly little wife of a rich man. Did I tell you I've been asked to chair a fundraising committee? I'm no more sensible than I was two years ago, but somehow, because I care about how I look, people care about what I say.'

She sighed. 'But I can't be connected with you in any way if you continue to see that man. I will no longer be credible.' She picked a piece of fluff off her coat. 'I'm sorry but that's just the way it is.'

She fussed with the buttons on her coat, put on her gloves, checked her hat in the mirror.

'I'll come back next week, when you've had time to come up with some new designs and to make some...' She winced. 'When you've made some changes in your life.'

'I obviously have some thinking to do,' I said, haltingly, trying to fill the space, furious at my deference.

She turned and stared at me. 'There's nothing to think about. You leave him. I'll continue my business with you, keep recommending you to the likes of the Vanderbilts etc. Your business flourishes and I keep my illustrious dressmaker. Simple.'

She turned to leave and then halted suddenly. When she turned there was a large smile on her face. 'I have the perfect solution. Of course, why didn't I think of it until now?

'You need someone to take you in hand, help you get your priorities sorted. And...' Here she gave me a sly smile. 'I know *exactly* the right man for you. He'll bring you back to your senses.' She clapped her hands in glee, like a little girl who's just been promised ice cream, before hurriedly leaving the room.

She called from outside the door. 'You'll find my matchmaking skills are amongst the finest in this grand city.' And as she began to make her way down the stairs she said in a fatuous singsong voice, 'You know I'm never wrong.'

Holding in my temper, I shut the door as quietly as I could and leaned back against it. Which was I most angry about? The fact that Julia Marshall had noticed my waning ability to design or that she had ordered me to get rid of Joseph. As I stood behind the door, I couldn't tell, both issues so intertwined. Joseph had begun to take over my every thought. Had my work, the very thing that I loved to do, become secondary? Had my ability to understand the colour, shape and line of a dress, the drape of a fabric, the finer detail of a piece of embroidery, been muted by my desire for Joseph? Did I believe that Mrs Marshall had been able to see what I hadn't?

No. I clenched my fists and balled them into my eye sockets, suppressing a roar of rage. Nobody was going to own me, nobody was going to tell me how to live my life.

## Chapter Four

### The Secret Dress

*A pale-yellow chiffon full-length day dress, with a full swathe from waist to hem. The full-length sleeves have long satin pointed cuffs that when turned back reveal the embroidered initials M&J. The yellow chiffon pleated belt is double sided, the reverse made from a burnt-orange slubbed silk with the initials M&J embroidered at the centre. The daffodil-yellow satin underdress is made in a sheath style and has M&J initials embroidered down the side seams, interspersed with tiny embroidered daffodil heads.*

# Determination

## 1912

There was no one I could tell about what Mrs Marshall had said. Certainly not Oti, definitely not Joseph – I knew how he would react. I simply gritted my teeth and ignored her.

'You're looking all grouchy – a great big frown on your face and tight lips. Joseph been mean to you?' Oti asked.

'No,' I growled.

'See, there you go. I just asked a question. What's up with you anyhow?'

We were going through fabric samples, deciding on what was needed for the next season – a difficult task, having to anticipate future tastes well in advance. I was feeling lacklustre, with little energy for anything but antipathy towards Mrs Marshall. What had happened to the Maisie who had left Joseph's house floating on a cloud? Where was the Maisie that day she'd found her studio?

Considering how to respond to Oti, my eye was caught by a pale-yellow silk chiffon.

'I'd like to get some of this,' I said.

Oti frowned. 'We're looking at autumn and winter fabrics, not floaty summer fabrics. What are you thinking?' She kept her voice even but I could see she was irritated by my lack of focus.

'I'd like to experiment on something. I just need a few metres, plus I'd like some of that bright-yellow satin.'

Her mouth twitched. 'You're the boss.'


When those fabrics were delivered I rushed back to my room at the boarding house, leaving work a couple of hours early. I'd had an idea for a dress and spent the next few evenings obsessively working late into the night.

I had replaced the small table in the window with something much larger, too large for the room, but a good size for laying out fabric, perfect for cutting out a pattern, ideal for keeping a delicate fabric away from wooden floorboards with splinters and nails. I began with the bright-yellow satin, making a full-length sleeveless sheath under-dress, slightly fitted to my shape. The smooth coolness of the shiny fabric is so difficult to hold, requiring patience and concentration to ensure seams don't slip, to guarantee the shape stays true. When using the sewing machine, I had to run it slowly, careful that the seams didn't pucker.

With the chiffon dress, the delicate fabric needed equally careful handling. I wore cotton gloves to ensure nothing caught at the sheer material, a sharp needle was needed to make sure the edges didn't fray. The rhythm of the hand-stitching had me in a trance as my mind wandered as to what this dress was for. Truthfully, I wasn't sure. I only knew it was a dress for Joseph and me, something I would only wear for the two of us. But it wasn't a Sunday afternoon dress, it was surely for something more elegant, something more celebratory; maybe our first tea at the St Regis, I thought rather grandly. The later I worked into the night, the more I became frustrated, tutting at my work, dissatisfied with what I was producing – something bland, nothing Maisie McIntyre would wear. Was I trying to be someone else?

I put the finished dress on my tailor's dummy and placed it in the centre of the room. I walked around the dress, trying to work out what I had made it for. As I circled it I found myself envisaging myself and Joseph, arm in arm, laughter and smiles, on the steps of a church. This made me stop. No. I couldn't think that. Not yet.

But once the thought was there, it wouldn't go away, it needled its way into every thought, took away my sleep, nudged at me on my walk to work. When I returned that evening, the dress was still there, still waiting to be identified. I circled it again talking to it, asking it what it wanted, what it needed.

Finally, the simplicity of it hit me. All it needed was a bit of Maisie McIntyre. It needed colour, it needed embellishments, it needed character. Quickly I rummaged through my bag of scrap fabric and found the perfect foil. A burnt-orange slubbed silk, just enough to make a splash. I took the yellow chiffon belt with its irregular pleats and invisible fastening and turned it over. Yes, I had enough of the orange to create a hidden reverse. Then I looked at the sleeves. Plain chiffon sleeves, just hemmed simply at the cuff. I huffed at my lack of vision and scrambled around my bag for any of the leftover yellow satin. Pulling it out of the bag I could see there was enough to create two deep cuffs, pointing on the top of the hand, which could be folded back if required.

I smiled. This was more like it – this was making me feel lighter, more like me. Mrs Marshall was wrong. Loving Joseph didn't make me lose my ability to design. It was just that I needed to admit to myself that I had dared to love him.

I could imagine Oti rolling her eyes at me, laughing at my inability to read my own feelings. Yes! I took out my sketchbook and begin to draw, my heart skipping several beats. I rummaged through my drawers for some metallic thread, found a packet of seed beads, discovered a few crystal beads of the right size. I looked at the yellow sheath under-dress and almost laughed. Yes, of course, I knew what this dress needed.

The following week, I was again up late, finishing the hem of the outer dress. My eyes were tired, the lighting not as good as I would have liked it to be, but I felt that there was a time limit on this dress and that it needed to be finished shortly, ready for the right time, ready, perhaps, for some spontaneity. There was a sharp knock on my door and my landlady, Mrs Majewski, let herself in.

'You have a visitor. A male visitor.' She sniffed with disapproval. 'There'll be no men in this boarding house, especially men of his sort.' She sniffed again, narrowing her eyes.

'What sort?' I asked. But as I said this I realised, from her look of outrage, that she could only have been talking about Joseph.

She shuffled her feet, unable to meet my eye. 'I suggest you go down and see him. I don't want him in my house.'

Hurriedly, I put my sewing down and followed my landlady downstairs. She opened the front door to reveal Joseph, hands in pockets, feet kicking the pavement, eyes to the street.

'What are you doing here?' I asked.

'I needed to see you.'

'Why? What's happened? Is Oti all right? Audrey?'

Mrs Majewski frowned at me. 'You know this man?'

I grabbed Joseph's elbow and led him down the steps, onto the street and walked a few yards away from prying ears.

'Joseph, what is it?' I was beginning to get scared, worried that something terrible had happened to Oti.

He pulled his arm away from mine and stepped back, sighing, shaking his head, his mouth in a downturn, his eyes shining.

'We have to stop. We can't do this anymore.' He was looking at my shoulder, then at my hands, finally at his feet as he put his hands back in his pockets and lowered his head.

'I don't understand. What did I do?' Panic was rising. That self-satisfied feeling of achievement, that smug way I'd been seeing the world over the last few days, the way I'd felt that I'd sorted everything out between us, that we were going to be fine, that we were going to get married, to have children, that we were invincible, that we could face anything together... I began to feel nauseous because it was gone, I couldn't even reach for it. Remarkably, it already seemed out of sight.

'You didn't do anything.' He let out a long, controlled breath, then looked up at the night sky, as if for help. 'I don't want to see you anymore.'

'No. That can't be true. I know it's not true.' Alarms were screaming in my head. 'What happened to make you say that? You were happy when I saw you three days ago, you wanted to be with me. You said so.'

'I'm scared.' He looked down again, his shoulders sagging. 'I don't have the energy.' Now he looked back up at me. 'It would be easier for both of us if we didn't do this.'

'No, Joseph, it would be easier if we faced it... them... all those people who disapprove of us. It would be easier if we did that together.' I grabbed both of his hands and held them in mine. 'We can do this. I love you and I need you.'

There it was. I'd said it out loud. I'd always thought I hadn't needed love. I was Maisie McIntyre who only wanted to work, who wanted to be better than all the rest at design, who wanted to be a couturier, someone who was talked about for her creations, not for her love affairs.

Joseph gave me that nervous blink: one, two, three, four.

'No,' he said. 'It can't be. I watch you when you're with me and then Oti tells what you're like when you're at work. You're two different people. When you're with me you're restrained, you're muted, you're pale.' He said the word 'pale' as if it was a bad infection. 'You aren't you when you're with me. I hold you back.'

This felt like a hard slap to the face. 'No, that's not true.' But as I said this I recalled the words of Mrs Marshall and I felt an unexpected tendril of humiliation creep up my back.

'Yes, it *is* true, Maisie, and I don't want to put you in that position. I want you to be that world-famous designer, a couturier of note. You won't be able to do that with me by your side.'

'No,' I repeated automatically. But I couldn't say any more because mortification was worming its way into me, intermingled with an unanticipated sense of relief, telling me that his words were entirely true.

He brought my hands up to his lips and kissed them. 'I have to go.' He breathed in the smell of my skin. 'We shouldn't see each other again.' He closed his eyes as he took another deep breath.

'Is this man bothering you?' came a harsh voice beside me that made me jump. I turned to see a large gentleman in a top hat and holding a cane as if ready to beat Joseph.

'No, sir. He is a friend.'

Immediately Joseph dropped my hands, stepped back onto the road and gave a small bow, before turning on his heel and walking away.

'Miss. Are you all right?' That harsh voice had softened.

'Perfectly,' I retorted absently, watching Joseph disappear into the night. I should have run after him, but instead I turned back to my boarding house and, ignoring the stranger's enquiries, I walked up the steps, through the door and up to my room.

Shutting my door, leaning on the doorknob I was confronted with the yellow dress. My heart sank. Why hadn't I been able to see it? That dress was a perfect representation of what Joseph had been trying to tell me. If I had been making myself a wedding dress wouldn't I have made the most sumptuous, intricately embroidered, colourful dress I could imagine? Wouldn't I have made a dress that epitomised me and everything I stood for?

With leaden limbs I slowly and carefully picked up the dress from the table, folded it with tissue, taking care to use extra layers around the embroidery on the cuffs and belt. Finally, I put it in a cardboard box, fastened it with ribbon and placed the box underneath my bed.


My life now seemed to be lived in a dense fog. There was a muted silence, a heaviness in my limbs that made simple tasks difficult; threading a needle became impossible, I made mistakes when cutting fabric, I spilled tea on a toile. Nighttime became my enemy as I inevitably ended up re-living those precious moments I'd had with Joseph, that jolt of electricity when we touched, the butterfly flutter of his eyelashes as I'd run my fingers over them when he blinked nervously, overlaid with images of my bland designs, and Mrs Marshall and the taut skin on her bony hands. Those images became pin-sharp in the dark, like the moving pictures in the cinema, only in vibrant colour.

Walking became my only liberation. I began pounding the streets of Manhattan at all hours, often with my head down just watching myself put one foot in front of the other, the rhythm numbing my chaotic mind, a mind that didn't know whether it was devastated or relieved, shattered or comforted, a mind that wouldn't sit still.

Ten days after Joseph had left, I was pacing my boarding room. I'd stayed in bed as long as I could, trying to rest, but nothing would let me sleep. I'd dressed absently in a plain green dress and my flat boots, ready to walk, to exhaust myself so that I might be allowed to sleep later that night.

It was a fine May Saturday, but as I was leaving I grabbed the shawl Rosa had made for me, thinking it might be cold later, and by the time I'd made it outside, the late afternoon shadows were slanting across the streets. With resignation I began my usual walk, head down, one step in front of the other, but I kept bumping into people.

'Sorry,' I gasped, before another bump. 'Sorry.' I whirled around and noticed that I was surrounded by women all moving in the same direction, all wearing white, many adorned with flashes of yellow, purple and green on their hats or draped as sashes.

I stood, open-mouthed, turning to watch the river of women of all ages, sizes, even skin colour, the tide only going in one direction – Washington Square. I closed my eyes as shame began to creep up on me, so bad that my whole face flushed.

I had forgotten. The suffrage parade. I was supposed to meet on West 9th Street with all the garment workers as well as friends and family of those that had died in the factory fire. My stomach dropped away.

'Come on, love,' came a voice as I was jostled forward. 'No good hanging around here, you'll just get marched into line. Might as well join in.' The woman laughed at me as she walked on.

Jolted into action, I picked up my skirts and ran the three blocks to West 9th Street. Halfway down the street, as arranged, stood some of my old Triangle Factory friends as well as Nonna Bassino.

'Sorry I'm late,' I said, breathlessly, as I slid into line, taking the arm of Nonna Bassino.

'Maisie,' she said, patting my hand. 'I knew you'd make it.' She gave me a sad smile as she ran her hand over Rosa's shawl. She looked so frail I wondered if she would be able to walk the block, let alone all the way to Carnegie Hall.

'Not to worry,' she said as if she'd read my mind. 'If I get tired, I stop. But I think Rosa will be with us, she'll keep me going.' She patted my hand again. 'But your arm is good.'

Soft, warm little fingers took hold of my other hand. I looked down. Annina. I hadn't seen her since the mass funeral for all those who'd died in the fire over a year ago.

She had changed dramatically. Now five years old, she'd shot up in height, her grey-green eyes seemed to have intensified. Her dirty blonde hair was tied back neatly in a long plait, tied at the end with a lavender ribbon, her white tunic dress had been neatly pressed and I could tell that the hand sewing was of a high standard. She gave me a shy smile, just like Rosa's when she got embarrassed over any praise of her knitting. That smile cut a tiny path into my sore heart.

For the first time in days I felt an easing in my chest, a softening of my rib cage. I squeezed Annina's hand. 'I'm sure we'll manage. It's the least we can do for your mamma.'

At that a cry went up and a loud whistle. Ahead of us a black and white banner was raised.

WE WANT THE VOTE FOR PROTECTION.

I pulled myself upright, proud of Rosa's shawl, even though I wasn't wearing the obligatory white, relieved that I had accidently made it to the parade, thinking that perhaps my subconscious had pierced my wallowing self-absorption and let me pick up Rosa's shawl and pointed my feet in the right direction.

We made it to Carnegie Hall, propelled by the claps and shouts from the crowds of women lining the streets and hanging out of the building windows, by the pennants and banners and flags and ribbons and handkerchiefs that waved us on for the two hours we walked, by the cheers and laughter, by the tears, the grand old ladies in their carriages, by the babies in their perambulators, by the songs we sang. I was driven forward by Annina's warm hand in mine and her wonder at the spectacle we were part of, by the weight of Nonna on my right arm, by her tears as she began to understand how many people had turned out to support the rights of women, of people like her, of women like Rosa.

By the time we had dispersed at Carnegie Hall, kissed our tears away, given Annina a hug, and squeezed Nonna's frail hands, I was a different person. My introspection had been checked. During that afternoon, where I'd witnessed the daring dedication of so many women, I'd put my fears and heartbreak, relief and shame, away in a box, just like I had with the yellow dress. When I walked away, I could again look around, see what was in front of me, see the stars in the sky. With a lighter step and a strength I'd almost forgotten I had, I took the trolleybus home. That night I slept an uninterrupted, dreamless sleep.

Back at work on Monday, re-invigorated by that long overdue sleep, ready to tackle the backlog of work, Oti was surprised to find me at my desk.

'You've got some colour back in your cheeks. Looks like you made the most of your weekend.' She spoke warily, looking at me as if she was trying to find the real me.

'I did,' I declared. 'I went to the suffrage parade. It was extraordinary.'

'You did?' She put her hands on her hips, smiling. 'You didn't come find me,' she admonished. 'I was looking out for you the whole time.'

I laughed. 'There were ten thousand people there. I'd have been difficult to find. Truth is, I had completely forgotten about it. It was just luck that I turned up in time. I got swept up in the whole thing. It was...' Inexplicably I began to cry.

'Oh Lord. What's going on with you, girl? Can't cry about

Joseph, but you can cry about a bunch of women marching and singing.' She rolled her eyes. 'You're a hot mess if ever I saw one. But that's okay, because' – she did a drum roll on the desk with her fingers – 'I made you something.' Standing up and walking over to the cupboard where we kept rolls of fabric, she opened the door and pulled out a dress on a hanger.

'I made you a dress,' she declared as she laid it out on the table.

Slowly, I stood up from my desk and went over to look at it. A day dress made from a vibrant print of many bold and coloured flowers, with a white frilled collar and matching cuffs. Although the skirt narrowed at the hem like those hated hobble skirts, she had introduced a split at the centre of the hem, about ten inches long, making walking easier. I rubbed the fabric between my fingers, a soft brushed cotton, perfect for spring-time but also with a comforting warmth. The pattern made it noteworthy, the cut ensured it was stylish, but the fabric would make it feel soothing and homely: just what my tired body needed.

Nobody had made me any clothing since Rosa had given me her shawl. This kindness that I didn't deserve, Oti's thoughtfulness whilst I had been so self-centred, made something break inside me and those tears now flowed, a dam burst.

'Come on, none of that,' Oti said, catching my arm. But that contact, that sympathy made it even worse. Nobody had touched me since Joseph.

'You're an idiot, you know that?' She squeezed my arm as the tears ran down my cheeks.

I nodded, sniffing, looking for my handkerchief.

'Good, we should all know when we've been idiots. So, it's time to get that dress on, let me sort out that red and blotchy face and I need you to go out and look for some of that Maisie McIntyre inspiration.'

. . .

In my new dress, designed and made by Oti, I walked fifty blocks uptown, virtually the same route I'd made on the parade two days previously. As I remembered the solidarity, the cheers and the support, my back became straighter, my steps lighter, and I started to feel the fresh air, see the blue sky, the newly laid pavement, Bryant Park, Fifth Avenue, until I found myself in front of the entrance to the St Regis Hotel, the place where Joseph and I had once stood, wondering whether we'd ever be able to visit together. Watching the doormen with their black armbands on, still mourning the loss of Mr Astor on the *Titanic*, something flipped inside me, a page turned, a decision was made, and a door finally shut. Gathering my courage, touching the necklace made from the shard of tortoiseshell, I walked up the steps, into the dining room and asked for tea for one. There was no hesitation from the maître d', no raised eyebrow or concern for my appearance. A wearied heaviness lifted, letting me breathe a little easier as I held my head a little higher. The pleasure at walking through the tables in the tearoom, the soft swish of my new dress, the click of bone china teacups on their saucers, the hum of conversation, the ease with which I slipped into my seat at a corner table, the effortless manner in which I ordered a pot of tea and a slice of cake.

I'd always loved to watch people come and go: the old widows in their black attire, sipping their tea with the measured gentility of aristocracy; the well-groomed wives, with their healthy complexions and shiny hair; the young debutantes, some shy and self-conscious, others loud and silly; the aloof literary ladies who wore too many scarves; the artistic women, actresses and showgirls, who glittered, all too aware of the effect they had on the room.

I brought out my notebook and drew, sketching whole outfits with small insets showing the tiny details on a hem, neckline or a sleeve, made notes on some of the fabrics I saw, noted the accessories, experienced an increasing rush of excitement, my whole body thrilling at this stream of creativity. It was as if the walk, the fresh air, the new dress, the lace tablecloth, the elegant cake on the delicate tea plate, all produced some kind of stupor, allowing me to wholly focus on my designs, forgetting about my tea, not considering whether I was a spectacle sitting on my own. My fingers were tingling as they sketched.

My pencil became blunt and I needed to ask the waiter for another, but as I looked up I was confronted by the sight of Mrs Marshall standing right in front of me, just a little too close.

'Miss McIntyre? Yes, it is you. What on earth are you doing here?' That girlish voice, so penetrating and loud, pulled me abruptly out of my design frenzy, as if I was being hauled out of a deep, profound sleep.

'Mrs Marshall, how lovely to see you,' I stumbled, my voice croaking.

She sat down beside me. 'Darling, are you here by yourself?' she whispered, as if she was ashamed of my loneliness.

I smiled at her, regaining my equilibrium. 'I am. This is a good place to think about new designs, to get inspiration.'

'I'm glad to hear it. I think you still have some work to do on those new ideas you had for me. They weren't quite right, were they?' Her brow furrowed slightly. 'You are a strange creature, Miss McIntyre. I can't fathom you at all.' Then her face cleared and she leaned forward, her eyes now bright. 'But there is an argument that women should have some mystery about them. It works a treat when you're trying to catch a man.' Suddenly she gasped. 'Talking of which, now that we've sorted out that little issue, it's high time you found a *suitable* man and settled down.' She patted me on the hand. 'You see, a single woman beyond a certain age begins to look ugly. How old are you now?'

I almost choked on my tea. 'I'm twenty-two.'

'Oh, darling, some would say you're already on the shelf.' She leaned in as she spoke, her voice again low. 'I hadn't quite understood how urgent this was. Well, thank goodness I'm on the ball. I told you I'd found just the man, listen, he's even from Scotland,' she panted. 'His uncle, that darling old Randolph, is one of our very own minor railroad barons, who just happens to be a great friend of my own Rex. The nephew, you know, he's quite a catch. He's just finished at Columbia and is now wondering quite what to do with himself. I'd say finding a good wife will do him the world of good. And now that you're back to your old feisty self, I think he'd benefit from a woman who challenged him a bit.' Here the horse-like laugh rang out across the room, a few heads turning.

'Really, Mrs Marshall, you don't need to go to the trouble.' I was beginning to feel like a fly caught in a spider's web.

'Dear, it's no trouble. Anyhow, in a few weeks' time it's our annual Fourth of July picnic on the yacht, I'd just love you to come. I've invited him especially. It'll be the most idyllic situation in which to meet the man of your dreams.' She closed her eyes. 'Just think how marvellous it would be to be wooed on a yacht on the Hudson, the sun shining, the girls in their summer frocks, the men in their boater hats. Oh, it's just too delicious an opportunity to pass up.' She gave a little squeal before pulling herself upright and picking up her parasol.

'Must dash, my darling. Sukie will be wondering where on earth I am.' But as she was about to leave me, she stopped to say, 'Now that dress, you've outdone yourself. Very fetching. You clever thing.'

'I didn't design this one,' I said, rubbing the fabric on the sleeve between my finger and thumb.

'Well, I'd like to meet whoever did. They're obviously very talented,' she gushed.

I smiled. 'One day, I will definitely introduce you.'


The next morning Oti found me fast asleep on the small sofa in the studio.

'What's all this?' she said as she surveyed the mess, her mouth twitching with irritation.

I sat up and rubbed my face. I hadn't been home, I'd hardly eaten since breakfast the day before and was in the same clothes I'd worn to the St Regis, the beautiful dress Oti had made, now rumpled and creased. I'd been designing and constructing new gowns and outfits most of the night, finally falling asleep at about five o'clock in the morning. I felt a little light-headed. My hair fell down onto my shoulders and my breath smelled.

'It's the new season of Maison McIntyre designs,' I said standing up, walking stiffly around the cutting table and picking up a sheaf of papers. Each piece showed a design that had been worked into a detailed coloured illustration, with cuttings of fabrics affixed to the edge of each drawing, along with suggested finishes and adornments. 'We'll work from a book of designs for each season. I believe Lucile calls it her *Book of the Season*. When these are completed, I will bind them into our own book, and we can show it to our customers. We will also make up a sample of every design and employ a mannequin to show them off, walk around the salon, showing the dresses as they should be seen.' Now I was talking fast, excitement bubbling up, going through each design, explaining how every dress should be made, the type of body shape each would suit, where we could change the colouring to flatter each customer.

Oti's face was difficult to read. There was interest, the occasional twitch at a detail that she'd never seen before, but there was also a threat of annoyance in her stance, her hands on her hips, her lips puckered, her brow deeply lined.

'So, let me make sure I'm understanding you,' she eventually said, clearing her throat. 'We're no longer simply dressmakers and seamstresses. No longer making dresses that our ladies have asked for. We're now making gowns that we need to persuade them that they want.'

'Just like the couture houses – like the House of Worth, and

Paul Poiret's maison de couture, like Farquharson & Wheelock on Fifth Avenue and Lucile Ltd.' I moved around the table, unable to stay still and picked up one of the illustrations. 'I'll take Mrs Marshall, or one of our other customers, through the book. She can discuss what she needs for the season. We agree on colours, what events she needs new gowns for. It isn't really that different to what we're doing now, but it will make us a bit more efficient; this season we'll have twenty designs to work to rather than a different design for every single customer. Each gown will still be bespoke, will fit each of our ladies to their exact measurements. But, Oti, you're right. I no longer want to be just a dressmaker or a seamstress. I want us to be a couture house, I want to design dresses that matter. That's what I've always wanted to be.'

'Maison McIntyre, huh?' she asked, pulling back as if to get a better look at me. 'I haven't seen you like this for a while, head-long, nothing but work, not thinking about anyone else. There's some kind of madness that takes over you, turns you into this wild creative machine. You scare me when you're like that.'

I smiled, almost blushed. No one, not even Netta, had ever understood me so well as Oti did. 'I'd forgotten how much I want to do this, how much I love to design, how I love to make someone look the best they possibly can, how I love to make them feel better about themselves. I've drifted back into accepting requests to copy designs from Paris or London. I don't want to do that. I want to be an original. I want people to copy a Maison McIntyre dress because that's what they want to be seen in.'

Slowly a hint of approval spread across her face and she leaned forward, picking up a design for an evening gown, the skirt almost completely covered in feathers. 'This is going to take one hell of a lot of hand work. You trying to break us?' And then there was that broad Jackson smile, her whole face changed, all hint of doubt erased. 'These are going to make your name, Miss McIntyre. But how are we going to get the customers to make this work? We barely have enough work as it is, now we have the new girls.'

'I even found a solution to that last night whilst I was firing off these new designs.' I began talking too fast. 'We need to put on a fashion parade. Just like the ready-to-wear parades you see in some of the department stores. But this will be like the parades Lucile puts on, for invited customers only. It will be an exclusive event.'

'Do we know enough people? Seems like we'll have to top up the numbers with Mr and Mrs Franke and their children.'

'Oh, I'm going to get Mrs Marshall to organise it.' I said this in a very offhand, casual manner.

Oti almost scoffed. 'I can't see her doing that.'

'She won't be able to resist. We'll make it an exclusive fundraising event, selling, say, only fifty tickets. The ticket price will cover all the costs of the event plus extra towards a favoured charity. That way we shouldn't make a loss, even if we don't sell a single dress. Once the fashion parade is over, we will serve champagne and it will become a party. The mannequins can mingle with the ladies, and they can look at the dresses up close. Mrs Marshall will love to be seen organising such a high-profile event. Everyone will want to be there, it'll be something different, a new event for the season, something to talk about, and hopefully, we'll come away with lots of orders. And the best thing about it is it'll be seen as a charitable event, rather than some high society trade show.'

'And, finally, I'm introduced to the ambitious Maisie McIntyre,' Oti said, not unkindly. Her arms were crossed as she leaned against the tabletop, an amused expression on her face. 'I knew you were in there, but something's been keeping her hidden away. I've met the driven Maisie, the hardworking Maisie, the slightly bawdy studio Maisie, the salon Maisie who can keep up with the best of the society girls, the homely Maisie who kept my brother company, but I've only just now met the single-minded, slightly ruthless Maisie.'

I put the designs back down on the cutting table, considering her words, trying to understand if this was a compliment.

She unfolded her arms and came towards me. Quietly she spoke. 'I always thought you'd leave him because of his colour. Because he didn't fit with your plans. You work with too many influential women who wouldn't like to be associated with a woman who *has relations* with a man of colour. We both understand the reason I stay in the studio when Mrs Marshall has her appointments, but you never introduced Joseph to any of your friends.'

That shame flickered at my collar.

She looked down at her feet. 'You and Joseph did the right thing.' Her voice was almost a whisper. 'I prefer this Maisie.' She pointed to the pile of drawings. 'She's the person I want to spend time with. She's the person I want to work for.'

She turned her gaze back to me. 'So, Miss McIntyre.' Her voice now loud and confident, her smile filling the room. 'I think we'd better go across the road and get ourselves a coffee before the others get here, so that we're ready to break the news.'


Fuelled with strong coffee we got back to the studio just as everyone was arriving for work.

As promised, I had taken on three new seamstresses two months previously, giving Oti the opportunity to step away from some of the day-to-day sewing and allow her to find new fabric suppliers and work out ways of getting our order of works running more smoothly. We'd had a few weeks to settle them in, find out their weaknesses and strengths, just in time for my suggested changes to the business.

Simone and Rebecca had worked with Oti in the haberdasher's and were more than competent on the sewing machine, but it was their hand sewing that had struck me: swift, neat and confident. Then there was Flavia, another distant cousin of Rosa's, who'd managed to escape the fire, but not without terrible disfiguring burns to the right side of her face and body. The three of them entered the room, Simone talking loudly.

'Have you seen the news? That woman who flies aeroplanes, she hasn't just gone and got herself killed.' Her tone was sombre but with an air of conspiracy.

I stared at her, hardly able to understand what she was saying, my mind was so filled with fabric, colours, mannequins and fashion parades.

Simone frowned at my lack of interest. She was taller than me, much like Oti, but she had a twisted smile that made her seem more approachable. She held up a copy of the *New York Times*. 'This morning's paper. The headlines are all going on about Baltimore and that professor, but why would I care about Mr Woodrow Wilson? It's not as if I can vote for him anyway.'

'This much smaller headline,' said Rebecca, pointing with her tiny hands to the more obscure article on the front page.

'*Miss Quimby dies in airship fall,*' read Simone, mimicking a solemn radio presenter.

'*Falling from a height of one thousand feet into Dorchester Bay soon after six o'clock tonight,*' Rebecca continued to read. So much shorter than Simone, she had to look around her shoulder to see the article. '*Miss Harriet Quimby of New York, the first woman to gain an aviator's licence in America and the first woman to cross the English Channel in an aeroplane which she operated herself, met instant and terrible death.*'

'*Five thousand spectators witnessed the accident...*'

I lost track of the story, mesmerised by the double act that was Rebecca and Simone, taking it in turns to read. This was what they did; they finished each other's sentences, they ate each other's food, they lived with each other, they swapped clothes. It was as if they were one and the same person.

'*Both victims were found terribly crushed when extricated from the mud of the shallow bay, into which they had sunk deeply.*' Simone let the newspaper drop onto the table.

There was silence in the room, everyone staring at Simone and Rebecca, until Oti picked up the paper and looked at the article. 'Isn't that the woman we talked about only the other week? The one who wears some kind of purple silk uniform, to make sure people will notice her?'

Harriet Quimby was a woman we'd been following in the news, a woman who dared to do the things only men had previously done. She wasn't just a woman of firsts when it came to aviation, she wrote scripts for Hollywood films, she was a journalist, as well as being someone who wore the kind of clothes that made her stand out.

'I would have liked to dress her,' I sighed. 'However, we've got plenty to take our minds off bad news.' I sat down at one of the tables. 'Come over here and look at these.' I indicated to my pile of designs.

Oti, Simone, Rebecca and Flavia gathered around the table whilst I began telling them of my plans for the future, what work they were going to need to do over the next few weeks, asking whether they'd be able to put in any extra hours and explaining how the fashion parade would work.

'Ooooh! Real live mannequins! In here? In our salon?' asked Simone.

'With a roomful of society ladies in their best clothes?' asked Rebecca.

'Yes,' I replied. 'We'll seat them along the length of the salon. The mannequins will come in from the studio and walk up and down so that the dresses can be seen up close, our potential customers will see how the fabric moves, how it rustles, how the light catches the glitter on the finishing. After the show, we'll just keep the party going, make sure the women have plenty of champagne and get them to buy our designs. Simple!' I beamed at the girls.

'Will we get some champagne too?' asked Rebecca.

'Careful,' Oti chided, playing the part of manager.

Out of the corner of my eye, I noticed that Flavia had silently moved over to the stack of designs and started looking through them, carefully inspecting each one, her face changing from its usual air of melancholy to a hint of excitement, a small upturn in her now thin lips. Eventually she looked up at me.

'Can you show me how we'll be attaching the feathers. There are so many, I wonder how we can do it without making the skirt seem bulky. Also, I wondered how are we going to find them in so many colours? There will have to be a pattern we work to, showing how we lay them out so that we can get the fading of the colour from skirt to hem.'

Rebecca and Simone abruptly stopped their chatter, their gazes directed towards Flavia. Nobody in the room had ever heard her speak so many words all at the same time.

I felt a quiver of exhilaration inside of me; I loved it when someone else understood my designs immediately. Flavia had by far the best understanding of complicated gown structures out of all the girls, including Oti, but she kept it quiet, didn't shout about her abilities, unlike Simone and Rebecca, who were prone to letting me know that their ideas were superior to my own.

As the day wore on, the enthusiasm in the studio built up to a rumble of animated discussion, every design being closely examined, ideas about the best way to make each one, who would focus on which dress.

'I think we need some of that tea,' said Oti eventually, picking up a sheaf of papers that she'd been writing notes on. She took me into the tiny kitchenette. I added some coal to the range fire, filled the kettle and put it on the stove.

'You know just how much work we've got to do here?' she

hissed. 'I'll need to re-work the schedules, get the fabric suppliers back in, ask everyone to do a bit of overtime. That's okay, that'll work to start with.' She was talking to herself now, pacing the tiny room. 'But we're going to need more outworkers for the embroidery, Flavia can't do it all herself, much as she'd like to. And we're going to need more seamstresses. You're gonna need to make use of your friends from the factory, those women you spent time with last weekend. Hopefully they can help us.'

I watched the kettle, noting the tarnished tin, wondering who would clean it. 'We'll find them,' I said gently. I turned to the noise coming from the studio and went to the door. Leaning on the doorframe, folding my arms, I gathered in the scene in front of me. My once bare studio was now brimming with colour. Three dressmaker's dummies stood in one corner, each dressed in a different design – a new forest-green riding habit for Mrs Marshall, a baby-blue evening gown for Miss Milholland, and my favourite, a very simple, pale-pink summer day dress. There was a low rack for the rolls of fabric at one end of the room, with a large pinboard above them, my favourite sketches pinned up, swatches of colour and ribbons decorating another wall.

Rebecca, Simone and Flavia were sitting at the large sewing table, wearing their aprons, Flavia with soft white gloves on so that the roughness of her scarred right hand wouldn't catch on the fabric she was working on. The way she stroked the material reminded me of the evenings when I used to work with Maw on her dressmaking, when she was teaching me what she knew, when she'd show me how to understand a fabric by running my fingers over it, to feel the alternating twists in the yarn on a chiffon, the complete smoothness of a silk, or the grainy feel of a georgette. Rebecca told a joke and Flavia gave a tiny smile as she nudged Simone.

'Just look at that,' I said to Oti, as the kettle began to whistle.

# Matchmaking

There was nothing Mrs Marshall liked more than a matchmaking project. She thrived on her ability to successfully pair up a girlfriend of hers with one of the many single men in her set. There was an art to her endeavours, I will give her that. She checked each person's background thoroughly to ensure there were no unexpected skeletons and she made it her business to understand their likes, dislikes, political leanings and hobbies. Listening to her discuss these marriage projects used to make me smile, that world of weddings and children and setting up a home so far away from my own. But now I was the focus of her artifice.

I was flattered to be asked to her annual Fourth of July picnic, women of Julia Marshall's set rarely even considered socialising with her couturier, and I welcomed the break from the hot and humid city. And, perhaps, I might find myself a new customer or two.

The day was idyllic, a slight breeze accompanying the cloudless sky, the Hudson River calm and asking to be admired. I wandered the deck of the Marshalls' yacht, glass of champagne in hand, considering my luck. Here I was, again pulling the wool over everyone's eyes. I could dress as well, if not better, than every woman on this boat, I'd learned to hold myself in the correct manner and speak with just the right kind of soft Scottish accent to be appealing. What would Maw think of me now, passing myself off as a woman of note? I could hear her cackle of laughter, see her pat my hand. Thinking of her gave me a sudden feeling of freedom, a realisation that I was no longer that girl from the Edinburgh tenement, no longer the girl who had to share a bedroll with her sister; I would never have to wash a sheet again. I was Maisie McIntyre, couturier.

The ladies lounged so easily in their pale, flowing chiffon dresses and broad-brimmed hats trimmed with wide satin ribbons. Their comfort in the situation was a little unnerving, their smiles, gestures and conversation all seeming so effortless. The gentlemen were perhaps a little more buttoned up, as if they were all in uniform: pale long trousers, dark jacket, white collared shirt, tie and boater hat.

'Daaaarling.' Mrs Marshall wriggled up to my side. 'Don't all the ladies just look a picture?' She patted me on the shoulder. 'And aren't you glad to see there are more than a few Maisie McIntyre designs here?'

I nodded, shading my eyes from the sun.

'Darling, you must wear a hat. It'll do your complexion no good; you'll look like you've been working out in the fields.' She drew out a length of my hair. 'And it'll turn your hair to straw, you know.'

'I've been indoors for six days in a row, I think I've earned the right to a little sun.' I gave her my sweetest smile.

She took me by the arm, and we began circulating the deck. 'You know, I really think you should start calling me Julia from now on. You've seen me in my underwear, after all. I think we can drop the formalities.' She squeezed my arm. 'Now, there's someone you simply *must* meet.' She squealed like an excited schoolgirl and pointed to the one man on the boat who was not wearing a dark jacket. 'Mr Cruickshank.'

Something about his name and the way he held himself made me stiffen. I pulled away from Julia.

'What is it, honey?' Mrs Marshall laughed. 'Oh, my dear Lord, don't tell me you're scared? Now, where's the decisive Maisie McIntyre when you need her?' She took my arm again, patting it gently and we continued on our walk.

'Please don't worry, I've thought this through very carefully,' she continued, taking my silence as approval. 'I told you his uncle is one of the minor railroad barons. Not a Vanderbilt, but he's the third son so they're not expecting him to marry from the very highest of society, nor do they need him to marry for money. He's intelligent, just finished at Columbia.' Julia Marshall gazed at him. 'I think he's a dream. If I wasn't married to Rex...' She trailed off, her expression wistful and far off. 'Oh, but listen to me,' she said hurriedly, reddening slightly. 'The best part, as far as you're concerned anyway, is that he's a great lover of the arts. I'm always bumping into him at the theatre and the opera, at concerts and art galleries. So, you'll see, he'll love you for all that creativity. A match made in heaven.'

She pulled me towards him.

'Aidan, darling. I need you to meet the world-famous Maisie McIntyre. Miss McIntyre, may I present Mr Aidan T Cruickshank.'

'Miss McIntyre.' He clicked his heels together and gave a slight bow. 'I have been hearing great things about you.'

The rakish, slightly too long dark hair, the hooked nose, that easy confidence, the cut of his suit that I'd noticed on the ship. I recognised him all too well.

'Mr Cruickshank.' I gave him a very slight bow of my head whilst all I wanted to do was run. But we were in the middle of the Hudson River and I couldn't swim. As the panic began to bubble up I suddenly wanted to laugh, realising that the whole preposterous situation called for an entirely preposterous response.

'If the résumé that Mrs Marshall gave you about me was as thorough as the one she just gave me about you,' I quipped, 'then there's hardly a thing we need to tell each other. I suggest we set the wedding date right away.'

There was an awkward silence and Julia Marshall's eyes widened with concern as she looked between the two of us. A slight twist of his mouth hinted at amusement. But despite my own anxiety at being caught out, being discovered as a fraud in front of all these important guests, my attention was caught by his jacket, made from an olive-green lightweight material with the slightest hint of yellow threaded through the weave. It was refreshingly different and stood out amongst the sea of dark-blue blazers.

'You see,' I hurried on, trying to catch my rapidly disappearing breath, 'I have no mother who'd interfere with the arrangements and no father whose permission you need to ask; you only need mine and, well, it seems I've already given it.'

I was trying to keep my voice playful, as if I was flirting, but in reality it was the only way I could fend off Mrs Marshall. I wasn't in the habit of being herded around, however well-meaning her intentions may have been. But I *was* attracted to this man: the mischief in his eye, the cut of his suit, his Scottish roots, despite that ever so languorous English accent. It didn't seem to matter how much of a threat I knew him to be, however much I wanted to thwart Mrs Marshall's plans. He had film star looks, a voice that felt like oil being poured on my rusted heart, and a dress sense that turned my head.

Aidan T Cruickshank let a slow and generous smile take over his face, whilst Mrs Marshall frowned with confusion before looking down at her feet.

'Why, Miss McIntyre, I'm glad to see that you are not predictable, no blushing or false pretence. I cannot stand that in anyone, let alone my chosen wife. Thankfully Mrs Marshall has kindly filled me in on all the details I could possibly need to make an informed decision for my future nuptials.' He mirrored my playfulness, and I thought I could detect an echo of my own annoyance at being played by our hostess. 'I understand that you are a woman of independent means and will not be marrying me for my money. I've learned that you have a brilliant creative mind and are a hard worker. God forbid that I would have a wife who only wanted to stay at home and entertain. If that was the case, I can't imagine what we would talk about. You are from Scotland, not Manhattan. Halleluiah! Us Scots must stick together. Why, surely there is nothing more for it? I insist that we set the wedding day for two months from now.'

We glared at each other without saying another word, eyes gleaming. Mrs Marshall looked from me to Mr Cruickshank and back again. I could see that she had no idea whether we were joking or not until, finally, she said, 'Well, that's settled. I'll leave you two to go over the finer details.' And she fled.

I was glad of the offshore breeze as I was beginning to feel too hot. Finally, I broke his gaze and looked across the water at distant Manhattan, letting a discreet giggle slip out. I had to squint at the reflection of the sun on the water. The brilliant colours of summer, the sparkle from the sea, the feel of the wind on my skin: all these sensations had heightened my perceptions, had made me feel a little reckless.

Keeping my eyes on the horizon, I flattened my lips, trying to suppress another snigger.

'I think, perhaps, on second thoughts, a long engagement is preferable.' I did my best to sound contemplative, the feigned nonchalance scattering into the sea. 'I need to reacquaint myself with how life must be when there is a man in tow.' Finally, I turned to him. 'And you would probably like to know what it's like to be with a woman who spends all her time at work, who is self-centred and ambitious. I suspect you'll find these traits abhorrent and call it all off. So, it would be sensible to give you that opportunity.'

He turned his back to the sea, leaned against the boat's highly varnished railings and folded his arms. He watched the party in progress, the high-pitched laughter, the clink of glasses, the slow current of sexual tension under the surface of good manners and polite conversation.

'Miss McIntyre. I don't wish to be in tow to anyone. Nor do I wish to have my marriage arranged by Mrs Marshall any more, I suspect, than you do. But.' He turned to face me square on, patting down his tie as the wind caught it. 'She might just have a point. There's something here, a spark, a whisper of what's to come. Why don't we act upon it? What do you say?' And now a smile, the annoyance gone, those dark eyes plucking at my heartstrings, making something inside stir. The playfulness, the light-heartedness, the semi-earnest petition, those dazzling good looks, the beautifully made clothes, all making me feel as if I'd taken off a particularly tight corset and let my posture relax.

'When did you inherit the T in your name? Or is that just something Mrs Marshall likes to do, to give you some gravitas?' I said, avoiding the question.

'When did you become world famous, *Miss* McIntyre?'

Touché.

I couldn't explain my immediate attraction to him, when my heart was still so sore, when I had so vehemently decided that I had no need of male interaction in my life. He was dangerous and knew things about me that no one else did. It would have been sensible to stay away, but sensible wasn't a word that I used very often.

But perhaps the wiser thing to do was keep him close to me, where I could see what he was doing, maybe keep him under control.

'If we're going to be seen together, if we're going to show

Mrs Marshall that we can do her dance of courtship, then perhaps we deal with the important stuff right away.' I kept up the tone of joviality, as if we were talking of things of no consequence. 'Perhaps you can tell me what you were doing on that ship, tell me why you were not being truthful about who you were? You seemed to have some idea that we were "like two peas in a pod". How so?'

'Isn't everyone around here being someone they are not?' he retorted, equally as offhand.

'Oh, come now, Mr Aidan T Cruickshank,' I said, mimicking Mrs Marshall's southern drawl. 'You have likened yourself to someone who was passing herself off as a rich widow, a single woman who grew up in the tenements of Edinburgh and should have been in steerage.'

A broad smile before he gave me a formal bow. 'Miss McIntyre, you a one-off. No wonder Julia likes you.' He turned back to the water, looking down at the effervescing foam as the boat's keel glided through the water.

'I'm the wayward child of a wealthy man of the cloth, sent to the Americas to atone for my sins and be put out of sight where I can do no harm.' Leaning heavily on the handrail he continued. 'My father thought it was a punishment to banish me to the New World.' He turned his head to me. 'In reality he sent me to a land that is more forgiving than my strict Presbyterian homeland, leaving me to mix with the very people he sent me away from.'

I pictured gambling debts, family shame, the problem hidden under the carpet. 'Does Mrs Marshall know about this?' I asked, tipping my head to one side in mocking wonder.

'No,' he laughed. 'My dear uncle Randy is the very definition of discretion. Our Mrs M believes I'm squeaky clean.'

'So glad to hear you aren't. How dull would that be?' I teased.

'Well, well. There's no lack of spirit in you, Miss McIntyre.

Perhaps we can discuss that as we do a turn of the deck, along with answering my questions about how a tenement girl from Edinburgh suddenly finds herself on one of the largest yachts on the Hudson.' He held his elbow towards me, indicating that I should take it.


Aidan Cruickshank was a welcome distraction, but I didn't have the time for what Mrs Marshall called 'the serious business of courtship'. I had a fashion parade to prepare for, designs to finalise, fabrics, buttons, ribbons and gauzes to source; I had to find the right women to use as mannequins, more seamstresses, more tables, more sewing machines, more tailor's dummies, more of everything.

I put up barriers, my head filled with colour, thread and sketches, but he battered those defences, wooing me with that lazy English accent, that clean, well-dressed smell of sandalwood and leather, those deep-set brown eyes with their hint of mischief, those perfectly fitting suits. There were suggestions of a train ride to Long Beach, a trip out to the newly fashionable Hamptons, taking tea in one of the coastal tearooms, offers of an evening at the theatre, a concert at Carnegie Hall, dinner on the rooftop garden at the Waldorf Astoria. Occasionally I would submit, enticed by his sense of humour, his wit, always able to liven up a dull party.

'How I hate these parties,' I sighed as we stood by the bar of yet another Coming Out ball. 'I wish you wouldn't insist I trail along behind you. I'm not entirely sure what they're for.'

'Drumming up business, you know that.' He looked at me incredulously. 'Silly debutantes, ingénues, sparkling society women, serious wives of serious men. You'll find them all here. It's just like the first-class salon on the SS *Furnessia*. You just need to find your mark.' His eyes teased. 'This' – he gestured towards my dress – 'is the best kind of promotion a girl could find. Don't knock it. One or two of these a month will make all the difference. We'll have those women running through your doors.'

'Just the people I wanted to speak to.' Mrs Marshall burst into our little bubble, her voice urgent and serious. 'Now tell me, when *are* you two going to announce your engagement?'

'All in good time, Mrs M. There's no point in rushing these things.' Aidan batted the question away before taking me by the hand and bowing to my patron 'You must excuse us. I've been promising Maisie a dance all evening and can put it off no longer.' Leaving Julia Marshall with her mouth open he pulled me away and led me past the dance floor and out onto the terrace.

'That woman is persistent; I'll give her that,' he muttered, dropping my hand, continuing down the steps and onto the lawn.

'At least it means I'm no longer introduced to the most unsuitable men I've ever met. All those hideous mothers think I'm spoken for.'

'Glad to be of service.' He bowed towards me as he spoke, his voice a little caustic.

'Watch out. I believe our hostess is on the warpath,' I warned.

Mrs Aston, rake thin with a permanent look of disapproval, swept down the stairs and headed straight for Aidan.

'Mr Cruickshank.' She held out her hand for the obligatory kiss.

'Mrs Aston, may I introduce Miss Maisie McIntyre. I believe your daughter-in-law is a patron of hers.'

She peered at me as if she was having difficulty seeing me. 'Ah, yes. The woman of colour.'

There was an awkward silence.

'You... mean my use of colour,' I stammered.

'Yes, you're the one who put Tattie darling in those fabulous bright colours. What a clever girl you are. Now I need to introduce this darling boy to my niece, Minty.' I was immediately forgotten as she turned to reveal a young woman, perhaps of sixteen or seventeen, with enormous doe eyes and tumbles of brown curls. She wore a tastefully alluring, pale-yellow evening gown that showed her slender figure to its best, her jewels discreet but notable.

The girl fluttered her eyelids, a blush rising up her pretty cheeks. 'Mr Cruickshank, my aunt has told me so much about you.' She held out her hand.

Minty, despite the name, was easily the most beautiful woman at the party, but a minimal shift in Aidan's manner showed me that he wasn't struck by her, the telltale sign being the undoing and doing up of his jacket buttons, the amused smile on his face. But only I could tell this as he did his duty, kissed her hand, bowed and held her gaze, ensuring she almost melted into the ground.

He seemed to be holding back, hiding something, and it was this knowledge that held me to him. We were both hiding something; perhaps that was why we made such an appealing couple to the outside world.

'Miss Aston, I do hope you'll join me for a dance later. But would you excuse me just now? I have promised Miss McIntyre an introduction to some dear friends, and I must do this before it's too late and we miss them.' Again, he kissed her hand, let her swoon over his touch, whispered in her ear, 'I'll come and find you later.' He gave her a conspiratorial wink before turning to me and indicating we should walk to the end of the garden.

'Oh, how I wish these mothers, aunts and grandmothers would stop trying to muscle in.' He turned to me. 'They've backed off you. Why haven't they backed off me? Aren't we supposed to be an item?'

'Are we an item?' I asked. We occasionally went out together, he was attentive and alluring, but he never went a step further, never tried to kiss me, never stared at me with a look of hunger, never quite set my heart alight. I didn't long for him like I had with Joseph, my stomach didn't twist at the thought of him, I never daydreamed about his smile, about the way he'd hold me during a dance, about how we might, one day, be together. He was entertaining, good company, but in a best friend kind of way.

He walked ahead with his hands in his pockets before turning back to me. 'Maybe we should just get married, then all of this would stop.' He threw out his right arm gesturing to the crowd.

'Not quite the marriage proposal I had once dreamed of,' I said, trying to keep my voice light as a sudden sadness descended on me, an image of Joseph, and then me in the yellow dress, flickering behind my eyes.

Still with his hands in his pockets he looked down at his feet and kicked the gravel like some petulant schoolboy. What did he want? Despite the fact that I must have known him better than anyone else, there was part of him that he kept locked away, fiercely guarded as if it would do him harm if let out.

'Anyway,' I said, shutting away the emotion, 'I have an important question for you.'

'Fire away.' The sulky expression left him, interest took over.

'I need your help with the fashion parade.'

'How are the arrangements going?' All thoughts of marriage quickly abandoned, thank goodness.

'Everything is going to plan. Mrs Marshall has done as I asked, inviting fifty of the most influential women in New York. The editors from *Vogue* and *Harper's Bazaar* are expected, even a few politicians and their wives are on the list. She's organised floral arrangements, champagne and canapés for the after-party, there's a seating plan and we've discussed the order in which the gowns should be shown. We're frantically busy in the studio, but it's all coming together, everyone having worked so hard. But there's a problem I need to deal with.'

He turned to me, an expression of amused surprise on his face. 'Finally, the inimitable Miss McIntyre asks for my help.'

My mouth twitched, a thread of annoyance catching my heart.

'What do you need? An injection of cash? Entertainment for the mannequins?' He was enjoying himself, his voice a touch patronising.

'No, I need you to make sure Julia Marshall never makes her way into the studio.' I held his stare.

'Ah, I see. Something to hide, some little secret that will have Mrs Rex Marshall running for the hills. Am I right?'

'Come to my studio tomorrow and you can see for yourself.'

# The Fashion Parade

Now I employed six women. Oti, with her fierce pride, held
everyone together, directing the workload, keeping all our work
on schedule. Simone and Rebecca, a perfect partnership,
complementing each other, their skills improving every day, one
better at cutting, the other more skilled at tailoring. Yulia, a loud
Russian mother of five girls, was our quickest worker, always
able to complete those rushed jobs to the deadline, always able
to sew and tell us a stream of funny stories about her family all
at the same time. And then there was quiet Anna, still too trau-
matised by the night of the factory fire, who rarely spoke, but
her ability to focus was beyond anything I'd ever seen, to block
out any noise, including Yulia's stories, and concentrate fully on
her work. And finally there was Flavia, who was taking on
much of the embroidery work, who absorbed everything Oti
taught her, looking up to her as if she was a big sister. These
women made up my studio, brought together by the designs, the
fabric, the colour, cocooned behind closed doors. When we
were working – fitting, stitching, designing, folding, packing,
tidying – we were safe, nothing bad could happen to us; we

fitted together like the pieces of a dress pattern. I had all I needed in these extraordinary women. But they were kept away from our customers, kept hidden from those white judgemental eyes. I knew that many of my clients would not appreciate their garments being handled by a black woman, would be frightened by the disfigurement of Flavia, would worry at the sadness in the eyes of Anna. But now I was opening the doors and letting Mrs Marshall and her band of influential women come within ten feet of my mixed, troubled workforce.

Aidan arrived at the studio the next day at ten o'clock, exactly as asked.

'Good morning, ladies. I trust you're all well?' he inquired as if he'd been in there twenty times before.

They all muttered an embarrassed greeting. Men were almost never seen in the studio, the landlord, Mr Franke, only ever able to hover by the door, seemingly too uncomfortable to come in, almost as if he thought the room was full of women only wearing their underwear.

'Miss McIntyre. What a delightful studio.' He began to walk around the room, looking out of the windows, inspecting the tailor's dummies, scrutinising the pinboard and finally looking up at the overhead glass domes, his hands clasped behind his back.

'I have never seen such a fine example of ceiling lanterns. They really are magnificent. You must find this the most welcoming studio to work in.' He brought his gaze back down to me. 'I now understand why I can never prise you out of it.'

I let those words sink in. Looking across at Oti and the others, I could see there seemed to be a silent letting out of held breath, a collective sigh of relief. I'd had no need to worry. He understood the situation immediately.

I didn't have to open my mouth before he said, 'I'll keep her distracted. Both of us will tell her that there simply won't be room for her in the studio whilst your mannequins are being dressed, whilst you are seeing to the finishing touches, whilst you keep everything running to time. I will ensure she is kept busy entertaining the ladies, checking everyone is in their correct seat and is well lubricated with champagne. She can oversee the waiting staff and the food – that should keep her distracted. She'll have no time to worry about what's going on in the studio. And then, if necessary, we can give her some excuse that everyone must be out by a certain time, as dictated by your landlord.' He then turned to the door that led into the salon.

'I suggest we build a mini corridor with a second door into the studio from the salon. That way anyone who comes in and out of the studio will have to go through two doors and that negates any possibility of your girls being seen when the first door is open. It also means there's a holding room for the waiting mannequin to come in, whilst she waits for the girl who is already walking through the salon. This will give her a chance to have a moment to gather herself after all the mayhem that'll be going on in the studio.'

I stared at him. He had read my mind, understood exactly what needed doing.

Laughing at my speechlessness he said, 'You'll come to understand, Miss McIntyre, that those of us who have secrets have learned very well how to conceal them.'

It should have been a disaster. After the final pinning, checking, last-minute sewing, the nerves and the waiting for guests to seat themselves, the excitement in the studio, the riot of butterflies in my stomach, we then had a power outage. No light.

That moment of silence as we were held in terror. What could we do? Beautiful outfits could not be seen without light. But I had Oti, and I had Aidan, and all worked out better than I could have ever imagined.

Oti had a large stash of candles ('I've never trusted those electricity companies') and sent me out to the salon to set them out around the room, whilst Aidan kept the ladies entertained and reassured that our show would be imminent. Oti gave each mannequin her own candle and when we were ready, they were sent out, in our new Maison McIntyre creations, lit by candlelight.

An unexpected evening of shadows, each dress, coat, and jacket seen in a new way. The candlelight picking out only the sharpest of lines on a purple velvet gown, the lighter fabrics given an added depth and a quality of boldness that might have been lacking in the electric light, the dim light on the sharp pleated sleeves of an evening shirt enhancing its two-tone effect. An evening of ethereal images, pale chiffon appearing ghostly and mysterious, the lace given added dimension on the sleeves of an organza blouse, the sculpted folds of an apricot silk taffeta displaying an illusion of fire. The contrast between pale skin and the sheen on a duchess satin gown became more obvious, the gold and silver beading on an evening dress noticeably more eye-catching. Our guests were stunned into silence at the atmosphere we had created, meaning the swish of a dress became the background to the evening, the whispers of the silks, the murmur of the velvets.

By the end of the night forty dresses were in the order book and more promised.

Afterwards, Mrs Marshall, so different from the woman I'd met two years previously, worked the room: sparkling when chatting with the congressman's wife, holding forth with Elizabeth Jordan, the editor of *Harper's Bazaar*, giggling with the models, ensuring no guest was left unattended to. I'd made her a pale-pink silk dress with a swathed skirt and high waist, and mid-grey silk stole creating a satisfying contrast. She had outshone a host of bright starlets and authoritative women, no longer the wallflower she had once been.

Putting on her coat to leave, she'd said, 'Maisie, darling, I can't tell you what a time I had tonight. My mother-in-law will go *on* that I don't have the stamina that she has, that I'm simply not clever enough.' She pulled herself up straight. 'Well, do you know, she's just goddamn wrong!' And then she shrieked at her own audacity. 'Yes goddammit, she's just wholly wrong.'

'Did you have a glass of champagne tonight?' I asked her, amused by her language.

'Oh, dear Lord, no. I haven't touched the stuff since our honeymoon. But you're right, I do feel quite drunk.'

I began to usher her out of the door. 'I think you'd better get home, before Rex discovers what's been going on.'

'I'm far too excited to go home. Rex can be such an old fuddy-duddy in the evenings. All pipe and slippers and some dusty old book. No, I'm off to my club to have a victory dinner with my girlfriends.' With a triumphant smile, she turned and flew down the stairs.

'What have you done to that woman?' Aidan asked from behind me as I leaned over the banisters to watch the whirlwind that was Julia Marshall disappear.

'I do believe she's discovered her confidence,' I said, walking back into the salon.


Two hours later I sat at the head of our dinner table, hastily set up in the salon after all the chairs had been cleared away, the waiting staff dispatched, the gowns carefully hung on the racks in the studio, the order book returned to my desk.

Oti, Simone, Rebecca, Flavia, Anna, Yulia and Aidan were seated around the table, their plates almost empty, their glasses half-full of leftover champagne, a row of candles down the centre of the table, reminding us of the ordeal we'd just been through. For the first time in weeks, I'd simply stopped and was just soaking up the sound of friendly chatter and laughter, enjoying the fire that was keeping us warm. I had a glass of single malt in my hand and felt full up, replete with achievement. Aidan had completed his duties to perfection, keeping Mrs Marshall busy and away from the studio. He'd played the chaperone and the fixer, as if he did that kind of thing all day long, relishing his role in the event. Oti had masterminded the behind-the-scenes schedule, keeping all the mannequins on time, each one of the seamstresses had been assigned a number of outfits and had been responsible for dressing the mannequins and ensuring they kept to Oti's strict timetable. There hadn't been a single hitch, despite the power cut. And now here they all were, being entertained by Aidan, as if he'd known them all his life. The light of the fire flickered across their faces as they laughed at the memories of the evening, the noise of knives clattering on plates, glasses being filled, the creak of the chairs as they sat back in satisfaction.

As the conversation faltered, Rebecca stood up.

'I could be one of those mannequins. It can't be that difficult can it? Just watch.' She began walking up and down the room in the style of our mannequins, hips slightly forward, left hand on left hip, a swinging walk. Being egged on by the other girls at the table she made a comical sight, her short, squat shape seeming to mock the whole process of modelling.

As she walked, Aidan piped up. 'Miss Rebecca Styles is modelling our most à la mode uniform. A white over-jacket made from the very best cotton, with mother of pearl buttons down the front, a pocket on each side as well as a breast pocket for holding items such as thimbles, sewing scissors and tailor's chalk. To complement the jacket, Miss Styles is wearing our prescribed dark-blue serge skirt, with darts at the front for additional flattery and a dark-blue belt to ensure everything is kept in place. The whole outfit is finished by a pair of brown leather lace-up boots with a small heel, just enough to ensure that Miss Styles reaches the height of her esteemed friend's shoulder.'

Rebecca could no longer keep a straight face and collapsed back into her chair, hand over her mouth, eyes crinkled.

Goading her on, Oti said, 'You'd make the perfect mannequin.'

Rebecca retorted, 'Now you're just plain lying to me, Miss Oti. I know I'm too fat. Even if I wasn't, I'm certainly too black. Can you imagine one of our skinnier sisters taking part in the parade this evening? Especially that purple evening dress where there's a lot of flesh showing. Someone we know would be having an opinion right now.'

Everyone laughed, but there was an edge to it. Yulia, perhaps having had one glass more than she was ever used to, perceptively jumped in with another of her stories about one of her girls. She was a large round-cheeked woman whose smile never left her face. Mother of five daughters aged from sixteen down to four years, living in a tenement apartment with her husband, mother and sister, she would always have some story that would keep away the gloomy world of bad landlords, rotting tenement apartments and the price of coal.

'I must tell you the latest about my little one, Katarina. Last Sunday, we were listening to the sermon being given by Father Antonov and he was getting a bit heated, you know, throwing his arms around and raising his voice. In our house, whenever someone shouts, which you know I don't like at all, I will always say "Keep your voice down, God can hear you."' Here she shook her head. 'After a while Katarina got up on the pew and said, "Keep your voice down, Father, God can hear you already." Can you imagine my embarrassment? Well, at least I didn't swear like that Mrs Marshall. What would her husband have said?'

I sat back watching these women who now made up my life as the steam from Yulia's famous shchi soup, with its warming sauerkraut and hint of dill, mingled with the pepper and spice from Simone and Rebecca's stew. When Anna brought out her *torta margherita*, the sweet sponge reminding me that Rosa had been there at the beginning of this family, this family that were at my workroom table, their voices, languages and foods weaving together just like the threads we worked with each day. These women who helped me shape fabric into dreams had, stitch by stich, sewn themselves into my life.

Forty dresses turned into fifty-five – word of mouth and a good write-up from the editor of *Harper's Bazaar* helped the orders flow in. We took on more seamstresses and already we'd outgrown the studio; we were tripping over each other, too many tables, too many sewing machines in too little space.

The apartment below the salon came up for rent. Before Mr Franke had drawn breath from telling me, I took it, turning it into an open-plan space filled with cutting and sewing tables, ten more tailor's dummies and a large blackboard showing each customer's order and where in the schedule of work it was. The light-filled studio became the finishing space, making the most of the natural daylight provided by those extraordinary ceiling lanterns. This was still the room I loved, the room that reminded me of where it had all started, the room where I felt most at home.

Julia Marshall continued her patronage, always recommending us to her friends, but we were now garnering customers from all over New York and beyond.

'Darling,' she said during another fitting, 'I noticed a woman leaving that I've never seen before. Who can she be? She can't be one of your customers, maybe she's one of your girls, one of those seamstresses you keep so well hidden away. But she was *so* well dressed, I can't imagine you let your girls dress as well as your clients.' Her voice was a little sour, as if she had bitten into an unripe plum. 'Aren't all your customers friends of mine?' She peered at me, a little too closely, as if she was trying to see into me.

'Oh, that was Miss Hineman. She's visiting from Boston; I expect that's why you don't know her.'

'She came all the way from Boston to see *you*? What extravagance.' She sniffed with disapproval, but then seemed to dismiss the thought as soon as she'd had it. 'Anyway, darling, I need to have a little heart to heart.' She was sitting on one of my sofas holding a half-drunk cup of tea. Putting down the cup she clasped my hands as if they needed warming up, looking at me earnestly. 'It's about you and Aidan. I do think you two should be getting on with it and naming the day. What happened to all that sudden enthusiasm when you first met? Here we are eighteen months later and all I see you do is talk to each other at parties, the occasional dance and that's it! Where's the engagement ring? Where's the big announcement? I do so want to preside over your big day. Since you don't have a mother to take control of the wedding, I can do that for you, darling.' Here she patted my hand, as if I was some poor orphan who'd been left out in the cold.

'Maybe we don't want to get married,' I retorted, trying to keep the irritation out of my voice.

'Now, darling, don't be so ridiculous and stop trying to pretend to be so...' here she hesitated as she looked for the word '...modern. Every decent young woman needs a decent young man. And our Aidan T Cruickshank really is a decent young man. If you don't succumb to his advances some other gorgeous young thing will swoop in and take your place. Now, take my advice and force the issue, threaten to cut him off or flirt with another man. That always does the trick.' Her concern was replaced by a look of triumph, as if she'd solved all my problems.

The truth being that he *was* decent – kind, attentive, funny and entertaining but also interested in the way my business was going, often giving me useful advice – somehow he'd become sewn into my life. One day I'd find him in the studio, entertaining the girls, making them laugh with stories of great society downfalls and disgraces, the next he'd be looking at my books to see where I could be more financially efficient, then he'd be in Mrs Vanderbilt's salon, talking with her as if he'd known her all his life. He was as at ease with the likes of Mrs Vanderbilt as he was with the seamstresses in my studio. His ability to switch from ballroom to storeroom was a trait that I could admire, something I'd always wanted for myself.

'That man, he's just like you,' said Oti one afternoon, as we were both embroidering the cuffs of a woollen winter coat. 'There are so many sides to that Mr Aidan Cruickshank, and I can admire that, but there's something I can't put my finger on, there's something that's missing. Don't get me wrong, I appreciate having a man around here sometimes, but I just can't figure out what he wants with you, Maisie?

'But what I do know is that you don't love him. I can see that. And I don't think he loves you. He's just useful – charms that Mrs Marshall when she's in the way, butters up our girls when they're in need of a bit of attention, even buys us food when we're too busy to eat. But you're not like you were with Joseph. I see that once he's out of the room you've forgotten all about him, whereas sometimes I see you still thinking about our poor old Joseph.' She let out a little laugh, almost as if it were for herself only. 'You think I haven't seen you wanting to ask after him, wondering what he's up to. I can see those questions on the tip of your tongue, but I can't tell you. I won't tell you 'cos I know that it won't help, it won't make any difference. He still doesn't want to see you.'

Only Oti could be so outspoken, only Oti was able to articulate what I couldn't. Her plain-speaking made it so obvious; Aidan *was* a handy man to have around, he played a part in my little business, he looked good on my arm. But he never made my heart skip a beat, I never once anticipated his visits as anything other than whether he could do something for me. What did I do for him, why did he spend so much time with me? I had no idea. It was as if our relationship was mutually convenient, a strange symbiosis existed with no recognition of what it was for.

## Finance

War in Europe was looming, but most were happily ignoring it, believing it could never happen. Orders were still flowing in, parties were on the increase, dresses were always in demand. My customers were starting to change as the suffrage movement gained momentum, thoughtful women wanting to be taken seriously whilst they mixed with men of political influence.

Soon, we were again outgrowing the space in the studio, the salon and the floor below. Now I had fourteen women working for Maison McIntyre, we had a continual flow of work, gaining new customers every week, struggling to keep up with the demand. Yet again we were tripping over each other and in need of more staff.

Mr Franke appeared in the studio one morning, hanging back in the doorway, always reluctant to step in.

'Miss McIntyre. I need to speak to you on a rather urgent matter,' he said, trying not to hitch up his trousers, a habit he could never quite break, despite my careful sewing.

'What can I do to help you?' Always giving him my best attention, knowing what an effect it had on him, I took him by the elbow and led him into the salon.

'I must tell you that I am selling this building. We are looking for a buyer just now and I suggest that you will need to move out soon.' His voice was hesitant, his German accent stronger than usual.

He must have been expecting me to be upset because when I greeted this news with a great smile he responded with a confused frown. 'How is this good news?'

'It means that my space problems have been solved,' I announced.

'But how? You haven't found anywhere to move to.' He scratched his red beard in puzzlement.

'I will buy this building. Then I will have the use of all three floors and the basement for storage. It's the solution I've been looking for. Thank you, Mr Franke. That's the best news I've had in days.' I kissed him on the cheek.

His mouth fell open into a perfect 'o'. I held on to the temptation to shut it with my index finger.

Eventually he managed to say, 'You can't buy this building.'

'Mr Franke. Believe it or not, I can.'

He stared, mouth again open.

'I just need to find someone to loan me the money. Would you give me a few days to sort that out before you look at any other buyers?'

I had no idea whether this was true or not. Would anyone loan me the money? I knew that women who wished to borrow money needed a man to guarantee her loan. Who would do this?

'Miss McIntyre. You surprise me every day,' said Mr Franke and he gave me a shy smile. I don't think I'd ever seen his smile throughout the whole of my tenancy. Usually his face was sad, as if he had a yoke of burdens that would never be released from his shoulders and being in his company always made me feel melancholic. But here was a smile, so unusual, so unexpected that I could only join in.

. . .

That night I arranged to meet Aidan to discuss the finances. A table was booked at Delmonico's, his favourite haunt. I loved eating there, still feeling the thrill of walking through the door of that fabled restaurant, walking beside the women of the Four Hundred, eating in the same room as Mary Pickford and the Rockefellers.

I was late arriving, leaving Aidan in his seat for too long, rushing up to the maître d', insisting I make my own way to the table, wanting to greet Aidan without all the fuss of my chair being pulled out, a napkin being placed on my lap, the menu presented with a grand gesture. I approached the table without him noticing me, as he was intent on watching something off to his left. I slowed my pace, noting a look of desolation on his face, and turned my gaze in the same direction to see a couple walking arm in arm to a corner table – Minty Aston and Joe Fitzwarren. Frowning, I continued towards Aidan as he turned to see me. He froze for a moment, as if he didn't know who I was, before hurriedly producing his usual genial smile, the usual welcoming greeting.

'I'm sorry I'm late,' I said. 'So much has happened today that the day ran away with me.'

He wasn't listening, as his gaze was pulled back to the corner of the room. But Minty was now talking to someone at a different table and her companion, Joe Fitzwarren, was left by himself. He caught Aidan's eye and he too, momentarily, had that look of desolation, where his cheeks seemed to sag, and his eyes became too bright.

'It's not Minty, is it?' I whispered.

Unable to keep his gaze from Joe, Aidan shook his head almost imperceptibly. 'They announced their engagement yesterday. He's a man in need of money and the only way he could see his way out of it was to marry a rich heiress.' Finally, he tore his eyes from the far end of the room and back to me, a crooked smile on his face, sadness in his eyes.

'Now you'll understand why I was sent away, so my dirty little secret could be pushed to the other side of the Atlantic, where I should have been able to keep my unnatural urges to myself.' His words were thick with emotion.

'It seems your father has little knowledge of New York.' I smiled at him. 'Come,' I said, holding my hand out to him, 'let's celebrate. Now we're even, neither of us has anything to hide, and we can be true friends.'

Finally I understood why he hadn't wanted more from me. Relief flooded my body. No expectations. So much easier. Until then I hadn't realised how much I had unknowingly been resisting the idea of a husband, someone to share my life with.

'I wanted to ask your opinion about something,' I said, eager to get onto my finances.

He took a large gulp of his bourbon and swiftly signalled to the waiter to bring him another. 'Anything for the inimitable Miss McIntyre.' His voice was a little slurred, as he raised his glass to me and knocked back another mouthful.

Wary of his tone, I continued. 'The building on MacDougal Street is up for sale. I want to buy it, solving all my problems over space in one go. It means I can stay in the studio and I can finally leave that awful boarding house and move into one of the apartments.'

'Well,' Aidan sighed. 'Congratulations, Miss McIntyre, what good news.' His words were monotone, with no emotion as he drank more whiskey.

Ignoring his petulance, I carried on. 'But there's a problem. I don't have the money and I'm going to have to borrow it. As I understand it, I may be able to secure a loan, but I will need someone to guarantee it for me, a man. I don't want to approach Mr Marshall, that would be getting myself into a tangle with his wife, I'd rather not go there. I was wondering if you had anyone you could recommend?'

The new glass of whiskey appeared at the table and Aidan picked it up, swilled it around carefully, watching the swirl of brown liquid. Slowly a smile spread across his face, but it never quite reached his eyes. It made me feel cold, almost vulnerable.

'I know exactly what we should do, Miss McIntyre.' His voice was too formal, too reserved, so unlike him. He leaned forward and took my hand. 'I think we should get married.'

His hand was icy, slightly damp, making me feel as if I was holding a dead fish. 'Why would we want to do that?' I asked, staring into those dark-brown eyes, looking for some of that old Aidan Cruickshank mischievousness, thinking perhaps he was joking. But they were stony, hard and without feeling.

'Isn't it obvious? It'll be a marriage of convenience. Plenty have done it before us. A sham to hide my dirty little secret, a financial backer for you. I can guarantee you your money, I can even lend you some if you'd rather, in return you'll turn a blind eye to my assignations.' Suddenly he was animated, those dead eyes now sparkling as he pushed his floppy hair off his face.

'Can't you see? This is perfect. Those terrible mothers will stop parading those insipid girls in front of me, Mrs Marshall will stop nagging you. She'll be in her element, organising the wedding, arranging the trousseau, inviting all her friends. We'll play the couple about town, go to the theatre, be seen in the park, we could even take a place out on Long Island and have our own famous parties. Think about it; we'll be hiding in plain sight, I can keep seeing my lovers, you'll have your studio.' He was fidgeting in his seat like a little boy getting excited about going to the circus.

I swallowed and looked down at my lap, running my finger and thumb along the edge of my napkin, my mind numb at the proposition. I felt as if a cage door was shutting on me.

'No. I can't take you up on your offer of marriage,' I finally managed to say. 'I don't think that would be a good idea.'

He stilled himself, a frown darkening his face. 'Why would you say that?' His voice was too controlled, too measured.

The general din in the restaurant seemed to die away, my hearing only narrowing in on Aidan's words, as if I was in a shaft where all other distractions were blocked out.

'I feel I would lose control of my independence, especially my financial independence.'

He blinked and put his head on one side, a slight smile on his face. 'Why would that bother you? Women shouldn't expect financial independence.'

Those words felt like a physical blow to my chest, as if I had been winded.

'Why shouldn't women be allowed to expect financial independence? I've been financially independent since the day I arrived in New York, and I intend to stay that way. I know what dependence feels like and I don't want to have to go back to that. I'm luckier than the majority of women in my position, but the world is changing, and I'm certain women will become more and more independent.'

He gave a little snort of derision, leaning forward on the table.

'What do you plan to do with your business? Have you thought about how it might be affected by this oncoming war? Do you think that high-end women's fashion will be something people care about during a world crisis? Surely, you're going to need to expand into the wider market, so you can cater for the everyday woman? I think you might find that the frivolity of the couturier may have had its day.'

'Are you trying to goad me?' I asked.

'No, I'm just talking to you as if you were a man.' His voice had now become patronising, needling under my skin. 'You need to think hard about expanding your business and how you finance it. I'm giving you the opportunity to have the freedom you're looking for. Look, my dear.' He patted my hand, that shallow smile back on his face. 'This is the best offer you'll ever get. No one will want to take on Maisie McIntyre. You're too opinionated, too independent. Men don't like that.'

If I let Aidan guarantee my loan I would be tied to him until the day I paid it off. If I married him then I would be committed to him for the rest of my life, putting up with his dalliances on the side. I watched him as he picked up his whiskey glass, as his eyes never left mine. I had lied, cheated, stolen and fought for that independence; I wasn't going to give it up that easily.

My mother had discovered her own freedom when my father left. Despite the hardship and occasional bouts of misery, she was far happier without him. With a clarity that comes when you put on the correct prescription glasses, I knew that I would be better off without Aidan T Cruickshank as my husband or guarantor, however witty, incisive or supportive he may have been.

I stood up from the table, taking care to do it quietly and without fanfare.

'Thank you for the offer. I will not be taking it up. I will seek financial advice elsewhere.' I picked up my gloves, turned and waved to the waiter to get my coat.

I walked out onto the street, looking for a cab, but before I could find one Aidan was by my side.

'Maisie. What are you doing?'

'Isn't it obvious?' By now the anger was effervescing inside of me.

'Why are you making life so hard for yourself?' he pleaded. 'We could get married. Together we could make your business into something to rival the House of Worth. But you're throwing that away, throwing aside my help. You can't possibly know what you're doing. Nobody will back you, of that I can be sure. Buying real estate, managing money, that's what we men are good at. You design the dresses for girls. I can deal with the money. Can't you see, we'd make a great team.'

The temptation to slap him was so great I had to clasp my hands to keep them still.

'Come back and see me when you've learned not to be so patronising. You need a quiet wife who will not challenge you, who will cover up your misdeeds and make you look good. I am too self-sufficient for you. You would hold me down and ask me to do things your way.

'Maybe your way has some merit, maybe a sham marriage and a financial guarantor could work. I like you; I like you a great deal and I think we work together very well. But I do not want to be obligated to you or feel that I must do things the Aidan Cruickshank way. I need to do things the Maisie McIntyre way.

'Sorry, Aidan, but there will be no wedding, no cover-up, no happily-ever-after.'

I leaned forward and kissed him on the cheek, catching the notes of cedar and leather on his neck, closing my eyes, wishing I didn't have to let them go.

# Chapter Five

## The Protest Dress

*White silk wrap skirt with a wide opening to show a pale-purple underskirt and gold silk partial overskirt. White chiffon shirt with a deep v at the front and short sleeves studded with purple beads. Pale-purple under-bodice. The high waist is embroidered with purple beading to look like a cummerbund. There is a gold flower with a white centre at the waist made from velvet. The gown is finished with a large, white bow with intricate purple embroidery down each tail.*

# Impetuous

## 1914

Aidan was right in one respect. Finding a financial backer was difficult. I visited at least fourteen banks, all of whom turned me down merely for being a woman. I couldn't possibly be responsible for owning a building, running my own business and employing many staff. But the fifteenth banker, a Mr T J Capriani, welcomed me into his office and took me seriously. He loaned me all the money I required at a good rate, acting as my guarantor. He treated me exactly as if I was a man and never once considered I couldn't do what I was setting out to do.

Mr Capriani was from an Italian immigrant family and set up a bank which served the many immigrants who couldn't get loans from other American banks. Of course, in New York, he was a busy man, serving the many Italians, Russians, Poles, Irish and British. A short, rotund man, with a bald head and round glasses, he was a jolly, reassuring presence for all those customers who were nervous that they wouldn't be given access to money. He was a fastidious dresser with a neatly waxed moustache, a deeply lined forehead and a shiny face, sitting behind a mahogany desk that was too big for his stature, always courteous and respectful. I may not have been his first woman customer, but I believe I might have been his most profitable one.

May 12th, 1914, I sat across the desk from Mr Capriani in his tiny and overcrowded office. He always sweated a little too much when he was excited, wiping his face with his pristine white-cotton handkerchief. Just as I signed the document he opened the bottom drawer of his desk and brought out a small bottle and two tiny glasses.

'A little limoncello. To celebrate your future, Miss McIntyre, and that of Maison McIntyre.' He handed me my glass and held his own up towards me. 'Let's hope this is the first of many beneficial investments.'

He took a sip and put his glass down and wiped his face again, more sweat beading on his forehead. 'As a banker I am not supposed to feel any emotion about my transactions. But every now and again I get a sense that I am doing something good, something that is going to matter. And I have one of those feelings today. You're not just about making clothes for important ladies, Miss McIntyre. I think, perhaps, that there is a bit more to the eye than we're able to see. I look forward to finding out what that is.' And with that he downed the contents of his glass, handed me the deeds to 130 MacDougal Street and ushered me out of his office with a grand bow and a flourish.

At twenty-four I owned a whole building: a studio, salon, two floors of sewing and cutting space, a basement for storage and an apartment all to myself, I now employed fourteen women and needed to find more, the orders were backing up. I was a woman who had no family money, no husband to hold the trapeze artist's net. Five years previously I had lived in a tenement in Edinburgh with no prospects other than a lifetime of colourless grind.

Standing outside Mr Capriani's office on East Houston

Street I couldn't move, stunned by my achievement. Suddenly I craved my sister's company. I wanted to be back in the bed that we'd shared, telling our whispered dreams to each other before we fell asleep, Netta wistfully murmuring her craving for thick gravy on a hot roast dinner, peppermint creams and somewhere she could warm herself by a roaring fire. She'd curl my hair around her index finger, willing my straight locks into a hopeful and elegant twist as she told me of her dreams of working in an office as a clerk or as a companion to one of Edinburgh's old ladies, I'd tell her of the luxurious gowns I would make, the sumptuous fabrics, the complicated embroidery, the frivolous feathers and unnecessary fur trimmings, we'd laugh about the ladies I would dress, the great houses they lived in, the ostentatious carriages they rode in. Now all I wanted to do was let her know I'd done it, I wanted to send her a cable: MAISIE McINTYRE STOP BUSINESS OWNER STOP. But it wasn't worth it. Despite my sending the occasional letter, offering to send money to help out or presents for her girls, she'd never replied, most likely still furious with me for leaving. I knew I needed to work harder to win back my sister, but sending a triumphant cable wouldn't do the trick.

However, I needed company. I needed to celebrate my triumph. Aidan was keeping to himself, regrouping after the devastation of his pal Joe Fitzwarren's engagement, licking his wounds after my rejection. Rosa would have understood how to mark the occasion. We'd have had the whole family around her tiny kitchen table, there would have been a cramped, noisy dinner with comforting food and enticing smells. There'd have been a warm sisterly hug, sensible advice mixed in with enthusiastic declarations. I touched my tortoiseshell necklace, pressing my thumb against one of the teeth of the broken comb, pressing as hard as I could to remove that absence, like sewing up a tear in a fabric that no one sees.

Suddenly I realised who I wanted to be with.

Across the road was a delicatessen Yulia had introduced me to, full of every kind of Jewish food imaginable. I have never been a good cook. As soon as I discovered places like this I had resolved never to attempt to cook again.

I ran in and ordered rye bread and bagels, hot pastrami and corned beef, potato salad, egg salad, chopped liver and mustard. The store was loud, people shouting their orders, food hurriedly being packed in paper bags. I ordered more food than I'd ever ordered before, round knishes and square knishes, pickles and sauerkraut, matzoh ball soup and my favourite, chicken noodle soup, emptying my purse to cover the cost.

With an armful of food-filled paper bags and all thoughts of Rosa, Aidan and Netta pushed to the back of my mind, I strode out of the delicatessen and found a taxi cab to take me to MacDougal Street.

'We're finishing early today. We're stopping for dinner. We have something to celebrate.' Breathlessly I put my parcels in the kitchen.

Everyone was tired. We seemed to have been working endlessly to fulfil the last of the summer orders and we were already gearing up for the August show. There had been no let-up, there had been no time to stop since that evening of our first fashion parade the previous year.

'This entire building now belongs to Maison McIntyre,' I announced triumphantly. 'We're going to expand into the other parts of the building, take on more staff and if things go well, maybe we'll open a shop on Fifth Avenue.' This idea had just appeared as I said it, spur of the moment.

There was a general murmur of surprise and, once all the fabrics and garments were safely put away, Oti and I dragged one of the large sewing tables into the salon and set out the food. Simone and Rebecca brought in chairs, along with glasses and cups. Makeshift plates were made from the paper bags and others used the pails that they'd brought their lunch in. With hardly any effort, the room was transformed into a scene of a great, noisy feast, that loud family dinner I'd been so longing for, the food softening everyone's fatigue. Soon there were passionate but friendly arguments, the laughter becoming boisterous, even quiet Anna could be seen giggling at some of Oti's more riotous jokes, Yulia managing to find yet another family story to keep the laughter on tap, and Josephine, one of our new seamstresses, entertaining us by juggling the knishes, slowly popping one into her mouth until they were all gone. Flavia had rushed home whilst we were setting up and had arrived back, breathless, with one of her polenta cakes. Just as the cake had been passed around, I stood up with my glass of water.

'Here's to Maison McIntyre and all of you who work here. I may have just bought the building, but it would be an empty shell without you. This is a business which caters for the needs of women. Because of that I need women to help me run it, women who understand how our customers think. You are those women. Men may dismiss our business as frivolous and unimportant, they may say we're not an industry that matters, that we're not an industry at all. I suggest we show them otherwise.'

I raised my glass and we toasted 1 30 MacDougal Street. We cheered all that we had achieved, our little collective, every woman in that room with their own individual talent, be it Oti's organisational skills or Rebecca's tailoring, Yulia's ability to keep our spirits up when hard deadlines loomed, or Flavia's flourishing flair with colour. Together these women transformed my designs from sketches to reality, working together with so much goodwill and unity. They had created something rare, a place where skill mattered more than background.

As the afternoon wore on and our voices became louder, our cheeks a little rosy, our stories a bit more boisterous, we missed the knock at the main door to the studio, we failed to notice Julia Marshall slip into the salon, until suddenly there she was, standing in front of the fire, her face full of bewilderment, her mouth slightly open, those dark eyes turned pale.

Seeing the shock on her face, I was suddenly able to see the room with her eyes. Black skin, scarred faces, uninhibited laughter, and unusual accents.

Getting up from my seat, I hurried over to her, standing between her and the table.

'Mrs Marshall. What are you doing here? I wasn't expecting to see you until tomorrow morning. Is everything all right?' I caught her elbow and tried to turn her back towards the door. Her eyes were darting from side to side, wide and alert, her face pale, her breathing irregular. It was as if she was a wild animal caught in a cage.

'Well, I was just...' Her voice faded out as she pulled her arm away from me, looking over my shoulder, looking at my table of unconventional women.

'Who are they?' she whispered. 'Have you turned your salon over to some sort of Lower East Side soup kitchen?' She let out a half giggle, half sob.

I held her gaze. 'These are the women who work in my studio, my seamstresses, my Premier, my finishers.' I battled to keep my voice calm and soft, as if I was explaining to a child. But as I spoke something shifted in me, a crack in my chest, and a feeling of recklessness stabbed at me. Grabbing her wrist I said, 'Come, why don't I introduce them to you?' I turned her to face the room. 'I've kept them hidden from you for so long, I should have introduced you months ago. How remiss of me.' There was a false jollity to my voice as I pulled her towards the table, pulled her towards the silent, wide-eyed women.

All too quickly she jerked her arm away from me. 'Oh, no. I couldn't possibly. I couldn't possibly interrupt your...' I could see she was struggling for the right words as she turned her back on the table. 'Is this a party?' she whispered, shrinking back from me, a look of disgust on her face.

Now I couldn't control the anger as it coursed through me. I took her wrist again and spun her around to face the girls.

'Yes, we are celebrating. Let me introduce you,' I said too loudly.

Oti, Simone and Rebecca froze, stunned into silence, watching me with widening eyes. Anna, Flavia and Yulia and the others were all looking down at their plates, cheeks red, fists balled together on their laps.

'No!' Mrs Marshall gasped, recoiling, staggering back towards the door.

We all stared at this woman, who had helped make our business, who had grown in stature over the last four years, who now seemed to shrink under our collective scrutiny. As we watched the shrivelling of Mrs Marshall, I could hear the bell of a fire engine, the hum of automobiles, the clip-clop of horses, a laugh, a baby's cry, a street vendor's shout to get rid of his final items of the day. These familiar noises appeared to bear down on our visitor until she was unable to tolerate it any longer.

She gathered herself, pulling herself upright, holding her bag with both hands in front of her. 'I can see I'm intruding.' She turned, suddenly looking down at her bag. 'I'll come tomorrow as arranged, as I should have done all along.' And with that she fled the room, her colour high, her hands shaking as she twisted the handle of the door.

The door slammed shut, we listened to her quick footsteps running down the stairs. We all looked at each other, no one daring to say a thing. Finally, Oti leaned back in her chair and let out a long, loud sigh, the air pushing her lips outwards, her whole body appearing to sag. Not knowing what to say I started to stack the empty plates, scraping any leftovers into an empty bowl, needing something to occupy my stunned mind. But as the bowl filled, I threw the knife I'd been using onto the table, a loud crash filling the silence.

'To hell with her,' I shouted, a sudden giddiness coming over me.

Oti crossed the room and took my arm. 'Maisie,' she hissed at me, steering me towards the studio, 'you know why we work the way we do. This isn't about you.' She closed the door behind us, her voice now a rigid growl. 'We all made choices about how to survive in this city. Don't throw that away because you're angry.'

I ignored her. 'If we're going to expand, if we're going to employ enough staff to fill up all the rooms in this building, if we're going to bring in enough orders to make that happen, I'd need to have you out there meeting the customers, taking the orders, maybe Rebecca and Simone too. I can't keep you hidden away forever, it's not fair on any of you. It's also not fair on our customers.'

Oti sat down hard on the last chair left in the room, putting her head in her hands. 'You're either a damn fool or braver than I ever took you for. Don't you know this town thrives on lies and falsehoods. Difficult to get along without them. We all spend our time hiding from someone. Why should you be any different?'

I could hear the others shuffling around in the salon, chairs scraping back, an embarrassed murmuring, perhaps packing up their bags getting ready to go home.

I put down the bowl I was still holding, full of the debris from the table. 'Shouldn't we be honest for once?'

A sound escaped Oti's throat, sharp as broken glass. 'When did you start being honest? Being honest hasn't done you any good. Haven't you learned that already? You've been spending too much time in those genteel ladies' drawing rooms, thinking they're respectable and sincere in everything they say. They're no better than you are, and they'd be the first to turn on you and take away their business if they thought you'd damage their reputation.' She sighed. 'Black girls are going to damage your reputation, therefore being associated with you will damage Mrs Marshall's reputation. It's a miracle we haven't been found out before.'

Oti infuriated me when she was so right, but I couldn't argue with her. I knew the moment Mrs Marshall stepped into the room that evening that we were in trouble. I'd been living on a knife edge for the past two years, shutting the door to the studio whenever a customer walked into the salon, always taking the measurements myself, never delegating the front of house jobs. I was Maison McIntyre, but Oti was my Premier and should have been the one taking the orders, measuring up, discussing the finer details. But I'd never allowed it because I feared how our customers would react to Oti and the others, scared that all my hard work would come to nothing as my customers vanished.

But as I considered what might happen, I found that my fierce loyalty to every single one of those women working in my studio outstripped any unease, a ferocious determination to protect them surged up inside me. I clenched my teeth and stood up.

'I no longer care what Mrs Marshall thinks.'

## Colour

The next morning Julia Marshall arrived late and in a hurry, keen to get on with the final fitting of two summer day dresses. The fashion at that time was to have a long straight skirt, with a much shorter overskirt that almost ballooned at the hips. This worked well with tall, willowy women, but not with Mrs Marshall, so short and petite. The dresses I'd made her had high waists with long, straight skirts and deep slits either at the back or off-set at the front so that she wasn't hindered when walking. This style made her seem taller, more authoritative; it was a style that gave her confidence.

That day she seemed unusually shy about undressing in front of me.

'Would you mind going into your studio whilst I change?' she said as she inspected the dresses hanging in front of her. She hadn't met my eye since her arrival.

'Don't you want help dressing?' I asked.

'No, don't be ridiculous,' she snapped. 'I'm perfectly capable of dressing myself.'

I took a slow, deep breath, keeping my frustration inside. Sometimes this was the way it was with customers. There were days when they weren't in the mood for chitchat, didn't want fussing over, had no time for fun and frivolity. This was rare for Julia Marshall, she'd recently told me that her afternoons with me in the salon would give her renewed energy, a boost of confidence, as if the act of dressing was putting on a fresh layer of paint, bright and hopeful.

'Of course, Julia. I'll just go and find the organdie roses we've been making that go with the sash and can be applied to your hat.'

'I would suggest you refer to me as Mrs Marshall from now on.' I could almost touch the frost in her voice.

As soon as she said this, I knew that this would be our last meeting.

'I assume your behaviour last night means that you won't be getting rid of those...' It seemed as if she couldn't bring herself to say what she was thinking. '...those girls.' She spat the words out. 'I assume you've been laughing at me behind my back ever since they started working for you. I won't have them touching anything that I wear. I won't have them anywhere near my outfits. Do you hear me?'

'I'm afraid that's impossible. They work on every gown we make.'

'Then get rid of them. Get rid of them or I take my business elsewhere.'

'But surely you still want this dress. Oti has spent hours over the hand-stitching on the sash. Have a look.' I grabbed the dress off the hanger, trying to curb my rage. 'Can you see those tiny stitches so that the gathers on the organdie sash ruffle up naturally.' I wanted to bring the detail up too close to her face, but I held back, holding on to the shake in my hands.

Julia Marshall blanched, as if I had pushed a tiny dagger in under her ribs and then twisted it.

She looked at the sash, then down at the sleeve of the dress she was wearing, one we had completed about three months previously and touched the lace.

I couldn't help it. 'Yes, Oti made that dress too. And while we're talking about Oti. Do you remember that dress I wore when you bumped into me at the St Regis and I promised I would introduce you to the person who had designed it?' I was so angry now that I couldn't stop. 'Oti designed it. Why don't I go and get her and I can introduce you?' I made my way to the door between the salon and the studio.

'Miss McIntyre,' she almost shouted. 'I do not want to meet this so-called Oti. I do not want this dress, nor the other one on the hanger. From now on I will be taking my business elsewhere and I will be telling all my friends what it is that you do here, what kind of women you employ. It won't be a secret anymore.'

Furiously, she picked up her bag and left the building.

That rage, roaring in my chest, quickly turned to a strange euphoria. I wanted to laugh openly, knowing she would have been able hear me as she went down the stairs. I felt light-headed, giddy with childish glee, with an unexpected relief; I wanted to throw open the salon window and shout out to her as she reached the street, shout about her prim rigidity, laugh at her shock that someone with black skin had made her dress, had made so many of her outfits. But, of course, I couldn't do that. Those were the reactions of a hysterical person, someone who didn't know what to do next.

But now I had a large mortgage to pay as well as an increasing wage bill. That euphoric anger quickly dissipated, leaving me shaking and needing to sit. Losing Mrs Marshall as a customer was a catastrophe for my newly expanding business. Not only did she commission us to make most of her wardrobe, but she encouraged all her friends and acquaintances to come to us too; she was our sales department, she helped us organise our fashion shows, she influenced the guest list, she had all the connections that we needed to get our work to the right audience. And now she was gone.

The ending of my working relationship with Mrs Marshall brought on a prolonged period of creativity. It was a kind of mania. I didn't sleep, I worked long hours, and my ideas went well beyond my usual everyday designs. The atmosphere in the salon became more relaxed and, finally, I was able to make Oti our official Premier and introduce her to all our customers.

But, as predicted, we quickly began losing customers. Soon there were days when we didn't have enough work to keep everyone busy.

About two weeks after Mrs Marshall had resigned her business, I was moving into the apartment that had belonged to my old landlord, Mr Franke and his family. It was a Saturday and I had the building to myself. The apartment vacated by the Frankes was glum and sparse: the ground floor window shutters were painted black, the walls a gloomy grey, spiderwebs in every corner, mould in the kitchen. The only furniture was a table carrying my old sewing machine, no longer used in the studio, new and more efficient models having been bought, but I loved that old sewing machine and I'd had it brought down to sit in front of the main window and where I could use it to make brightly coloured curtains for the main living area, and smaller, more discreet café curtains to hide the open shelving in the kitchen. My first job was to paint the small apartment – a living area, kitchen, bedroom and tiny bathroom. Since I had little work to do I'd decided I should do the painting myself, so was happily spending the morning up a ladder painting the room white. Paint was expensive, especially coloured paint, so using white and then dressing the room with colourful curtains, cushions and wall hangings was how I intended to turn the dark, cheerless area into somewhere that I wanted to be, somewhere that would be my very first home.

I'd completed one coat and was just preparing to get started on the second when there was a knock on the front door and a man's voice saying, 'Hello! Anyone at home?'

Frowning, I recognised the voice but couldn't quite place it, I put my paintbrush down and went to the door to find Carter, Mrs Marshall's chauffeur.

'I have a delivery for you from Mrs Marshall. Going to need your help to get it in.' He turned to the street where there was a small truck.

'What is it?' I asked, unable to think of anything Mrs Marshall would want to send me.

'Every single dress, coat and skirt you have ever made for Mrs Marshall.' The tall, ruddy-faced man gave me an uncomfortable look. 'She's been in a terrible rage these past few days, there's nothing her staff can do that's right. Even Mr Marshall has decided it's best to keep away from her just now, staying at his club. She was going to throw these all away but, you'll be surprised at this, Mrs Marshall Senior persuaded her to send them back to you. She thought you might appreciate them. I'm not so sure. Have you got the space?'

'Space is about the one thing I do have,' I said as I trotted down the steps towards the back of the truck. There were six hanging rails filled with Mrs Marshall's wardrobe. The very first dress I saw was the peacock-blue evening dress. I climbed up onto the back of the truck and held the fabric between my fingers. A rush of nostalgia hit me: the terror after I'd stolen the bolt of peacock-blue material, the feeling of triumph as I found myself in first-class on the SS *Furnessia*, the whirlpool of emotions on my arrival in Manhattan, my first visit to The Plaza Hotel. All these sensations rippled through me, temporarily blotting out my lack of customers, my reputation, my need to look after the women who worked for me. That blue silk conjured up the optimism and naïve confidence I once had in myself, reminding me that I could have that all over again.

'Well, we'd better take them in,' I said to Carter.

Half an hour later, Carter and I had wheeled and carried all the hanging rails into the other empty ground floor apartment.

'What will you do with them?' asked Carter.

I walked around the rails, picking up a skirt of chiffon, a dress of pale-green silk, a burnt-orange military-style coat. Just as I was beginning to think that I was flattered that she'd kept everything, every single outfit I'd made, I noticed that on the skirt I was holding there was a long cut from the hem to the waistband. I picked up another skirt and again, a long, precise cut had been made in the middle of the skirt. I looked at every piece on the hanging rails. Each one had been cut, just one long cut, in the front of the skirt so that it couldn't ever again be worn as it currently was.

I looked up at Carter, showing him a large yellow satin skirt cut right up the middle. His face turned a deep red.

'Oh, miss. That's the behaviour of a spoiled child. Bad manners, that is.'

What spite. I never knew Julia Marshall capable of such malice. But an idea suddenly occurred to me and I started riffling through all the outfits again, noting the jumble of colours, textures and weights of fabric, and I began to think of how these dresses could be re-used, how I could keep everyone in work and how I could bring in some money quickly. I wasn't sure that it could work, but it might just create an immediate stopgap for our current crisis.

'Well, Carter, I think I'm going to cut them up. Destroy them.'

He took his hat off and nervously scratched at the back of his head. 'Is that wise? Can't you do something with them? Maybe patch them up? Re-use them.'

'Don't worry, Mr Carter, I have a plan. Please tell Mrs

Marshall, with as much pleasure as you can muster, that I'm thrilled to have every item of her wardrobe and I'll look forward to cutting them up into little pieces.'

I ushered Carter out of the front door and sat down at my sewing table to draw, all thoughts of painting gone from my mind.


Monday morning Oti found me in pile of cut-up dresses, skirts and coats.

'Lord in heaven, what *are* you doing?' She rushed over to the pile of fabric. 'You're cutting these up? Are you mad?' It seemed as if she was stricken, her face full of horror as if she'd discovered pieces of art being defaced.

I told her about the delivery Carter made. 'She doesn't want them. We need work and we need money quickly. These have presented the perfect solution.'

'How?' She picked up Mrs Marshall's pink dress worn at our first fashion parade.

'Look at these,' I said, pointing out five cushions that I'd made the day before. 'These cushion covers have been made out of the fabrics from these dresses. And here.' I pointed to a lamp-shade. 'I've made this out of one of her summer coats. There's a whole treasure trove here and we can quickly make cushions, lampshades and other small household items, using these fabrics. There's nothing like these out there. If you look at the cushions in the shops you'll see that they tend to be made from upholstery or curtain fabric. But here we've got all these wonderful colours, silks and satins, tweeds and jerseys. No two cushions will be the same, and we can combine two different fabrics, say two tweeds of differing patterns or a combination of three different coloured silks in a bold patchwork. The patterns and combinations are endless. We've got so much fabric here, all for free. All we need is the cushion pad, some thread, sewing machines and our women upstairs to work them up. We could get through this work in just a few weeks and we'd have enough stock to sell up to Christmas. Don't you see?' I stood up and started pacing the room. 'We can open a small shop selling home goods, completely different to anything anyone has ever seen before. Do you remember Elsie de Wolfe? The woman who's designing the inside of the new Colony Club. I bet you she'd be interested. And there must be others who'd take these. We'd have to think up a name to sell them under – not Maison McIntyre, that name isn't too popular right now. Maybe something like Maison Rouge, or something else French, then that would give it some sort of mystery, make the customers think these have come from France. Then, maybe one day, we could branch out into furniture, other soft furnishings, turn it into an emporium. Oh, that's what we should call it! An emporium, maybe the French Emporium, then that gives it an oriental feel. And we can use the cushions in the salon, give the room a little bit of a lift, and hopefully some of our customers will ask where they came from. We can send them to the emporium and they'd buy some for themselves.' I was becoming a little breathless and the ideas bubbling over.

Oti put her hand to her forehead. 'You're giving me a headache, you in one of your design frenzies. Can you stop for just a minute?'

She picked up one of the cushions. I'd made it out of a bright pink, deep pink and an almost maroon, all of a thick silk, three large stripes graded in colour. The back of the cushion was one piece of bright-yellow taffeta.

'I can tell I'm not going to change your mind on this one,' Oti sighed. 'Haven't we got more important things to be dealing with, like finding new clients?'

'We've got the new designs to finish for the August parade, so we'll keep most of the staff on those. We only need a few to make up these cushions and lampshades and anything else I come up with. Once we get going I think we'll only need two or three weeks to use up all the fabric we have on these dresses, and when those are finished, then, hopefully, I'll have found a few new customers and we can get on with the business of haute couture. It's just a stopgap, something to generate some money and keep everyone busy. I couldn't bear it if we had to let any of those women go, it wouldn't be fair, just because Mrs Marshall doesn't like the look of some of them.'

'How are you going to organise all of this, when we've got all the autumn designs to oversee or do we get one of the others to take charge of it?'

'Flavia. She has a good eye for colour and design. I think that once I've told her what ideas I have she'll easily work out what I'm trying to do.' I picked up a piece of green fabric. 'Wouldn't it be lovely to have a cushion with these sequin embroidered birds on?'

Oti tutted, shaking her head, but there was a smile in her eyes. 'Okay, have it your way. Just when we thought we might have a moment to catch our breath, you go all frantic and come up with new ideas.'

The next two months were spent creating a range of soft furnishings unlike any I'd seen in Manhattan. Having given Flavia the role of managing the project, the first thing she did was take the empty apartment across the hallway from mine and turn it into her own workroom, where she could work with me to create the designs and then supervise three of the women who were not busy in the upstairs sewing room. Cushions and table linens, lampshades and wall-hangings were soon piling up in what had once been a bedroom. Giving Flavia this responsibility made her stand taller, draw her head higher, no longer keeping to herself; now we could hear her voice and see her face. She used almost every single scrap of the material from

Mrs Marshall's dresses, producing a hum of excitement in the studio that I hadn't heard since our first fashion parade, everyone seeming to understand that what we were doing was different, something that might get noticed. What would Julia Marshall think of her dresses being turned into household items? That simple question always made me smile.

But at the same time, we were still a couture house, albeit with far less customers. We were at the beginning process of designing for the autumn/winter season, agreeing fabrics, number of designs, anticipating our customers' wishes. Appointments had dried up so we were surprised when we received a knock on the door a few weeks after Mrs Marshall and all her friends had deserted us. Oti and I were in the studio, working on the new season's designs when a Mrs Bailey Parsons was announced, requiring an appointment.

Oti and I stared at each other. Harriet Bailey Parsons, a recent New York resident by way of her even more recent marriage to the wealthy Maximillian Parsons from an old and well-established shipping family, was seen as one of the beauties of her age. But she had a reputation for being intelligent, thoughtful and empathetic, used to dining with senators and presidential candidates, wealthy industrialists and financiers. A member of the WSP, she clearly took her responsibilities seriously, often photographed in the papers lobbying influential politicians for the women's vote, and, I'd noticed, her sense of style was astute and singular. My ideal customer had just walked through the door.

'Go,' I said. 'She's all yours. You talk to her and then I can pop in later and introduce myself, I need to finish up here.'

Oti blinked. With a slow intake of breath, then an even slower exhale, she stood up, hung her tape measure around her neck, picked up our most recent *Book of the Season*, a pad of paper and perfectly sharpened pencil, and opened the door into the salon.

I couldn't help myself, but I tiptoed to the door and kept it ajar just slightly, enough to be able to hear their conversation.

'Miss McIntyre?' a kindly voice asked.

'Oh, no, I'm Miss Jackson, Miss McIntyre's Premier,' Oti said. Only I would have noticed the slight wobble in her voice.

'Good, just the person who I need to speak to. I wondered if you'd have time to show me some of your designs. You see, I rather urgently need a suit for a lunch party I have to attend with our senator, a coat for an outdoor event I must speak at and also an evening gown. I know I haven't made an appointment, but I was hoping that you might be able to fit me in at the last minute.'

I finally let out my breath. Oti was on her way, and she didn't need me.

'You cannot imagine how terrified I was,' she said after Mrs Bailey Parsons had left. 'She's taller than me and big boned too, a booming voice – a presence in any room. But she was all smiles and kindness and proceeds to cosy down with me on the sofa, discussing these important lunches and dinners she needs to attend with stuffy politicians and fusty old men.' Oti was sitting at her newly created desk, her pens and pencils neat and her notebook lying open, her tidy handwriting and a few small sketches filling the page. She was wearing her new Premier's uniform – a black woollen suit with a tie-fronted shirt.

'She was telling me that she's been invited to give a street speech for the WSP, saying how nervous she is as she's never had to make a public speech before, so she wants a coat that's tailored "to perfection". Those were her words.' Her eyes were sparkling now. 'I'm going to make sure we get it just right.'

That session with Harriet Bailey Parsons was Oti's first as a Premier. And it wasn't long before Mrs Bailey Parsons began sending her friends to Maison McIntyre.

Meanwhile we'd found a small shop for the proposed Colour Emporium, as we'd decided to call it, on the corner of

Fifth Avenue and 38th Street, just across from the new Lord & Taylor Building. We were able to get a lease for only a few months, not expecting to need the shop beyond Christmas. Having the shop opening to look forward to was a welcome distraction from the strains of holding up the struggling couture business, and organising a fashion parade that we weren't sure anyone would turn up to. We might invite customers to an opening party, but we didn't have to entirely rely on their custom. Passers-by could be enticed into our Colour Emporium with inviting and inventive window displays. Once customers were through the door, I had no doubt they'd want to buy; our household range was eye-catching and radically different.

Two days before our autumn/winter fashion parade, I picked up my usual *New York Times* on my way into work.

ENGLAND DECLARES WAR ON GERMANY; BRITISH SHIP SUNK; FRENCH SHIPS DEFEAT GERMAN; BELGIUM ATTACKED; 17,000,000 MEN ENGAGED IN GREAT WAR OF EIGHT NATIONS.

We all stared at the headline in the workroom, a quiet depression covering us all.

Simone picked up the paper, reading aloud the detail with a kind of fascinated glee that had me feeling a little sick.

Yulia crossed herself as Simone continued to read. 'There are days when I curse the Lord for giving me five girls, but today I'd like to bless him. I'm sure we'll be getting involved at some point. How can they ignore so much bloodshed in such a short time?' She crossed herself again.

As the women chattered, surmised and speculated, I took myself into our tiny kitchen and put the kettle onto the stove.

'You all right?' came Oti's voice from behind me.

I hardly knew what to say. 'Just a little shocked at today's news,' I said, unsure how to tell her my real feelings.

She looked at me, crossing her arms, leaning against the wall. 'Maisie McIntyre. I know you. You may well be shocked at what you've heard today, but surely this isn't anything that you haven't been expecting? I think you're worried about the fashion show and if anyone's going to turn up.'

I couldn't help but smile. 'Are you accusing me of being a ruthless businesswoman who only thinks about her profits?' I teased.

'Well, yes, ma'am, I do believe I am!' She gave a little snort, looking down at her left arm and pulling a stray piece of wool off her jacket. 'I know you better than anyone. I know you're worried about how this business is going to survive without Mrs Marshall and now this happens. Couldn't be worse timing. How can we possibly expect our customers to be going out and enjoying themselves in a brand-new Maison McIntyre dress when Europe is being decimated?' As depressing as all of this sounded, she said this all with a wry smile on her face, as if she'd been expecting this reaction from me all along.

'Maybe we should call off the fashion parade,' I said quietly, checking through the door that no one was listening. 'Since we hardly have any customers anyway, it's probably the sensible thing to do.'

'Oh no, don't you dare.' Oti wagged her forefinger at me. 'Don't you go getting all morose on me.' She gestured towards the studio. 'Think about those women out there, what would they think? What would Mrs Bailey Parsons think of you. I know what she'd say, she'd say you've got no gumption, no sticking power.' She shook her head. 'Oh no, missy, we're all ready to go, there's no backing out now.'

. . .

Three o'clock, the time for the parade to begin, was fast approaching and only ten women had made their way up our three flights of stairs into the salon, laid out with forty chairs. My stomach was churning, and my breath shallow. I would look a fool having to do this show with so few to watch. No press had even turned up. But just as I was thinking disaster had fallen on us, we heard running footsteps up the stairs and a young boy burst into the room.

'There's a note for you, miss,' he blurted, so out of breath he could hardly speak, and thrust a piece of crumpled paper into my hand.

'How do you know it's for me?' I asked, amused at the boy's determination, his insistence that it be for me.

'She said you'd be the lady that looked ill. She said your face would be white and that you'd be holding your stomach as if you wanted to be sick,' he said at the top of his voice.

I had to smile.

'I came all the way from the Colony Club,' he breathed, still struggling for air, now bending over with his hands on his knees.

'But that's almost thirty blocks away. Surely you didn't run all the way?'

He looked up, a cheeky grin overtaking his face. 'I hitched a ride on the back of a carriage for twenty blocks, until they noticed and made me get off, so I only had to run a few blocks.'

I looked down at the note.

*Miss McIntyre,*

*Please delay your fashion parade by half an hour. We'll be with you as soon as we can. I couldn't postpone our meeting at the Colony Club, but I've arranged for several cars to bring us to you the minute we're finished.*

*Yours*
*Harriet Bailey Parsons*


Again, I had to smile. I turned to the small group of women who had gathered in one corner.

'We're going to be running a little late, but perhaps you'd also like an exclusive preview of a couple of our dresses?'

Half an hour later, Harriet Bailey Parsons and twenty other Colony Club members made their way up our stairs and into the salon, chattering and full of enthusiasm for an intimate fashion parade.


Every single woman who attended that fashion parade ordered at least one of our autumn/winter models. Thirty-nine designs ordered, including three for Mrs Bailey Parsons. How on earth were we to deliver all of those *and* open a shop?

As we were putting together the last-minute touches for the opening of the shop, a note was delivered to the studio.

*Dear Miss McIntyre*

*As you may know, Paris is too seriously occupied with war responsibilities to consider the question of dress, and this maybe for some time to come. Mrs Vanderbilt, Mrs Stuyvesant Fish, Mrs August Belmont and myself have decided to organise a fashion fête as an incentive to create new designs in New York, which has become the logical successor to Paris in fashion, with London, Berlin and Vienna also cut off.*

*The proceeds are to be devoted to the Committee of Mercy organised by Mayor Mitchel and Mrs J Borden Harriman for the relief of women and children made destitute by the European war.*

*I would like to invite you to submit two designs to this fashion fête for the approval by the committee. These designs should be available for our perusal on October 4th, with the fête taking place over three days, beginning on November 4th at the Ritz-Carlton.*

*If you could contact me at your earliest convenience for a meeting to discuss the event.*

*Yours,*
*Mrs Woolman Chase*
*Editor-in Chief, Vogue*

Oti held the note in her hand.

'You're going to have to say no to this. How in God's name are we going to manage that as well as deliver all those outfits? We're overstretched as it is. No, you've got to refuse this one.'

'Too late. I'm seeing her tomorrow,' I said briskly.

We were having our regular early morning coffee, in the coffee house across the street from the studio, before anyone else arrived. 'We can't turn this down. All those ladies who buy their fashions in Paris and London, they can't get there anymore, no designs are coming over, no fabrics are making their way from Europe. Don't you see? We can't wholly rely on the patronage of Mrs Bailey Parsons – look where that got us with Mrs Marshall. We need to make sure we secure the jobs for everyone in the studio, not just for the next few months, but for the foreseeable future.' I paused, taking a sip of my coffee. 'Besides, we should be doing something for the war effort. Making dresses for well-to-do women doesn't exactly make us seem sympathetic to the war. I'm worried about Yulia, with all her extended family back in Russia. What if my sister's husband gets called up? I want to be able to look them in the eye and say I did something to make a difference.'

Oti raised an eyebrow. 'Look at you getting all selfless and big-hearted. You sure this isn't just about you trying to prove yourself to Mrs Marshall? You know she's going to be there, don't you?'

'Ach, who cares. We've moved on from her already. We have a new type of woman to dress. Women who are independent, women who have jobs, women who can think for themselves, women who want to stand out because they want to make a difference. *We* will stand out at this fashion fête, because we are like the women we want to dress, and we will produce designs that suit their frame of mind.'

'Oh, Lord. Here you go.' She stood up, straight and assertive in her Premier's suit. 'Well, you better let me go and find some more hand-sewers, and we should start looking to finding embroidery and finishing companies outside of our studio. We've got too much work to do it ourselves.'


Two days later the Colour Emporium opened. The display window was filled with piles of cushions, draped wraps over armchairs, tables laid up with the linens and other homeware items we'd bought in to fill the space: candlesticks, picture-frames, table mats, crockery and cutlery, jugs and jars. Once inside, the room was a riot of colour, a mishmash of furniture, lighting, paintings, wall-hangings, tableware and more. It was the complete opposite to the organisation in the studio: nothing matching, everything appearing to have been thrown together, but in truth, Flavia had spent hours curating this space, she'd brought in all her family to help with dressing the shop, the women who'd worked on making the cushions and the other items had also come in after work to help. There was an air of excitement and exhaustion that you could almost touch.

We'd sent out invitations to all the old and new Maison McIntyre customers, not letting it be known who was behind this new venture. I didn't keep it any particular secret, but I certainly didn't mention my name on the invitations.

'Oh Lord, look who's coming through the door.' Oti turned to me, her eyes narrowed. 'Did you invite Mrs Marshall?'

A dual feeling of delight and horror swam through me. Smiling I said, 'I might have mistakenly put an invitation through her door...'

'Maisie McIntyre, you're a wicked individual. You could ruin all of Flavia's hard work, she could condemn this whole event, tell all her friends never to come here, spread the word that we're frauds, that we're taking advantage of her, that we're...'

'Oh, I don't think so,' I said as I watched Julia Marshall slowly walking around the shop floor. She greeted a few acquaintances, she frowned as she rubbed the fabric of a table cloth between her thumb and forefinger and then she became still. As she stood there, staring at a pile of cushions, all fashioned from the clothes we had made her, I could hear the banging of my heart in my ears, drowning out all other noise.

Slowly and deliberately she looked up and turned, watching to see what the other customers were doing. I could see her mind working at a frantic pace, her eyes taking in every item in the room. And then someone came up to her, greeting her effusively.

'Julia, darling, have you seen these exquisite cushions? Can you imagine the use of these kind of fabrics? It's as if they've taken my latest ball gown and rustled up a few soft furnishings because they had nothing else to use. I can't work out whether it's the work of a genius or someone who goes through the garbage bins of the Four Hundred. What do you think? Look at that embroidery on that pale-blue silk cushion. I could swear I've seen that somewhere before.'

Mrs Marshall blanched, doing her best to hide it as she coughed into her hand.

'Well, I'd certainly say it's the work of a clever seamstress.' She threw a thunderous glance at me. 'But I'd say it's a bit of a fad, I can't imagine how anyone would want these seen in their drawing rooms.'

As she spoke, I picked up one of the large paper carrier bags we'd had made, with the words Colour Emporium printed on the sides, and rushed over to Mrs Marshall and her companion. I picked up two matching cushions made from the luscious olive-green velvet we had used in a sumptuous winter evening gown she'd worn only a few months earlier. It was embroidered with dark-green velvet birds' nests, twigs sewn from metallic threads, the clusters of pearl eggs nestled between the fibres.

'Mrs Marshall,' I cried at the top of my voice. 'How wonderful of you to join us today. I just wanted to make sure you got these two cushions, the ones we discussed. I know you wanted them for your drawing room as soon as possible.' Carefully I placed them into the bag. 'You know these are completely unique, you'll never see another pair of cushions like this. I do hope they garner as much praise as you were hoping for.' I handed her the bag. 'Please do keep looking around, I'm sure you'll find other items that will please you.' I squeezed her arm before passing her the bag.

If it was possible for her to have become any paler, she would have done. Instead, her shoulders sagged, her hat seeming to follow suit.

'The Lord will find a way of punishing you, Maisie McIntyre,' Oti hissed at me as I returned to her side. But there was a smile in those dark eyes, a hint of impishness on her face. 'Don't you ever pull a stunt like that again or he'll strike you down right in front of me.' She crossed herself as if she was in front of the altar at church.

# Protest

The Colour Emporium, despite its unlikely foundations, became an overnight success. We'd never be able to use second-hand gowns again, we'd certainly get found out and lose our Fifth Avenue clientele, but it had given us the springboard for creating a different kind of homewares, that made us unusual and set us apart from the slightly stuffy and musty colours currently in fashion. Flavia took on the job of sourcing and designing full-time, we found a shop manager and lengthened the lease.

Dress commissions were running at full steam, new hand-sewers and seamstresses were employed, we started working with a new outsourced embroidery company. I had two designs to work on for the upcoming fashion fête in November.

My recently re-found creative mania suddenly focussed itself on the idea of protest. I wanted to object to the fact that a woman couldn't hold a bank account without a male signatory or take out a line of credit. I wanted to oppose the fact that we were treated in the same manner as so-called criminals and imbeciles who were also denied the right to vote. As a woman who ran her own business and had to pay taxes shouldn't I have the right to choose whether I agreed with them or not?

What better place to protest than at the Fashion Fête in five weeks' time, creating a dress full of subversion. It would be a statement of rebellion and a banner of defiance, a white evening gown of sumptuous fabric but full of so much detail that admirers would need to look at it closely. And when they did they would see the insurgence, they would see my message of insurrection. They would see that I was making a statement for women's suffrage.

But I needed to do this in secrecy. The Fashion Fête was being organised in aid of the war, it was about giving a boost to the American garment industry, making those women who would only consider French designers aware of the wealth of design and dressmaking talent in America. The press would be present along with virtually every well-known society woman within a hundred miles of Manhattan. It was an ideal moment to promote our work. It would not be seen as the time to hijack the cause and inject it with an atmosphere of protest.

There was a jury of imposing women, including Mrs William K Vanderbilt Jr, whose job it was to accept or politely reject suitable models of clothes. If I showed them my finished design they would, without a doubt, reject it. To ensure my gown would pass the inspection of these indomitable women I had to leave the subversive embroidery and beading until after the jury inspection, which would only give me a month to finish it. I didn't tell anyone, not even Oti, what I was doing.


'Have you seen this?' Oti asked, bursting into my office the day after the fashion parade, brandishing a newspaper.

'No, I decided to avoid the papers today,' I replied, looking up from my sketches.

Oti rolled her eyes at me as she sat in the chair opposite my desk, sighing. 'I'll just read the bit that matters:

'*As the model took to the floor the guests were trying to peer more closely at the detail of the dress. A white silk wrap skirt with a wide opening to show a pale-purple underskirt with a gold silk partial overskirt and a white chiffon shirt with a deep v at the front and short sleeves studded with purple beads covering a pale-purple under-bodice. The high waist was embroidered with purple beading to look like a cummerbund and a gold flower with a white centre at the waist. On close inspection, the white silk satin bow at the back had wide tails with the bold purple wording "Votes for Women" written down the length of each tail.*

'*With the model continuing to walk through the tables, murmurs began to spread until, at the model's final turn, a large banner dropped from the ceiling and hung in the middle of the room. A highly decorated, beautifully embellished piece of needlework ran the same slogan "Votes for Women" as well as being adorned with feminine images of love, flowers, and those of historic women of influence such as Boadicea and Florence Nightingale.*

'*There was an audible gasp and some women left the room. The model was hurriedly whisked away and the orchestra was asked to strike up some rousing music.*

'*The dress, designed by Maison McIntyre, has already become known as "The Protest Dress".*'

'The press exaggerating so they can sell more papers. There were no gasps, just a few murmurs of disapproval, nothing to get excited about.'

'So much for you being all charitable and big-hearted. What happened to you wanting to look your sister in the eye?'

'The women who went to that fashion parade paid good money, money that will help those poor orphaned children. And, thank you for asking, Miss Otella Jackson, haven't I secured jobs for our women and some more? Won't we be needing to hire new seamstresses as soon as possible? In fact, I believe the telephone has been ringing all morning. Don't tell me that's concerned friends just checking up to see if we are all well.' I twiddled with the pencil in my hand as if it was a high school girl's baton.

'You make me so mad when you're right,' Oti said, laughter in her voice. 'All right, we've already had ten enquiries this morning. It seems you've all too quickly become known as the Suffrage Designer and they're queuing up to have a Maison McIntyre dress.'

I smiled. 'What would Mrs Marshall say?'

## Chapter Six

### The Black Trouser Suit

*A two-piece women's trouser suit. A fitted jacket, finishing at low hip, made from black wool crepe with finely ribbed, glossy, black silk sleeves and double cuffs fastened by three self-covered buttons in bright-pink silk. The jacket is fastened by one link button, made of the same bright-pink silk. The high-waisted, wide-legged, black wool crepe trousers are fastened at each side with three large pink buttons.*

*From the personal collection of Ms Maisie McIntyre.*

# War

## 1917

'He's gone and signed up,' Oti said one morning as we drank our coffee before the start of work, looking down at her hands splayed out on her lap, her eyes blinking furiously.

I didn't need to be told who she was talking about. Joseph. The man I once loved, who I'd tried to keep out of my mind. For six years Oti had kept any conversation of him away from me and my memories of him were becoming hazy, only to be brought into focus every time she gave me one of those Jackson smiles that transported me back to our Sunday afternoon outings.

In April 1917 the United States declared war on Germany. Less than one hundred thousand men had signed up, meaning millions had been drafted.

'Why?' I asked, a numbness creeping over me. At least up until now I knew he was safe, still living with both of his sisters, still working as an architect's apprentice, still woodworking in his spare time. But Joseph was no fighter. What was he doing willingly signing up? War was against his principles. He'd never even thrown a punch – how was he going to shoot a man? It felt as if there was concrete in my stomach.

'He's just another of those idiotic boys out there.' She gestured towards the windows facing the road. 'All of them thinking they owe this country something. What loyalty does my brother owe this country that rarely gives him a moment's thought?' There was real anger in her voice, her mouth tight, her eyes on the windows.

'He's joined the 396th Infantry regiment of the 93rd Division. He leaves tomorrow.' She looked right at me, desperation in her eyes. 'He's a peace-loving man, never harmed an insect in his life – always steps over them or picks up those great big spiders and puts them out in the yard, only for them to come marching right back in again.' She pressed her lips together as she began massaging the muscle between her thumb and forefinger.

'Have you tried to talk him out of it?'

She gave a snort. 'My brother, never one to rock the boat, suddenly decides to stand up for himself and become all brave and stubborn.' She looked up at me. 'What are Audrey and I going to do without him? How am I going to get rid of those spiders? We'll be overrun.'

'A wide-mouthed cup and a piece of card. Then you can take it down the road and release it onto the street or outside someone else's house. It works every time.' I leaned in towards Oti. 'You'll work it out. If Joseph can get all big and brave, then so can you.' I grabbed her hand and squeezed it, too hard, not believing my own words. 'We're all going to have to get big and brave.'

Slowly everyone sent a loved one off to France, life was about waiting and hoping: waiting for a letter, hoping for the best, terrified of the worst. But we decided on a rule – no talk of war during our day at work. This gave us the opportunity to lose ourselves in the colour, in the rhythm of couture, from the sketches to the finished item. The feel of the fabric soothed us, the beat of the sewing machine, the quiet of the hand-stitching, the concentration required kept us all in check, allowed us to forget the terrible business of war for a few hours a day.

But at the end of the day we'd gather, bring out our letters and our news. Flavia would often bring one of her cakes; it was her way of smoothing out the creases of war.

'I brought my favourite today, *sbrisolona*. I'm sorry, Maisie,' she said as she handed plates out, 'I know it's too crumbly for the studio, but I couldn't help myself. You see we got word that my brother's been injured in Belgium. We don't think it's too bad, they aren't talking about sending him home, but my parents are tearing their hair out. You see we've still not heard from Lorenzo, my other brother, for weeks – it's too much for them. I spent all night baking.'

Flavia would never say if she was upset, or sad or worried. We knew when she was struggling because she would bake. Baking calmed her, feeding her friends and family gave her the ability to deal with her own traumas after the factory fire. Eating her delicious creations, sitting round in a circle, also gave the rest of us a way of coping with the increasing bad news.

Oti seemed more reluctant to give us news of Joseph, although she knew this was part of the deal – share and share alike – so she'd keep it short and to the point, always precis his letters, never read them.

'He's still not been deployed, although there's talk of France in the next few weeks. But he's bored, doesn't find training in the freezing cold much fun, thinks the food is terrible, can't get to grips with the weapons.' She rolled her eyes. 'I could have told him that and saved him the trouble of all those regrets he's having. I think he'd just like to come home to his own bed and some good down-home cooking.'

On November 6th 1917 the men of New York state granted the women the power of the vote. I wanted to yell and shout, jump up and down, I wanted to go and see Mrs Chapman Catt address the women of New York, to celebrate in their success. I wanted to wear my suffrage button like every other white woman in the state, but I didn't feel that I could, not if Oti, Rebecca and Simone couldn't. It didn't feel like the victory that it should have.

As our designs became more serious, as suits and day-dresses became more muted, our early evening sessions with tea and cake became darker with Joseph finally deployed to France, Anna retreating into her silence again as news of her little brother's death arrived, and Flavia producing more and more cake, her older brother now missing presumed dead. The laughter that had once been such a part of our day was now absent.

And then Joseph wasn't safe.

I knew something was up when Oti hadn't arrived at work. She was always the first one in after me, we always went for our coffee before the others arrived. The telephone rang.

'He's been badly injured. I would have come into work but I can't leave Audrey, she's too upset.'

'Where are you?' I knew she didn't have a telephone.

'I'm at the neighbours', they let half the street use their phone in emergencies. Listen, I can't talk for long, I can't leave Audrey just now, but I'll be back to work as soon as I can. Could you send Mrs Aston's embroidery over? I can get that done whilst I deal with Audrey.' She sighed. 'That girl. We don't even know how bad it is and she's gone into some sort of hysteria.'

'Don't worry about the work, we can get...'

'No! I need to be doing something. I can't sit around all day doing nothing. Get it sent over straight away and hopefully I'll be in tomorrow. We can't sit at home waiting for more bad news.'

I put the telephone receiver down and began looking for the work Oti needed. As I folded up the fabric, slipped in the pattern, used the brown paper and string to package it up, I felt as if I was moving in a strange fog. All the background noises had receded, but the crackle of the paper, the snip of the scissors as I cut the string, seemed heightened, seemed to bore into me. I had pushed all thoughts of Joseph away as much as I could, doing as he'd asked, cocooning us both from the *what-if*s and the *what-could-have-been*s. But Oti's telephone call had brought him back into focus: his very particular hand movement when he'd point out some little detail on one of the buildings we'd visited, the way his left eyebrow would twitch when he was amused, his low chuckle that was so infectious.

His injuries were so severe he didn't arrive back in America for six weeks. Whilst we waited for news we insulated ourselves, our everyday use of fabric and threads creating a cushion for the fall that we knew was to come. Oti worked longer hours, ate less and less of the cake Flavia put in front of her, her cheekbones became more pronounced, she pulled her bun tighter and tighter, as if she wanted to pull away any unnecessary thoughts.

'Oti, you need to go home,' I said the evening before Joseph was due home. 'You need some sleep.'

She looked at me as if I was far off in the distance. 'They say his right side is shattered, that he has trouble breathing 'cos of the gas, I've been told he has constant nightmares. I'm scared about what we're going to find when we get to the hospital tomorrow.' She brought her focus back onto me, her pupils darkening.

'Maisie. You'll help me out with this, won't you? What with Audrey being about as worthless as gum on a boot heel just now, I don't think I can do this without you.'

Twice a week Oti made the long bus journey up to the Columbia War Hospital in Williamsbridge to visit, often returning without him having spoken a word. Twice a week I did the same. For six months we took it in turns, the journey exhausting, but the strain of watching him refuse to talk to either of us, anger raging in his eyes as we all learned that he would probably never walk again, became a different kind of exhausting, making each of us feel as if we'd been cutting logs all day. Often Oti would take her finishing work to the hospital, working on it as she sat silently with her brother. Somehow her embroidery became all the more intricate, more detailed and of a higher level of quality than I had been able to imagine. It was as if it was a release from the trauma she was watching, a way of blocking out the worry, using beauty to counteract the ugly truth.

I learned to lock away my own emotion, this wasn't my trauma. My job was to be there for Oti, to cover her work when she had to leave and pick up the pieces of Audrey, when I sent her home to make sure she got some sleep, when I ate the corn-bread that Joseph had refused.

I tried to break through the wall of Joseph's fury, at first bringing him news of what was going on in Manhattan, telling him of the latest buildings going up, such as the Racquet & Tennis Club and the half-timbered Tudor style building on Central Park West, but as I spoke I'd watch him turn away, sometimes a tear trickling down his face, I realised that my attempts at cheering him up were only making him worse.

So, I decided to do what Joseph had done for me. I brought him a library book and because he couldn't yet concentrate well enough to read himself, I read it to him.

At first it was an ordeal that I dreaded – I still wasn't a proficient reader and I knew others would also be listening. The book was P G Wodehouse's *Uneasy Money*. A film of the book had recently been released, people were talking about it and I

thought it might be distracting. As I started the slightly ridiculous story of a penniless lord who inherits a fortune from an
American millionaire, my reading was slow and halting, but
soon, when Joseph no longer turned away from me, I gathered
confidence, giving the characters accents, sometimes acting out
the scenes. He could only manage half an hour's listening, but I
read every visit, until nearly two months later, I finished.

'The end,' I said, dramatically closing the book. 'That's it,
Joseph. They lived happily ever after.'

Suddenly the ward came alive. Claps and wolf whistles,
shouts and cheers and, for the first time in months, a tiny, almost
imperceptible smile broke Joseph's perpetually sad mouth. I
laughed, embarrassed at the attention, thrilled that the anger in
Joseph's eyes had temporarily receded.

When he finally left the hospital, Oti invited me over to
their new ground floor apartment in Harlem. His right leg had
been amputated below the knee due to gangrene, his right arm
was beginning to heal with intense physiotherapy. I'd become
used to his still-haunted, sometimes furious look, where his once
full face was now haggard, his hair always clipped tight was
now in patches on the right side, burn marks showing through.
There had been no sign of the famous Jackson smile since the
day I'd finished the book and his once beautiful hands now
always fidgeted and never lay still. He had so much pent-up
energy, yet he still couldn't concentrate, was unable to focus.

I arrived, a small bunch of daffodils in my hand, my
stomach filled with butterflies, worried about the effect of him
moving home. I placed the flowers in a jam jar in front of him.

He visibly flinched. I tried not to close my eyes, did my best
to stand my ground.

'No,' he growled. 'Not here. She doesn't get to come here.
This is my house!' he yelled at Oti. 'Get her out!'

Oti pulled herself upright. 'Joseph Jackson. You don't get to
talk to me like that. Just 'cos you've had those kind nurses

pandering to your every need for the last six months, doesn't mean you get to speak to anyone like that. I'll have you know this apartment is in my name, the rent paid by me. So I get to choose who comes here and I choose Maisie.' The two of them glared at each other until Joseph seemed to collapse, his shoulders slumped.

'I just want peace and quiet and I can't get it when she's around. She's always talking, reading... always going on. There's too much colour, too much buzzing around. I just need...'

'What you need, Joseph Jackson, is people. You need things to do, people to speak to, people to read to you, colour to see. I don't care what those doctors said. You're going to be surrounded by the people who love you. We're going to help you get better, and one of those people is going to be Maisie.'

He looked down at the jar of daffodils and I could see a whisper of memory flick across his face. 'All right,' he said begrudgingly, 'but she only gets to come because I'm going to get sick of the sight of you, Otella Jackson. I'm going to need to have some kind of break from your bossy ways.'

Oti smiled. 'Likewise, my baby brother, don't you go thinking I won't be feeling just the same way.'

I arrived every Sunday morning, at ten o'clock so that Oti and Audrey could get to church and then visit their friends. At first it was excruciatingly awkward. It was as if we'd gone back to those first few visits in the hospital. Joseph wouldn't talk, wouldn't let me make him coffee, refused the cannoli that I brought from my local delicatessen – such a marked contrast to our old Sunday afternoons when we'd walk and walk, talk and talk, admiring the magnificence of Manhattan. Now we were still and silent.

But just as the whole world slowly began to resume some kind of normality, just as we began to wake up from the gruesome nightmare that had been the Great War, Joseph too began to soften. I began reading to him again: more P G Wodehouse, *Tarzan of the Apes* and, my favourite, *The Secret Garden*.

'I brought you the latest copy of *Architecture*,' I said one day, nervously laying the magazine on the table in front of him. 'Thought you might be interested.'

Worried that he'd turn away as he had done in the hospital, I pushed it towards him. Holding my breath, I watched him lean forward and run his hand over the front cover.

'Not much point in reading this. It's not like I'll be able to work at that kind of thing ever again.' His voice was sad, resigned, his eyes no longer blazing but almost drooping.

'Why not?' I asked carefully.

'Some days I don't even have the energy to do anything but stare at that blank wall. Can't be drawing new buildings if I can't even concentrate on holding my pencil.'

'Well, I'd better get you something to stare at then.'

The next Sunday I brought with me a large, flat, brown paper parcel and laid it out on the table.

'You should open it,' I said. 'Something for you to stare at.' I had my hands on my hips, chewing my lip, so nervous at his reaction.

'You open it.'

'Oh no, you bring yourself over here and open it yourself. I've got coffee to make.'

Standing over the coffee pot in the kitchen I eventually heard him wheel his chair over to the table, then the crinkle of the brown paper as he unwrapped the parcel, followed by silence. There was such a long silence that I could no longer keep down my curiosity. I stole over to the door and peered around to see Joseph leaning right up close to the framed picture that lay in front of him. He was running his finger along one side of it, his mouth moving as if he was talking quietly to himself.

'Don't think I can't see you spying on me, Miss Maisie

McIntyre.' His voice boomed like I hadn't heard it in months. He looked up and there was just a hint of amusement in his eyes. Not that dazzling smile, not yet, but this was enough. I almost dropped the coffee cups I was holding.

'An architectural map of Manhattan showing every fine building I can remember.'

And suddenly I was back on our old Sunday walks, the way his voice would curl around me as he'd tell me the story of this building or that high rise. I had to blink hard to stop the tears.

I brought his coffee to him. 'Perhaps you could tell me about some of those fine buildings. I'm sure we never did get to see them all. Now we can.'

As we slowly began to see improvements in Joseph, a state of giddiness began to emerge throughout America, as if all the nervous energy that had been stored up during the war now had to be expended. The recession was ending, women had the vote and it was becoming increasingly accepted for women to work.

And with that giddiness, Maison McIntyre grew. We now found that our customers fell into three categories.

The first were the frivolous, empty-headed girls who had yet to emerge from their cocooned, silk-lined drawing rooms. These girls, on their way to 'coming out', were only interested in catching as rich a husband as they could manage. And in doing this they needed to wear the most attention-grabbing outfits and ensure their rivals were left in the shade. These girls were usually accompanied by their ambitious mothers, the kind of women who'd had well-laid plans for their daughters since the day they were born: scheming, often shrewd and always willing to do whatever it took to outmanoeuvre her opponents. In truth, I preferred these customers. They luxuriated in their wealth and their duplicity, they were open about their belief and felt that there was nothing wrong with their ambition.

The second type of customer was more thoughtful and more sincere. Often, they were well educated and had been to university. Many were now working, some even had political ambitions. I should have liked these women more than the silly little girls and their indomitable mothers, I should have identified with these well-meaning women and understood their determination – they wanted to make a difference and they realised that by wearing beautiful, tailored clothes, by being well-presented they would be taken more seriously. But I didn't enjoy dressing these women as much. I could mould those air-headed girls, I could help shape their characters, but it was too late with the older, more serious women.

In the early 1920s a third type of customer emerged. Prohibition had quickly shown itself to entice bad behaviour rather than temper it. Alcohol was everywhere, you just had to know where to look for it, synthetic liquor being the alcohol of choice, the cocktail the fashionable way of drinking it, parties had changed from the formulaic debutante balls or staid dinner parties to outlandishly lavish and excessive cocktail parties. But extravagant and bounteous parties required sumptuous and luxurious cocktail dresses. Confident, eager girls who had time on their hands and trust-funds to spend were delighting in the freedom of dress: dropped waists, flat chests and cropped hair that seemed to go hand in hand with a new sexual freedom, excessive behaviour and the thrill of drinking when it was forbidden. New fabrics such as synthetic silks made evening wear more affordable, finding the lower echelons of society now able to keep up with the higher, modes of dress cheaper, money more readily available. Which meant many of my clients wanted to stand out with all the embellishments we could possibly provide on their flapper dresses: ostrich feathers, sequins, brilliants, rhinestones, metallic threads and jewels.

. . .

With the increase in customers and increase in work, by late 1920 we were sorely in need of more space, better organisation, more hand-sewers, more finishers, more embroiderers. We were taking on more and more staff and outgrowing 130 MacDougal Street. I had already given up the apartment on the ground floor, turning this into an office, whilst the adjacent, bigger apartment had been turned into a new salon so that our customers no longer had to climb the wearying three flights of stairs. Now we had a new open-plan area, decorated with mute colours on the walls but brightened by the now well-known soft furnishings from the Colour Emporium. Flavia and her team of seamstresses had moved to their own workshops down the street to continue the increasing homewares business, with a bigger shop on Fifth Avenue and a smaller one in Brooklyn. But our most difficult problem was finding another embroiderer. The embroidery house we had been working with was never quite as good as Oti on the complex work, and Oti was too busy; working as our Premier and seeing to the needs of Joseph gave her little time to concentrate on such detail. We had yet to find someone who was as talented as her, the intricacy of her work having always been a level above anyone else we used.

One day, coming into work a little brighter than usual, her dress just that bit sharper, her eyes less weary, she said, 'I think I've found someone who will be able to do some of the most difficult embroidery for you.' She was a little breathless. 'Eveline Patience, she lives near me. I've brought some of her work for you to see.'

She picked up a bag from her table and pulled out some pieces of embroidery to show me. Laying them on the table I leaned over to take a close look. The first was an appliquéd flower, where the textures went well beyond the traditional usage of thread. Beads, ribbons, card and even raffia had been used, with clever contrasting stitches outlining the flower, the mixture of stitching styles and textures making it almost pop out of the fabric. It was innovative, surprising and, in places, humorous. Then there was a piece of black organza embellished with mother-of-pearl petals held in place by metallic outline stitching, coloured brilliants sitting in the centre of the flowers. This was embroidery like I'd never seen.

'I'd like to meet this friend of yours.'

'I'm afraid she won't leave her home.' Oti sighed. 'She doesn't take visitors. But she'll take in work. If you give her a commission, I can take it to her. I know it will be returned better than you'd expect it.'

I frowned. 'Why won't she leave home?' I wasn't sure I wanted to work with anyone who wouldn't even meet me.

'She doesn't like big spaces. She gets frightened. She doesn't like crowds of people, they scare her. She's better in her own home.' Oti picked up one of the pieces of work and inspected it carefully. 'She's better than me. She's faster than me too.'

'Where did she learn to sew like this?' I asked, curious that someone apparently so confined could produce work that seemed so worldly.

'She told me that she used to work for a dressmaker before she became ill and that they aren't happy about her always working at home.'

I was sceptical. Would someone who only ever stayed at home lose their touch, wouldn't you need the influence of the outside world to improve your work?

'Let me take her Mrs Bailey Parson's coat. She will be able to complete the appliqué quicker than I can. It'll be better too.'

Harriet Bailey Parsons, the woman who had been Oti's first appointment as Premier, had continued to be one of our best customers. A successful writer and poet, she led a wealthy but rather bohemian lifestyle, which required many colourful outfits, most of which were becoming more and more intricate as the decade went on. She loved being seen in heavily embroidered dresses, jackets and coats and her latest commission was no different. We were running late with it and I needed to have it ready in five days' time. Sending it out to an untried worker was too much of a risk. I'd rather have done it myself.

'If she can't do it, I'll have completed it by the time it's needed,' Oti said, seeing exactly what was running through my mind. 'I can brief her; I know what's required. Let me take it today.'

I put my hand on her arm. 'Are you sure this isn't just you in need of more money to help with Joseph, you doing this at home? If that's the case you know I'll pay you more, I need you here.'

'No.' She pulled her arm away, her voice gruff. 'You'll just have to trust me on this.'

My frown deepened, confused by her behaviour. 'Oti—'

'Just let me do this,' she interrupted. Her voice was strained as she gave me a flat grimace before walking to the back of the studio, carefully folding up the pieces of fabric for the coat, putting it in a Maison McIntyre box, tying it with string and wordlessly leaving the studio.

All my bewilderment was forgotten when the coat was returned. The finishing was exquisite. But it hadn't only been finished exactly as I'd expected, there was a little bit of character in there. The colour of the fabric and the shape of the coat was enhanced by the finishing, the stitching immaculate, the texturing more superior than I'd expected. Eveline had even added in a couple of tiny, covered buttons within the embroidery giving it added depth and completing it as if it was a piece of artwork.

Despite the strange request that we never meet, Eveline Patience was employed as an outworker and began to produce some of the most extraordinary work that I'd ever seen. True to my word, I didn't insist on meeting her, she was adamant about that. But she, like Oti, never missed a deadline, never misunderstood a brief, always interpreted it with a little Eveline 'twist', perhaps adding in a tiny little embroidered mouse on an appliquéd collar, allowing a squirrel to hide amongst the leaves embroidered on an overskirt, include tiny beads that looked like bees visiting handmade flowers that sat on a sleeve. Her work nearly always surprised me, repeatedly made me smile and ensured my customers were increasingly happy with their commissions. They loved the added character that was introduced to their gowns, making them feel even more special than they did when wearing a Maison McIntyre dress.

But as we settled into the 1920s, Oti had another bombshell to deal with. Audrey became a single mother.

'Three people to look after,' she said over our morning coffee. 'Just when we were getting into a good routine, when Joseph was sorting himself out, just when I thought I could breathe.'

'I can help,' I said. 'I'll come over one evening a week, as well as my usual Sunday morning with Joseph, once Audrey's had the baby and settled back home.'

Oti sat back in her chair, threw her head back and roared with laughter. 'I don't think so,' she eventually said, catching her breath. 'You have not one idea what to do with children. Look at you when you used to take Annina Bassino out for the day. You just wanted to dress her up like a doll and have her sitting there looking beautiful.' She let out another roar of laughter. 'Oh dear Lord, no. You'd dress up Audrey's baby and it would be sick everywhere, I know it. I can see you now, holding that baby away from you.' She held her hand out in front of her, her thumb and forefinger together as if holding an imaginary dirty dishcloth, her face scrunched up as if there was a bad smell. 'No, I don't need your help, thank you kindly. I know you mean well, but you'd just cause more chaos than there already is.' She wiped her face and with wide eyes she said, 'Would you just promise me you won't be having babies any time soon. We've all got enough to contend with.'

'Well, I'm so glad I can oblige you, Oti Jackson,' I said, relief running through me. 'There'll be no wee bairns coming from me.' I crossed my legs firmly. 'No chance.'

But I didn't want to ignore Audrey, and a few days after Laura Jackson was born, I arrived at their apartment with several Macy's bags, full of baby clothes and toys.

It was five thirty on a Wednesday evening, Oti was still at work and I thought that Joseph and Audrey could probably do with a surprise, could do with someone to take their minds off the new chaos in their lives. I'd pictured myself whisking the crying baby off Audrey's shoulder, somehow managing to calm Laura, making coffee for both her and Joseph, bringing some temporary order to their evening. Instead, the door was opened by a man I didn't know with a haunted look and a thimble on his right forefinger.

'Is Audrey in?' I asked, peering behind him.

'No, but Joseph's here. You want to come in?'

Tentatively I walked into the main room of the apartment, recently made bigger with unnecessary walls knocked down and doors widened so Joseph could use his wheelchair more easily.

The everyday refectory table was laid out with a wide swathe of a pink fabric on one side with thread, ribbons and beads laid out in neat lines on the other. I recognised this as part of the skirt of a dress we had designed. Joseph and another man looked up, Joseph working on a metallic thread pattern on the sleeves of a black dress for Mrs Bailey Parsons.

'Get out,' he snapped. 'You can't be here.' He turned his wheelchair so that he could make his way towards me, around the table. 'Get!' He waved his good arm at the door.

'But...' I was completely disorientated. 'I came to see Audrey, to see the baby...' I said, weakly holding up my Macy's bags.

'I'll see you out.' Oti's voice came from behind me. She took me by the shoulders and turned me around. 'Come on, outside.' And herded me out the front door.

'What was that?' I choked.

'Just what your eyes saw. Three men doing the job you're so satisfied with.' She crossed her arms, still in her coat, bag on one arm.

'But, what do you mean? What are they doing with Eveline Patience's work?' And just as I'd said the words I understood. 'It's Joseph.' I put my hand to my mouth. 'It's Joseph,' I repeated. 'But the other two, who are they?'

'Both veterans, both injured, both in a mess, just like Joseph. Don't you dare go taking that work away from them; that work has saved them, given them something to live for, something meaningful to do, no longer having to stare at the walls of their apartment, no longer having to feel sorry for themselves.'

I gawped at her, still confused by what I'd seen. 'But how...?' I stumbled. 'How did this happen?'

Oti ran her hand over her forehead, sighing. 'Joseph's right arm wasn't working so well and the physiotherapist suggested he try some needlepoint. As you can imagine he wasn't too keen on doing such a "female pastime" as he put it, so I asked him if he'd help me out with some simple embroidery. I lied and said the *man* who owned the embroidery company we used was too busy, I told him I'm brought some work home. Of course, it wasn't anything we were working on, I just made it all up. But, God darn it, he was good. It didn't take long before he was able to concentrate, he stopped fidgeting, then one day he slept through the night without a nightmare for the first time since he came home.' A smile spread across her face as she spoke and she looked towards their window, seeing the men sitting at the table. 'He picked it all up right away, got better than me in a short few months. So, I started bringing home real Maison McIntyre work and he just ran with it. Makes me sick to be honest, how someone who's never picked up a needle in his life can get so damned good at something so difficult so quickly.'

'And the others?'

'Veterans. In the same position as Joseph. Couldn't concentrate, needed some work to do that wasn't physical. They both suffered from the gas. They can't move around too quickly, so sitting doing this kind of work really helps. We've been training them up. They've only started working on the real designs in the last few weeks.'

'Why didn't you tell me?'

'You listen to me.' Her hands were on her hips, she was leaning towards me, those eyes ready to pierce me with their fury. 'If you'd known you'd have been full of pity, treated Joseph all sorry-like.' She changed her voice to a stage whisper. 'He did this without you, without your help and do you know the difference that made? He's got his self-esteem back. I can see little bits of the old Joseph now. He works on his own terms, produces beautiful embroidery, trains up men to do the same. Those sweet boys in there, who have had their whole lives ruined, who've been shattered and let down by this great country, have found something to keep them alive. Do you have any idea of the ugliness they've seen? Do you understand how the beauty that we ask them to produce has turned their otherwise valueless days into something worth living for, something to look forward to? That work that you and I give them has turned them back into men.' She was breathing heavily, almost out of breath after her diatribe. 'Now you best get on out of here, before I beat your sorry white ass.' As she said this last line, she began to laugh, first a small chuckle, her shoulders shaking as if she was absorbing the movement of a subway train, but these delicate shakes quickly turned into full body-wracking howls that then developed into great tears and loud, sloppy sobs.

Alarmed, I quickly took her in my arms and gave her a hug, a full enveloping hug but the harder I hugged her the louder became the wails. The two of us stood there, in the middle of the street, soaking up that human contact, the warmth, our muscles relaxing with the sad relief.

Eventually she pulled back, sniffed, wiped her face, shrugged off her sobs and wiped her face again, sighing.

'Would you look at me? Howling like some hysterical old spinster.'

'Look. I don't care who does the work, just as long as it gets done. And now I know that it's being done by someone I love, by friends of someone I love, then I'm happy.'

Oti wiped her face again. 'You still love him?'

I couldn't hold Oti's gaze and looked down at my hands. 'Of course I do,' I whispered, biting my lip, willing my emotions to stay hidden away. I took a deep breath, straightened my shoulders and looked up, a breezy smile on my face. 'But, don't worry, I won't be taking him off your hands anytime soon.' My voice was now airy and casual. 'I've got enough on my plate as it is.'

She blinked but said nothing, just nodded as I turned to leave.


Every few months I took myself to have dinner with the Bassino family. My attempts to keep up with them became increasingly difficult, our differences in circumstances becoming greater every time we met.

'I do like your suit,' said Annina, with envy in her voice as she fingered the wool fabric of my jacket. 'I would like to wear something like this.' She kept her voice low with her back to her father as we were doing the washing up.

'I've told you that I'll make you a suit,' I said. 'I used to make you dresses when you were younger. I don't understand why your father won't let me do that any longer.'

She sighed. 'He says we're intruding on your time, Anyway, he says I'd look out of place in one of your suits. Where would I wear it?' She stacked the plates and put them on the shelf under the sink. 'He has a point.'

In 1922 Annina was fifteen and her brother eighteen. Roberto was now earning, working in construction as an iron-worker. Dinner with the Bassinos, without Rosa and now without Nonna, who had died the year previously, was a stilted affair. Annina was the reluctant cook, the unwilling house-keeper, her ideas about her future in stark contrast to her father's.

'Why can't I come and work for you?' she asked, a question she raised every time I came for dinner.

'You know why. You're only fifteen. You should still be in school. I won't take anyone on who isn't seventeen, and even then, you need to have some experience.'

'I can sew. I bet I can sew better than some of the girls you've taken on. Anyway, I've got experience. I've started working in one of the garment factories.'

Flashbacks of those terrible thuds on the ground outside the factory, the thick, acrid smell of burning flesh, the pavements awash with blood. My first reaction was to grab hold of the scrap of tortoiseshell comb I had on my necklace, a necklace I still wore most days.

'Annina, it's illegal. You shouldn't be working there,' I gasped before turning to Matteo. 'You can't let Annina work in one of those factories – not after Rosa...' I couldn't finish my sentence.

'We need the money,' he replied gruffly. Matteo's job as a janitor produced a consistent but flat wage. Despite the money that Roberto was now bringing in, I suspected that he had loan sharks that needed paying off.

'Matteo,' I sighed. 'You know I'm happy to chip in. Please, let Annina stay at school.'

'No!' he almost shouted. 'Is blood money.'

Matteo, once the kind and loving father, was now unpredictable and irrational. Some days he was welcoming and cheery, happy to talk of Rosa, other days he was furious, then remorseful, teary and pathetic. Without Rosa and Nonna to ground him he was unable to make any decisions, to move on or let his family live again. He simply wanted Annina to stay as a little girl.

I was reluctant to cause any greater rift in the family, knowing what I was already responsible for. I felt helpless and the only way I could support them, I thought, was to keep in touch, make sure Annina was safe.

# Tori

The after party of the autumn/winter parade of 1924 was mirroring the success of the show, the order book was filling up and the noise in the salon was getting louder as I took a step to one side, leaning on the doorframe, and watched my clientele: those ambitious mothers and their hopeful daughters; the editors of *Vogue* and *Harper's Bazaar* as well as the fashion editor of the *New York Times*; serious women; working women; those extravagant and outlandish women seeking frivolous embellished dresses to enhance the excesses of the season. Men were increasingly seen at my fashion parades, men like Bunny Hoptoun, all gaudy and showy, only here to make the most of my discreet serving of whiskey before he headed off to his favourite speakeasy. But tonight there was a very different man attending, a tall, broad-shouldered, sandy-haired man who seemed to mesmerise every woman he met. There was something about him that held my attention, an aura that surrounded him, producing little bubbles of interest in my chest. I followed his journey around the room, greeting and cajoling, laughing and encouraging, until he arrived before me with a petite, taut woman.

'Miss McIntyre. I'm Marianne Monte Smyth and this is my husband, Senator Torridon Smyth. We wanted to congratulate you on such a colourful show.' The smile didn't reach beyond her lips, the words had a hollow ring.

Senator Smyth, impeccably dressed with shiny patent shoes and a sparkling diamond tie-pin, thrust a large hand out to me and, shaking my hand enthusiastically, said, 'Tori Smyth. Pleasure to make your acquaintance. I'd just like to say I've not enjoyed an afternoon so much in months. Your talent seems to increase every year.'

I frowned. 'Have you been to one of my shows before?' I enquired.

Just as he was about to answer his wife interrupted. 'My husband simply can't get enough of you. He's been following your career ever since your Protest Dress appeared at Mrs Woolman Chase's fashion fête. I frequently find him with my copy of *Vogue* or *Harper's Bazaar*, critiquing the latest fashions, but whenever he sees one of your creations, he never has a bad word to say.' She sniffed slightly before continuing. 'Unfortunately, our views on dress do not match. He loves colour and grand flourishes, I abhor colourful pattern and far prefer the darker, plainer colours and the subtle, clever draping of Chanel. I'm afraid I have now taken a vow never to buy anything that isn't Chanel.'

Confused as to why this woman was even at my show, I decided to ignore her slight. 'I'm flattered that you've taken the time out to come and see us this afternoon, Senator Smyth. And I'd just like to say I followed your work closely on the Factory Investigating Committee and I'd like to thank you for your persistence in getting the laws changed on stricter regulation for the safety and health of the garment workers in New York and also for making sure people are now more aware of the terrible conditions the women have been made to work in.'

His eyes twinkled but his wife gave me a look as if she'd just bitten into a lemon.

'We should talk,' he said. 'Perhaps you could help with our continued work.'

Before I could reply, his wife touched his arm and pulled him away. He gave me a wink before turning his attention to her. I couldn't help but watch them, such a strange mismatched pair – she so tiny and uptight, keeping a sharp eye on her husband, he so congenial and open, enjoying the attention of the many women who fawned over him.

A little later I noticed him whispering in his wife's ear and then stepping outside onto the front steps of the building. I picked up a teacup, patted my pocket to make sure I had my hip flask and slipped out of the room.

Senator Torridon Smyth was sitting on the steps to our building smoking a large cigar, enjoying the early evening scene in front of him: the busy street filled with cars waiting for some of my guests, customers in the restaurant opposite, the summer heat abating. I sat down beside him and brought out my hip flask.

'You look like you might want some of this,' I said, pouring whisky into the cup and handing it to him.

A wry smile accompanied a quiet chuckle. 'Why, I do believe you have the measure of me already, Miss McIntyre.' And he downed the liquid in one and pushed the cup back in my direction. 'May I?'

I smiled and poured another shot. Without a word he savoured this portion more carefully, looking down the street at nothing in particular, a strange look of contentment on his face.

'A fine Highland malt. But I guess I should expect nothing less from a lass from Edinburgh.' He handed the cup back to me. 'I won't ask where you could have possibly obtained such a thing.' He winked. 'Genteel ladies wouldn't have a notion.'

Without looking at him, eyeing the coffee-drinking

customers across the road I said, 'There is nothing genteel about me.' I held the teacup in both hands in front of me, laying it on my knee. I hit the side of it with the nail of my right middle finger, considering my next words.

'I admire a man who can appreciate women's fashion, especially one who has such an interest in the workers behind it all.'

We sat silently on those steps for a good while, enjoying the background noise of Manhattan. Our silence was easy and companionable. For the first time in over ten years, I realised, my heart was beating a little too fast and I was nervous, a little self-conscious. I kept my eyes on the shop front ahead of me, not entirely knowing what to do. My romance with Joseph had happened slowly, over time, little by little, sneaking up on me. But here, I was prepared to jump right in, to be impulsive and reckless, to do something wholly unexpected.

'I'll ask nothing of you, but I'll never wait for your call. I'll never insist on you regularly visiting. I have my own life to live, an all-consuming business to run. If you want to see me, you'll have to come to my house. I imagine it's best not to be seen in public. I'm discreet and I'm not demanding. You'll need to give me at least two days' notice and I'll let you know if I can't see you due to a prior engagement, because I won't drop everything for you.'

He took a deep drag of his cigar and as he blew out the smoke he gave me a huge smile that overtook his features and made my heart leap.

'So, Miss McIntyre isn't demanding?' He eyed me sideways. 'I have only one question.'

I held his eye.

'Am I allowed to smoke in your house?'


The first time we met alone was laughably nerve-wracking. I'd already moved out of my apartment in MacDougal Street into a small three-storey townhouse on West 17th Street, between Sixth and Seventh Avenues. I couldn't sit. Pacing up and down my bedroom, wondering how this first so-called 'date' would go. We didn't have that first casual meeting, maybe a walk in the park or dinner at a favourite cosy restaurant, there was no opportunity to gradually get to know each other. We were charging down the helter-skelter, feet first.

Over time, without fully realising it, I'd turned my whole house into a sort of display area for all the things that inspired me: fabrics, dresses, coats, hats, shoes, belts and buckles, lamp-shades, crockery, rugs, curtains, tableware, wall hangings, books, the occasional painting and an eclectic mix of furniture – all things I'd collected during the fourteen years I'd been in New York. I'd curated this colourful, slightly chaotic private exhibition which I would spend my spare time updating, adding to and taking out anything that I'd outgrown or lost favour with. I knew it was eccentric but it was a place that calmed me, took me away from the noise and commotion of running a business, of having to produce two collections a year and employing coming up to one hundred staff.

I rarely let anyone into my home, I wasn't someone who entertained, who liked to show off their personal effects; it made me feel vulnerable, as if I'd been stripped bare and cold air was running over my skin. This was the place I retreated to after a long day at work, where I could take off the mask of Maison McIntyre and become the real me. It was difficult enough admitting to myself that I again had a man in my life, but showing him my house, my strange, eclectic collection was unnerving. As a child, Netta had poked fun at the little odds and ends I used to keep in the corner of a drawer: scraps of colourful fabric, a china thimble I'd found on the street painted with tiny buds of lavender, an ivory button, a smooth and perfectly round pebble, a green-glass bead. These were the few things I owned, and they felt as precious as if they were made of gold. She used to say that I loved these things more than our family, that I could easily collect things, but found it more difficult to collect friends.

'Let me show you around,' I said on that first visit, my heart beating a little too fast as I wondered what he would think. 'Mind you behave. No one has ever seen the whole of my house before. You should take it as a compliment that I'm even allowing you beyond the front door.'

Wordlessly he slowly toured the house, his fingertips touching a tassel here, a feather there, smelling a piece of carved sandalwood, appreciating the silky touch of a small elephant whittled out of soapstone, admiring a mahogany wardrobe from India, opening a Japanese parasol, trying on an Afghan Pakol hat.

'Your very own museum,' he said in a whisper, turning around and picking up a bright-green feather boa, a note of envy in his voice. 'If I had a house to myself it would be full of every kind of whisky made by man, every different kind of cigar and old law books. Yes, old law books and a fine leather chair, a mahogany drinks cabinet with a never-ending supply of ice and an ashtray that would be emptied frequently by a fine-looking maid.' We were in one of my reception rooms, walking around the room until he suddenly came to a halt in front of a small bookshelf. He pulled out one of the books and flicked through it.

'Have you read this?' he asked, holding up my copy of *The Wizard of Oz*.

I gave him a slight shake of my head, biting on the inside of my mouth, embarrassed at possessing a book I'd never read. 'You remember that green and red dress at the fashion parade? It was inspired by the cover and some of the colour plates.' Terrified he'd think me stupid and laugh at my inability to read a children's book, I carried on talking, trying to hide my embarrassment. 'Sometimes I just buy a book because I like the way the title has been embossed onto the leather or the style of the pictures – I don't even read the text.'

He held my stare until a smile began to creep across his face and then, in that great booming voice that I was getting used to he said, 'There is nothing monochrome about you, nothing black and white about Maisie McIntyre.'

We had an unspoken agreement that we would meet every six weeks or so, always at my house, neither of us wishing to be seen together in public. I'd leave work early on the Friday of his arrival and dismiss my cook and maid for the weekend. I'd stock up on food, drink, and cigars. As I waited I would relish those last moments to myself, sitting by the fire with a glass of whisky, enjoying the fact that I wasn't needed, no customer required my attention, nobody wanted to discuss finances or the latest schedule. I was so rarely alone I'd become unused to it. These moments before Tori arrived became my way of transitioning from one life to another, from very public couturier to private mistress.

Three knocks, wait a beat, and another knock signalled his arrival.

I double-locked the door behind him, and we hugged, a long, silent embrace. That touch, his large enveloping body against my light frame began the process, the mechanism for drawing out all the bad stuff: the late nights, the political meetings, my own business worries, the continual deadlines.

'Sorry I'm late,' he said. 'The train from DC was delayed.'

I handed him a tumbler of whisky and led him upstairs. We'd stay in that bath for over an hour and gradually he'd come alive, the hot water slowly taking away the grime of the week, the whisky taking on the role of reviver. Often, we didn't say a word until he'd sloughed off the skin of his life as a senator and begun assimilating the serenity of a weekend with me. It wasn't until after our bath, until after we'd made love, until we lay together in my bed with another whisky and a plate of bread and cheese that we'd begin to talk. We'd cleansed ourselves of reality. We could commence forty-eight hours behind closed doors where no one could see us.

'You know we don't have to be here every time,' he said. 'We could take a suite at The Plaza or the Waldorf. I have to take a suite anyway, otherwise Marianne will get suspicious. If she telephones, I've asked the staff to take a message and send it over. But she hasn't telephoned yet. I think she likes having the weekend to herself.'

I looked up from my plate, staring at him. 'You pay for a suite at The Plaza that you don't use, every single time you come here.' I was wrapped in my satin dressing gown, sitting cross-legged on the bed.

'I do. I know... it's a little ostentatious, but it's worth it to make sure there is no inquisition when I get home. It also means there are no questions from my office. I'm, supposedly, accounted for.'

I was silent, slightly stunned by his level of deception. But when did I get so worried about that? Whether I liked it or not, I was part of this ruse.

'I worry that you should be out there, having a good time with some young man,' he continued, 'building your life together, getting married, having a family, not stuck behind closed doors with someone almost twice your age.' He was sitting up in the bed, propped up by the pillows.

I smiled and took a sip of my whisky. 'Are you worried that I'm going to demand you leave your wife and insist you marry me?' I laughed. 'Because if you are, let me put you straight right now. I could never be your wife. I could never attend election rallies, host dinners, glad-handle politicians, sweet-talk your rivals or potential political enemies. I can admire your wife for having the stamina, the conversational deftness, the iron smile, and the selfless ambition for her husband; political wives are a breed of women that are furlongs apart from the person I am. I would fail at the first hurdle: I would insult the guest of honour, misunderstand the political nuances, or show a face of extreme boredom during an important speech. I am not built for that life.'

'You are nothing if not brutally honest.' He shook his head with a rueful smile.

'Well, if you want me to be brutally honest then I should tell you that I don't believe I'm someone who can maintain a full-time relationship. I'd find it too exhausting, too distracting. It would use up too much of my energy, energy that I want to use on my work.' I sidled up to him and nestled into his shoulder.

'You see, when you're not with me, I can forget all about you.'

'Well, that's so good to hear,' he said with a sarcastic grin on his face. 'Not even for a few minutes each day?'

Truth was, when I was in the frenzy of work, I didn't consider him at all. Perhaps when I went to bed at night, I'd wonder where he was, what he was up to, but there was rarely the kind of longing I'd had with Joseph. I never dreamed of Tori, but I often dreamed of Joseph, sometimes I thought I could smell his skin, feel his touch. Sometimes I'd wake with the weight of Tori beside me, wishing it was Joseph.

I avoided the question. 'Don't tell me that you're thinking about me all the time. Not when you're in one of your committee meetings or those party meetings.'

'Have you ever been in one of those meetings? Of course I think about you, more often than you'd imagine. When I see a woman wearing a dress I like, I wonder if it's a Maison McIntyre. When I hear of a good tip on the stock market, I make a note to tell you, because I think it would be good for your portfolio.'

'I don't have a portfolio.'

He sat up. 'We'd better rectify that. If ever there was a time to invest in stock, shares, property, honey, now is the time. I'll make you an appointment with my broker.'

'So, you're only thinking of me in business terms.' I narrowed my eyes at him. 'Don't you ever think of me in... how shall I put this?' I pretended to think. 'Hmmm... sensual terms.'

That booming laugh that would hit me in the chest, deep and resonant. 'Oh, Miss McIntyre, I always think of you in those terms. There's nothing unusual about that.'

I frowned. 'Do all men do that?'

He laughed again. 'Now, I've never taken you for naïve, but, yes, it's our biggest failing. How did you *not* know that?'

'When you leave on a Monday morning, I shut the door on you both physically and metaphorically because I'm raring to get to work. It's as if my creative reservoir has been filled to the brim. Being with you seems to regenerate me. You revitalise me.'

'Well, I'm glad to be of service, ma'am.' He gave me a salute, a twinkle in his blue eyes.

'Seriously. I know that if we lived together it would be altogether different, I think I would find it...' I was worried about saying the word, but we seemed to be into the truth, so I just went ahead. 'Stifling.'

He smiled, that crinkle of skin beside his eyes, those dimples in his cheeks. He pushed the hair off my face. 'That's what I love about you, Maisie McIntyre. You're wholly independent, not in the least needy. You don't want to be seen on the arm of a powerful man because you have your own power. You have Maisie McIntyre power and I find that incredibly arousing.'

He pulled me toward him, his hand in my hair, pressing into me.

Was I only attracted to him because I saw him so rarely,

because I felt no responsibility towards him? Perhaps the same could be said for him, perhaps that's why we worked so well.

The breaking down of social barriers since the end of the war, the increasing independence of women, the mixing of new money with old and a certain acknowledgement of the working woman made it easier for me to socialise with my clients. Occasionally I would gather my courage and make the effort to be seen at some of those wild cocktail parties, always with an eye to finding new clients. There was an element to these parties that I loved; they were full of colour and sparkle, energy and effervescence. The men and the women dressed in wild, gaudy colours, jewels displayed in melodramatic fashion, peacocks wandering the grounds of those grand Long Island mansions, champagne fountains glittering, dancers iridescent and twirling, the laughter even appeared to be a shimmering shade of silver. I would dress in a fairly low-key manner, hoping to fade into the background as I watched the evening change gear, a strange mania take over; the noise increasing, glasses smashing, women thinking nothing of jumping into the swimming pool in their expensive evening dresses, high-jinks the order of the evening.

'You look as if you'd rather be anywhere but here.' A whisper in my ear, that voice that had once poured oil on my rusty heart, the smell of sandalwood and leather, hair cream and whiskey.

'Aidan Cruickshank.'

He kissed my cheek, lingering a little longer than he should have.

'How is it that we've managed to avoid each for over ten years? I hear so much of you, I see a Maison McIntyre dress practically everywhere I go, I see flickers of you in the distance. Do you make it your life's ambition to hide from me, to hide in the shadows of fabric?'

I smiled at his words. 'Maybe I do. Maybe I find fabric is a better companion than most.'

Simultaneously we both looked over the garden, at the floating cocktail glasses, the cigarette holders, the feathers and shawls, listened to the shrieks, the laughter, the orchestra, the feet stamping on the dance floor; the highly strung exuberance just kept on increasing, building to a crescendo of frightening proportions. He turned to me, his dark, penetrating eyes looking straight into me. 'I've realised that I find Maisie McIntyre a better companion than most.' Then he grabbed me by the hand and said, 'Come on, we need a drink.' And pulled me into the maelstrom and towards the bar.

'Two whiskey sours.' He nodded at the barman.

'And where has the elusive Aidan Cruickshank been?' I asked, taking a sip of my drink.

'He flits from light to dark, his favoured place being in the shadows, where he can indulge in his fantasies. Occasionally he emerges into the light just to make those that matter think he's living a heterosexual life: he takes out a debutante, flirts with a bored wife, has a dalliance with an enlightened artist. It covers the trail to his real life.'

'You sound sad,' I said, seeing a lost little boy, vulnerable and in need of affection, no longer the confident, cool Aidan, once so smooth and charming.

'Only you would know that. Only you can see beyond the well-cut suit and well-used patter.' He sighed. 'I've missed you,' he said, before downing his cocktail in one.

'Damn it.' He turned to the bartender. 'Another.' And then back to me. 'Why couldn't you fall in love with me, and I in love with you? Wouldn't our lives have been so much easier? It seems I'm doomed to love men, complicated men who want to bully me, use me and keep me under wraps. Life would be so much more fun if it could be lived with the notorious Maisie McIntyre.' He picked up the newly filled glass and held it up.

'Here's to a life of whiskey sours in the shade.' And promptly drained the glass.

'So melodramatic!' I laughed. But as I did so the inkling of an idea began to form, a whisper of a plan that might suit the both of us, but it wasn't allowed to fully gather, the swirls blown into the night by an interruption from a tall, bulky woman with a loud, slurred voice.

'Don't you know Miss McIntyre here made me this slick new dress, she's a genius. You really should go and see her; she'll make sure you stay part of the right set.' She pulled her companion towards me, so that she stood directly in front of me. 'Miss McIntyre, I absolutely insist that you take on Marion and sort her out.' She swayed slightly holding a cocktail glass in one hand and the girl in her other.

I made my polite thanks, thrust my card in the trembling girl's hand, reassured her that we could fit her in as soon as possible before Aidan deftly manoeuvred me away.

'Does that happen often?' he asked, clinging on to my arm.

'Yes, all the time. Wasn't it you who told me I should come to these dreadful events? Ideal for drumming up business?'

'I'm so sorry to have done that to you.' He bowed in mock contrition before taking my arm. 'But onto more important matters. Any romances on the horizon?' There was a wicked glint in his eye but before I could answer, we found ourselves face to face with Senator Tori Smyth and his wife.

'Miss McIntyre,' said Mrs Monte Smyth more warmly than I ever remembered her being. 'Mr Cruickshank.' She appraised us. 'What a perfect couple you make. Don't you think so, darling?' She turned to her husband.

Tori and I had not met in public since that day of the fashion parade after-party. We made an effort never to be at the same event; if I had an inkling that he would be there, I'd avoid it, if I saw that he was there, I'd leave. I had no desire to create an awkward situation, I had no desire to be found out. I clung on to Aidan as if he was my most treasured possession, I gave Mrs Monte Smyth my best attention, I greeted Senator Smyth warmly but absently, I pawed at Aidan, laughed with him, drank with him until they finally left us.

He pulled back from me, appraising me through narrowed eyes, a twisted smile and an air of satisfaction.

'You are having an affair with him, aren't you?'

'Is it that obvious?' I trembled at the thought.

'Not in the least, darling.' He took my arm again and led me down to the swimming pool, all lit up from underneath, lights festooned around its edge. 'There is no one else out there that would understand what effusiveness means when it's coming from Maisie McIntyre. You've got it seriously, haven't you?'

I sat on one of the sunbeds and lay down, crossing my legs and closing my eyes. 'Yes, I do believe I have. I didn't mean for that to happen, but somehow it did. We only see each other every six weeks or so, maybe less. I can get on with my work, uninterrupted, without having to think about what he wants, what he needs, I don't have to worry about being home, about bringing him his pipe and slippers. And when he calls, I'm ready for a break, I'm ready for a few days of indulging in the selfishness of being with another. We shut ourselves away in my apartment and don't speak to another soul for two days.'

'That's what some would call having their cake and eating it.' He smirked, but then he put the back of his hand to his forehead. 'Now, all my hopes are dashed. At no point will I ever be able to relinquish my Maisie because I don't smoke cigars. Don't you find them a little overpowering?'

'No, I don't. I find them rather endearing.'

'Oh, now you really are in trouble. Nobody finds cigar smoke endearing.' He fell back onto the sunbed he was sitting on, as if he'd been struck by a blow. 'You know, I only ever wear these suits, these beautifully made shirts, just in case I bump into you. I know the effect they have on you.'

'Now, I know that's not true. You were wearing them on the SS *Furnessia*, in Jenners. Your attempts to flatter won't work on me, Aidan Cruickshank.' But I wanted to lean over to him and pull him into my arms, I wanted to feel that summer wool on my skin, breath in his subtle flavouring.

'If I knew you weren't out there, I'd slide into my old silk pyjamas. If it wasn't so frowned upon, I'd never get out of them. Doing the foxtrot in a pair of silk, tie-waist pyjama bottoms would be the ultimate indulgence, the freedom of movement would make it so much more enjoyable. Dinner at the Ritz would be infinitely more bearable, tea with my uncle might even be tolerable. But I know that I could run into you at any minute and that Miss Maisie McIntyre cannot resist a well-dressed man. I've been on the lookout for you since the day you so carelessly tossed me aside at Delmonico's.'

Tears began to prick at my eyes. I gave him a mournful smile. But that whisper of an idea began to return, gathering around my head, circling like a mini tornado, swirling to a point until I was able to catch it.

'I have an idea. Why don't you and your pyjamas come and work at Maison McIntyre.'

Aidan suddenly sat up, facing me, his face glowing in the poolside lights, those deep brown eyes glittering, the air of repression wiped away. 'I thought you'd never ask.'


The twenties roared and the business soared, and by 1926 we were rapidly outgrowing the building on MacDougal Street.

'There's a building I know of that's up for sale in the Garment District,' Tori dropped into the conversation one weekend. 'It's on West 38th Street. It would give you much more factory space, so you could look at a big expansion, maybe open a Fifth Avenue store.'

I looked at him with his sandy hair and confident wide

shoulders, honed by rowing at Harvard. 'Are you turning into my financial adviser?'

He stuck his chin out. 'Amongst other things.'

Of course, it made sense, but it was a huge step. 'I suppose I'd have to sell MacDougal Street to finance it.'

'Oh, no. Don't do that. You should be investing in property. Keep it and turn it into apartments. You'll never regret that, especially with that top floor and those beautiful ceiling lanterns. One day that building will be worth a lot.'

Suddenly I was considering a world that was way beyond anything I'd imagined. Wanting to be a couturier was easy to envisage, when all I needed to worry about was designing something beautiful, consider shape and line, colour and fabric, a customer's character, whether they'd be able to pay. But owning a large business, where I'd be responsible for possibly hundreds of employees, needing to distribute worldwide, find more investors, open shops in cities across the states. That took my breath away.

'Now come on, Maisie.' Tori laughed. 'Don't tell me you've never considered this kind of expansion. You're a woman who looks to the future, I know that.'

What would Netta say? Her baby sister running a global company. I blushed at my shameless desire to boast. It seemed that I only thought of Netta when I wanted to tell her how well I was doing. How often did I consider how she was faring? I still wrote to her occasionally, sending her presents of shoes and hats and scarves that I thought she might like: nothing too showy, but something a little out of the ordinary. I still hadn't heard from her, but I hoped that she wore them, that she thought of me when she did. Perhaps, if I expanded my business abroad I'd go and visit her.

I turned to Tori. 'Yes. I think we should look into it.'

. . .

Business was doing so well Joseph's embroidery atelier was also expanding rapidly. His reputation for fine and detailed work was spreading throughout Manhattan and beyond. He, Oti, Audrey and little Laura moved to a bigger house in Harlem with the whole of the first floor given over to the business of embellishment. Now he employed ten men, all veterans of the Great War. But he was still wary of me, and would only see me on a professional basis.

'I don't have the energy to see you outside of our work. You're too exhausting,' he'd said to me after I'd once tried to persuade him to let me bring him dinner.

In 1927 we opened a store on Fifth Avenue, just as Tori had suggested, with Aidan masterminding the whole process. Women of a different type began to frequent the store, we began to produce some ready-to-wear dresses to appeal to women with a little less money than our usual customer. But the appetite for exquisite gowns continued, the demand for heavy embellishment, requests for brighter and brighter colour wouldn't abate and I began to tire of it.

'I think your weariness is a symptom of the time,' Tori said seriously one evening. 'You may be ahead of the game, but I believe that this ridiculous frenzy will be called to a halt in the not too distant future. You should start planning for it now.'

'What do you mean? My customers are as confident as ever.'

He blew out a long breath of cigar smoke, high up into the air, watching it as it curled its way through the room. 'I had a long meeting with my broker yesterday. We're pulling out of most of our stocks. If I'm right, this crash is going to be bad. The things we should be investing in is commodities, the things that people need: food, fuel, manufacturing. We had a long, long argument about putting our money in the movie companies. He disagreed, but I firmly believe we'll be in need of some escapism.

'This is going to be bad, Maisie, and you may be among

some of the worst affected. Most people aren't going to be able to afford to use a couturier. You need to think about scaling back or doing more of the ready-to-wear.'

'You really think it's going to be that bad?'

He sighed. 'I do.' He ran his hand through his hair. 'I think it'll be like nothing we've seen before. I just want to make sure you're protected from the worst of it.'

'I've noticed that when a woman can't afford the outfit she wants, she'll buy an accessory, something to liven up what she already has. Maybe a belt or a scarf, perhaps a handbag. Now that cosmetics are becoming easier and cheaper to make, I've noticed that women are using lipstick and nail polish much more. I feel better when I've painted my nails and my lips, even if I'm wearing that old skirt I've had for years. If I can expand into these smaller things, then, if it gets as bad as you say it will, perhaps we can keep our customers even when they don't have much money. Hopefully, when things have recovered, they'll remember us.'

'Just like that Chanel woman. You know, she has a good head for business on her.'

I gave Tori a flat smile. I did not like be compared to, or accused of copying, Coco Chanel. Of course, he was right, she'd been in the business of perfumes and cosmetics for several years. I was late in coming to the party.

Just as Tori had predicted, over the course of a few weeks in October and November 1929, the use of lavish embroidery, brilliants, diamanté and sequins became obsolete; a skirt made entirely from feathers or cuffs studded with jewels was now seen as bad taste. The Crash and following Depression ensured that the cocktail party was in limbo and life became more serious.

'So many orders cancelled,' Oti moaned as December

loomed ahead of us. 'We should be inundated with holiday season outfits just now. This is when everyone relies on the overtime to help pay for Christmas. Instead I'm wondering whether we should be sending people home.' Her eyes were too bright, her usual tight bun just a little loose.

'You've got to stop reading the newspapers, Oti,' I said, trying to keep the conversation light. 'It's not good for you.'

'Don't you make light of this situation!' she demanded. Oti rarely raised her voice. 'Those women out there, they rely on you to give them a good wage each week, especially now, when most of their husbands are out of work.'

I held my hands up in surrender. 'Hold on. You know we have a plan. We've discussed this and now is the time to get rolling with it. We need to up our production of accessories, and we need to do it fast. If we can catch some of the Christmas market, then it will help.' But I was as scared as Oti looked. How easy it would be to lie down and be steamrollered by the disaster that surrounded us. How easy it would be to just walk away, perhaps jump on a ship and go home to Edinburgh, let all those women on the factory floor join the lines for the soup kitchens, put newspaper in their shoes to block up the holes.

No, nothing would let me admit I'd been defeated by the actions of those men in their board rooms on Wall Street, loaning money to people who couldn't pay, encouraging the man on the street to buy stocks they couldn't afford.

'I've spoken to Aidan and we're ready to do the changeover. But I'm worried about Joseph. How's he faring?'

Oti flattened her lips. 'He's going to have to let several of his men go. Their work is drying up rapidly. I'm worried about how we're going to keep paying for that house. Without the business, it's much too big for us.'

'What if he could help with some of the accessories? I know it'll be boring work, but it could tide him over until the worst has passed.'

. . .

Dressmaking too had to change its direction and become more about discretion and immaculate tailoring. By 1932 the couture business was at its worst, just like the stock market, but our expansion into accessories had saved us, had now become our mainstay. Staff had been retrained in the making of the belts, bags, scarves and costume jewellery, we even had a small unit making cosmetics.

My office in our West 38th Street factory and workshop overlooked the main factory floor where the accessories and jewellery were now being made. Once the floor had been filled with tables for hand-sewing, cutting and machining. Now only a quarter of the floor space was taken up with the creation of couture.

The building was much more utilitarian, not as beautiful as my first studio. I'd worked hard to turn my office into some sort of replica of that first workroom. I'd put two large ceiling lights into the roof, letting in as much daylight as possible, painting the plastered section the same bright-pink paint from those first days of my studio. The room was decorated with Colour Emporium soft furnishings – sofa, two armchairs, bright cushions, colourful curtains, my old tailor's dummy, a gilt floor-to-ceiling mirror, and two large oil paintings of a riot of colour. I loved those paintings; they made me feel as if I was a million miles from the Depression.

There was also a large table at one end of the room, for spreading out fabrics, cutting, drawing or, often, eating at. This room had become my second home. I even had a chaise longue for those days when I never made it home.

In the summer of that year, as the Depression seemed never-ending and the heat unbearable, Oti, Aidan and I were having our usual Monday morning meeting, going through the week's schedule, sorting out staff issues, working on initial ideas for the next fashion show.

'We'll make sure there are doormen to keep out the uninvited customers, but by putting on the show in the store we can create a buzz. People on the street can look in, those on the inside can feel they are part of the elite, even if they can't afford it anymore.' Aidan was responsible for the organisation of our twice-yearly fashion shows and he never failed to bring something extra every time. 'We're going to have to work doubly hard to make many sales this year. I suggest we have a good amount of the accessories dotted around the store.'

'Do you really think our usual customers will turn up? Things just keep on getting worse, I can't imagine where they get the money from,' Oti commented.

'Yes, I do. Even if they can't afford couture, they'll want people to *think* they can still afford it, being seen in a Fifth Avenue store with a large glass frontage, where they can leave the place with a Maison McIntyre bag, even if it's only containing a scarf. They'll be back buying clothes, as soon as they're able. I'll bet my silk pyjamas on it. Oh, and can we ask if any of the women on the factory floor would like to earn some extra money by serving the drinks? I'd rather give them our money than bring in someone else.'

'Yes, good idea,' I said. 'Since we're on the subject of catering, I want to build a canteen here in the factory. We have the space now that the storage area is hardly used. I thought we could at least serve lunch, and if we thought we could afford it, I'd also like to have breakfast available too.'

Aidan raised an eyebrow. 'I do believe you're turning soft, Maisie McIntyre.'

A smile tugged at my mouth. 'It makes good business sense. If everyone is well fed their productivity will be higher, their concentration will be better and their happiness seems to increase. I bet you the day we introduce the canteen will be the day you see bigger smiles and hear more laughter around here.'

'Don't try and disguise your apprehension about your workforce with the pretence of that old Maisie McIntyre ambition. It doesn't wash with me.' His eyes, though, were twinkling as he said this. 'But either way, as much as I like your idea, we can't afford it.'

'Not a problem. I'll pay for it. The money won't come out of the business. Once we're back in the black then Maison McIntyre can take on the expense of feeding our staff, but right now, that's my responsibility.'

Both Oti and Aidan stared at me, neither able to speak.

'Well, if you've had enough of catching flies with those open mouths, are we done? Aidan, perhaps we can meet up tomorrow to discuss the canteen.' I stood up. 'I have to go, it's my turn to be at the shop this afternoon, I'll be late if I don't leave now.'

'Sure would appreciate a few sales this week. It's eerily quiet down in the sewing rooms.' Oti walked over to the window overlooking the factory floor. 'I hate to say this, but I could do with some drama around here.' She stood watching the women at work. 'That canteen's a good idea,' she said quietly, almost to herself before pulling herself up straight and turning to the door. 'I'll see you later.'

Aidan lingered, pulling at the edges of his shirt cuffs, straightening his tie.

'You need to say something?' I asked, recognising the signs of discomfort.

He sighed, putting his hands in his trouser pockets and looking down at his shoes before continuing. 'Word on the street is that Senator Torridon Smyth is in the pocket of the Mafia, is involved in illegal bootlegging, amongst other things.'

'I told you the subject of Tori is out of bounds,' I hissed. 'But you know as well as I do that Tori Smyth is a staunch upholder of the Prohibition Law.'

'Maisie, listen to yourself. Tori Smyth, a man who loves his single malt more than any I know, is the staunch upholder of the law of no liquor. Come on. I know how much the two of your put away during your little trysts.'

'Drinking it is one thing, everyone does it. But it doesn't mean they're in with the Mafia. Hey, I drink the stuff, but I have nothing to do with them!' My voice was getting louder, my colour rising.

'Whoa, hold your horses.' He took hold of both my shoulders, looking directly at me. 'I'm only telling you what I've been hearing; I just want to warn you, make sure you're not getting caught up in anything untoward.' His voice was now gentler, more understanding. 'None of us want anything to happen to you.' He gave me a warped smile. 'You're in deeper than you think.'

I sat down at my desk, defeated by Aidan's empathy. 'The truth is, I've suspected it for some time. He's so embroiled in the workings of this city; it would make sense if he's in with them. And when I bought this building, it was all made just a little bit too easy. Mr Capriani was constantly surprised at how quickly permits went through. He even accused me of being in with the Mafia.' I played with the ring on my left little finger. 'Lately he's been distracted. We talked about the Sam Seabury investigation into Tammany Hall. He may be the senator for New Jersey, but he seems nervous about the outcome.' I shivered as if someone was walking over my grave. 'How do you know this anyway?'

He searched my face, silently assessing me. Finally, he said, 'Underground places that you never want to know about, that I never want to show you, places best kept hidden. Just take my word for it, Tori Smyth keeps some unsavoury company.'

. . .

I almost ran to the Fifth Avenue shop, running from Aidan, from his unwelcome words, from having to think about Tori. I wanted Tori to be the good guy, the sheriff that came to the rescue, not the bad guy who caused all the trouble. But how was I to know for sure? We never stepped into the real world when we were together.

Arriving at the store breathless, I was quickly able to push Tori to the back of my mind as I noticed one of our regular couture customers walking through the door.

'Mrs Walker, how good to see you,' I said. She was one of those pushy mothers I so despised and admired all at the same time, but she'd never been into the shop – several times during fittings she'd berated me for letting my standards slip by becoming 'retail'. A tall, thin woman, who normally held her herself rigidly, she now had an air of fatigue about her, dark circles under her eyes, her usually bright skin seemed paper thin and devoid of colour. She gave me a relieved smile as she realised the shop was empty and sat down on one of our brightly coloured sofas.

'My feet are a little sore today. I need to take the weight off.' She sat bolt upright, still with that mother's eye for first impressions, most likely aware she could be seen through the shop window.

'How is your daughter, Rosalind? She must be coming up to twenty-one any minute. Will there be any kind of celebration?' I asked carefully.

'I don't think so,' she said quietly, her lips tightening almost imperceptibly. And then she seemed to sag, as if I'd cut an invisible cord, falling back into the sofa, her face drooping slightly.

'What you need is one of Flavia's famous hot chocolates,' I said.

In the back of the shop we'd built a tiny kitchen, a place to boil a kettle of water or a saucepan of milk. Flavia had taught us how to make the best Italian coffee as well as the richest hot chocolate, no expense spared. She'd keep us well supplied with one of her famous polenta cakes used to bolster even the most dejected of our customers.

'Here you go,' I said, placing the cup and saucer and plate of cake on the table. This little ceremony would invariably have the effect of opening the sluice gates; out would come the upset, the confusion, the loss. These were women who had grown up with immense wealth, who suddenly found themselves in the position where they had to cook and clean for themselves, perhaps even try and find a job, unable to afford to buy new clothes, having to move from a Fifth Avenue mansion to a two-bedroom apartment, walk or use the subway instead of being chauffeured everywhere. Having to live off a meagre budget and consider whether food was more important than a delivery of coal was embarrassing and upsetting. Perhaps these women weren't entirely destitute, but they were having to adjust to a life that they'd never had to consider before. A comforting drink in a bone china cup surrounded by the accoutrements of a life-style now only remembered was a moment of relief that they could appreciate, feeling that perhaps everything wasn't as bad as they thought.

When we first opened the Fifth Avenue store, it was for selling couture, but now, several years into the Depression, our range majored heavily on the textile handbags, scarves, belts and cosmetics that were still affordable to our customers; they could still act the part of women of means with a Maison McIntyre bag or scarf. They'd match this season's red lipstick to last season's suit, something they'd never considered before. The accessories, initially created to bring in the aspirational woman with a little less money, were now helping us hold on to our original customers, letting us keep in touch with them, making them feel as if they were still being looked after by a couture house.

. . .

Two weeks later I was woken at five a.m. by a knock on my door. I'm an early riser, but even this was too early for me. It was the tentativeness of the knock that gave out the air of foreboding. No urgent banging, no shouting to open up, just the feeling that the intruder didn't want to be the bearer of bad news.

'Aidan, you look terrible.' His shirt collar was undone, his black bow tie hanging around his neck, his eyes bloodshot and his beautiful hair ruffled and unkempt.

'What's happened? Is Oti okay? Has something happened to the workshop or the store?' He shook his head and stepped through the door, sorrow in his eyes as he handed me the *New York Times*.

*Senator & US Attorney Murdered in Cold Blood* the headline screamed. The *Times* still had no pictures on the front page in those days, but I knew who this was about.

That dropping feeling in my stomach, my breath taken away. I leaned against the doorframe to steady myself.

'I didn't want you to find out on your walk to work, I know you like to pick up a paper on your way, I know you like to...' Aidan paused, watching me carefully. '...read the social pages.' He finished in a whisper, knowing I wasn't listening, knowing I was scanning the article.

Tori Smyth was murdered, gunned down in his favourite restaurant in Murray Hill, having dinner with his oldest friend, Johnny Stillman, the US Attorney for the Eastern District of New York. Both men were killed, both men filled with bullet holes and callously left sprawled across their food.

I staggered as a violent nausea billowed up from my stomach. Aidan caught me.

'Let me go,' I protested as I stumbled out of the front door and was sick onto the pavement. It was as if my body was rejecting the words, vomiting them back onto the street, eliminating the contaminated meaning, ridding myself of the truth. I stood there for several minutes, being sick again and again. I couldn't stop it.

Eventually I grabbed the redbrick column beside the door, wiping my mouth, breathing heavily.

'I've told Oti and she's on her way. She's told Rebecca and Simone that you won't be in for a few days, and she'll stay with you today. Don't worry about the studio, we'll sort everything. We'll just say you're unwell, no need to give any detail.' He guided me back into the house.

'Does Oti know about Tori?' I asked.

'She's known for years. You can't work that closely with someone without her understanding your worst secrets.' The kindness in his voice brought back the nausea but I pushed it down, pushed down my horror at the whole scenario.

'Those Fridays when you leave early, in a flurry of hurried instructions, so opposite to your usual self, who virtually lives in the studio, who prefers her own company. She understood what was going on, she just didn't know who it was.'


Oti stayed with me for three days coaxing me through my inability to keep anything down, finally able to feed me tiny morsels of toast, water and her own homemade chicken broth.

A vicious circle of questions simmered away inside me, eating into me so that I couldn't sleep properly. I began pacing the whole house, up and down the stairs, in and out of every room, picking up items I knew Tori had handled, an antique perfume bottle, a red velvet cummerbund, an opulent fan made from peacock feathers. Why would he be involved with the Mafia, why was he killed, how had I been so blinkered?

'All right, that's enough·now,' Oti said gently on the third day, as she carefully pulled a heavy glass ashtray from my fingers, the one Tori used most often. 'It's time for you to have a bath and get dressed. You look like some kind of witch. Three days is long enough wallowing in your own sorrow. It's time to pick yourself up and get on. You've a funeral to get ready for.'

'Oh, no, I can't face all those people, especially his wife. All those politicians, all those grey men. No, I'm not going,' I said as I pulled the blankets up to my chin and closed my eyes.

'Why don't you think about what you could wear to the funeral. I know black isn't your colour, that you never use it, but maybe creating a dress that's a little different, a true Maisie McIntyre dress, would be good for you, would help you focus, help you recover. You could think about what it was that Tori would have liked to see you in.'

'But he would have liked some colour.' I rolled away from Oti. 'He hated black as much as I do.'

'How about a jacket with a coloured lining? Then no one would see it, it wouldn't cause a stir, but you'd know it was there, you'd know it was what Senator Smyth would have liked. Maybe you could make it a reversible jacket, so that you can re-use it, make it something that would remind you of him.'

'The *Other Woman* relegated to the back of the church in a minnow's dress, trying to blend into the stonework. You know that's not my style, Oti.' But as I said this an idea began to needle its way into my mind. I did want to go to Tori's funeral. I wanted to say goodbye.

'You'd feel better for going, there'd be some finality to it. When did you last see him?'

'Six weeks ago,' I said absently, getting out of bed, walking over to a table where I kept a pad and pencils. 'We had our usual weekend, quiet, self-involved, hardly taking any notice of the world outside.' I could still smell the faint lingering of his cigar smoke, I could see his smile across from me in the bath, his big hands gesticulating, one holding the cigar, as he spoke, the sandy hair slicked back across his head, those oh-so-kind eyes that couldn't possibly have been engaged in any wrongdoing. But he had been on edge, constantly checking out of the window, saying he was worried he'd been followed. He hardly slept the whole weekend, drank far more than usual, smoked nonstop.

I opened my sketchbook and began to draw.

'You'd always come back from those weekends a different person, you'd be full of energy, wild new designs pouring out of you. Whatever they might say about him, he did you good.' I heard her rummaging in her bag before coming over and putting a newspaper on the table. 'It's time you saw this.' She put her hand on my shoulder.

*Senator in the pocket of Mafia gang*, read the bold headline.

Unwillingly I read the article, telling me how the man I loved, Tori Smyth, had been in the pay of a New York Mafia gang for years, how he'd pushed through building plans that would never have been approved if it hadn't been for his endorsement, how he'd ignored the illegal bootlegging, the import of whisky and gin from Europe into New Jersey, how he and countless officials, police and members of the coastguard were in the pay of a large ring of organised crime, how his well-known investment success was helped along by his Mafia friends, how he'd been rumoured to turn evidence against his Mafia connections. How they were having none of it.

I felt queasy. The Tori I knew hadn't appeared capable of any of this – the open-hearted, life-loving man who lived for public service. It seemed that I'd spent eight years loving someone who didn't exist.

I looked down at my pad and continued to sketch, the soft scratching of the pencil on the paper soothing my bruised memories.

Oti leaned towards me. 'You designing your dress for the funeral?'

'Almost done,' I replied, picking up one of the coloured pencils and adding a few touches to the sketch, before pushing the pad towards Oti.

'A pantsuit?' she sighed, but there was a twinkle in her eye. 'Well, at least I know that our Maisie is back. I was beginning to wonder whether I'd ever see that feistiness again. You sure know how to cause a scene, Miss McIntyre.'

Despite the accusations being splashed all over the papers, Tori's funeral was a big affair. His political allies were out in force denying that he could possibly be involved with the Mafia, his wife vigorously refuting the so-called 'false accusations', the newspapers whipping up a storm of conflicting opinion. Most of Congress, the president, the New Jersey State Senate, the US Attorney's office, and many, many more attended the funeral. Tori had been a well-loved man, always able to recall a name, even if he'd only met someone once, always making them feel heard. With such a large attendance, with such a storm brewing over his possible Mafia connections, I made the naïve assumption that no one would notice me. But a woman wearing a trouser suit to a funeral in 1932 was something that would never go unnoticed.

Women had been wearing trouser suits for some time: Chanel had championed them for years, popularising palazzo pants on the Riviera, Marlene Dietrich was famed for the male attire she'd worn in her film *The Ship of Lost Men* three years previously, but her appearance at the premiere of the movie *The Sign of the Cross* just a few months earlier, wearing a masculine tuxedo, had caused outrage in the press and even in Congress. I'd never understood why her appearance had caused such a stir, why politicians would care, and I made the mistake of thinking the world had surely got over their puritanical shock.

My trouser suit was impeccably tailored, fitting me like a glove. It was feminine, discreet and understated. But, as I've already said, I don't like black. The only other time I had worn black was on the passage from Glasgow to New York, feigning a recent widow. I needed to wear colour. I couldn't bring myself to be seen in only black; it wasn't me, it wasn't the Maisie that Tori knew. I put those pink buttons on there as a tribute to the man I'd loved. But in 1932 women still wore full mourning to funerals; they wore respectful black dresses or a jacket and skirt, with a hat and most likely a veil. Women didn't wear trouser suits with bright pink buttons. In the haze of my grief, my anger at Tori, at the Mafia, at the whole ludicrous situation, I didn't consider how people would notice my suit, how it might have been interpreted as disrespectful; I was only thinking about wearing an outfit that would have meaning for Tori, that he would have understood.

Nobody spoke to me at the funeral. I didn't care, too caught up in my own sorrow. I was only there to say goodbye to Tori. It was a funeral full of pomp and showy display, entirely suited to the character that Tori was. He would have loved the attention, the fact that the president and all his entourage were there, that his political enemies came to pay their respects. I didn't attend the reception afterwards, happy to slide away, thinking no one would make the connection between the two of us.

The next day the press had made the association. The picture newspapers had photographs of me looking like the forlorn mistress in my absurdly eye-catching outfit, the *Daily News* with one particularly close-up image, just one picture of Tori's coffin and nothing of his wife. Tori had not deserved that, nor had his wife. The story should have been of his life's endeavours and achievements, instead, it was all about me and my fashion faux pas, it was about us, the secret lovers and all we had done to keep our affair hidden away.

## Chapter Seven

---

## The Hollywood Dress

*A full-length, figure-hugging dress made from white silk crepe and black silk chiffon, with two sections of black bugle beading. It has a halter top and is skilfully draped to cling tightly to the body from hips to knees, ending in a bouncy flare.*

# Netta

## 1932

'Oh, good Lord. How do you not know that you're pregnant?'
Oti asked incredulously, her hands on her hips as she stared at
me with wide, unbelieving eyes.

This question caught me completely unawares. All I
wanted to do was laugh off such a ludicrous suggestion. I sighed
because it explained why I had been nauseous and constantly
sick over the last three weeks, it explained why strong smells
brought on the nausea, why I could no longer drink my beloved
coffee, and it explained the sore nipples. Why hadn't the
obvious answer occurred to me before now?

Over the weeks since Tori's death I had started to find it
difficult to be in my house – everything reminded me of him. I
could no longer sit down or take a bath or sleep in my bed
without remembering the way his hand would stroke my arm as
we sat on the sofa together, or his sleeping breath would brush
my back at night or how he'd close his eyes as he relaxed in the
bath, his toes wiggling gently by my sides. No corner of the
house was immune to these memories, every piece of furniture,

ornament or piece of fabric making me recall some comment he made, funny, flippant, or serious, all of them crystal clear in my head and refusing to leave.

My office had become my home and I was spending as many hours there as I could, shutting away the newspapers, any talk of the Mafia, any thoughts of Tori Smyth. By pushing away all that ugliness, all that grief, I could become the Maisie I had almost forgotten, the one that loved beauty, colour and simply making dresses, I could almost pretend I was that young Maisie, twenty years ago in her first studio with nothing but good things to look forward to. Here I could almost be normal. Except I kept on being sick.

Oti had popped into my office to try and persuade me to come out for lunch. She was in and out of my office more than usual, checking up on me, making sure I was not sliding into some sort of depression – she'd found a new fabric that she thought I might be interested in, wanted to ask if I'd seen the pictures of the Chanel diamond jewellery show.

'Why do you think I'm pregnant?' I asked, stupidly.

'You can't stand coffee no more. You keep being sick. You just look different.' She gave me her *do you think I was born yesterday?* look. 'When did you last have your period?'

I had no idea. It wasn't something I kept close track of. 'No, Oti, this can't be. I'm getting too old to have children, I'm forty-three, women don't have children at my age.'

'Oh, so you're more stupid than I thought you were,' Oti replied. 'Please tell me you were being careful. Surely you weren't trying to trap the senator by getting pregnant. That doesn't sound like the Maisie I know.'

'No! Of course I wasn't trying to trap him. We've been having an affair for eight years, if I'd have wanted his child I'd have done it a long time ago. Do you think I want a baby at forty-three?' But as I spoke, the hysteria was beginning to show in the rising pitch of my voice, the reality starting to dawn on me. 'But...' I sighed, '...I thought it was the shock. You know, when traumatic things happen to you, parts of your body try to protect you from that trauma. I just thought... I just thought... that's what was happening...' I held my head in my hands. 'That's what I've been telling myself these past few days.'

Of course, she was correct. It all suddenly made sense. The only thing, outside of my working life, that made any sense.

Oddly, as I sat there staring into a future I couldn't compre-hend, I realised that for the first time since Tori's death the nausea had gone and I wanted a drink. But it was nine thirty in the morning, and even Oti would have raised an eyebrow if I'd made myself a whiskey sour just then.

'I don't want a child,' I said, bluntly. 'I was not put on this earth to bring up another human being, I'm too selfish.'

Oti rolled her eyes. 'Maybe you're selfish, but too selfish to bring up a child?' She leaned forward on my desk. 'You can't be thinking that you want to get rid of that poor, innocent child. Not its fault who his or her mother is. This is the child of the man you've been in love with for years.'

I tried to interrupt her, tried to protest, but she continued.

'That child is a part of him, you'd have a small version of him to look after, a bit of him in your life every single day.'

Could I love a child that looked like him, that might have his blue-grey eyes, his infectious smile, his sandy hair and big hands?

'No.' I shook my head. 'There are too many reasons not to become a mother: I want to design for the theatre, for Holly-wood, perhaps expand my business overseas. What about London, Paris, perhaps even Rome? Having a child would ruin those ambitions; it would just get in the way.'

Oti seemed to rise up as I said these words, anger flashing in her eyes. 'Don't you say another word. You'll regret it, I know you will. You act too quickly, too impulsively. That Senator Torridon Smyth, does he have any other children?'

'No,' I said, looking down at the floor.

'You look at me, Maisie McIntyre,' Oti ordered. 'You look at me good and proper.' I looked up, at her blazing eyes, her voice heavy with warning.

'This is his child. No one else has that, not even his wife. This child will be yours. Before you only got to enjoy him every few weeks, now you've been given the opportunity enjoy a part of him every day for the rest of your life.'

As soon as I had made the decision that I would become a mother, I found myself wanting to see my own family. In the twenty-two years that I had been in New York I had yet to hear from my sister. At the beginning I had written brief letters, sending presents for her and her girls. I'd describe New York, my boarding house and grey landlady, the wonders of Central Park, the shops on Fifth Avenue, but I only told her briefly how my work was going. I'd pictured her rolling her eyes if I'd have described my studio and Oti and the women who I employed, if I'd described the kinds of dresses we were making. She would never have believed a word of it; I could hear her saying how letters were for telling lies. During the Great War I'd sent money but because I'd heard nothing I began to think she'd moved, perhaps to somewhere better. In 1929 I'd even gone as far as booking a passage home, thinking it was time to confront our silence, but then the Crash had occurred and I felt I couldn't leave Oti and the others – my New York family. Suddenly it seemed less important to run away to a sister who hadn't bothered to contact me in over twenty years, than it did to ensure the business survived, to be certain that the more than one hundred women I now employed were safe, that we could look after them. But now, all I wanted was to talk to my sister, Netta, my big sister who might even be a grandmother, I wanted to tell her what I had achieved, of the women I dressed and, of course, I wanted to tell her about the baby.

It took me five months to summon up the courage to contact my sister, eventually writing to Richmond Place, half expecting no response, surprised and relieved when I received a reply one month later.

*Maisie,*

*I will come to New York, but I can't afford the fare. If you send me the ticket, I'll come. It will help Ava. One less mouth to feed and more space for the bairns.*

*I could do with a change of scene. Duncan died a month ago. I don't want to be in that tenement any longer than I have to.*

*Netta*

Unmistakenly my sister: blunt and to the point. I smiled. I'd loved my sister who was candid and outspoken. I hankered after that curt sisterly love. I suddenly found myself yearning for those days when we'd run through the streets of Edinburgh, delivering my mother's dress commissions, when we'd sit in the Meadows, when I'd mimic our customers with their stuck-up Morningside accents, Netta rolling in the grass, laughing until her sides hurt. In those days we were almost the same: thinking alike, laughing and moaning at the same things; we wanted a better, brighter life.

How do you greet a sister you haven't seen for more than twenty-two years? My sister who, undoubtedly, had led a harder life than me, who'd probably spent her days with raw hands in cold laundry water whilst my soft hands gathered and draped delicate and silky fabrics. My sister who never knew about the money our mother had saved for us. My sister who hadn't grabbed, or been able to grab, the opportunities that may have come her way.

As I stood on the quay waiting for her to walk down the gangway, I wondered how she was feeling. Was she excited by the future or was she frightened by the tall, overbearing buildings, unlike anything ever seen in Edinburgh? Could she see the opportunity or was she overawed by the unknown? For a moment I was back on the ship's deck all those years ago, with my heart in my ears, my stomach doing somersaults with the fear of discovery, of being sent home, a known fraud.

What would her reaction be when she saw me? Shame at having let her sister pay for her passage, or delight at seeing me. Just as then, my stomach was doing acrobatics as I searched for her, nervous at our reunion, scared that there'd be no love left, worried that she'd be someone different.

Standing on the quayside I suddenly felt conspicuous in my showy fur coat, hat and patent leather high heels, eight months pregnant and fully made up, red lipstick and long eyelashes. There was Netta with her crumpled coat, her ashen-red hair spilling out from under her creased, grey felt hat, holding a faded carpet bag.

We both smiled warily, neither of us able to find words that adequately described how we felt. I swallowed down the mix of emotions: shock at her appearance, her apparent lack of care at the way she looked, the fact that she seemed twenty years older than me, but all I wanted was a rush of sisterly love, a desire to grab her and hug her, feel that filial closeness again. Instead I felt strangely detached, a forlorn pity for this frumpy, middle-aged woman who stood, rather pathetically, in front of me. And relief, enormous relief, that I had left that life when I did.

Eventually we hugged, a slightly awkward embrace. When you're eight months pregnant it's hard to give a proper hug to someone five inches shorter than you. She smelled of biscuits, a smell from home, a smell I'd have recognised anywhere and despite the relief I was feeling, the recognition of that smell brought tears to my eyes, tears of homesickness, for our dead mother, for the kitchen we used to spend so much time in, for the way Maw had once patted my hand, whispering 'Ma Maisie'. All these emotions were in danger of overpowering me.

Holding on to her longer than necessary, I discreetly wiped my eyes.

'Look at you, all big and grown up,' she said, pulling herself away. 'All dressed up as if you're going tae the races.' Her bluey-green eyes twinkled with amusement, but her face was drawn, no hint of make-up, her skin shiny and sweaty, the whites of her eyes more yellow than white.

'Well, I thought I could take you out for lunch, celebrate your arrival in style,' I said, forcing myself to sound cheerful and excited.

'Ach, no.' She sighed. 'I'm beat. What I'd really like is a big cuppa tea and piece a cake, sit down on a comfy chair and put ma feet up. I'm knackered.'

'How can you be so tired?' I asked, thinking only of the whiskey sour I'd been hoping for before ordering our lunch. 'You've been on a boat for twelve days with nothing else to do but put your feet up. Aren't you desperate to get out? Can't I take you to my favourite restaurant and show you my New York?'

She gave me that Netta twitchy smile of annoyance.

'It's exhausting trying to fit in where you don't belong. What were you thinking of, sending me a first-class ticket? I didnae have the right clothes, didnae have the right words. They only realised that I was someone tae reckon with once I'd told them you were my sister. But even then they looked at me strangely, as if they thought the sister of Maisie McIntyre should be dressed better, should look after herself better. I ended up sitting on the deck or in my cabin knitting baby clothes for Carla. You know she's expecting again.'

I pushed down any ungracious thoughts and smiled, putting my arm through hers and leading her to my car.

'Well, I'll show you New York tomorrow, when you're rested. I'm sure my cook can rustle up some cake when we get back. I've just moved into a new apartment and your bedroom is all ready for you.'

She stopped suddenly and unwrapped my arm. 'Your cook?' And then she looked towards the front seat of the car. 'Your chauffeur?' she said in a high Edinburgh society voice, a sneer creeping in. She stepped back to inspect me.

'Who is this person who's pickin' me up in her posh car, with her fur coat and high heels, who has a cook? You dinnae even sound like a Scot. Did you hide your accent, embarrassed by where you came from? Do you have a maid tae help dress you? Perhaps a secretary tae write yer letters for you?' Her voice was harsh, her accent broad. 'You better not have gone all high 'n' mighty on me. Are you still capable of rolling your sleeves up and doing your own washing?'

Too easily I quipped back, 'I havenae done ma own washing for the last ten years.' And regretted it as soon as the words left my mouth.

Netta turned to look at the ship. 'Maebe I should just get back on there right now. You're not the sister I once knew. She'd never have thought about embarrassing me with a fur coat and a chauffeur.'

I flushed at my thoughtlessness. I walked around to face my sister and took her by the shoulders.

'Please stay,' I said, doing my best to give her one of my old sisterly smiles. 'You're right. Working in the circles that I do, it's easy to forget where I once came from. My days are filled with ladies who have never done the washing, never cooked an egg, wouldn't know where to buy the milk from, couldn't even begin to understand how to darn a sock. I spend most of my time pretending, flattering them with expensive silks and satins, feathers and brilliants, veils and trains. My hands have gone soft, my pillows are made from down and I buy a newspaper every day.'

She scoffed, turning her gaze wistfully back to the ship.

'But I haven't forgotten that my big sister looked after me, that she let me help Maw out with the sewing, let me make clothes for Ava and Carla. Because you did that, I was able to come here and start my own business, become a dressmaker, become a couturier.'

'A what?'

'A couturier. It's just a posh name for a dressmaker,' I explained hurriedly.

She wrinkled her nose at me, but hesitated. Before she could make up her mind, I took her arm and turned her towards the car. 'Come on, let's go home for that cup of tea and cake.'

'Aye, that's best, before you start talking about "circles" and "couturiers" again.'


That evening and the next morning Netta exhausted me by rejecting all the food I offered, except cake, every drink except tea. She found fault with the way I'd furnished my apartment, the way her bed was made, the way the windows had been cleaned, the towels folded. Eventually, over breakfast, as she refused the toast and marmalade on offer, I lost my temper.

'What *do* you want?' I almost shouted.

Just as loudly she quipped back, 'What's wrong with a bowl of porridge?'

'I haven't touched porridge since the day I left my boarding house, it was grey and tasted of dishwater. I won't have it in my home.'

And finally, Netta smiled. 'Didn't Maw call you Fussy

Maisie? You'd not eat sommit you didn't like even if you were hungry. Glad to see you haven't changed that much.'

At last, I'd found the sister whose company I craved.

'I tell you what. Why don't we walk over to the grocery store on our way to the garment factory? We can get you something you'd like; I'll even get some porridge. Then we can make a stop at Macy's on the way. You're going to need some new clothes. You'll be surprised how cold it is here in late March and that coat you were wearing yesterday won't be warm enough, or that hat.' This wasn't necessarily true, but I wanted to make sure she had some clothes that meant she wouldn't stand out so much, where perhaps she wouldn't feel uncomfortable when surrounded by cashmeres, tweeds and beautifully draped jersey.

She took a breath in obvious objection but I put up my hand. 'No, I insist. I'm not having my sister freezing to death out there. And it's on me. I've made you come out to this cold place, so I'll buy your new clothes.'

Three hours later we stepped into the heart of Maison McIntyre. When I'd bought the building on West 38th Street in 1924, I'd had it fitted out to mirror some of the smartest couture houses in Paris. Unlike my original salon, where I'd filled it with a riot of colour, here the walls and curtains were a discreet cream with a more subtle use of colour in the other soft furnishings.

Netta, in her new knitted, calf-length dress, matching coat and dark cloche hat, was silent, her mouth slightly open as we walked through the grand columned entrance and then into the high-ceilinged salon, the showy front to the business, the place where customers came to indulge their desires with the clothes that they wished to be dressed in.

'I thought I could get the mannequins to show you our latest designs,' I said, heaving myself onto one of the sofas, trying not to think of the bottle of bourbon in my desk drawer.

'I dinnae wanna see your fancy models. Cannae you take me into the workrooms? I want to see how those dresses are made,' Netta grumbled. 'An' I'm gasping for a cuppa tea.'

'I'll show you the workrooms, but you'll have to wait for your tea. No food or drink goes anywhere near the fabrics. House rule,' I said more firmly than I felt.

She grunted but said nothing.

'Why don't I get Oti to show you around. I need to go and check in at my office.'

The baby was kicking me as we walked up one flight of stairs to where the work was done: vast workrooms for hand sewing, machine sewing, cutting and finishing, as well as the small canteen and kitchen, rooms for the staff and mannequins to retire to and have a cigarette, a stockroom and a packing room, and, of course, my own design studio and office. Our first stop was the main workroom with its rows and rows of tables, up to seventy women, sewing at a table, or fitting one of the many tailor's dummies. There was a low hum of concentration.

Netta stood stock-still as she surveyed the room, then looked up at the ceiling, at the zigzag of the glass roof, letting in as much natural light as possible. 'Is all this yours?' she asked, awe in her voice.

'Yes.' I watched as realisation dawned on her face.

'All of it?'

I smiled. 'There's more. Come on, I think Oti is in the other workroom.' I tugged at her sleeve, walking her to the other end of the room and through a door into an almost identical room – more tables and chairs, more busy working women, more sewing machines, more tailor's dummies. But Netta stopped at a table to look at a dress that was being made, picking up the fabric.

'Please don't do that,' I asked. 'You need to wash your hands before you handle the fabric, and you might need some gloves too.'

Netta's face turned a bright red. 'Ma hands are clean,' she said loudly, showing me her splayed-out hands, stubby fingers, calloused and dry. 'You saying ma hands are too ruined to work here?' she huffed.

'No,' I said patiently, as if talking to a child. 'I'm not saying that. If you look around you'll see that some of us here also wear gloves. Sometimes we wear gloves when we're handling a particularly delicate fabric, or someone might have cut their finger at home the night before. We need to make sure that the fabrics don't get damaged or marked. After all, we're working with expensive fabrics every day. We can't afford to waste any of it.'

There was fury and humiliation on her face, but I wasn't backing down. This was my business and she'd have to conform and do as I asked.

But before either of us could decide how to continue this conversation Oti called to us from the other side of the room.

'Maisie. Thank goodness you're here. We need to discuss... Oh, I'm sorry, this must be your sister.'

She leaned forward and put out her hand. 'I'm Oti. I'm your sister's Premier. It's so good to meet you, we've heard a lot about you.'

Netta didn't move, simply stared at Oti. 'But... but, you're bl —' She didn't finish her sentence as Oti continued it for her.

'Yes, I'm black. But you'll see that it doesn't hinder anything that I do.' Here she winked at me. 'And, actually, I think you'll find that I'm better than your sister at embroidery, way better than her.' Oti had been my main Premier for nearly seventeen years, and she was used to this reaction, but she was never quite as playful as this with our customers.

Netta blinked, her cheeks flushing. 'I'm... I'm sorry,' she stuttered, looking down at her feet. 'I didnae...'

Oti gently slipped her arm through my sister's and began to

walk her towards the finishing room. 'Don't you go getting all
het up about that. Now, I've heard that you might be in need of
a cup of tea and some of the best cake in the Garment District.
Let me take you to the canteen.' She turned back to me. 'I'll
come find you in a bit,' she called, giving me her most complicit
smile as she led a stunned Netta away.


'I've left her in the finishing room, listening to some of the girls
telling her wild stories about life in the city, about the parties,
the secret drinking dens, the Macy's parade, the subways and
tunnels and bridges. I don't think she'll be needing you for a
while,' Oti said as she walked into my studio ten minutes later.

I groaned. 'She's already driving me mad. The women in
Macy's couldn't make head nor tail of her as she refused to be
dressed by the personal shopper, shrieking at her to get out of
the fitting room.' The baby again kicked me in the ribs, and I
had to take a sharp breath. 'I'm not sure if this is going to work
out. She's too...'

'Forceful, opinionated, knows her own mind?' Oti interrupted with a large grin on her face. 'I know someone just like
that, but it's what you need when you have a baby, someone to
tell you what to do when you're so tired you can't even stand,
someone to tell you what to wear when you've forgotten to get
out of your nightclothes for three days.'

'Oh no, I'll not be having that.'

Oti laughed. 'You'll not have any say in the matter.
Audrey's girl, Laura. She was a screamer. None of us slept for
months. It was restful just coming to work. Poor old Joseph,
couldn't ever get away.'

I looked down at my hands, smooth and clean, long red-
painted fingernails and one ring of plain twisted gold on my left
little finger. Poor old Joseph. Mention of him still hit me in the
throat, despite Tori, despite my own child being on the way. We

saw little of each other, our relationship strictly professional, no allowance for everyday chatter, no room for once held feelings. If there was no place for Joseph and what could have been, where was I going to find the space for a child?

'So, I'm thinking your sister wants to work here,' Oti declared.

My heart sank. 'No, she's here to look after the baby.'

Oti raised her eyebrows. 'You sure about that?'

'No... Yes,' I insisted, 'she's here to look after the baby.' My voice rose. 'She can't work here. That's what I'll be doing.'

With difficulty I got up off the sofa, and slowly made my way out of the studio and into the finishing room. Netta, sitting with a group of girls being shown how to embroider a piece of leftover baby-blue satin using dark-blue beads and seed pearls. Netta, talking as she worked, taking instruction from Yulia, so completely at ease, so different from the Netta at breakfast that morning and in the fitting rooms at Macy's. Netta, whose face was soft, her eyes twinkling as she spoke, her companions hooked by her breezy chat, her funny stories. A tiny stab of jealousy hit me at her ability to make friends.

I leaned on the doorpost, taking a deep breath, feeling too tired to think about our prickly relationship, wondering why Netta was so harsh with me when she had made no effort to contact me over the years.

'Netta. It's time to go. I have booked a table at The Plaza for lunch.'

The shiny smile on her face dropped and the darkened eyes re-appeared. 'Do we have tae?' she asked, disappointment in her voice.

'Aye, there's work to be finished here and we need to leave everyone here to get on.' I gave her my best smile.

She quietly put down her sewing, took off the white gloves she'd been given and placed them neatly on the table in front of her. 'I'll be back,' she said before coming over to me.

'Shall we?' she asked, through gritted teeth.

As soon as we stepped onto the street, she rounded on me. 'Why did you have to do that?' she growled. 'I was enjoying myself.'

'Netta, they have work to do. I have customers who are expecting the best dresses, finished with the best embroidery. That wasn't some ladies' sewing circle; those were precious fabrics and some of those dresses take hundreds of hours to finish. We have women who are waiting on those gowns, who have important events to attend – parties and fundraisers and dinners with the president. They can't afford to be distracted by your tittle-tattle. Mistakes tend to be expensive.'

'Ach, just listen to yourself. All puffed up and important.' She glared at me, breathing hard, much like a charging bull. 'Did it occur to you that I might like to sew in your studio? I'm sure I could be as good as any of those girls.'

'But you were never interested in doing the sewing or the embroidery for Maw. You did the housework; I did the sewing.' She'd always rolled her eyes at Maw and me, when we got excited about a new idea we'd had or a different fabric we'd seen. She'd always retreated to the cooker or turned her attention to washing the clothes.

'That's because no one else wid do it!' she shouted in exasperation. She turned away, as if she needed to gather her patience. Eventually, she continued, her voice quieter. 'You were too distracted by the cut of a dress or by making a simple shirt more intricate. You were never happy with the ordinary, always trying tae be different. So, whilst you were trying tae be noticed, I got on with keeping us warm, dry and well fed. I did it because I had tae, not because I wanted tae.'

Of course, Netta spoke the truth – I still didn't worry about my own need for food or warmth, all I ever cared about was colour and design. I broke her stare, looking away, down the street, my eye caught by a woman wearing a simple, slimline, three-quarter-length coat, the sleeves with triangular 'fin-like' inserts at the wrists. How was I ever going to be able to bring up a child?

'Let's go and have some lunch. I want to take you to The Plaza Hotel, the place where all of this started.' I put my best smile on, ready to start again, trying to push away my feelings of guilt.

'What is The Plaza?' Netta asked.

I blinked, trying not to laugh at her ignorance. 'It's one of the biggest, smartest, most expensive hotels in Manhattan and I'm going to take my sister there for lunch,' I announced proudly, taking her arm and turning her towards Seventh Avenue. But she wouldn't move.

'No,' she said, her jaw set square, her mouth tight. 'I dinnae care for smart hotels, silver service and ladies in fur coats,' she continued with disdain. 'I want tae see the places you worked in when you first came here. I want tae see where you lived, where your friends lived, I want tae see the New York where the real people live.'


More tea and more cake. I was never one for cake, but at eight months pregnant I was happy to eat anything that came my way. Besides, it was a good distraction from looking at the irritated face in front of me.

We were in a loud tearoom, Netta sighing and gulping down her tea. 'And what about our Aileen? You havenae said about her.'

For a moment I had no idea who Netta was talking about, but then I realised. Slovenly Aileen. I sighed.

'Once she found out that I ran my own business as a dressmaker, she came to ask for a job. She arrived at the studio in a filthy dress, her fingernails were black, her hair was unwashed, and she smelled. She couldn't even sew. I wasn't going to let her anywhere near those beautiful fabrics. I sent her away, told her I wasn't having her and her slovenly ways in my studio. I haven't seen her since.'

Netta stared, the frown on her face deepening. 'But she's family. You have tae look after your family.'

Before she could start on at me, I interrupted her. 'That's why I want you to stay, why I *need* you to stay. I need my family, I need you, Netta. I need you to stay and help me look after this baby. I don't know what to do. I know how to sew, how to make a dress, how to make someone look good, but I don't have a single idea about babies.'

'You know that I loved all my wee bairns, and I've loved Carla's too, God knows they were a tricky lot. I know that when I see yours I won't be able to resist helping out, but I'm not sure that I want tae be your nanny. It'll not be a good idea. Couldn't you get someone else, and I could come and work in your studio?'

'But you are so good with babies.' A horrible prickling feeling came over me, a sudden knowledge that I'd made a terrible omission. Instinctively I stroked my own bump.

'Netta,' I whispered, shame flooding through me, 'when I left you were pregnant. You've never told me what you had. Was it a boy or a girl? Does it have a name?'

The colour drained from her face and that hardness left her eyes to be replaced with a terrible desolation. I leaned towards her, touching her wrist. 'What happened?' My mouth had become dry, my tongue sticking to the roof of my mouth.

'He died three weeks after he was born, that poor wee bairn.' She swallowed loudly, her eyes bright as she pulled a handkerchief from the inside of her sleeve, wiping her nose. 'We named him Donald. He was a wee sickly thing, didnae want tae feed much. So quiet, never quite right. Oh, but he had his father's eyes.' Here she gave me a helpless, twisted smile, her crow's feet wrinkling as she tried to hold back the tears. 'He'd have been a bonnie wee boy.' She turned her gaze towards the large window of the tea shop, looking to the other side of the road, staring, as if the grown-up Donald was there watching her.

'Just when I'd got used tae having him around.' Her voice broke. 'Just when I'd learned tae love him.' She looked back at me. 'You'll find, when you've had your own, that even when you're so tired and want nothing else but tae go to sleep, the thing that makes you feel better is a good long cuddle, when they wriggle on your chest, when they sigh with contentment, when they smell all clean and milky and innocent.' She wiped her eyes, mouth turned down, her shoulders drooping. But then, suddenly, she sat up, took a deep intake of breath and looked at me, the hardness back in her eyes. 'After that I wouldnae let Duncan anywhere near me. No more babies, no more tears.'

In response, my own baby seemed to stretch, kicking me with impatience in the ribs, whilst its head clashed with my bladder, causing me to wince and shift in my seat, rubbing at my ribs.

'Nine months of anticipation only tae be given three weeks of joy. Not a great payoff in my books.'

I rubbed my stomach, trying to subdue the kicking, unable to meet my sister's eye. 'I can't imagine how that would feel.'

She sighed. 'I hope you never know.' She looked down at her hands, picking at her bitten fingernails. But all of a sudden, she looked up. 'You never told me about the baby's father. What happened?'

'He died,' I said. It was much easier to give this simple statement than run off with some spiel about who and why and when. 'I had an affair and he was killed by the Mafia.' The more blunt the statement, the less likely people were to ask details.

Netta gaped. 'Do others know about the father?'

I snorted. 'The whole country knows who I had an affair with and most have been able to put two and two together and work out who the father is. I haven't kept it a secret.'

Netta gaped again. 'I didnae know,' she whispered, fiddling with the knife on her plate. 'What about your customers? Surely those high-class ladies weren't too pleased to be associated with a woman of "low morals"?' Here she put on her best Morningside accent and looked down her nose at me, her eyes twinkling with mischief.

I laughed, thankful for the heavy atmosphere to have been broken. 'We have lost a few customers, but, surprisingly, most, especially the ones who were hit hardest by this Depression, have been very supportive. They haven't forgotten that I was the supplier of a shoulder to cry on and hot coffee and cake when they were amongst the disgraced and fallen.'

Suddenly Netta blurted out, 'I'm sorry I never contacted you.' She kept her eyes firmly down, the colour rising in her face. 'I was so ashamed.'

Her unexpected words sideswiped me.

'There were you living your dream, doing what you'd always said you'd do and there was me, stuck. I'd failed, whereas you were winning. We stayed living in the same tenement, always short of money, Duncan finding it more and more difficult to work 'cos of his lungs, the girls increasingly wild. I had to go back to the laundry at the North British to makes ends meet.' She looked up. 'Maisie, I was too embarrassed. What could I say to my baby sister who has a chauffeur and owns her own home?'

I picked at the crumbs on my tea plate. 'I sent money home to help but you never replied so I wasn't sure if you still lived at Richmond Place. I didn't want to keep sending my money to another family by mistake, so I stopped...' My voice petered out as we both sat in an embarrassed silence.

Eventually, I took a deep breath, sat up straight and said, 'What you need is a Bassino family meal.' Gingerly, I got up from my chair and picked up a paper bag filled with a large cake from the nearby delicatessen, a cut of ham and some focaccia bread. 'Everything always used to seem better after I'd eaten with them.' But, of course, this was no longer the case.

I still had an unsettled relationship with the Bassinos. My guilt and Matteo's accusations had never left me. Annina had often pleaded to work for me, but I wouldn't go against Matteo's wishes. He insisted I was bad luck and he wouldn't let his girl near my studio. Nothing I could do would persuade him. And once the business had moved from MacDougal Street to the Garment District and I'd moved further uptown, I'd found it easier to not see them, my visits becoming more and more infrequent, my presence becoming less and less appreciated.

But after telling Netta about the fire, about Rosa and her family, she'd insisted that we go. 'You shouldn't forget all about them.'

I told her of the shawls that Rosa used to make, of the food she cooked, her enveloping hug, the way she'd teased me about being so skinny, about how she was going to work with me in the studio at MacDougal Street, how she had been my friend, a sister, a mother, all of those things I'd left behind in Edinburgh. And as I talked, as I told her of all the things that Rosa had done for me, Netta said, 'She was your family. You look after your family.'

The door was opened by Annina, now a young woman in her mid-twenties, tall and too skinny, with muddy blonde, exceptionally straight hair, deep-set grey-green eyes and a snub nose. She had a haughty look, eyeing us with a contempt that filled me, again, with shame.

'Come in.' It wasn't the overwhelming greeting that I'd received when Rosa was alive, it was more measured, as if she was wary of two strangers on her doorstep.

We walked into the same tenement apartment that they'd been living in since I'd known them, but it was shabbier, slightly grubbier, paint peeling, a smell of muskiness, of disillusionment. But this time there was a hint of that life before the loss of Rosa, that constant family discussion: raised voices, wild gesticulations, fast speaking always tempered by smiles and laughter, good food and hugs and kisses and the general sensation of goodwill. Now that Roberto was married, his wife, Francesca, had brought back some of that warmth and there was a smell of good food, that smell that had been missing from this family for so long.

I sat on an upturned crate, Netta on a wobbly stool, both of us leaning on the same old kitchen table, now worn and pitted. We were introduced to Francesca, round and dark haired, so like Rosa that I almost caught my breath. She had that homely aura that made you want to touch her, made you feel that you were amongst family and would be well looked after. As she began to cook, the smells and the bangs and crashes she made around the kitchen as she worked brought Rosa right to me. The feeling that she was in the room so strong, as if she was standing just behind me, telling me that I couldn't possibly be warm enough, that I wasn't wearing enough clothes and questioning why I hadn't got my feet up because I needed to give that baby a rest. At that moment my need to see, to feel, to smell Rosa was unbearable, becoming a physical pain in my back and brought tears to my eyes. I stood up, the crate being too uncomfortable to sit on.

'Annina, tell me what you are doing now. Where are you working?' I shifted my weight from foot to foot, rubbing the small of my back, trying to ease that persistent ache.

'I've moved to a new factory. Same work, different place.' She said this with an indifference that I'd become used to when I worked in the factory, that resigned acceptance, that tone that said you knew it was awful but what else was there to do.

I glanced at Matteo, sitting in the corner on their battered and tattered sofa, hunched and silent.

'It's not far from your studio. I often walk past it on my way to work. Do all the women who work for you get a uniform? They look very smart.' Annina spoke with a raw New York accent with no hint of the Italian she'd grown up with.

'Yes,' I said, trying to ignore her underlying bitterness, 'anyone who works at Maison McIntyre gets given a uniform that fits the position they're working in, a uniform that's comfortable but smart. If they're producing some of the best outfits in New York they need to feel good about what they're wearing.'

Annina looked at me blankly. 'Why would you care what they think? Aren't they just there to get the work done? Don't you just want them to sew and get the garments out the door?'

She looked so tired, this young woman, with sallow skin, lank hair and the cuffs of her white shirtwaist frayed and greying. Up until that moment, I had never thought that I had a maternal bone in my body, or had any kind of protective, parental instinct, but just then, all I wanted to do was take her in my arms and give her a big, motherly hug. Maybe it was because I was heavily pregnant, maybe it was because she was the daughter of my dead best friend.

I suppressed the urge, knowing how awkward it would be, how embarrassment would fill the room. Instead, I smiled at her, my best, most patient smile and explained. 'Every single person who works for me needs to be interested in the work that they do, needs to understand exactly what the customer wants, exactly why they're doing it. If they're just there for the money, for the food at lunchtime, for the free work suit, then I don't want them. They need to love the work that they do.'

Annina frowned and for the first time that evening seemed to soften. 'I want to have a job that I love,' she said quietly.

'Food's ready,' Francesca announced and plonked a large pan on the table. There was a scurrying as the children brought plates and cutlery, glasses and a jug full of water.

For the next hour I was able to indulge in home-cooked food just like Rosa's, I could sit quietly and watch my sister relax and enjoy the family atmosphere that had been missing during those awkward dinners after the fire: the chatter of the children, Roberto gently teasing his father, the feeling of satisfaction after a well-loved meal, and finally, at Matteo's opening up and his ceremonial bringing out of the limoncello. I again saw my sister as I remembered her: without anger, bitterness or rancour, a tenderness in her face, her eyes twinkling. She had once again become the girl I'd shared a bed with, nursed our mother with, shared our teenage hopes together with.

'Can I show you something?' Annina asked once we'd cleared the table and helped with the washing and drying up. She disappeared into the tiny bedroom and returned with a folded piece of knitting. She opened it out and spread it on the now cleared table. It was a shawl, similar to those that Rosa used to make.

'I've been teaching myself to knit the same way she did, copying Mamma. Now I've started to make my own designs. This is one of my own.'

I fingered the shawl, very similar to Rosa's, the quality of the knitting not as good, the designs not as refined as her mother's. However, they were still different from anything that could be seen in the shops or in the fashion houses.

'Do you have any others you can show me?' I asked.

She brought out three more. 'This is all I have. I sell everything I make. But I don't have much time to make them, what with the job at the factory.' She pulled a dejected face.

I looked at all the shawls carefully, inspecting each design, noting the colours and patterns. 'These have real promise.'

She looked at me pleadingly. 'Please can I come and work for you.'

I glanced at Matteo. Annina turned to her father.

'Please, Papà. Please let me go and work for Maisie. I'm old enough to make my own decisions now and this is what I want to do.'

There was silence around the table then Matteo suddenly started talking very fast in Italian, he and Annina having a disagreement, their voices getting louder as Netta and I watched with a complete lack of comprehension.

Eventually Matteo turned to me, his face a conflict of emotions. 'No,' he said quietly. 'It's best she stays where she is. It's better money than most of the factories. We need that money.'

'Annina can come and work for me,' I said quietly. I wouldn't normally have gone against Matteo, but I could no longer stand the thought of Annina in one of those dangerous garment factories.

'But...' he tried to interject, but Netta went over to him and sat beside him.

'She'll be well looked after. I went tae see her studio today and everybody who works there is given good wages, they get fed at lunchtime and they're careful about where all the fabric is stored, and where all the fire exits are. Those girls that work in her studio are looked after better'n any I've seen before. They get uniforms, they get breaks. If you ask me they get mollycoddled, but I expect that's what you'd like tae see.' She took his arm, as if they were about to go out for a walk together. 'I think that your Annina's maw would be proud tae have her working with our Maisie. I think you might be too.' She searched his face for some chink in his armour and as soon as she saw his eyes soften, she said, 'Aye, you should be proud of your girl, she's got some fight in her. You know, I'd like tae to work in her studio, but if it came tae it, I think Annina would be more suited.'

Netta caught my eye and held my gaze.

'Can I, Papà?' Annina asked. 'Please?'

Matteo stared at his daughter, a tear slowly falling down his left cheek. He nodded. 'Sì.'

Annina shrieked and hugged her father tight. '*Grazie mille, grazie mille.*'

As I watched them I realised how exhausted I was. I needed to leave. I hugged Matteo and Roberto. I took Annina's hands and looked her straight in the eye.

'You come and work for me, but I won't be able to be your friend. It won't be like working with the girls in the factory. I'll need your total commitment and loyalty. You understand?' I didn't want to see the haughty Annina we'd met at the beginning of the evening, I wanted to see Rosa's daughter, who would work hard and understand colour and the principles of design.

'Come on, Netta. We need to go.'

We climbed into a cab and as soon as the door was shut she said, 'It's no wonder you don't have any friends. That family, who had their world devastated by the loss of their mother, the woman who looked after you when you first arrived here, who fed you and mothered you, the family that just welcomed you when they hardly have anything, and you treated their daughter as if she was just another job applicant. You should have taken her on years ago.'

'But I didn't want to go against her father,' I pleaded.

'Oh dinnae give me that. You just didnae want tae get involved. If he was so worried about the safety at your studio you could have taken him there yourself and shown him around. You could have persuaded him, I didnae think there was a person on this earth you couldn't persuade.' She tsked. 'You just didnae try. You didnae bother.'

She huffed at me, glaring, breathing hard. 'Not one single friend, I'd be certain of that.' She sighed and, with her bag held tightly to her chest, she turned her head to look out onto the street. 'Just work and ambition. That's all you've ever had. Nothing has changed. Nothing at all. And what about Aileen? You did the same to her. She's family, for goodness' sake!'

I wanted to take her by the shoulders and shake her, tell her she had no idea what she was talking about, did she have a clue about how guilty I felt about Rosa, about leaving Netta in Edinburgh, about...? But I was suddenly overwhelmed by a pain in my lower back followed by the sensation of wetness in my underskirts.

As soon as I was able to catch my breath I said, 'Netta, I think the baby is coming.'


The day Jessica was born should have been joyous, heartwarming and a blessed relief from the discomforts of pregnancy. But she took three days to arrive, eventually being hauled out by an indifferent doctor, she and I both exhausted, Jessica too weary to feed, me too shattered to care. At least a nurse would take her away and let me sleep whilst I was still in the hospital. At least, with the presence of those slightly disapproving nurses I could pretend at playing mother, I could hand her back when the sound of her angry mewling became too much.

During my pregnancy, in those rare moments of quiet, when I'd let myself think about life with a child, I'd found myself daydreaming that Tori's offspring would receive the world with open arms, just as Tori had, that she'd greet her mother with her father's subsuming smile that had been the undoing of me. But she was born with a frown on her face and screamed for what seemed like months. I'd feed her, wind her, change her, but still she'd scream. I'd pick her up, walk around the apartment, sing a song, dance, make faces. I'd put her in the pram and walk miles through the city. Rarely did she stop her continual yammering, incessant shrieking that only got louder as she got older.

If I wanted something, I'd set my mind as to how to achieve it. If I wanted to work with a particular woman, I would woo them with my skill and lure them with my designs.

But I didn't know how to make my daughter love me, nor did I know how to love her back. I could dress her and make everyone's heads turn. But she wanted love, not beautiful clothes. Every day I'd wake up determined to try again, determined to be a better mother, but, against all my wishes, I couldn't help but find motherhood agonisingly boring. The daily grind of feeding, washing, clothing, feeding, washing, clothing was monotonous, was grey and dull. There was nothing fun about motherhood, I found very little colour in it.

I'd wondered if the love I'd had for Tori could be rekindled by his daughter, if I would revel in the time I was able to spend with her, look into those eyes that were Tori's, see some hint of him in her smile. But I could see nothing of the man I had loved, not in those early days, in those days which are supposed to be the most important. All I could see was a red, scrunched-up face, the soaking nappy, the kicking legs. She couldn't possibly be Torridon Smyth's child. Surely she would have had his calm temperament, his openness, his love of a hot bath. No, she was angry, she shut me out, beat me with her tiny fists and hated being bathed.

The only person who was able to give her any consolation was Netta: Netta the natural mother with infinite patience; Netta, the warm and cosy mother-figure, who smelled of warm milk and scones and who could envelop my child in her expansive bosom, giving her the comfort that I was incapable of. I should have been jealous of her as she consoled Jessica, changed her, played with her and took over the feeding after I gave up, failing with both breast and bottle. I should have been upset when Netta took Jessica out for walks in Central Park and came back glowing with what seemed like a real parental love and pride. But I was secretly relieved, oh so thankful that someone was able to keep Jessica amused when I couldn't, delighted that I didn't have to deal with the day-to-day monotony of child rearing, so pleased to be able to wear a dress that didn't get ruined by baby sick.

If I'd been a mother in the Lower East Side, I'd have been surrounded by a myriad of other mothers in the same position as me, who understood the loneliness of motherhood. I'd have been part of a community who looked after each other. If Rosa had been my neighbour I'd have visited her for company, for advice, for five minutes' sleep; she'd have teased me for my lack of resilience whilst feeding me good food to nourish my soul, she'd have told me how difficult Annina was as a baby, how Roberto was so sweet but never slept, she'd have made me feel better about finding motherhood so difficult. The only community I had was at Maison McIntyre and I was convinced that it was no place for a child. Of course, if I'd have allowed it, even considered it, those women would have jumped at the chance of mothering my child, they would have gladly welcomed her into our assortment of brilliant seamstresses, they would have loved her in the way I found so difficult. But I wouldn't even contemplate it. No baby should be seen anywhere near those precious fabrics, tiny brilliants and sharp needles. My customers didn't want to walk into the haven that was Maison McIntyre to be confronted by the cry of a baby in the background. Couturiers demand perfection and children do not engender the type of excellence and commitment to work that we require, causing havoc in a world that compels us to be neat, tidy and immaculate in everything that we do.

Six weeks after Jessica's early arrival Netta announced, 'I need tae go home. I've done my job, helped you with the first few weeks, let you heal after that long labour, but now it's time for you tae spend time with her. You're her maw after all.' She tickled Jessica under the chin, gave a little giggle and blew on her naked tummy.

'No, Netta. I need you here, please, can you stay?' Trying to keep any hint of panic out of my voice.

'I need tae get back to Ava and Carla and help with their bairns. I was hoping you could book me on a ship in the next week or so. Can you do that?'

'No.' I went right up to her and took both the tops of her arms, almost shaking her. 'I can't do this without you. Look, I'll pay you and then, well... when Jessica's a bit older, when she's more manageable, then you can go home. But not now. Can't you see I have work to do, important work and I can't have her screaming at me all day long, I have to concentrate, I have to come up with the next collection over the next three weeks. This is a crucial time for me, I...'

Carefully Netta took my hands off her arms and then took my hands in her own. 'My baby sister,' she said patiently, as if I was a small child, looking at me directly. 'I will not be your nanny, I will not work for you paid or unpaid, I will not let you ignore your daughter, you need tae be the woman that you say you are and take on the job of being a mother. Those women can live without a new dress this season, they'll survive. But Jessica will not survive without her mother. That poor bairn has tae grow up without a father, don't let her be left behind by her maw.'

She turned and efficiently put a clean nappy on Jessica whilst she continued to speak. 'If you won't book ma ticket on the next boat tae Glasgow, then I'll go tae your studio and ask Oti tae do it for me.' She said this in her sweetest singsong voice, all the time looking at Jessica, teasing her and tickling her. 'I'm sure you'd rather I didnae do that, so why don't you just get on down tae the booking office and pay for a third-class ticket. None of that first-class nonsense, I just want tae be Netta, not some la-di-da lady who dresses for dinner.'

At this she picked up the now re-dressed Jessica and handed her over to me. 'Now, you best get her into that pram and take her off tae the park, I'm sure she's sleepy and could do with the rest and some fresh air. I'm off to finish knitting those booties I've been making for her, need tae get them done before I go.'

The first work that must be done on creating a collection is seeing all the regular textile manufacturers and choosing the fabrics for that season. This is no small job, spread over several days, involving appointment after appointment with their travelling salesmen arriving with suitcases full of tweeds, woollens, coat fabrics, velours and duvetyns, followed by velvets and furs, then the silks and satins, taffetas and organzas, gauzes and crepes. As I inspect the bolts of fabric, designs begin to whirl around inside my head, whispering to me which tweed is best or which taffeta is the most eye-catching. Then we have to consider the embellishments, the lace samples, the new buttons, the latest belts and updated beads and sequins, the newly made fabric flowers.

Keeping all of these fabrics, details and designs in my head as we spend the days working through all the samples, noting which ones we want, changing an order because we've just found a silk in a more subtle pink, or a tweed with a more prominent purple thread running through it, becomes complicated and requires our full attention. So, when I arrived in the main workroom, ready for our first appointment to look through the textiles, with Jessica fast asleep in the pram, Oti rolled her eyes and shook her head at me.

'Oh, my,' she said. 'This is going to be an interesting day.' She looked down into the pram. 'She's a cutie.'

'That's because she's asleep; you might not think so when she opens her mouth.' I put my hand in and stroked her cheek. Jessica snuffled and wriggled a little in her pram, the momentary trace of a smile crossing her lips. Just for a second I felt a tiny stab of love for this surprisingly quiet daughter of mine.

'Shall I get Yulia?' Oti asked. Yulia, still working for us after those very first days in the studio, was now a grandmother. She still regaled the girls with stories of her ever-growing family, whose antics constantly entertained the workroom staff.

'Yes, maybe that would be a good idea.'

Oti left and I pushed the pram into the elevator and took Jessica silently into my studio on the first floor, shutting the door behind me. I put the pram beside the large picture window that looked over the workrooms and stood there watching: the long rows of tables where dresses were carefully laid out, in various stages of construction, being hand-sewn; sleeves being attached, hems being finished, pleats being neatly folded. I could hear the gentle hum of voices, sewing machines, of scissors cutting fabric. I felt safe, cocooned. In this room I could think what I liked, and nobody would know. I could look at my daughter and search desperately for something of her father: the crooked smile he'd crack after he'd told a joke, the flick of his wrist after he'd lit a cigar, the glint of red in his sandy hair and the little sigh he'd make when he lay down in bed. But she had none of these mannerisms or characteristics. She was resolutely serious, dark haired, and stiff wristed. I could see nothing of him in her, no hint that she was his child. I could sit in my studio and let myself feel the weight of all my conflicted mind – how some days I wanted to hold her close and others I wished I could forget she existed. Nobody would know. I could ask myself if Tori hadn't been killed, would I have kept the baby? And acknowledge with a piercing clarity that the answer was *no*. I would have found a discreet doctor, paid whatever it took to keep my life intact. That thought should have shamed me, but in this room, where I was protected from the outside world, I could let that shame exist alongside everything else: my grief, my well-hidden love, my fear of being a bad mother and my long-held guilt.

I leaned back and closed my eyes, tired of the struggle that had been going on inside me since Jessica had arrived, tired of trying to be someone I was not. As I did this a terrible idea began to form in my head, an idea that both seemed appalling and the answer to my problems.

What if I asked Netta to take Jessica with her, back to Scotland? What if I gave her enough money so that she could live comfortably and bring her up in a manner that would be consistent, homely, and full of love? Netta wouldn't have to contend with her difficult sister, she could bring Jessica up in the way she wanted, but she'd never have to worry about affording it, she'd never have to worry about money again. She'd be able to move to somewhere more suitable, somewhere bigger and newer, warmer and cleaner. She could even find somewhere that Ava or Carla could move in with her too. Jessica would have a family, have cousins to grow up with, be allowed to get dirty and make noise. She'd be loved.

I could picture the scene in my head. Saying goodbye to Netta on the ship, tucking her bags away beside her bunk and just as the warning was given for visitors to leave, I'd hand Jessica to her. She'd give her the usual cuddle, a raspberry on the tummy, an Eskimo kiss, and then she'd try to hand her back, perhaps a slight tear in her eye. But I'd say, gently, 'No. You're better at this than I am, you can give her a better life than I can.' I could clearly see the tears and the pleading, perhaps a bit of anger, but I'd refuse and extricate myself, running down the crowded corridor and down the gangplank before Netta could even bundle up Jessica and get up off her bunk. It seemed so easy, such a neat solution.

But even as these thoughts filled my head, they frightened me – these thoughts of abandoning my child, of making her an orphan. Looking back into the pram at that now angelic face, pink and sweet, breathing gently, for once sleeping soundly, could I really do that to Jessica, to Netta? Wouldn't it make all three of us happier in the long run?

Oti came into the studio and shut the door behind her.

'Yulia will come over shortly, she's just finishing up with a customer. Hell, you look awful. What's up with you?' She sat beside me on the sofa, concern on her face.

With my head in my hands I said, 'I've made the most terrible mistake. I shouldn't have done this. I can't be a mother. I'm just no good at it.' And then I told her of the thoughts I'd just had, the plan that had formed in my head, the plan that seemed so rational and sensible, that would solve everybody's problems.

'Oh, now you cannot go on thinking like that. You've just got the baby blues, you aren't thinking straight,' Oti said. 'You'll work this out, this is just another of those Maisie McIntyre conundrums.'

'No. This isn't just some passing feeling that will wear off next week, I'm sure of that. I don't feel that I can be trusted around that child. She doesn't like me and, to be honest, I'm not sure I like her.' I couldn't look at Oti, knowing that my words would be shocking, would probably turn her away from me, make her look at me in a different light. I could feel her intent stare, but I kept my head in my hands, looking at the pattern of the wooden grain in the floor.

'Audrey felt the same way about Laura. It near killed her for a while. That girl hadn't a clue. She cried and cried, couldn't hardly get out of her bed, telling me and Joseph that she didn't want the baby, that she wanted her to be taken away. But she made it, in the end, and so will you.'

Finally, she stood up. 'But I wonder if this calls for a break. For you to go away and live a different life.' She walked over to my desk as I sat up, surprised by her words. I couldn't go away; I had a business to run.

'This arrived yesterday and I haven't had the chance to speak to you about it.' She opened the top drawer of my desk and pulled out an envelope.

'This came from Samuel Goldwyn Productions.' She pulled

the letter out of the envelope and brought it to me. 'They're asking if you'd like to head up Costume Design and re-organise the wardrobe department. You could start immediately, pending salary negotiations.'

Slowly I took the letter and read it. Costume design in film had become an important business. As the Depression continued, audiences were looking for escapism and Hollywood delivered that in spades. Extravagant films such a *Palmy Days* and *The Kid from Spain* had romantic sets, lavish costumes and fairy-tale endings, all for twenty-five cents a go. The big movie theatres on 42nd Street, like the Roxy and the Paramount, were packed during several showings a day, entertaining thousands of people.

But I would be following in the footsteps of Coco Chanel.

'I know what you're thinking,' Oti said as if reading my mind. 'You know the bad press that woman's had. They're gonna be relieved to have you there. Her style is too muted for Hollywood, her demands too much. I heard they parted ways without much love lost.'

I re-read the letter. Mr Samuel Goldwyn was giving me the opportunity to move to Hollywood and get away from the feeling of claustrophobia that was engulfing me. New York had become nothing but an enormous construction site, filled with the noise of jackhammers, steam-shovels and blasting crews as they built more skyscrapers, public projects and the new subway system. The place was being torn down and built back up again, only bigger and higher, the traffic on the streets becoming more and more congested as everyone bought their own automobile. I craved peace and anonymity, retreating to my fabric-filled office, my apartment no longer being the haven it had once been. The letter that I was holding in my hands was giving me the opportunity to stretch again, to extend my range and see another side of life.

Since I'd arrived in New York, twenty-three years previously, I had rarely left the city. I'd loved it too much to want to leave. I'd never felt the need to take time away from my work, to go and walk the hills, sit in the sun or soak up another culture. I had everything I needed in this busy, crowded, noisy town. But now the idea of a different climate, different people, different work was appealing.

But what about Jessica?

'Jessica will like the climate better there, it'll be quieter, she'll be calmer. You'll be able to have a house with a garden, she can play on the grass, she'll be able to breathe the fresh air, not this city of dust and car fumes.' Oti again seeming to read my mind.

'But what about Maison McIntyre? I'd be too far away.'

'I think we could manage. If you came back twice a year, at the time when we see the fabric suppliers and we work on the designs – so, say you come back for three to four weeks every April and October. I know how to do this; I've been putting these collections together for as long as you have. I can do all the fittings with the models, I know what you want, I know how you think. If you're happy leaving me in charge, we can make this work.'

I stood up and walked over to the picture window, again looking at the busy women in the workroom below, the scene I looked at every day, that made me feel safe and secure, just like the rainbow-coloured reels of thread that I still kept in a cupboard in my apartment.

Would a change of scenery, change of lifestyle give me the time and patience to become a better mother and bring me back to a more instinctive way of designing, less rushed and more natural? Oti knew every part of the couture business, I knew she could run it without me.

.   .   .

'Netta,' I said that night at the supper table. 'I wondered if you'd consider staying on a little longer. I've got to start working on designing up the new collection and will be busy for the next two to three weeks, depending on how things go but then...'

Netta put down her knife and fork and took a deep breath.

'Before you start, please, hear me out. You might be interested.' I put my hand on my heart. 'I've been offered a job in Hollywood, to design for one of the studios. I think we should go. We'd move to a house, there'd be a garden, we'd be near the sea, it's much warmer over there and I think I'd be able to spend more time with Jessica. But I need your help getting us settled in, and helping me learn how to be a mother.' I tried my best to keep myself from pleading, but whilst I spoke my eyes began to prick and I couldn't keep a wobble out of my voice. 'Once I've found someone who'd be good with Jessica,' I sniffed, 'then, if you wanted to, you could go home.'

She opened her mouth but no words came out. It was like a fish that has just been landed, floundering for air, a confused frown, her mouth opening and shutting.

'They've signed stars like Anna Sten and Eddie Cantor, and they've made some of the biggest musicals in the last year. I'm sure you could come and visit me at work, perhaps take a tour around the studio, maybe even work in the wardrobe department if you wanted to stay. Can you imagine? You might be able to dress some of the stars.'

Netta began to redden, to blink furiously.

'Netta, are you all right?' I said, leaning towards her, touching her arm. A tear slowly fell down her cheek.

'Aye,' she eventually said, wiping her nose on her sleeve. 'Aye, I'm all right.' She sniffed loudly and wiped both her hands on her upper thighs. 'Aye,' she repeated. Sniffing again she said, 'I want tae go home, but...' She smiled lopsidedly at me. 'I'd like tae go and see Hollywood.' And then she burst into tears.

'Netta, what on earth is the matter? You shouldn't go if the idea of it upsets you. I just thought that you might like to see what it's like.'

'Ach, ye nugget,' she laughed. 'You know I love the pictures. I've always wanted tae go and see where they are made and see the life those film stars live. But I never thought... no, I never thought...' She shook her head. 'I canna say no tae that. Carla's gonna have tae wait. Her bairn will survive a few more weeks without her gran.'

# Hollywood

In early September 1933, Netta, Jessica and I moved to Los Angeles and into a newly built mock Tudor house in Laurel Canyon with a large garden and a terrace overlooking the city, a swimming pool and a separate cottage. Up in the hills, we were away from the noise and dirt of downtown Los Angeles, the air a little cooler, the privacy unexpected. Coming from the constant rain in New York, the dry heat was a welcome relief.

My grief over the death of Tori and the shock and fear over the birth of Jessica had begun to slip from my shoulders and I'd started to see glimpses of happiness. Netta again had a smile on her face and had discarded her old felt hat and scuffed lace-up shoes and put on a light summer dress and a straw hat. At five months old Jessica had finally lost her permanent frown and suddenly, almost overnight, had stopped screaming, transforming into a happy, gurgling baby who loved to sit in the garden with her little fat feet being tickled by the grass.

Netta had persuaded me to bring Annina as my assistant. Haughty Annina had kept away from my studio, instead diligent and hardworking Annina had turned up, ready to learn, impressing both Oti and I with her ability to concentrate and focus.

'That girl needs someone to believe in her. You had Mrs Marshall. Why don't you get rid of some of that guilt you carry around with you,' she'd sniffed at me. 'Here's your chance to redeem yourself in her father's eyes.' I was happy to bring her along. Not only would I have a promising assistant, but I could keep an eye on her and report back to Matteo on her progress and safety.

We decided she might like a place for herself, so I offered her the cottage.

'Don't you want me in the house?' Her voice had a touch of shock about it.

I was taken aback by her question, but before I could answer she whispered, 'I've almost never been by myself. I'm not sure I'll be able to get used to it.' In awe she wandered around the three rooms of the cottage: double bedroom, bathroom and kitchen-living area. It even had its own little terrace, hidden from the main house. 'It'll be too quiet. I don't know if I'll be able to sleep by myself.'

I felt a profound sense of relief. Normally I would have been annoyed by this, by the difference between us, me who had been so independent, so happy to have space in that tiny cabin on the SS *Furnessia*, to have my own room at my first boarding house on Jones Street, but now I just wanted to make sure she was safe. Is that what a bit of sleep and some time outdoors did to your sense of well-being or was it the effect of motherhood?

'Why don't you try it out. I'll get the maid to make up a bed in the house and you can always come and sleep there whenever you like. If you eat with us you don't really have to spend any time down here at all.'

. . .

After a week of settling in, unpacking our belongings and getting to know our neighbourhood, we'd been summoned to meet one of the producers. He sent a car, a gleaming Chrysler Imperial with wire-spoked wheels and a gazelle statuette leaping from the front of the bonnet. Annina and I sat side by side in the back, Annina overexcited, giggling and pointing, thrilled by the scent of the eucalyptus trees, not caring about the wind on her face or the dust from the road, riding in the back of a brand-new car, driven by a uniformed chauffeur through the meandering hills, until we reached a mansion with a winding driveway.

The car stopped and the door was wrenched open, our driver pointing us towards a set of double doors. Standing on the steps was a genial-looking man dressed in a well-cut grey suit and tie, with a balding head, dark, almost black eyes, and slightly pointy ears. Coming forward, he introduced himself as Harold Finerman.

'So sorry Sam can't be with you today, he has an important engagement that he couldn't break.' He kissed my hand in a showy manner. 'And who is this fine young woman?' he asked as he bowed too low at Annina.

'Annina Bassino,' I said, already distrusting this too ostentatious man. 'She's my assistant.'

'Ah,' he smirked. 'Nothing like a good assistant.'

I shuddered at the lewd intention in his voice, but Annina seemed not to notice, too starstruck by the whole show.

We walked into the house, through a huge open-plan seating area and out the other side into the garden where there was a large swimming pool occupied by six young giggling women in gaudy swimsuits and wearing too much make-up.

'Take a seat, ladies. Perhaps you'd like a drink?' asked Mr Finerman.

'A little early,' I said, archly, despite my own desire for a drink.

'Never too early in this business, my girl,' he retorted as he poured himself a quarter glass of neat bourbon.

I tried very hard not to dislike the man, but he had an oleaginous manner, his tone was patronising and he watched Annina a little too closely.

'Miss McIntyre. Unfortunately, we probably won't be working together that often, my film projects tend to be the less showy ones, more along the lines of government propaganda type films.'

My own inward sigh of relief as he took in a deep breath, as if sucking through his teeth. 'There is an important question I have for you. It's come to our attention that you have a young child.'

'Yes, I do. What has that to do with anything?' I tried to keep my voice even.

'Well, you know, the film industry is a very demanding industry. We work long hours,' he said condescendingly, as if I'd never worked a long day in my life. 'We didn't know you had a child. It's likely we wouldn't have offered you the job if we knew you were a mother.'

I let the words sink in, Annina was sitting bolt upright, next to me, her hands held tightly in her lap. I stayed silent for a moment longer, trying hard to push down my anger.

'Mr Finerman, do you have children?'

'Why, yes, of course I do. I have two fine nippers, a girl of two years and a boy of four.' He beamed at me as he took another sip of his bourbon, but those eyes, too small and too beady, didn't smile.

'Does anyone question your ability to do your job because you have children?'

'Well, of course not. That's different.'

'Why's that?' I asked, all innocently, as if I had no idea why.

'My wife, of course. She looks after the children so I can concentrate on my work. She deals with the housework, plans the meals with the cook, briefs the pool boy. But you don't have a wife, you are the wife.'

'I am no such thing, sir. I'm just as capable of concentrating on my work as you are. I have a nanny.' As I said this, Annina turned to stare at me, panic in her eyes.

'But how can you possibly organise the house, the garden, the dinner? How can you do that and make sure that you design and deliver costumes for all of our films?'

'I have a cleaner, I have a cook, I have someone who looks after my garden and cleans the pool. You are I are no different, except that I'm more capable than you.' I stood up, grabbing my bag, nodding at Annina to follow.

'And now that we've got that straight, I will take my leave. Perhaps you could tell Mr Goldwyn that I'd like to see him in the morning, it's obvious we have terms to discuss.'

We started walking back through the house, but I just couldn't help myself. Telling Annina to go on out to the car, that I'd be with her in a moment, I turned back to Mr Finerman. I walked straight up to him and leaned down to whisper in his ear. He smiled as if he thought I'd relented, was ready to be supplicant and malleable.

'Don't you dare belittle me in front of my assistant. Do that again and I'll return the favour. I don't suppose you'd like to be put down in front of all these badly dressed starlets. By the way, where *are* your wife and children? Do you always invite a posse of girls over when the cat's away? Do give her my love, I can't wait to meet her.' My voice was full of saccharin.

I couldn't stop the shaking as I walked back through the house of bad taste: chandeliers that were too large for the room, buffalo horns and tiger skin rugs. The place made me shudder and I couldn't leave it quick enough.

. . .

Mr Finerman aside, costume design in Hollywood had always been a difficult business. Because of the time lapse between approved design and release of the film, the costumes may well have already gone out of fashion. It's even more of a gamble than producing a collection twice a year and not everyone had succeeded, Coco Chanel being the latest. These were the days of black and white films, everything needing to be emphasised to make sure it stood out: a hat that may look perfectly balanced in real life with three ostrich feathers would need six to be striking enough, if an evening dress had the perfect equilibrium with a train two yards long, it would need to be double that to be eye-catching. If your designs were restrained and discreet, they'd simply fade into the background. Bold designs and a clever use of the shades of black and white were called for; cream looks muddy on screen, pure black too harsh. In 1932 the *Letty Lynton* dress became known as the iconic dress, described even by its designer, Adrian, as 'a trifle extreme'. A white mousseline de soie dress with enormous, ruffled sleeves, worn by Joan Crawford. Overemphasise the shoulders, exaggerate the waist. I didn't just have the legacy of Chanel to deal with, I also had to re-think the way I designed.

Where Maison McIntyre had women making the decisions, Hollywood studios tended to be run by men. In couture, I was used to focussing on the woman, what she wants, the event she goes to, her shape, colouring and her personality. When you are working as a Hollywood costumier your first port of call is the script. Is your heroine a Roman slave, a rich girl from Rhode Island, a woman who was brought up in a jungle, or a fashion model living in Paris? Once you've understood the script you must then work with the director, the stars, the producer, art director and camera man and learn to deal with their opinions as well as get their approval. Suddenly I was just another wheel in the huge movie machine.

But, somehow, this reset, this new way of doing things revitalised me. Normally, I like to be in complete control, to understand every detail; I don't want some man, whose job is to make sure he's within budget, telling me how to make a dress. Maybe it was the weather, perhaps it was Jessica's burbling giggles, but I relaxed and found myself enjoying working with this committee of men.

I designed for romantic screwball comedies, westerns, psychological thrillers, blockbuster musicals, sweeping love stories, wild farces and action adventures. There was a gaudiness and vulgarity to the work that the old me would have hated, but leaving behind the cold of New York, the social strictures of Manhattan, the rigid seasons of couture, had let me become a more accepting person, someone who pushed aside the frustration when a leading man decided he wouldn't wear what I'd given him, when the director changed his mind at the last minute, and I let my work become unrestrained. To keep the threat of boredom away, I got to run to New York twice a year and step back into the world of refined, structured couture for a few weeks, working with Oti on the next season's collection. I'd change gear, find new equilibrium, revel in those weeks without my family, without the constant noise and discussion of the film studios, re-becoming Maisie McIntyre, ambitious, outgoing, colourful. I'd work long hours, eat in my favourite delicatessens, sit in my studio with only the background noise of Manhattan to accompany me, surrounded by my designs, the colours, the fabrics and the threads of my New York life. Then I'd go back to California and change my colours. I became a chameleon and re-embraced the extravagance and garishness, again revitalised, like a snake having shed its East Coast skin.

Netta, like Jessica, blossomed in the heat of Los Angeles, becoming a lighter, less disapproving version of the Netta who stepped off the ship in New York. The more I heard her laugh, the more I didn't want her to leave. I told myself I was making up for all those lost years, giving her a life she'd craved by doing my best to turn her head with the impossible glamour. Every time she told me she must pack her bags and go back to Carla, I took her off to the studio for the day, accidently letting her bump into Anna Sten, Barbara Stanwyck or Humphrey Bogart. I even managed to persuade Cary Grant, pretty much an unknown in those early days, to inadvertently pour his cocktail over her and then take her to the Clover Club as an apology, introducing her to the hidden gambling rooms. They rolled in at five fifteen in the morning, two hundred dollars the richer and fast friends. The suavity of that man. In return I made him the most expensive and flawless suit he'd ever owned. He had an eye for a good suit; I appreciated the presence of my sister. Our arrangement benefitted the both of us. She dined off that evening for years and forgot to mention going home for many months after.

Annina quickly became my West Coast Oti, only without the sense of humour. But what she lacked in wit she made up for in organisational ability. She would know well before I did how many costumes would be needed for a film, how many hours of labour were required, what kinds of fabrics were available, whether there would be an issue with the schedule. She'd know exactly what the other studios were producing, whether Travis Banton or Dolly Tree would be dressing Carole Lombard, she'd find out that Adrian's latest designs were a little too close to mine and suggest that I'd need to tweak them. She'd forewarn me if I was likely to clash with one of the producers or directors on our new film and if so, then she'd do her best to fend them off, distract or protect them from the worst of my occasional avarice; she made it her mission to befriend every single leading actress, smoothing the way for an easy collaboration. By the time I left for my first stint in New York, she'd changed from a mousy-haired, opinionated New Yorker into a blonde, sophisticated woman with good taste and stamina, who could hold her own in a roomful of men.

But outside of work I noticed a troubling and possibly dangerous streak, that she could be reckless with men. I, who had virtually discarded any ideas of romance or involvement with a man, found her continuous need for male company disturbing: out dining and dancing every single night, gambling and drinking, partying and flirting until the wee hours and still capable of a full and productive day at work. There was a mania to her, some need to prove to the world that she was as glamourous as the very best leading ladies, that she was as capable as they were. Sometimes I'd notice bruising on her arms, as if someone had held her too tightly, occasionally her eyes were too bright, her wit and charm just a little too overdone.

Twice a year Aidan would visit. He was everyone's favourite, always swanning in with a flurry of presents and stories, treating us like he was our kindly uncle, dishing out wise words that he was able to produce because he lived on our sidelines and saw all our faults. His visits had become highly anticipated, and we always felt better for his presence. We'd be kinder, more tolerant, more open when he was in our midst, better versions of our everyday selves. There were impromptu parties, picnics and soirees, all of Hollywood wanting in on the feel-good factor that spread out from our Laurel Canyon house. Four years into our Hollywood stint his arrival garnered no less affection.

'Aidan is coming to visit,' I said over breakfast one morning.

'Uncle Aidan!!' Jessica shrieked.

Netta, knitting at the table, making a new cardigan for Jessica, said, 'I'd better get a new dress then.'

I smiled. Netta, never one to spend money on a new outfit, understood that Aidan meant parties, which meant visiting young, up-and-coming actors, because Aidan simply loved to be surrounded by beauty, especially beauty that was out to impress. When Netta first arrived in New York, she'd have been more than happy with her floppy hat and fading dress. Four years on and we'd managed some modest changes; she'd lost a little weight, sat up straighter, her hair was dyed a discreet blonde, she even wore a little make-up. But she'd go nowhere without her knitting, always looking to make a hat for one of her grandchildren, booties for whoever's newest baby, she'd even started making for the local Goodwill charity. But Netta and her knitting had become a bit of a Hollywood legend, the no-nonsense, sharp-witted observer who kept our heads level, laughed herself into the ground when some starlet was trying to impress, all with a ball of wool and a pair of knitting needles clacking away on her lap, usually sitting at the bar of some hot-shot producer with a whiskey and soda beside her.

'We have to throw a party,' Annina said. 'We have to welcome him in style.' Nina, as she'd become known, was now living in the cottage full-time but still ate breakfast with us every day, no matter how late she'd got in, always there to persuade Jessica to eat her fruit and porridge. They'd become like sisters, one more like the spoiling aunt, the other transfixed by the increasing glamour of Nina, her body sheathed in her black worksuit, her hair in a glamorous updo, her nails sensibly short but impossibly red. There was a sweetness in their exchanges that warmed me.

'Party!' Jessica interjected. She had a full understanding of the word 'party', it had become a way of life. 'Ice cream,' she continued, pushing her porridge aside.

'When's he arriving?' Nina asked, trying to put a spoonful of the rejected porridge in Jessica's open mouth. My daughter artfully ducked and flicked the spoon to the floor. Nina sighed.

'Next Thursday,' I replied, folding up the letter. 'Why don't you take Netta down to the studio to work on a new dress.' Netta's eyes lit up. 'Maybe we should make one for Jessica too,' I continued, kissing her on the top of her head as I grabbed a piece of toast. 'But only if you eat your porridge.'

Hurriedly, she grabbed a clean spoon from Nina and happily fed herself.

'Let's organise it for Friday night. I'll sort the guest list, the food, the drink.' Netta turned to Jessica. 'The ice cream.' She stuck her tongue out at my little girl, tickling her bare feet underneath the high chair. They shrieked at each other, fat giggles ensuing.

# The Party

Parties at the McIntyre household were relaxed, lazy affairs, only for our favourite people – strictly invite only – with strings of lights around the garden, a three-piece jazz band, a dance floor on the terrace, a bar beside the pool, canapés served by beautiful out-of-work actors, a juggler weaving in and out of the throng of guests on the grass, a magician showing card tricks. We set up a roulette table in the dining room, fireworks at midnight, breakfast served at dawn. We only did this when Aidan was in town. We only did this for our favourite person.

He swept into the drawing room just as the first guests arrived. Quiet jazz music trickled in from the terrace, the fire pit blazing in the centre of the garden, and I was flowing with a sense of contented well-being. My strange, unconventional family: Netta, Jessica, Nina and Aidan were back together. We sorely missed Oti, but caring for Joseph and running the business in New York left her little time for transcontinental visits.

At forty-nine, Aidan Cruickshank hadn't put on an ounce of weight, in fact he seemed a little wirier, perhaps a little more highly strung despite that always casual air of self-confidence. His features remained as chiselled as ever, the nose still hooked but the rakish brown hair was now flecked with distinguished grey, just enough to make him appear thoughtful and considerate to the crowds of elderly women who chased after him.

I'd made him a director of Maison McIntyre so that he could organise the twice-yearly fashion shows, move in the right circles and continue to bring in new customers, smooth over any tricky negotiations with local government officials, pay off the local Mafia, now that Tori no longer kept them at bay. In return I paid him a handsome salary. We made sure that we were occasionally seen together, letting the gossips think two old flames were back together so that he got to live his underground lifestyle, have his love affairs and grand passions with all the beautiful men of New York and now, sporadically, of Hollywood. He simply oozed charm, still dressing in Savile Row suits that always made me want to touch them, so right for his personality, for his shape; they made me jealous of the abilities of his tailor.

After the initial family greetings there was little opportunity to talk to him as the older women surrounded him. The mothers, the producers' wives, even the cook had taken a fancy to him. They gazed, he talked, they laughed, he touched someone's arm; I could see them shudder with pleasure. Watching him was like witnessing an Academy Award-winning performance, never missing a beat.

Netta was equally as popular, sitting at the bar with her knitting, holding court, telling stories of our days in the laundry, her trip over on the boat, ridiculing the life in Los Angeles. All the famous actors paid their respects throughout the evening, each one of them kissing her hand with great show, every one of them making her blush. I had never seen her so happy. Those frown lines faded away; she became sunnier. I noticed that she had one man giving her particular attention – a Mr Pound, the aptly named chief accountant at Samuel Goldwyn Productions, a small, portly man, about the same height and breadth as Netta, with a sandy comb-over and friendly blue eyes. Once he'd arrived she ignored her knitting, her gaze on Mr Pound only. The attentive actors sensibly stayed away; they could sense when they were not needed.

Eventually, Nina arrived, late as ever, bringing the party to a virtual standstill. She wore a new gown of her own making, a figure-hugging, full-length, pale-green satin gown with a halter neck and plunging back neckline. It was clear she was wearing no underwear. With her dyed-blonde hair pulled up, showing her slim, long neck, she drew more attention than any of the stars in the room, quickly surrounded by a posse of young actors looking for someone to help their careers along the way. She too played her part to perfection, touching them, whispering in their ears, pouting, and laughing at their jokes. But I could tell she was keeping an eye out for someone in particular, frequently glancing at the main door, a little frown appearing each time she was disappointed.

Jessica then sneaked into the party, wearing her sweet teddy bear patterned cotton pyjamas and hugging a very large soft toy, her hair tousled, her face still full of sleep. The increasing noise of the party must have woken her. Ronald Colman and his brand-new wife, Benita Hume, seemed enchanted, as if she was some sort of doll to play with. Swiftly and apologetically, I scooped her up and bundled her back to bed. Although Netta was supposed to be keeping an eye on Jessica, I was happy to let her concentrate on her new-found admirer. We lay on the covers together, thinking up stories about the guests, wondering which one of them still had their old soft toys. Finally, she fell asleep and I lay on her bed listening to the noises of the night and it became clear that the party had stepped up a gear, the tempo had increased to something more urgent, perhaps even a little menacing, almost like those parties in Long Island in the twenties, those frenzied affairs with wild dancing, an abundance of alcohol and an intensity that I always felt would cause injury.

Taking myself downstairs I noticed that the juggler was now using fire torches, his display more perilous, the reaction from his audience louder and more piercing. I could see couples downing shots of whiskey and immediately ordering more as if they'd never see the stuff again, then I noticed Nina with her back up against the terrace wall, mainly in shadow, with a faintly recognisable figure pressed right up against her, his mouth by her right ear, his hand on her breast.

'Annina!' I shouted, rushing over to her, a menacing feeling in my stomach. 'Would you come and help me talk to the men setting off the fireworks, they know you. It would help if you were there with me.'

The man lugubriously pulled away, as if he didn't care that he'd just been caught necking my assistant.

'Ah, Miss McIntyre. What a pleasure.' The man held out his hand, an oddly formal gesture in the circumstances.

'Mr Finerman,' I said coldly, ignoring his hand. 'I had no idea you'd been invited to our little party.'

'Your fine assistant here, the inestimable Miss Bassino, gave me the heads-up. I wouldn't have missed it for the world, such distractions. How could I have refused.'

Unease prickled at the back of my neck.

'Nina, would you mind?' I asked. 'Mr Finerman, I'm so sorry to drag her away from you, but we have a little business to attend to.'

I grabbed Nina's arm, too harshly, pulling her away as fast as I could.

'Ow,' Nina whined, as I pulled her into the garden, 'you're hurting me.'

'Not as much as that man will hurt you,' I growled, my Edinburgh accent suddenly re-surfacing. 'You shouldnae trust that man. He's nothing but trouble.'

She laughed, pulling her arm away from me, rubbing her

flesh. 'He's no trouble, just a pussycat. I'm a big girl, I can fend for myself.'

'Well, you didnae look like you were doing a great job. His hands were all over you.' I was trying not to shriek at her, surprised at my own fear.

Just then the fireworks started, everyone's attention pulled to the sky. Explosions of every colour filled the air, fountains of light, whirling Catherine wheels like sparkling flowers in the dark. Heads tilted upwards, oohs and aaahs, claps and laughter with each explosion. We were mesmerised, enthralled, our attention caught for the next twenty minutes.

At the end of the show, Nina was no longer by my side. Guests were beginning to leave and I was distracted, saying my goodbyes as Aidan sidled up to me, a look of concern on his face.

'Have you seen Nina? I can't find her anywhere.'

Instantly a cold dread came down on me. 'No, I haven't seen her since the fireworks started. Have you seen Harold Finerman?'

'That weasel. Why do you ask?'

'I last saw him feeling up Nina, looking as if he had every intention of finding out what's below that satin dress.'

Aidan blanched. 'I'm going down to the cottage, that's the only place I haven't looked.'

I followed, my stomach churning, my hands already a little sweaty, the worry increasing, thinking of Nina's vulnerability that she hid so well.

There were no lights on at the cottage.

'Perhaps she's sleeping,' Aidan said. 'Lights off would mean she's asleep, right?'

I shook my head. 'She sleeps with the lights on. Always has done. It's the only way she'll sleep down here by herself.'

'Nina!' I shouted, my heart in my throat. Something was very wrong, something that perhaps I could have stopped.

The door was unlocked and I burst in, shouting Nina's name. There was a heaviness in the air, as if the oxygen was solidifying around me. I flicked on the hall light. Although sparsely furnished, the room was a wreck. The chair, side table, mirror and a pair of shoes thrown across the floor, wooden splinters and glass shards mixed in with spatters of blood.

'Nina?' my shaking voice asked tentatively. 'Nina. What did he do?'

Then I heard a faint whimper coming from the bedroom. Crossing the hallway, pushing aside the mess with my feet and turning on the light, I saw her curled up in one corner. Completely naked, her head on her knees, her arms hugging her legs, her hair dishevelled, a patch where it had been pulled from her scalp, her left foot bleeding, her arms already showing severe bruising.

'Nina. Nina. Look at me,' I said, panicking, as I squatted down beside her.

She was shaking hard, otherwise unable to move.

'Did he do this? Did Harold Finerman do this to you?' I whispered as I stroked her hair.

She gave a slight groan.

Carefully I put my hand under her chin and pulled her head up so she was facing me. Immediately she jerked away and hid her face again, giving out a cry of pain. But I'd seen the swelling on her face, crusting blood around her mouth, the ripped ear, the gash across her left cheek.

Aidan wailed in anguish, trying to pull Nina into his arms. She resisted, retreating even further into the corner.

That smell of blood, fear, sex, terror and resignation, a heavy, animal smell overwhelmed us, a smell that has never quite left me.

'Aidan, can you go back up to the house and find Netta and bring her down here? Make sure no one else knows what's going on,' I said, articulating the words overly clearly. 'She'll know what to do.'

Three hours later I sat in the garden, drinking a large whiskey. The guests had departed and finally everyone was in bed. I'd felt so dirty I'd had a long bath, needing to scrub away the guilt that was blanketing me. I'd yet again brought tragedy to the Bassino family. How was I going to tell Matteo?

The full moon was throwing its eerie light over the city as I nursed my glass, the constant nighttime noise pushing into my thoughts: the lazy buzz of the cars, the continuing parties, a cat wailing, a glass smashing, a shout, laughter, the slam of a door. This was the skin of the city, a city that could never be quiet, would never stop and contemplate its legacy, what immorality it emitted, what harm it created. It continued to thrust ahead, to forge its own new paths of destruction in the name of entertainment, innovation and money.

Rolling the cold glass along my forehead, the ice cubes tinkling gently, I tried to soothe the voices in my mind. Nina, now in her early thirties, was a responsible adult, but she was under my protection. I'd brought her to this town. I knew the reputation Harold Finerman had – the rumours of his infidelity, the late-night pool parties, the hint at orgies, the whiff of drug usage. I'd seen them together before and had said nothing.

Refusing to go to the hospital, too ashamed, believing she had brought it all on herself, believing her naïve flirting had made him do what he did and that by fighting him she had been the cause of his anger, she sobbed as she told me that she'd thought that if she'd taken her punishment meekly, he'd have been gentler.

The pain became too much, the internal bleeding not stopping. Knowing a discreet doctor lived just a couple of houses away, I'd walked down the street and banged on the door. Her left cheek had been broken, several ribs cracked, she'd needed stitches in her head, a couple of toes had been shattered and we never fully understood the damage to her womb.

The sun began to rise over the city and I got out of my chair to pour another drink. The clink of the three ice cubes on the sturdy cut-glass tumbler was soothing, the gurgling sound of the pouring brown liquid healing. There was a packet of cigarettes on the side and I took one out. I rarely smoked, believing the smell of smoke ruined a good outfit. But I needed a distraction. I found a lighter, appreciated the sophisticated rip of the flint wheel, the whoosh as the flame flew up, lit the cigarette and inhaled deeply. I was hit by that dirty, woozy sensation you sometimes get when you haven't smoked for a while, but as I drank and inhaled, the ache of guilt began to subside and the bones of a plan began to form.

## Revenge

Six weeks later, Netta, Annina and I were surrounded by packing crates in the living area of the Laurel Canyon house: boxes and packing paper, piles of crockery and paintings, bags of fabric and a tower of hat boxes. We were preparing to leave Los Angeles and return to New York, Hollywood now tainted by Mr Finerman. It was time to return to normality.

I stood amongst the chaos, chain-smoking, a habit I hadn't been able to break since the night of the party. 'This seems never-ending,' I moaned.

'Good morning, my fair chickens!' Aidan chirruped as he burst into the room.

'You're a little too cheerful,' I said, although it was a relief to feel some happiness with the last few weeks having been joyless and bleak, feeling as though we'd failed Annina, failed our time in Hollywood.

He slapped a newspaper down on the coffee table, a large red ring hastily drawn around a small article.

'Our revenge has been enacted,' he crowed. 'Mr Finerman is done for.'

Annina frowned but put down the ornament she was wrapping and moved over to the table. She picked up the paper. 'What do you mean?'

'Well, my darling girl.' Aidan took the paper from her. 'Nobody gets to treat my Nina in that way. Nobody, but *nobody*. So, I have it on good authority that Mr Harold Finerman will never work in this town again. Here, let me read this:

*Charges have been filed against Harold Finerman, the much-lauded Hollywood producer, in connection with the attempted assault of an unnamed, young movie starlet at the Beverly Hills Hotel. According to sources at the hotel, Mr Finerman was discovered in a compromising position by the girl's mother. Mr Finerman is currently being held in jail whilst he awaits a hearing for bail.*

A look of concern crossed Annina's face. 'Was the girl all right? She wasn't hurt?'

Aidan patted her shoulder lightly. 'Don't you worry, I made sure the whole sting was planned down to the very second her mother arrived.

'Maisie spent weeks making a dress she knew that Finerman wouldn't be able to resist, a shimmering dress of alternating black and white shaped sections, clinging and leaving nothing to the imagination. She told me that the black and white symbolised the good and the bad, the white being the dominant colour. Who'd have thought Maisie would be putting oblique messaging in her work?'

'But was the girl all right?' Annina insisted.

'Please my darling, not a hair was harmed on our little starlet's body. He didn't have a chance to get anywhere near her. Just the very implication of being alone, unchaperoned, in a bedroom with that young girl and a half-drunk bottle of whiskey was enough to send the mother wild, shrieking through the grounds of the hotel, chasing him with her not insubstantial handbag.' A look of mischief. 'And it may just have been a coincidence that the *Times's* Read Kendall was in the Polo Lounge whilst this was all going on, where he had a prime view of Mr Finerman's not inconsequential beating.' He let slip a girlish giggle. 'Oh, and he just might have had a photographer with him, just to make sure there was photographic evidence.'

Annina took the copy of the *Los Angeles Times* from Aidan and re-read the article. I looked at Netta and we both held our breath. There was silence as we watched a slow but cautious smile spread across her face. The first smile we seen since before the fireworks at our party.

# Chapter Eight

## The Cashmere Cardigan

*A dark-blue seamless, crew neck, cashmere cardigan with contrasting bright-pink button placket tape on the inside edges and eight Murano glass bead buttons, each a different colour.*

## Knitting

**1938**

Netta decided that getting married in white would be ridiculous for a woman of her age. Instead, she wore a British racing-green silk velvet suit: a straight skirt that came down to the middle of her calves, a hip-length jacket nipped in at the waist with big gold buttons, and a high Chinese collar. She looked ten years younger than when she'd first arrived in New York, four years previously.

Finally, things had come good for Netta. My no-nonsense, practical, say-it-like-it-is sister who had a girlish blush on that once wearied face, was practically skipping down the aisle as she hung off the arm of her new husband, Eric Pound, whose own smile was so wide I was concerned his face might split in two.

'You'd never think that man was the same grey, unobtrusive accountant who could hardly get a word in edgeways at Goldwyn Productions,' Aidan whispered into my ear. 'What has your sister done to him? Whatever it is, I'd like some of it.' He winked at me as we linked arms.

'Well,' I said as we turned and followed Netta and Eric down the aisle and towards the back of the church, 'it seems that hiking and spending Mr Pound's not unsubstantial fortune is their secret.'

Aidan stopped dead in the aisle. 'Don't be ridiculous. Falling in love on a canyon trail when you're in your fifties. No.' He shook his head, his eyes following the couple.

I shushed him as I pulled him along. 'If you'd bothered to come over on the same ship as us you'd have known all this beforehand, instead of insisting on gossiping at the back of the church. Just because you'd rather woo your men friends over a martini and caviar, doesn't mean to say that's what everyone else wants to do. Poor Eric, used to sitting at a desk more than twelve hours a day, dealing with the likes of Harold Finerman, looking at figures well into the night. It's no surprise that days out in the fresh air have turned him into someone entirely different.' I leaned into Aidan. 'To be honest, I find their constant chatter and incessant laughter quite exhausting. Sometimes I wish for the old Netta, always criticising. It's less wearing.'

'Don't be such a grouch.' Aidan play-punched my arm. 'I thought you were happy for them.'

'I am. I'm thrilled that she's decided to come back to live here.'

'Ah, now the truth comes out. You've had enough of the big bossy sister,' he said, giving me a sideways smile.

'Now, Aidan Cruickshank, I'm not rising to that,' I laughed.

Los Angeles couldn't keep Netta; the call from Edinburgh had finally been too strong, and she only agreed to marry Eric if he moved to Scotland with her. Delighted to find that he could move to colder climes, with a ready-made family in situ and grandchildren to bounce on his knee, he'd whooped with delight and declared himself a happily engaged man.

Now back in that freezing church in my home city,

watching those two happy people bobbing down the aisle as if they were twenty-one, I couldn't help but think of the stark contrast with Netta's first wedding – heavily pregnant, in her Sunday best, nerves and no smiles, she and Duncan standing stiff and upright, flowers from the park, only Maw and myself present, straight home after the service to pie and cake. Second time around, no expense had been spared, Netta almost regal in her green outfit, discreet flowers, a constant relaxed smile, always touching Eric on the hand, sleeve, knee. I'd never seen her so happy.

We waved Netta and Eric off in their outlandish Rolls-Royce, and now, with Jessica's hand in mine, my other on Aidan's arm, we walked back to our hotel.

Being in Edinburgh for the first time in twenty-eight years, I hardly recognised the places I used to frequent: Richmond Place that had once felt homely now appeared shabby and dirty; the haberdasher's on Cockburn Street, once so comforting, now gone and replaced with a sweet shop. With talk of war, everywhere felt nervy and even Jenners, the place that had soothed and comforted me, now seemed in limbo, unable to make up its mind. And finally, here we were at the North British, the hotel we'd found ourselves staying in.

As Oti took Jessica to get her tea, I slumped into a chair at the bar, desperate for a drink.

'Poor Eric,' I said as Aidan passed me my single malt. 'How was he to know Netta and I used to work here? What would he have thought of us if he'd seen our younger selves all red in the face and sweaty with our raw hands and our wild frizzed hair?' I looked around the bar with its views over the park. 'Until we arrived two days ago, I'd never been upstairs, never seen these rooms. We only ever worked in the three underground floors that housed the massive laundry, washing great vats of linen and uniforms for the hotel and all the trains that passed through. How could he have known that walking into a suite overlooking the Scott Monument, with four-poster beds, bathrooms and well-stocked bars was so improbable to Netta and me, so bewildering and unnerving, that neither of us could speak? Eric thought he'd committed some terrible faux pas, and it took all our powers of persuasion to reassure him that he couldn't possibly have us stay anywhere else.'

Aidan looked at me long and hard as he took a sip of his drink.

'So, tell me. What is the sister of the bride going to do with herself now? Will you be hightailing it back to New York, back to the fast-moving world of couture, back onto that merry-go-round of two collections a year, holed up in your studio, never seeing daylight, hiding from your high-society customers?'

'You make it sound like I'm a recluse,' I said as I lit a cigarette. I looked at its burning tip, feeling lethargic. It was as if the wedding had taken up all my energy and I was ready to collapse. I sipped my drink.

'This strange new Maisie,' I said with a sigh, leaning back in my chair, 'will hate it. The old Maisie, of course, would have loved it,' I added quietly.

'Who is this strange woman in front of me?' Aidan asked with a look of mock concern on his face.

I smiled. 'The whole experience with Mr Finerman seems to have shattered me, I've lost my taste for excitement, for the colour I love, for all that finery. I'm feeling like a forgotten rag doll that's been thrown into a corner, all limp and dusty.'

'I'm glad to see you haven't lost your taste for a bit of drama.' He leaned forward, grabbing my hand and squeezing it. 'But, my darling, you did a marvellous job today, if I hadn't known better, I'd have thought the old Maisie was back in town.'

I flopped my head against the back of the armchair, closing my eyes. I just wanted to curl up under a thick eiderdown and sleep. But I wasn't sleeping either. After a couple of hours, I'd be wide awake, sitting fully upright in bed, wondering what to do. To distract myself I'd start designing – sketching and drawing, but my designs were flat and I'd have to take myself out onto the dark streets of Edinburgh and walk briskly, clear my head and make myself tired enough to collapse into my bed and get a few hours of leaden sleep.

'What you need is a distraction,' Aidan declared. 'You need to do something completely different, and I think I've found the exact thing.' He sat up straight, beaming like some proud schoolboy who'd secretly gone and won the top prize but wasn't quite ready to reveal it to his parents. 'Be ready tomorrow morning at nine o'clock sharp. We're going on an adventure.'

Standing in the knitting room of a hosiery mill in Hawick in the Borders of Scotland, I was mesmerised: the hypnotic noise and the movement of the knitting frames, the cones of yarn jolting around, cashmere, lambswool, vicuña; the finishing rooms where rows of women were trimming, binding, linking and checking the finished items; the washing rooms where the men used large wooden paddles in huge vats of hot water to agitate the garments, the smell echoing those days at the North British; the drying room with racks and racks of underwear, pullovers, jackets and nightdresses; the extreme softness of the finished garments, softer than most because of the water from the River Teviot.

'Aidan, you've gotten me here under false pretences.' I leaned into his ear. He pulled back, winking at me, omitting to reply and wandered off to look at one of the machines.

For the first time in months, I was feeling a bubble of interest rise in me – my whole body alert, my brain beginning to come up with ideas, colours, patterns.

'Uh-oh,' Oti said as she walked towards me, a huge grin on her face. 'Praise the good Lord. I haven't seen that face for such a long time.' She grabbed me by my shoulders and almost shook me in her excitement.

'You've gone into one of your design frenzies, I can see it on your face.' She laughed. 'Aidan!' she called out. 'You were right, it's done the trick.'

I looked from Aidan to Oti and back. Our guide, Mr Farquharson, elderly in a shuffling way, wearing his brown warehouse coat, didn't seem to understand the laughter, seemed worried that he'd made some terrible mistake.

'Have you two been plotting behind my back?' I asked with mock outrage.

'My darling, someone had to sort you out, it was obvious you'd lost your get-up-and-go. Of course, Oti knew who to call. Aidan, your prime fixer, at your service,' he said, doing a sweeping bow.

I opened my mouth, but I couldn't speak.

'You see, Oti and I had been wondering where that ambitious, single-minded Maisie had gone, the one we all knew so well. Where did she go? The outspoken Maisie, the one who's a little too casual with the truth, a little too willing to overstep the mark. We were terrified you were on your way to being middle-aged and boring.' Again, he winked at me.

'So we decided to do something about it, and here we are.'

Amidst the noise, the shuffle of the knitting frames, the perplexed stare of Mr Farquharson, and the great smiles of my friends, my eyes started filling up. I blinked furiously, trying to push away tears. Unwillingly, I was being bombarded by the emotions of the last six years: the death of Tori, the humiliation after his funeral, the arrival of Netta, the birth of Jessica, the difficulties of running a business from the wrong side of the country, Annina's rape, leaving Los Angeles, the happiness of Netta's newfound love and marriage, the support of Oti and Aidan, of being back in my home country.

'Well, my sweet chicken,' Aidan said, taking me by the arm

and coaxing me away from the group. 'Let's not show our hand just yet. Let's pretend that you need to go away and have a good think about this. Let Mr Farquharson think that you're the weak link here and that I need to convince you that buying this company is a good thing. He believes you're my wife, and that the Mrs wears the trousers, that my job is to persuade you that this is a sensible idea.'

I took a deep breath.

'Oh no you don't.' Aidan put his chin up slightly and wagged his index finger at me. 'Not a word. You know this is a surefire thing, and so do I, we all do. The deal is as good as done. We just need your say-so.' He gave me a good hard stare, as if he was trying to dig the words out of me with his eyes.

'But who will run it? Who will run the business?' I asked.

'You, of course, with the help of Eric.'

'But he's retired, he doesn't want to do that,' I said, avoiding the real issue.

'Oh, don't you believe it. He couldn't be more excited. The man has been under the thumb of the Hollywood studios for far too long and finally he sees a project that he knows he can help make into something great. Look.' He took me into a corner where it was a little quieter. 'We have a war or we don't, either way this factory is going to be busy. If we don't have a war you'll be able to make the cashmere that you want, ship it out to Oti in New York and we can properly expand the ready-to-wear business, as well as give Oti some of the finest cashmere fabrics ever produced. If we do have a war, well, I suspect we'll be making uniforms or hosiery or something like that for as long as it takes, but if that's the case we'll make a killing. And when the war is over, you'll have all these ideas that have been stored up in that clever head of yours and you can storm the world with Maisie McIntyre's cashmere range.' He spread out his arms, like wings, his palms open. 'It's a win-win situation, Miss McIntyre, and I suggest you grab it with both hands immediately.'

'But what about you? Couldn't you stay and run it? I'm not sure that country life is for me,' I whined. Aidan was the fixer; this was a project that was more suited to his skills.

'Oh no. If my family find out that I've been back to Scotland I suspect they'll run me off to Timbuktu before I can pack my underwear. There are too many rumours about my lifestyle that don't suit them. I'm better off back in New York where I can hide in plain sight, doing my dark deeds in dark corners.'

'But where will I live?' I asked. Another stupid question.

He laughed. 'Funny you should ask that. I've also found you the perfect place that happens to be up for rent just now. It's a bit big, but I'm sure that won't be a problem, you can fill it with your Colour Emporium delights and shock the whole of Hawick with your outlandishly colourful designs.'

Six months later, Aidan had returned, and we were sitting in the dining room that I had turned into my workroom. A room filled with bolts of colourful fabric, two sewing machines, three tailor's dummies, two large worktables and a big pinboard covering one whole wall of the room, covered with cloth and knitted woollen swatches, buttons, brocading, a few ribbons and some sketches. A well-established fire kept the room warm.

'Your own personal studio,' Aidan said as he looked around him. 'Very Maisie McIntyre.' He turned back to me with a huge smile. 'See, I knew we'd get the old Maisie back.' A triumphant grin, chin slightly upturned, eyes narrowed in victory.

'All right, Mr Cruickshank. You were right. A little time away from the mess and mayhem in America has brought me back to myself, but I'm not entirely sure how much longer I'll last.'

'Oh, come on. You've only been here six months; you need to give it a little longer than that. Scotland needs to know that their finest living couturier is in town and intends to do great things.' He stood up and walked over to the window overlooking the garden. 'But I'm concerned,' he said less heartily. 'If you have no dining room, how can you be wining and dining the good and the great? Shouldn't you be holding great soirees to get to know your wealthy neighbours and your business rivals? Shouldn't I be hearing stories of wild parties, outrageous outfits and breakfast at dawn?' He turned to me, hands in his trouser pockets, a wry smile on his face.

I folded my hands on my lap. 'I've had my fingers burned by wild parties.'

'True.' Looking down at his feet he continued. 'I'm worried that you're taking life too seriously. You need to make the most of what you have just now. If war is on its way, things aren't going to be that much fun.'

'Well, it'll all be over by Christmas, that's the word on the street,' I quipped back in my best New York accent, not entirely believing the words that everyone was saying. In truth, I was worried that we were about to lose the colour in our lives, that everything would become drab and beige. I was beginning to wish I was returning to New York, that I could follow the threads that were gently pulling me back. But I couldn't, I had a job to do, and I needed to make sure it was done properly.

'So how does the textile community take to having a woman running the show in one of their larger mills?'

I twisted my mouth to one side, considering my answer. 'They're a bit wary, a little worried I have no idea what I'm talking about. I've learned to bring Eric with me whenever there are money discussions because they can't quite understand that I hold the purse strings, but what they aren't too pleased about is that I will insist on wearing trousers most of the time.'

He threw his head back and laughed aloud. 'Why on earth is that?'

'Women are not allowed to wear trousers in their mills and I, of course, have over-turned that rule in our mill because I don't want to be seen as a hypocrite. It seems I'm a troublemaker.'

'Glad to hear it. You wouldn't be Maisie McIntyre if you weren't up to no good. But tell me, how are the government contract negotiations going?'

I let out a long, frustrated sigh. 'Protracted. If war happens we will be forced into making hosiery for the military. But it seems our prices are too high and our quality is too good. The big mills in the Midlands can produce what the government want at greatly reduced prices with bigger gauge machines; we can't compete, but we must. If we don't take on the contract we won't be given access to yarn – it's that simple. The gun is to our head.' I leaned back in my chair and put my feet up on the table. 'I'm sure we'll come to some agreement but it's so time-consuming. Even Eric is exasperated by the whole thing, and we may have months more of this to go. Drink?'

Aidan snorted. 'It's that bad? I just mention the contracts and you turn to drink?'

Without replying, I got to my feet and went over to a small cabinet in one corner of the room, took out two glass tumblers and poured us both a single malt.

Handing Aidan his drink, I continued. 'Truth is, I'm feeling a little out of place. This is supposed to be my home country, but I've become used to the fast, easy ways of New York, to the warm, benign weather of California, I'm now accustomed to a variety in my diet and a diversity in the people I meet every day. Winter in the Borders of Scotland, in a house with rattling windows and no central heating, is trying. Cook insists on feeding me mulligatawny soup far too often because she feels that, since I've lived in a foreign country, I must like spicy food. And when I asked her whether she could make me a pomodoro sauce to go with some spaghetti, she looked at me as if I'd suggested we eat her children for supper. And on top of that, my housekeeper couldn't hide her initial horror at the colours

I've used in the house; I've been experimenting and have painted the walls with what she calls "dark and eccentric" shades. I sent fabric off to the local seamstress to be made in curtains; she was so scandalised by the bright and wildly patterned material, she almost refused to do the job.

'I'm a stranger in my own country.'

Aidan rolled his eyes. 'Still the perpetual drama queen.'

I grinned. 'You see, without you or Oti to keep me on my toes, I obviously lose my ability to see the lighter side of life. That's why I need to go back to New York. I'm not sure that hosiery lines and factory workers, country houses and tweed skirts suit me.'

'But look at you. All that fresh air and time with your daughter has made you all rosy-cheeked and blooming. No, I say you stay here, give that gorgeous daughter of yours a pony to ride and games in the garden. Make the most of a less complicated way of life and appreciate the beauty of all the nature out there.' He gestured towards the garden.

'Ha! Aidan Cruickshank, you wouldn't know a piece of nature if it hit you on the head.'

'Possibly true. However, talking of that gorgeous daughter of yours, where is she? I've missed her more than you can imagine.'

'She'll be down in the kitchen with Cook making you a cake – come on, let's go and find her. I'll give you a tour of the house on the way.'

I took him through the drawing room, parlour, and study before taking him upstairs, ending up in his own bedroom.

'Very bohemian. I can see why people are scandalised. You just need a set of Fiesta dinnerware and we'll be all set.'

I laughed, the first full belly laugh I'd had in months. 'How well you know me. I had a full set of that very same dinnerware sent over and Cook finds it distasteful. Far too much colour for her liking and she says it's cheap, which is true, but I like it. The good thing about cheap is it's not expensive to replace. Wedgwood, which I find a little staid, causes a scene when it's broken. Cook doesn't care if she breaks one of the Fiestas.'

'Sounds like you and Cook have a marvellous relationship.'

'Yes, it's one of mutual misunderstanding, but we seem to muddle along somehow.' I sighed.

'I get the feeling that you don't like playing lady of the manor. No headscarf and pearls for you?' Aidan teased.

'I'm saying nothing,' I said as we walked into the kitchen.

'Uncle Aidan!' Jessica yelled as she dropped her spoon into a large mixing bowl and ran over to him to give him a hug.

'Whoa, hold it there, little Miss Jessica. As much as I love you and am in need of one of those special Jessica Smyth hugs, I love my suit more and I need you to go over to the sink and wash those particularly sticky hands.' Aidan had stepped back and raised his hands in the air. 'This is a brand-new suit from Savile Row, it's on its first outing today. Buttery fingermarks won't be good for it.'

The suit was a perfect dark blue in a beautiful cashmere wool. As he ran his fingers down the sleeve I couldn't help but do the same on his other arm. Every piece of Aidan's clothing was exquisite and put me and my slightly worn woollen trousers and cashmere pullover to shame. Jessica had spent enough time with Aidan not to be upset or offended by his reaction and dutifully went to the sink and washed her hands. Presenting them to Aidan for inspection, he turned them over and then picked up Jessica and whirled her around shouting, 'And how is my favourite girl?'

She shrieked, he laughed, she giggled, and they both ended up in an ungainly hug and Eskimo kiss.

## Sister

Aidan stayed for three weeks, diligently working through every single detail of the business, how it might run whether we had a war or not, making contingency plans, deciding on the ratio of outerwear to hosiery, but when he wasn't working he kept Jessica busy, spoiling her with toys and ice cream, taking her to see Netta and her family.

'Are you sure you don't want to go and see your family?' I asked towards the end of his visit.

'Ooooh, no. I don't think that would be wise.'

After a busy day in the mill we were winding down over an early evening drink.

'Are you certain? I don't want you to get on that ship and have any regrets.'

He furrowed his brow, his head on one side. 'What makes you say that?'

I sighed. 'I'm finding that now I'm back here in Scotland, and perhaps because I'm now a mother and I want my child to know about her father, I've been wondering about my own father. What happened to him, why did he leave? Maw never, ever spoke about him. I was too young to know anything.

Netta always told me that Maw was better off without him. Is he dead or alive? Where did he go to? Is he still in Edinburgh? Maybe he never moved away, and was nearby the whole time, keeping an eye on us, making sure we lived a good life.'

'I think you'll find that I'm far better off without my family and they are better off without me. There are no regrets there.'

On Aidan's last day, with his bags packed and last-minute details finalised in the office, we had a few minutes to kill before we needed to leave for the train station. He was twitchy, unable to sit still, pacing up and down just like an expectant father, so I suggested a final walk through the factory to say his goodbyes.

His flamboyance almost brought the mill to a standstill as he kissed some of the girls, shook hands with the men on the knitting machines, chatted up the tea lady. As much as his constant presence had exhausted me and made me wish he was already away in America, I knew that we'd all miss him, his enthusiasm, his oblique ideas, his thirst for life.

In the linking room he chatted easily with Jack Lewis, who oversaw the linking and binding, eventually coming over to me, a query on his face.

'Who's that quiet girl beside Jack?' he asked, his voice full of curiosity. She was a slight woman with mousy-brown hair, straight and held back by a folded scarf, knotted at the nape of her neck. Her deep-blue eyes – strangely familiar – contrasted with her too-red lips and the dark circles under her eyes that spoke of sleepless nights.

'Maura Lewis. Jack's big sister.' I paused. 'Why do you ask?'

'She is the spitting image of you.' His words hung in the air between us. 'Any relation?'

'Not that I know of,' I said too easily, but now that I looked at her properly, now that he'd pointed it out, I could see the resemblance – the same dead-straight hair, the small, delicate hands, the way she held her shoulders. But she'd been so quiet, so easy to overlook, as if she'd been purposefully hiding in the shadows.

'Jack was telling me that he's expecting to be called up any minute. As a Territorial he'll be the first off.' He kept his gaze fixed on Maura. 'You know, she really could be your younger sister.' A heavy pause. 'Maybe your questions about your father could soon be answered.'

Those words echoed loudly in my ears as the implications of what he'd said sank in. I had to steady myself, feeling as if there was a shifting beneath my feet.

'Too much of a coincidence,' I replied a little more sharply than I intended. I checked my watch. 'We must go. I don't want you to miss your train. Hawick has had its fill of Aidan Cruickshank.' And I marched him through the front entrance and to my car. He gave me the warmest of hugs, so meaningful that I found my eyes filling with tears. We hung on to each other for too long. When would I see Aidan again – two months or two years? We all expected the war to be over quickly, but that had been said before. What would I do without his sharp wit, his brilliant brain, his immaculate dress sense and beautiful clothes, the way he could read my thoughts, and finish my sentences? In some ways we were so well suited, in others we were polar opposites. I gave an enormous sigh as he extricated himself from my lingering clutch.

'Now don't you dare get all sentimental on me, Miss Maisie McIntyre,' he teased, touching my cheek with a crooked finger, as if he was wiping a tear away. 'Remember, there's always the telephone. You can call me whenever you need, even if it's three o'clock in the morning my time.'

Telephone calls to America were hard work; the line crackled, the voices were distant, and you often had to shout to make yourself heard. I'd come off my weekly calls with Oti exhausted and frustrated, wishing I could simply find myself in our studio in Manhattan ready to talk, surrounded by the paraphernalia of couture, not sitting in a cold office encased by dark-wood panelling, earth-coloured tweeds and forest-green wool samples.

'I will sit in my colourful house with all my favourite things, reminding me that there is a colourful world out there. And when this war is over, I will jump on the first ship I can find. Hell, I might even jump on the Pan American Clipper service and see how hard a thirty-hour flight across the Atlantic can be. If Carmel Snow can do it, then so can I.'

'That's the spirit. That's the Maisie that I know.'

I saw Aidan off at the station like some forlorn, lovesick girl-friend. I had my handkerchief in my hand trying not to let the tears come again, feeling as if thick walls of fog were closing in on me and that my lungs were being stifled by poisonous gases. I shuddered, wiping my face with my hand and pushing away those negative thoughts, checking my watch and rushing to pick Jessica up from school, soothed by her soft, warm hand in mine, glad of her childish chatter and girlish laughter, as we made our way home.

One month after war had been declared and one month after the genial Jack Lewis had been deployed to France, I received a visitor at my office. Mr Les Lewis, father of Jack and Maura, appeared, red-eyed and puffy-faced, dressed in a rough brown jacket, buttoned at the front, a collarless shirt and trousers that bagged at the knees, falling below his paunchy stomach and shoes that could have benefitted from a dust-off. His hair had been wetted and was plastered across his head.

I asked him if he'd like a cup of tea and whether he'd like to sit down, perhaps he'd like a tour of the mill, see where his daughter worked. I don't think the old Maisie would have done this, I believe she would have cut to the chase and asked him what he wanted.

'I don't care where she works. It's you I want to see. It's Maisie McIntyre that I need to have a wee word with.'

The way he talked was unnerving, a little too familiar, as if he'd known me for years. I shifted in my chair.

'Well, Mr Lewis, what can I do for you?' I asked.

'So, Maisie,' he said, leaning back in his armchair as if he was in his own front parlour. 'It's about your sister.'

I frowned. 'What could you possibly want with my sister. She lives in Edinburgh; she wouldn't know you.' There was something about his expression that suggested smugness, the possession of knowledge that I had no notion of.

'Not that sister, your other sister.' He paused for effect, a gleeful provocation radiating from him. 'Maura.'

I put my palms calmly on my lap, made myself breathe. There was nothing about him that I recognised, nothing that pulled me to him, no paternal strings tugging at my heart.

'So, the penny drops. Your father is sitting here right in front of you. What a turn-up for the books, eh?'

Why was I so caught off-balance? That suspicion that Aidan had voiced, hadn't it been a joke? 'But...' I stuttered.

'But... how is it that I've risen from the dead? But... how is that we find ourselves sitting here, sipping dainty cups of tea? But... how is it that the infamous Maisie McIntyre finds herself lost for words?' His voice was bitingly unpleasant.

Quite suddenly, without fanfare or forewarning, a flash of memory, fuzzy and unformed – loud voices and unknown thuds heard through the thin walls, holding my sister in our makeshift bed, an unwanted fear. These fleeting images had followed my nighttime dreams throughout my life but, until now, I'd never understood what they were.

'What do you want?' I asked, keeping a façade of calm, pushing down that old fear.

'Isn't it obvious? I want the money, the equivalent of the one hundred and fifty pounds you stole. *My* money, money your maw was keeping from me, money she hid from me, money I risked all to get.'

My stomach dropped away; I had no idea that money had been my father's. I closed my eyes and thought of what my mother must have put up with, the repercussions of keeping that money from him, keeping up the lie.

I lit a cigarette, drawing so deeply I began to feel a little dizzy.

'Filthy habit, that. Dangerous in a place like this.' There was tangible vitriol in his voice.

I continued to smoke, drips of courage beginning to return with each drag as I started to consider what to do. I knew this man was a failure, a bully that had been thwarted by our maw. If she could do it, then surely so could I. Putting my feet up onto my desk, I feigned a nonchalance that I didn't yet feel.

'So, our maw kept the money from you,' I retorted with a bitter smile, feeling anger rising in my chest. 'I always knew she was a strong woman. But what about you? Seems like you ran away.'

'I had no choice, I had to leave.' He batted back his answer. 'You don't need to know the details. What matters is that you give it back, otherwise there'll be repercussions. Career-ending repercussions.

'I have it on good authority that you stole that money, never telling Netta, that you ran away, pretending to be a rich widow, lying and cheating your way into New York society, pretending to be someone you are not.'

I smiled at him, the kind of smile I'd learned in New York drawing rooms, the one that could cut like a blade. The evidence was long gone, the money spent, the old mourning dress sold. Let him dig all he wanted – he would never find proof of any of it.

'Mr Lewis. Is that your real name? Or is it McIntyre?'

'McIntyre.'

'Well, I think I'd rather call you Lewis.' I stood up and walked around to the other side of my desk, leaning on it so that I was towering over him.

'I will give you the equivalent of what was one hundred and fifty pounds forty years ago. In return you will never tell Maura who I am. You will leave today, right now.' My voice was rigid. 'I will drive you to your house, you will pack your bags, you will leave a goodbye note, I will drive you to the train station, buy you a ticket to wherever you want to go, and I will watch you leave.

'If...' I paused for effect, giving him my steeliest glare. 'If you *ever* dare return here, or tell Maura who I am, I will set the dogs on you.' I crossed my arms, my heart still racing.

We stared. Les Lewis's bravado wobbled slightly, he blinked, his mouth twitched.

I stood up and walked to the door. Opening it I put my head around the corner and said, 'Miss Brown, I'm just taking Mr Lewis back home and then I need to go into the bank. I'll be out for an hour or so.' I turned back to my office.

'So good of you to pop in and see me,' I said in my loud, efficient voice. 'So good to get to know you, Mr Lewis. I'll let Maura know you dropped by.'

As he stood up I took him by the elbow and walked him out of the room. Making our way to my car I said, 'Whilst you pack your bags I will go to the bank and get your money. Once I have seen you safely onto the train I will give it to you. And that, Mr Lewis, will be the last of it.'


Two hours later I stood on the platform of Hawick station and watched the train to Newcastle depart. Les Lewis and a brown envelope full of cash were on board.

As the train disappeared into the distance I lit a cigarette, my hands shaking. My bluster had been all show. A pretence of confidence and self-belief. If he knew about the stolen money, then there was a chance he could find out about the stolen fabric, about the lies I told on the ship to New York. Had he spoken to Netta? If I was exposed would it ruin me? Or would no one care?

I knew that he would return, I knew that he was not a man to pass up the opportunity to extort more money out of me. It had been too easy; I had given in without a fight. But, in the meantime, I could fill up my armoury and be ready to retaliate.

By 1943, with four years of war under our ever-tightening belts, we were all tired, hungry and perpetually anxious. We were sick of the lack of food, fed up with clothes rationing and just as Aidan had predicted, I was bored, not just by war and its deprivations but by the monotony, by the argument over whether we had eggs or porridge for breakfast, no longer cannoli or bagels, the lack of colour in our food, in our clothes, even in our conversation. The hush of the countryside would bang at my eardrums, and I longed for the reassuring discordant cacophony of Manhattan, my only way to counteract that silence being to walk the factory floor and let myself be bombarded by the clatter of the knitting machines. My life was so distant from that in New York: a life of gowns made from yards of silk, my favourite rich, luscious duchess satin, bead-encrusted jackets and the perfect finish of a couture gown; now we were reduced to trousers patched at the knee, faded shirts with turned collars, shoes lined with newspaper.

Putting colour into our days became an obsession. Far away, in New York, Oti and Annina were creating couture, still able to get hold of colourful fabrics, still finding demand for bespoke gowns. But in Hawick, in Scotland, we were suppressed by a severe shortage of fabric, we had no time or energy for embellishments. My own wardrobe became muted, full of flannel and tweed, my designs so dull that I could no longer imagine a life where we dressed in shimmering satins or heavily brocaded silks, beaded bodices or sequined belts. Once I'd described the evening gown as an opportunity for its wearer to blossom, now, in our grey wool suits, we were being made to wither.

Whereas designers such as Hardy Amies and Digby Morton threw their energies into designing uniforms for the women's services and the government-controlled utility clothing, I couldn't bring myself to embrace this new world of fashion with heavy regulations and limited choice. Looking back now, I had no right to criticise those garments which were masterpieces of invention in the face of severe shortages.

But colour could be found in unlikely places. Our twice weekly Make Do and Mend session, held in an outhouse next to the factory, gave us the opportunity to make clothes for the evacuees, patch up existing threadbare garments for ourselves, and use blackout material to make trousers, coats and shorts for the children. We were a group of misfit women making a round of misfit clothing using many of the leftover upholstery fabrics I had from the Colour Emporium and any Maison McIntyre material I had brought with me from New York.

We would patch schoolboys' trousers and our own work clothes with colourful squares of gaberdine, wool and cotton, turning Hawick's population into a troop of elegant tramps. We lengthened trousers with purple wool, let out skirt waistbands with patterned linen, patched up jacket elbows with fuchsia-pink corduroy.

Every Tuesday and Thursday evening a group of around ten of us would meet, making use of some of the older sewing machines from the factory, some spare tables and any fabric we could get our hands on.

There was Janice, mother of four boys, perpetually harassed, hair falling out of her bun, cheeks flushed, eyes too bright, always working on a wretched pile of boys' clothes, always recounting the latest mishaps, knee scrapes, fights, football scores, mother-in-law snipes and the noise that four boys under the age of twelve can produce.

Then came Mrs Elliot, a sixty-something, sturdy widow in a uniform of thick tweed skirts, with impenetrable skin-coloured, heavily darned stockings, and solid brown, lace-up brogues: a woman who couldn't sew, usually breaking a needle, creating a bird's nest of a mess with precious thread, but a lonely woman who needed these sessions as much as the evacuees needed their patched clothing.

Evie, our newest recruit, was quiet and unobtrusive, her skin sallow from working in the munitions factory, a talented seamstress who worked hard to clothe her three children, despite appearing to only be in her teens. She'd marvel at the colours she was being allowed to use, quietly rebelling against a husband who would have disapproved but was in Africa and hadn't been heard from for months.

And then there was Joan, always running late, always arriving breathless and dishevelled, always apologising.

'Sorry, sorry, sorry. Why can I never be on time for anything? You'd never believe it, my mam's dog got stuck in the outside lav – we couldn't open the door and it was whining and barking and sending the neighbours round the bend. I had to climb up on the roof and peel away some of the corrugated iron to get in so that I could undo the door from the inside. God knows how he got in there *and* locked the door!'

Joan's stories always made everyone laugh, would always suck out any bad air in the room. At twenty-one, she revelled in the freedom of volunteering for the WVS.

'Best uniform a girl could have,' she'd declared her first day in the service. 'I got two new suits, blouses and an overcoat, I've never had such good quality clothes, designed by none other than Mr Digby Morton himself! And look at these shoes; I've never owned a pair of shoes that didn't belong to someone else beforehand. When I put these on I knew that I was the only person to have *ever* worn them. God they hurt my feet for three weeks, but I didn't care, they were brand new!'

'Joan, I've left several pairs of trousers for you to make up at your usual machine,' I said. 'Mrs Elliot, can you take them with you this evening?'

'Yes, dear, of course I can,' she roared from her machine. 'Oh, hell and damnation, this fabric's too slippery for me. Can someone come and help me get out of this jam?'

Margaret, one of the four land girls billeted with Jessica and me, went to her rescue.

And finally, there was Maura.

'You said you might have some buttons for me.' She'd quietly sidled over to my side, a little glimmer of excitement in her eyes.

'Let me see,' I said, riffling through an old carpet bag filled with threads, buttons and as many embellishments as I could bring from home. These items were now highly sought after and mostly used to help disguise rips, tears and stains on old clothes that needed a bit of love and cheer.

'Here you go. I found these at home,' I lied, omitting to tell her that I'd asked a local potter to make them especially. 'The deep, shiny black will stand out against the red.' I handed over the eight oval buttons, two for each cuff and four for the front opening.

She held one of the buttons against her mother's old red coat that had needed considerable taking in, inspecting it as if it were a piece of gold. A shy smile spread across her face. 'Thank you.'

Since that day when her father had declared that she was my sister, I'd found myself keeping a close eye on her, nurturing her sewing skills, giving her more responsibility at work, trying to get a little closer. Even though her father had left and she was free of his influence, there was something fragile about her that

I couldn't put my finger on. I often wondered whether I should tell her about our father, that I should come clean about who he was, but I was wary about doing any further damage – she so rarely opened up, almost never joining in the girlish, joking conversation, never giving away any detail of her life outside of the mill. I brooded over what it was that kept her so buttoned up. Her brother, Jack, who used to work in the linking room, had left at the beginning of the war and hadn't been seen since, captured in Dunkirk, now languishing in discomfort somewhere in Germany. But after four years of working in the mill and these evenings that cushioned us for a few brief hours from the hardships outside, she had changed, become more confident and I didn't want her to lose that. In the mill she was one of the more competent workers; I'd done my best to give her the more interesting projects, begun to ask her opinion on new lines that we were trying out, brought her in on future planning meetings. In the evening Make Do and Mend sessions she'd become a skilful seamstress with a good eye for line and shape and I noticed that whenever she produced a finished garment for one of the evacuee children, she'd stand up straighter, her eyes would sparkle, and her voice would have more strength.

'You going to wear that to the dance next Friday?' asked Fanny, another of the girls who worked in the mill. 'You'd make a grand entrance in that, that'd be sure,' she said, envy running through her voice.

Maura blushed. 'Wouldn't that be a thing,' she said wistfully, but then looked down and quickly picked up the buttons and went back to her seat, threaded a needle and purposefully concentrated on her work.

Fanny, a robust, big-chested girl, rolled her eyes at me and mouthed the words 'Her father,' before going back to her own sewing.

Her words brought me up sharply. I frowned at Fanny.

'Her father?' I mouthed back at her.

She nodded with a grimace.

I retreated to my sewing machine, my heart slamming against my chest, my colour rising as I thought what to do. Les Lewis was back? Oh, why hadn't I told Maura about him? I put my hands on the sewing machine, steadying myself. I had planned for this day, I was ready, wasn't I? Quickly I made three pairs of shorts from a heavy curtain material Mrs Elliot had brought with her that evening, the rhythm of the machine soothing me, my plan ready and in place.

At the end of our two hours, all the women tidied up their work either giving any finished children's garments over to Mrs Elliot or taking their unfinished projects home. Joan rushed to get out, shouting her goodbyes from the street whereas Maura lingered, her frame shrinking as she slowly and purposely folded her fabric, overly careful as she put needles back in their packet and absently winding any loose thread onto its reel, as if she was trying to slow time down.

Suddenly the door burst open and in ran Jessica.

'Mummy!' She gave me a perfunctory hug before rushing over to Maura causing the physical shrinking to temporarily reprieve.

'Little Jessica,' Maura breathed, 'where did you come from?'

Jessica giggled. 'You know where. I've been at my friend Jenny's. I go there every Tuesday after school and have my tea. She's a much better cook than Mummy or Mrs Shaw.' She said this, rubbing her tummy. 'I love Tuesdays.'

Jessica, now nine years old, had lost her Californian accent and now had a slight Borders burr, making her seem softer, a little more serious. A life spent outdoors had transformed her into a vivacious, confident girl who was very happy in her own company, always willing to learn, albeit occasionally a bit of a know-it-all, always willing to tell me in great detail about the bugs, birds and animals she'd discovered at home or school.

Watching Maura with my daughter, I could see a hint at

family resemblance: the slightly snub nose, the rounded jaw, the furrow in her brow. Maura's face would light up in the same manner as Netta's when in the company of children, taking away the darkness in her eyes.

'I'm sure Jenny's mother is very happy to feed you when we send you over with a dozen eggs every week, whatever's available from the garden and even some of that sugar that Aidan included in his latest food parcel,' I teased.

'Oh, Mummy,' she shrieked with delight, 'she made a cake! It was soooo delicious.' Her lips pursed as if she was whistling, lingering on the long 'o'. 'A Victoria sponge with just a smidge of raspberry jam. I could have eaten it all. Can we go home for supper now? I'm starving.'

When Jessica first smiled at me in those early days of Hollywood, it brought her father to me so strongly it caused a deep physical pain that took my breath away. Over time, she'd grown into the image of her father: the way her blue eyes flashed and twinkled with amusement, the little twist of her head, a mannerism you would have thought could only have been instilled by the presence of the man himself. That sharp pain had, slowly, turned into light tendrils, like an indigestion that crept along my chest. One day, as I received another hug from my daughter, her laughter bubbling against my shoulder, I realised that the constant background pain had vanished, having been replaced by a fierce love for this small child who astounded me each day with her ability to see beauty in our increasingly gloomy world. She taught me how to see the detail in the muted colours of the wildlife in our garden: the neat, scaly pale fringes on the tail feathers of the drab female pheasant, the shimmering purple and blue chest feathers of the black pheasant that reminded me of the shimmer of that peacock-blue material I stole from Jenners. She showed me that there can be flashes of colour and beauty in a world of camouflage.

On good weather days, Jessica and I would cycle into

Hawick – petrol rationing dictating that we couldn't use the car every day. But on Tuesdays and Thursdays we always drove into town. I'd bring any fabrics, threads, buttons and embellishments needed for the Make Do and Mend session, we'd bring in food for Jenny's family and I could also give a lift to Maura, who lived on our route to the mill.

'Ready to go, Maura?' I asked, trying to keep a façade of normality as I watched her shrink, a hang-dog expression enveloping her.

The journey to Maura's house was less than five minutes. The once shabby, two-up, two-down terrace on the edge of the town had been slowly improved over the four years since Maura's father – my father – had left. She'd painted the door, replaced the putty in the leaking windows, put new curtains in the front room and dug up the overgrown front garden and planted it with vegetables.

'Thanks for the lift,' Maura said.

But just as she went to open the car door I said, 'I need to tell you something, something I should have told you ages ago.' Why hadn't I told Maura before, why didn't I tell her the night her father left? My heart was racing, I didn't want to be here, I wanted to run away and not have to face this... what was this? I turned the light on inside the car.

'We're sisters. Your father is my father.'

She looked at me with disbelief, confusion knitted across her brow, the yellow light giving her face an eerie quality.

'I have no recollection of him, he left when I was very young. But I think he used to beat my mother and I think he used to beat you.' She blinked but said nothing. 'I don't want that to happen again. He's come back because he wants money from me. He left my mother because he'd stolen money from a gang of men who he should never have stolen from. The kind of men who break your legs if you don't do as they ask.'

She swallowed. 'How do you know this?'

'After our father left I made some discreet enquiries. He's done a good job of keeping low but it seems that perhaps my queries have stirred up some long-held bad feeling. And' – I winced – 'I may have made a phone call just before we left this evening.'

She frowned. 'How do you know people like this? You're a couturier, a factory owner. You don't mix with those kinds of people.'

She was right. How had I ended up mixing with thieves and fraudsters? It was simple – Aidan. The man who somehow knew every corner, every level of life, who knew where to find out every single piece of information needed.

'You don't want to know.' I sighed. 'But we need to get you inside, get your bags packed and you're coming to stay for a few days. We need you out of harm's way.' I was beginning to shake.

'Mummy,' came a quiet voice from the back of the car. 'Are some nasty men coming?'

My stomach heaved. I had almost forgotten that Jessica was in the back of the car, she'd been so still and quiet. I rubbed my face, ran my hands through my hair and took a deep breath, turning around to look at her properly.

'Yes. So we're going to help Maura pack her bags in double quick time and she's going to come and stay for a while. While you pack, I'll talk to her father, make sure he understands that he needs to leave.'

Her eyes were wide, her face pale. 'Is he my grandfather?'

My too sharp, intelligent daughter. What was I doing involving this innocent girl in all of this... this sordid affair?

'Sort of.' I picked up her hand and squeezed it. 'Don't worry. We're going to run into the house, pick up what's needed and as soon as you've packed the bags we'll be out of there and back home in a flash. Okay? You ready?' I gave her my best smile. 'Ready, Maura?'

'Ready,' came the simultaneous answers.

. . .

Forty minutes later we arrived home. We lugged in Maura's bags and were greeted by the smell of mutton stew.

'I'm starving,' said Jessica, running off to the kitchen.

'Me too,' I said. Mutton stew was not my favourite, but rationing was so severe that there was little that I now found unappetising.

'Do you seriously think he's gone for good?' Maura asked, putting her bags at the bottom of the stairs.

'Yes. I think so,' I said as I walked into the drawing room and poured us both a glass of whisky.

'Was it true about those men?'

'Well...' I drew out the word, then taking a sip of my drink. 'Parts of it.'

She grinned. 'Maisie McIntyre, always embellishing the truth.'

I laughed. 'That's exactly what Oti would have said.' I looked at her with my head on one side. 'Perhaps there's a little bit of Oti's strength in you. We could all do with a little bit of Oti.'

'I'd like to meet her,' Maura said quietly, sitting on the sofa.

'Oh, you'd loooove Oti,' Jessica declared at the top of her voice as she ran into the room. 'She's loud, she's funny, she tells naughty jokes and she's black.' Jessica sat herself on Maura's lap and took Maura's face in both hands, staring into her eyes. 'Have you ever met a black person?' Her voice was full of earnestness. 'Because I haven't seen anyone like that since Oti was here for Netta's wedding. Did you know I was only five years old then. And tomorrow is my birthday; I'm going to be ten. Double figures! Will you come to my party on Saturday?' Jessica jumped off Maura's lap and almost shivered with excitement. 'Oh, oh, you can meet the rest of your new family.

There's Ava and her sister Carla, and then there's all my cousins...' She began listing them on her fingers.

For a moment Maura looked panicked, as if the idea of a new family was terrifying, as if she didn't know what she'd do with them. But quite suddenly her face exploded into a smile, a huge, disarming smile, just like that of her good-looking brother, a smile I'd never seen on her before.

'I *will* come to your party, *and* I can wear my new red coat.'


After dinner, after both Jessica and Maura had taken themselves to bed, I wasn't ready to sleep. I was restless, my mind in a spin, running through the events of the evening, worrying whether my father would leave for good, whether he'd ever return, whether Maura was safe, Jessica... Netta. I sighed at the thought of Netta, who I still hadn't told about the stolen money, who I was too afraid to tell. All her anger and bitterness had disappeared since her marriage to Eric and I didn't want it to return, I didn't want to lose her friendship again.

I poured myself another whisky and wandered through the house, unable to settle, until I came into the hallway and found a letter on the side table addressed to me.

When I saw the handwriting my heart almost stopped and I had to catch my breath. It was from Joseph. I hadn't heard from Joseph since I'd left America, he had never written me a letter the whole time I'd known him. When I'd last seen him in New York, he'd been stiff and awkward with me, only talking work, hardly meeting my eye.

Carefully I opened the envelope and pulled out the letter. His neat, precise handwriting matched the way he worked, just like his workshop, just like the way he did his embroidery.

*27 127th St*
*Harlem*
*March 2nd 1943*

*Dear Maisie*

*Oti has been nagging at me to write, and you know when Oti gets into one of her moods, she won't give up. I could say I'm writing this to save myself from her constant badgering, but that wouldn't be entirely true. I feel it's time I came clean and put aside my pride.*

*I couldn't face you. You who led such a busy life, who were so successful, who had everything. Me, who was in a wheelchair, who was half the man you used to know, who had nothing to give you. But it's been over twenty years and, as Oti says, I've got more to give than most, I've had a better life than most and it's time for me to stop being, in Oti's words, 'a darned idiot'.*

I put the letter down onto the side table and finished my glass of whisky and with a huge sigh I put my head in my hands.

———

I was in my office, Maura and I discussing schedules, deliveries, wool supplies, when Miss Brown burst in with the news.

'It's done. It's over. The war in Europe is over!' And as she said this I heard whoops and shouts and cries coming from the factory floor. She rushed over to me, this buttoned-up woman, always so strait-laced and sober, gave me a tight, meaningful hug, kissed Maura on the cheek and then blushed at her own boldness. 'Oh, miss, this is so...' She couldn't find the words, she was shaking so hard.

Laughing, I said, 'Tell everyone they must go home. We

can't possibly do any more work today, I'm sure they're ready to celebrate.' She ran out the room, but I shouted after her. 'And tell them they can come in late tomorrow!'

Maura and I stared at each other. We should have been jumping up and down, dancing with joy, but instead I felt empty. We'd become so used to living a half-life, ragged and skinny, cold and colourless, it had become normal, and I could hardly remember what it felt like to eat too much, to indulge in an overly hot bath, or to eat a tooth-achingly sweet cake and feel a little sick afterwards.

I pulled a cigarette out of its packet and offered one to Maura and, leaning back in my seat, put my feet up on the table and closed my eyes. If Oti were here, she would have made me get up, would have given me that Jackson smile that I so missed, and insisted on me revelling with everyone else. I heard shrieks and hollers outside. Smiling, I thought of the mischief small boys would be getting up to that night, assuming their parents were too distracted to bother with punishing petty pranks, thinking cuffed ears would be missed out on in favour of a few beers and a good old sing-along.

'I don't think I can face all that jollity,' I said, opening my eyes, seeing the water stain on the ceiling, ugly blotches that matched my mood.

'Me neither,' came the response.

We both sat smoking, saying nothing, listening to the distant sounds of joy. I wanted that elation to seep into me, but my body felt like a barrier, a brick wall shutting out the euphoria. I felt flat, willing myself to be happy, wishing myself into a positive frame of mind.

'Tell you what. How about a drink? I think we're allowed to, don't you?' Without waiting for an answer, I pulled open the bottom right drawer of my desk and brought out a bottle of whisky and two glass tumblers.

We chinked our glasses together. 'To life without war. To a colourful life without war.'

The whisky slowly made its way down my throat. As it made its way downwards, it seemed to open an old door that had been sealed shut, and I began to see flickers of colour in my mind, hear whispers of rustling fabric, the chink of a heavy belt buckle, the titters of beads as they rolled across a table. Suddenly I felt as if I was glowing, fizzing, as if there was a bubbling under my skin. My face flushed; my heart began to beat too fast. I sat up.

'Are you all right?' Maura asked. 'You look strange, you have this weird expression on your face. It seems as if you're about to take off, like some aeroplane.'

I laughed, too hard, almost manically. I grabbed a pencil, some paper and began to sketch. 'Can you pass me the coloured pencils?' I asked, without looking up, drawing as fast as I could.

'Which colour?'

'All of them, I need them all,' I said, like some greedy child. I could hardly breathe. I grabbed one colour after another, adding extra details with each one.

'Look,' I said, showing her the drawing, talking too fast. 'A cardigan, much like the ones we used to produce. Made from cashmere, as soon as we can get hold of it. Crew neck, with buttons on the front. But the buttons will be made from Murano glass, each one will be a different colour. And the placket tape on the neck and button seams will be a vibrant, contrasting colour to the cashmere. So, if this cardigan is dark blue, the placket tape will be bright pink, or if the cashmere is cream, the tape will be turquoise, so you'll get flashes of colour when you move.

'The glass beads will be especially commissioned and then, perhaps, we can produce a range of Murano glass bead necklaces, earrings and maybe even rings and bracelets, that would all match the buttons on the cardigans. What do you think?'

Maura held her neck with one hand, her mouth slightly open.

'I've never seen you like this.'

'I haven't been like this for years,' I almost yelled. 'This is what I should be like, this is how I am.'

'Maisie McIntyre, let off her leash,' she laughed, standing up. 'This *is* a cause for celebration. I'll go and get Jessica and I'll meet you at my house for dinner. It'll probably be Spam, but I'll see if I can find some sugar and we can make a cake. By the time you've finished here the cake will be made and supper will be ready.'

She skipped out of my office whilst I poured myself another drink. It was as if someone had taken the lid off my coffin, had let the air in and given me life all over again. I smiled to myself, looking forward to dinner, to tomorrow, to the next few months.

But as I put the bottle down on my desk I suddenly felt dizzy and lost my balance, falling onto the side of the desk. Picking myself up, I was still lightheaded, a little nauseous, I couldn't stand. Crawling to my chair, with a huge effort I pulled myself onto the seat, twisting to sit down. The room seemed to swerve at an angle, my legs felt unruly, the queasiness continued.

## Chapter Nine

### The Final Suit

*A two-piece suit made from a heavy dark-blue slubbed silk. A mid-calf straight skirt lined with red silk, a long-line single-breasted jacket with bright-red silk double cuffs, frog buttons and mandarin collar.*

*From the personal collection of Ms Maisie McIntyre.*

# Joseph

## 1958

I wish I could wear the trouser suit that I wore to Tori's funeral. I feel it's as relevant now as it was then. But even I know that it wouldn't be fair on Joseph and that I should wear something that won't call attention to me, that will let me be stylish but discreet; I have learned my lesson.

My black suit is hanging on the wardrobe at the other side of the room. My silk slip, underwear and stockings have been laid out on the sofa beside it. But that part of the room seems a long way off just now and, as I stand, I look around for my stick. Nowadays there are fewer and fewer days when I can make it across the room without it, a beautiful bone-handled ebony stick that will match the mood of the day. Stick in hand I shuffle to the other side of the room, my legs feeling heavy and sluggish, and I eventually make it to the sofa where I let myself fall onto the cushion, taking a few deep breaths to recover. Getting dressed has become a daily chore. Gone are the days when I could just throw on a dress, slide into a pair of heels and run out of the door, at my desk by six a.m., happily designing and ready to face the day, as long as I had a black coffee to accompany me.

I'm craving that black coffee.

Today is Joseph's funeral and the weight of our misaligned relationship sits heavily on me. His decline began eighteen months ago, and finally, inevitably, when he slipped away last week, it felt as if part of a weathered cliff had fallen away, a shocking gash in the landscape left behind. Despite a fifteen-year correspondence, ignited by that first letter received after saying goodbye to my father, we never fully made our peace, both of us too proud to face our inabilities, too ashamed of our inadequacies. Now I must close the door on Joseph Jackson, knowing I can no longer mend the tears in our differing fabrics.

'Good morning, Miss McIntyre,' I'm greeted by the always cheerful Mandy.

'Do you stand at the other side of the door and wait for the noise of my movement, so that you can make sure you come into the room just at the time I need you?' I ask, trying to keep any trace of annoyance out of my voice. Despite the intrusion that I often find so frustrating, because I don't like talking to anyone first thing in the morning, and because I quite like my own company and don't find the need to constantly have people around me, I have become fond of this woman who has the uncanny ability to appear exactly when required and disappear just when I feel the need to be alone. It's as if she can read my thoughts. She's unlike so many of those other helpers, who would talk at me as if I was deaf or stupid, often shouting, often talking in the third person. Their soft, sensible shoes irrationally infuriate me, simply because they remind me of their patronising way of speaking. I'm old, not stupid. Just because I can't walk as well as I'd like to, doesn't mean I've lost the ability to think or reason; I'm still able to have an opinion and decide what's best for me.

But it's that grumpy old woman talk that I've had to learn to keep in my head, the crinkling of my brow that I must smooth out and simply take a breath instead, count to ten. I've realised that life without Mandy would be dull and uninteresting. She's become my legs on the days when they don't want to work properly, and those days are becoming more frequent.

She ignores my question probably because she understands I don't want to know the answer. 'Here's your coffee.' She hands me the cup and sits beside me on the sofa. She knows she won't get me to do anything until I've drunk at least half of it.

'Looks like it's gonna be a beautiful day. I always think a funeral goes off much better when the weather's good. Seems like God has decided that he wants that person to have a good send-off, wants everyone who's made the effort to come along to have as smooth a day as possible and won't have to worry about getting wet.'

I take a long sip of my coffee, thankful that she's learned how to make a decent cup. 'Maybe I should order a good thunderstorm for my funeral. Seems like I've managed to upset a lot of people on the way, might as well make one last hurdle for them, remind them that I was a cantankerous old woman to the last.'

She snorts. 'I'd like to see that.' And she bursts out laughing, her laugh so infectious that my whole body starts shaking.

'Oh, now, honey, don't you go ruining those beautiful silk pyjamas.' She leans over and takes the cup off me as I throw my head back and roar with laughter, tears filling my eyes.

'There'd be some soggy skirts, bedraggled hats and ruined silk. What a revenge that would be!' And just as quickly as the laughter arrived, it disappears, and I realise that I'm being an old fool.

'Don't suppose Oti would appreciate it that much,' I say soberly. 'The older she gets, the fussier she's become about her appearance. I wouldn't like to be Audrey today; she and her sister never did get on that well.'

Mandy says nothing.

'D'you manage to get much sleep last night?' she eventually asks.

I sigh. 'Not much. My legs were throbbing like they had a pneumatic drill on them half the night. I know the best thing is to rest them up, but when they're behaving like that I just want to get up and go for a long walk, which is no good, because I can't. So, instead, I sat up and did a whole load of sketches. I'll send them on to Jessica when I'm happy with them. She'll probably throw them in the waste, but at least I'll feel as if I've done something useful.'

'Well, don't forget you've got an appointment with the doctor in a couple of days, maybe he can give you something for the sleeping.'

Now that I've drunk most of my coffee, I'm feeling a little less cranky, and I let Mandy help me get dressed. The black suit is from a few years ago, the one I always wear to funerals, made from black worsted wool. The jacket has a Peter Pan collar and is nipped in at the waistline. It's single-breasted but becomes double-breasted just below the waist. Oti wants us all to wear something that honours Joseph, so I've changed the buttons on the jacket, specially made ceramic buttons that show off the buildings that Joseph loved the best: the Dakota, Empire State, Chrysler and nine others. They're highly stylised, painted white with slim black brushstrokes showing the outline of each structure. You'd have to lean in to really notice what's on each button, each one the shape of the relevant building, not too big to be brash, but big enough to be obvious. Eight buttons on the front of the jacket, two on each cuff. And, as a nod to Joseph's brilliance with embroidery, I've added a 'J' on the front of each cuff, in black and gold metallic thread with jet beading.

As I struggle with the buttons on my jacket and look at myself in the mirror, I feel an unexpected sorrow, a nostalgia for those days in my first studio, for the daffodils Joseph brought

me, for those walks around Manhattan, as he used to show me
the architecture of New York, for the time when he took my
cold hands in his and blew on them, for the optimism and
certainty. Those were the days when I was fearless, ruthless,
ambitious and without much care for anyone else. Part of me
wishes I could still be like that, the other part of me knows that
cannot be. I learned through Oti and Joseph and all the women
I worked with that we need to help each other and we are all
better off for it.

Using my stick, I walk slowly from my bedroom through to
the kitchen. Mandy has made me another cup of coffee and I sit
at the table. The latest *Vogue* magazine is waiting for me, but I
don't have the heart for it today. Mandy sits opposite me.

She's spent the last year looking after me, working six days a
week, living in and only going home to her family on Mondays.
I always tell her she needs to spend more time with her children, she always tells me, with a glint in her eye, that I'm just
like the pot calling the kettle black and that she's quite happy
here, bossing me about. Mandy has come to understand my
every mood; she keeps people away when I haven't the energy
and has come to realise that I don't like to be fussed over, that I
want to keep up the pretence of independence. Her care has
made it possible for me to continue my work. If it weren't for
her I would have retreated into my shell, I would have become a
hermit, never leaving my apartment, never seeing anyone.
Mandy, much like Oti, is not only able to counteract my mood,
but has discovered what gets me up in the morning – a decent
cup of coffee and the best Italian food in Manhattan.

This morning, Mandy has brought me cannoli, the very best
cannoli from the Italian delicatessen a few blocks away. She
knows I have a weakness for these. Usually, she brings them
when she needs me to do something for her. Today I suspect
they're to give me strength for the day ahead. Normally my
breakfast is three cups of black coffee and that's it, but my love

for these pastries is illogical; I don't like cream or cheese, and I rarely eat sweet things. I take a bite, savouring the crisp crunch of the deep-fried dough perfectly complementing the slight lemon flavour of the whipped ricotta.

I feel tears prick at the back of my eyes. I used to hide this when it happened, but I know that Mandy will not comment, that she'll understand what's going on in my head.

This food, this food... made with such love, that has so much resonance with me, brings Rosa right to me, even though it's forty-seven years since she left us. When I feel her, I stop and close my eyes, picturing her gently chiding me for not putting enough weight on, for working too hard. And she reminds me that there is love to be found in everything that surrounds us.

'I hope you bought enough so that you could have one or two,' I say, as I manage to gather myself without my voice breaking.

'Oh, don't you worry, I've already had plenty.'

There's a knock at the door and then we hear it open.

'Mum,' calls out Jessica. 'You up?'

Mandy and I look at each other and both roll our eyes at the same time.

'Oh, here you are,' Jessica says breathlessly. 'Look at you, up bright and early.'

I resent her positive and too-breezy tone, her 'Mum's the patient and I should treat her as such' voice, but I know it's just a defence against a sadness that continually follows her.

'All dressed and ready for action right on time.' I make myself mirror her merry attitude, wishing I could take away that melancholy.

Mandy looks at me, narrowing her eyes in a warning manner, before she stands up and says, 'Good morning, Miss Jessica. Would you like one of your mother's favourite cannoli?' And without waiting for a reply, she finds another plate and places it on the table, next to the box of pastries.

Jessica, as predicted, says, 'Oooh, I'd better not. Got to watch what I eat.'

I barely recognise the Jessica that has grown up in this fast and unforgiving city, so different from the girl I brought back from Scotland. That Jessica lived her life with an open heart, with an abandon that used to take my breath away: that girl that revelled in the outdoors, the mud and the grass, the birds and the horses, wanting nothing more than to feel the wind on her cheeks.

Now she moves through life with a carefully constructed precision, her make-up perfect but severe, living her life mechanically, according to the rules of the increasingly impossible standards of the industry she works in. The fashion world both praises her and punishes her, every success taking away a bit of that little girl who showed me where to find beauty in the murk and cloud, removing that Tori Smyth smile that used to halt me in my tracks every time she used it.

I worry that she's trying too hard to prove herself, to live up to her mother's reputation. But I never wanted her to take on my legacy. She has my eye for beauty but not my resilience. There are days when she lets her armour drop and I catch glimpses of her exhaustion and my heart aches for what should have been, for the life she should have lived. But I have to find the positives and she's recently married an architect, of all things, who has begun to bring out the old Jessica, lets me catch flashes of that free spirit.

Before I can ruminate any further there's another knock at the door and Netta, Eric, Maura and Annina all appear together.

If Rosa Bassino had reached her fifties, she'd have looked just as Annina does now – soft, motherly, with those kind crinkles around her eyes. She's so changed from the girl who came to Hollywood with me, all brash and ambitious. Motherly she may look, but the worst of Harold Finerman made sure she'd never have children. Instead, the couture business has become her much-loved child, every woman who works there her ward, every dress that leaves the building sent off with the kind of fanfare a mother would give her graduate leaving home. She has made Maison McIntyre into a business full of love *and* colour.

Netta and Eric, now married for twenty years, have grown rounder and happier in the company of each other. Where Netta once appeared drawn and hassled, at seventy-one she now blooms. It's rare that a smile leaves her face, she's still so surprised that the second half of her life has turned out as it has – a grandmother seven times over with a husband who can rarely take his eyes off her, living the life of a wealthy woman.

I'd finally told Netta about our father and about the money, just before I left Scotland. I was so worried about what she would say, what she would do, we'd become close during our time in Hollywood and those days of the war. She gave me that Netta look of twitchy annoyance, didn't speak for what felt like hours as I held my breath, almost running out of air as I waited for her response. And then she threw back her head and laughed. She laughed so hard she told me she had a stitch. My confusion was absolute. I couldn't understand her reaction until she said, 'Your face.' She wiped her eyes, her other hand on her chest, heaving with mirth. 'That's the best present you could ever have given me. Maisie McIntyre fearful of her sister.' She wiped her eyes again. 'Oh dear. I can't wait tae tell Eric.'

'Aren't you angry?'

'No.' She giggled. 'How can I be angry? That was so long ago. Maybe if you'd told me after you left. Maybe I should be angry at you. But there's no point now.' She came over to me and gave me a big hug. Now I was beyond astonished. Netta, just like our maw, never hugged us. 'Duncan was a good man and we did all right for ourselves. Perhaps we could have done with a little more coal on the fire, but we didn't do too badly. Now we live a good life, Maisie McIntyre, and, in a roundabout way, that one hundred and fifty pounds did it for us. If we hadn't lived that harsh life we wouldnae appreciate what we have now.'

Now I watch my sister, talking quietly to her husband, and I marvel at the changes in both of us.

Maura, now running the ready-to-wear business, bright and in her late fifties has made the journey with Eric and Netta so that she can support Oti. She and Oti became fast friends when Oti travelled to Hawick after the end of the war, during my first episode, when nobody knew what was wrong with me.

The four of them pile into the kitchen, say their 'hellos' and kiss everyone in turn, including Mandy. As coffee is poured, we hear Aidan arrive.

Aidan is beside himself at the loss of Joseph. They didn't know each other that well, but he feels the effect it has had on the rest of us.

'What a terrible day this is,' he says as he kisses everyone in turn. As always, he is wearing the latest fashionable suit, black, single-breasted with a pale-blue silk handkerchief peeking out of the breast pocket, a matching black waistcoat and turn-ups on the trousers. The white shirt and black tie have the perfect sober sheen. The buttons on his suit cuffs have been replaced with covered buttons embroidered with metallic bees, a reference to Schiaparelli's famous bee dress that Joseph worked on. As Aidan leans in to kiss me on the cheek I cannot help but touch the lapel of his jacket, made of the very best wool, I'm comforted by the expensive aftershave.

'Thank you for coming,' I say. 'I don't think I could manage this without you.'

He squeezes my shoulder and sits beside me. 'We're just missing Oti,' he whispers as he looks around the table at our tightknit group. 'She'd be making sure we've all got our tokens of respect for Joseph, ensuring they are dignified but Joseph-like.' He leans in and inspects the buttons on my jacket, giving me an Oti-like look of approval and then winking at me.

The doorbell rings and Mandy goes to find out who it is. On returning she says, 'The cars are here, we best get going.'

Amidst the usual scuffle of coats, hats and handbags, I haul myself up off the kitchen chair, check my hair in the mirror as Mandy hands me my hat, large and wide-brimmed to ensure as much of my face is hidden as possible.

'Handkerchief?' she asks.

I pat my pocket, take her arm, and we slowly make our way to the elevator.


Oti Jackson has always been a woman who holds herself upright, can keep her emotions in check and who can cause those around her to be caught up in the subject she is speaking about.

She's standing in the pulpit overlooking a full house at the Abyssinian Church in Harlem. She speaks of Joseph's life, of the architectural apprenticeship that was cut short, of his service during the Great War, of his injuries and then how he discovered embroidery, how he used it to recover, how he became one of the best embroiderers in the industry, how he set up his own company and employed other injured ex-service-men, how it helped with their physical recovery, and overcame problems with concentration, how their self-esteem was given a boost when they could again earn a decent wage. My mind wanders back to those afternoon walks, that smile, those flowers on that first day in my studio. I've been reflecting on that time so much recently, those first few years in the MacDougal Street studio, that beautiful room, the excitement of a new venture, Joseph and Oti, Simone, Rebecca, and Flavia. Life was very black and white in those days, decisions seemed easy to make – you either did or you didn't. But that decision to never fight

Joseph for his love, to let him push me away because of his fears, because of what *might* have happened was, I realise now, the greatest mistake I have made. Occasionally I think of what we could have done together, find myself thinking of the children we would have had. But it serves no purpose. He found his calling, he was able to channel his creativity through his disability; that probably would never have happened if we'd stayed together. Oti was the one who gave him that gift. I would have been too impatient, too needy, requiring instant results and quick decisions.

But my age and my illness have begun to teach me about patience, about resilience and about the needs of other people.

Funerals are, by their very nature, events that cause you to reflect. I've never been one to look back, to regret, but as I get older it seems so much easier to do. I want to remember the triumphs, the dresses that made a difference, the women who I worked with who stayed with me for all their working lives, my friendships with Rosa, with Oti, Aidan, Annina and Maura, and now with Mandy. But occasionally the regret slips in, the death of Rosa, Annina's rape, my relationship with Joseph always overriding every other regret, the *what-if*s, the *could I have done it any better*s.

Aidan touches my arm. 'Time to go,' he whispers. 'You've been in a daydream the whole service.'

I take his arm, glad to have him with me, glad to have the support of this still handsome man, unfailingly loyal despite our rocky start. We walk to the end of the church, say our greetings and thanks to the pastor and out onto the street.

'I'm going to go home now,' I say. 'Don't think I've got the heart for the reception.' I turn to face him and touch his arm. His eyes reflect the heavy sadness in my own. 'Come for dinner the day after tomorrow. I've got much to tell you.'

# Oti

Oti walks around the room quietly picking up a cushion, a picture, a book, an ornament. Slowly a big smile spreads across her face.

'You've done a good job with this place. This is how it used to be. Glad to see you've come out of the cream phase.'

We are sitting in the studio of MacDougal Street, the day after Joseph's funeral, the whole building fully refurbished and the top floor now converted into an apartment for me. My Fifth Avenue apartment, where I've been living until today, will be sold as soon as possible.

'That was a reaction to coming back to New York after the war. I was tired and hardly able to get up out of my bed. Even though I'd been craving colour after all the drabness of the previous five years, surrounded by all my fabrics and cushions and ornaments, I couldn't settle. The calming influence of cream muslin curtains, white bedlinen, and pale furniture somehow soothed me, slowed down the whirling mass in my head, let me rest and recover.'

'Glad to see you kept the sewing machine.'

By one of the big windows is my mother's sewing machine,

the one I brought over from Edinburgh. It's been fully restored and is working again, years of neglect having made it seize up. After the funeral yesterday, I used it to make the skirt of a new suit I'd designed. It was a folly, just the nostalgic foolishness of an old woman, my modern sewing machine is so much more efficient. But by sitting at that machine, I could close my eyes and think of my mother, hear her voice. Handling the fabric, cutting the threads, sewing in the zip, all helped pacify me and take away some of the melancholy after the funeral.

Oti looks across at the wall where the large pinboard used to be. Now there is a big grid covering the whole wall of ten-inch square picture frames, each one holding a piece of fabric, ranging from the first years of Maison McIntyre to last season's show.

'It's good to see these again.' She puts her hand up and touches a frame with a red patterned fabric inset with threads of gold and silver, before she turns suddenly, her hands on her hips and declares, 'You've got your colour back.' And now she gives me that Jackson smile that I've so missed, something she doesn't give away lightly.

But then her brow furrows and she comes over and sits beside me. 'So, what's all this about? I know you've been unwell, but you've been keeping me at a distance, and I haven't really had the opportunity to come and give you a piece of my mind.' She pauses to clear the emotion in her voice. 'What with Joseph being so ill, you know I'd have been here if I could.'

I smile. 'Don't worry, I know that. We'll talk about that in a minute. But first, how are you?'

She leans back in her chair and sighs. 'I'm feeling mighty relieved and because of that I'm feeling mighty guilty. He's no longer suffering and I'm thankful for that. I'm sad he lived such a closed life, shut away from the city he loved. But I'm proud of what he did, how he managed to make something good... something beautiful out of such pain.'

'You did that, you helped him become that man.'

She turns her head and gives me a flat smile. 'You'd have done it too.'

'Oh, I don't think so. You know how impatient and selfish I am. I'm no good with responsibility.'

'You'd have learned it, I had to. You'd have managed.'

I close my eyes. It's time to tell her. This guilt that's been with me for so long is eating at me. It's time I told my best friend the truth even if she never speaks to me again.

'Am I a bad person to be relieved that I no longer have to take care of him?' Oti asks, her eyes bright. 'I can't say that to Audrey, she's too judgemental.'

'No, you're not bad. I'd be thinking the same thing. You've done this for more than half your life. It's time to get on, kick off your shoes and go dancing in a new dress.'

Oti, aged seventy, is still as trim and lean as she was the day I met her, her hair now speckled with grey, always pulled back in a neat bun. She favours the two-piece suit; in fact, I can't think of a day she isn't in a suit. Today's outfit is a brown bouclé highly tailored jacket with big brown toggle buttons and an orange lining, the pencil skirt showing its contrasting lining at the long slit at the back. She favours less colour than I do, most often seen in greys, browns or blacks with a trim of colour. I've never seen her wearing anything other than a formal suit or dress. God forbid she ever considers sportswear; I've never even seen her wear a Maison McIntyre cashmere jumper.

Oti snorts. 'Me dancing? I don't think that would be very elegant, do you?'

'Just before Joseph broke off with me,' I blurt out, 'Mrs Marshall told me she'd take all her business away if I didn't get rid of him. She saw us together.' I hold my breath. This has been eating away at me for years, that I've been less than truthful to my friend, the one person who has been by my side since my first days in MacDougal Street, who has stuck with me through everything good and bad.

'When Joseph said we shouldn't see each other anymore, I was relieved.'

Oti looks down at her hands, those long elegant fingers, the pale skin on her fingertips. 'I know. I've always known that.'

I sit up straight, stunned at her response.

'But you never said anything.'

She gives me a crooked smile. I can see that she's holding in her emotion. 'Why are you telling me this now? This was forty-five years ago. What Mrs Marshall said then made no difference to what happened. You're getting yourself in a stew over nothing.'

I take a deep breath. 'The sense of relief after he said he didn't want to see me was...' I twist the ring on my left little finger, twisting and twisting it. 'It meant I didn't have to face up to the bigotry, I didn't have to make difficult choices, I didn't have to defend my decisions. It was the easy way out.' I want to get up and walk around the room, but I can't.

'I'd always thought we'd be together, maybe even get married. You know I made a dress...' I feel my voice breaking.

'He was ashamed of his inability to fight for your love, to fight for your relationship.' Oti's voice is quiet now, but there's such passion in it that my eyes are beginning to prick with the emotion. I blink hurriedly.

'And then, when his right leg had to be amputated, he was even more ashamed of his physical inabilities. He knew that you wanted to spend time with him, even if it was just as a friend, but in the end, he couldn't do it. It was easier for him not to see you. To keep your relationship professional.'

I twist the ring on my finger harder and harder.

'I have a recurring dream. The older I get the more often I have it. It's of Joseph and a little boy. Maybe he's five or six. They are sitting on the bench in Central Park where I first met

Joseph. They're happy, laughing and at ease. I think it's our child.'

I've never told anyone about this dream. It's so vivid that when I wake up I feel as if it's just happened, as if Joseph and that little boy have just left the room.

Oti now has tears in her eyes. 'He told me that he used to have a similar dream, but it was you on the bench, with that little boy. He said it was your child, that you and he had a little boy.'

I feel as if someone has punched me in the heart, is now squeezing it so tightly that it's stopped working. The pain is excruciating, a paralysing pain that means I can't even breathe.

'He only told me this on the day he died. Said he'd been having that dream for near on thirty-seven years. He knew there was nothing he could have done, so never told anyone.'

Just under thirty-seven years ago I found out that Joseph was Eveline Patience, when he threw me out and decided we couldn't be friends.

Oti gets up. She goes over to the sewing machine and sits at the table. She opens the drawer and pulls out a scrap of fabric. The machine is already threaded up and she begins to sew a pattern on the material. She talks as she sews.

'He told me that leaving you was the biggest mistake of his life, but at the same time it was the best thing he could have done. He knows, considering the circumstances, that his life was as good as it could have been, and as much as he dreamed of a life with you, he knows it would never have worked out.' She pulls out the scrap of material, cuts off the threads and brings it over to me, placing it on my lap. She's embroidered a heart in red thread on the blue fabric.

'Why are you suddenly moving back here? Seems like you're making big changes, bringing the colour back, maybe becoming less of a recluse. What's brought that on? I should be worried, but, actually, I'm relieved.'

I play with my stick, with the ebony top, the shiny knob that fits so neatly in my hand.

'I have multiple sclerosis.'

She stares and then sits down too hard.

'Shouldn't you be in a wheelchair?'

'That won't be too far off.' I sigh.

'That why you need your stick?'

'Yes.'

'How long have you had it?'

'I had my first episode right at the end of the war, just before you came over, but I didn't find out it was MS until three years later. You remember I told you I had a bad bout of flu? I couldn't get out of bed for two weeks. It was after that I was diagnosed.'

'So it wasn't the flu?'

'No. I couldn't walk. I had a bad episode.'

'You get these often?'

'More and more frequently.'

Her jaw is even more square than usual, her lips flat, her eyes blazing.

'You make me mad, *so mad*,' she growls, like a lioness who's trying to protect her cubs. 'Why did you hide it from me? Am I not your friend?' Now her eyes are red and her breathing erratic.

'I was ashamed,' I say, unable to meet her gaze. 'I *am* ashamed. I thought you would see me as a failure. I'm Maisie McIntyre, I don't have weaknesses.'

She grunts at this. 'You've got plenty of weaknesses.'

'But you didn't need another burden. You had plenty of your own.'

'So, this is why you've spent the last ten years working yourself into the ground, proving to the world that you aren't a failure?' She's almost shouting now.

I nod slowly. 'I thought by building a worldwide business,

by creating something that was bigger and better than anyone else, no one would notice my physical failures. Be the biggest and the best and nobody will care if you're a cripple.'

She stares. Contempt, anguish, love swirling all over her face. 'You're a dogonne idiot. You and Joseph were just a pair of dogonne idiots. You were like two children. Maybe you should have been together, you could have been idiots together.' She runs both her hands over her hair until the back of her head is being supported by the palms of her hands. She breathes out heavily, slowly shaking her head.

'It's like you've had some kind of mania, as if you had to prove you could do this thing, take over the world, prove that Maisie McIntyre is better than anyone.' She shakes her head again, then looks across at me. 'Who else knows?'

'Only my doctor... and Mandy.'

She rolls her eyes. 'Oh, Maisie.' Now a tear rolls down her cheek. 'You didn't even tell Aidan?'

'Especially not Aidan. He's not a man who can deal with illness. Haven't you noticed he leaves the room at the first mention of needles or blood tests, he's in bed with the lightest of colds?'

'So, what happens now?'

My mouth twists in contemplation. 'There's so little known about this disease.' I wave absently at my legs. 'No real treatment. I just have to wait for the inevitable: a wheelchair and a gradual diminishing of my physical abilities. It won't be pretty. It's not as if living a healthy and fit lifestyle will keep it at bay, it doesn't work like that. Some days my legs just won't move, however hard I tell them to. I'm on this medical trial, on a very low-fat diet, which may slow the progression. I've been doing that since the war anyway, so it wasn't difficult to do. People say it helps with the fatigue and maybe that's why I've been able to stay fairly healthy up until now. I've occasionally had cortisone injections when I've had a relapse. But to be honest, it's all a shot in the dark. There's so little information that I sometimes think just hoping for the best might be the better option.'

'So how are you going to continue working? Surely you don't have the energy to be flying across the Atlantic a few times a year, to be in and out of the studio, down at the Colour Emporium warehouse in Brooklyn, visiting the shops across the country?'

'It's time to retire.'

Oti throws me a great smile and says, 'Praise the Lord. At last!'

'I would have liked to die at my sewing machine, but my body isn't even going to let me do that. I've finally realised that if I don't slow down now, I won't be on this planet much longer. I no longer want to be the head of such a big business. Deep down, I'm just an old woman who wants to make things.' I rub at an aching pain in my jaw.

'The paperwork's all done, and I'll be announcing my retirement in the next few days. Jessica gets control of the overall company and all of you, my loyal friends, get your fair share of the company you worked for. I'm also giving you the dress archive. I'm afraid that could be a burden, there are hundreds of dresses.'

Oti raises an eyebrow before asking, 'And Jessica?'

I sigh. 'However hard I've tried to dissuade her, she's determined that this is what she wants. I don't think it will make her happy, but she will probably run it better than I've been able, and most likely make an even greater success of it than I have.

'I've stipulated that although Jessica has ownership of all the real estate, the income must go towards a charity close to my heart, even after my death. You've heard of ClothesForce, the ongoing campaign to improve conditions in garment factories.'

'I have. They do good work.'

'Tori and I set that up in 1925 and it's been funded by the income from the increasing amount of real estate I've acquired over the years. I always felt a little uncomfortable at what seemed like effortless income, and with all my guilt about what happened on the night of the Triangle fire, we set up Clothes-Force. I never want another person to die from exploitation in the garment industry. That and I had to make sure Annina was safe. She was working in one of those factories at the time. I made damn sure inspectors visited more often than they should have done. It made me physically sick knowing she worked there; I had to keep an eye on her.'

She raises an eyebrow at me. 'You're a sly thing sometimes, wanting everyone to think you're just a greedy, ambitious woman.'

'How about you? Now Joseph's gone. What are you going to do?'

She looks up and around the room, slowly eyeing the ceiling lanterns, the surroundings recently painted with the very same fuchsia pink that was there when I first arrived, she notes the newly varnished wooden floor, the large oil painting on the wall behind us, an abstract of an apple orchard in full bloom with its pinks and whites, the luminous green grass, dark flowing waters of a nearby river.

'I want to live somewhere as welcoming as this,' she says wistfully. 'Our house is still like a hospital. I don't think I can stand it much longer. I need colour again; I need to make things again. You know? I've hardly made anything for over a year now. Not a suit, not even a piece of embroidery. It's all been about caring for Joseph, administering medicine, making sure everything happens on time so that he didn't get out of sorts. And I'd like to sleep. You know, I haven't had a decent night's sleep since... I don't know when. I'd like the opportunity to stay in bed all day.'

This is my friend. We haven't sat down and talked like this in too many years. I've been hell-bent on conquering the world before my body gives up on me, she's been caring for her brother, having retired from Maison McIntyre nearly eighteen months ago. I've never made friends easily, and of the very few friends I have, she has been the most constant, the most honest, the funniest.

'Come and live here,' I say.

She holds my gaze. I see a mix of emotions: amusement, fear, thankfulness, relief, astonishment. But she doesn't answer, only getting up from her chair, a little stiffly, and walking over to the bag she left on the table. She pulls out a magazine.

'Have you seen this month's *Vogue?*' she says as she passes me the magazine. 'There's a portrait in there you should see. I've marked the page.'

I take the magazine and it falls open to a sumptuous black and white photograph of an elderly woman, a tiny stick of a woman with a ridiculous bouffant hairstyle. She's standing in front of an austere marble fireplace, flowers in the place of a fire, huge silver candelabra on each end of the mantelpiece, a vase, possibly Ming, in the centre. She's wearing a full-length pale duchess satin gown, straight cut and sleeveless with a square neckline, and matching full-length satin gloves. She has a dark velvet cape which she holds back with both hands on her hips, a look of defiance on her wrinkled face, her chin slightly pushed upwards, an enormous diamond necklace adorning her neck.

'Mrs Rex Marshall,' I whisper, 'wearing Maison McIntyre.' Something dislodges in my throat, I have to cough to cover it, tears pooling in my eyes.

I have had no contact with Julia Marshall since the day the Colour Emporium opened. Aidan always relishes telling me of her latest insults, I have been told how many people have been warned off me by my very first client.

'Did you know about this?' I ask Oti.

'Yes,' she says, her eyes twinkling with mischief. 'She and I worked closely on the dress and cape. It was a little bit of sanity whilst Joseph was so ill. Let me remember what it was to create again.'

'You just said you hadn't made a thing for over a year! Did you just flat-out lie to me, Otella Jackson?' I ask in mock outrage.

'If you were listening properly, Maisie McIntyre, I said I'd *hardly* made a thing in the last year. There's a difference.' She says this with her dark, beady eyes crinkled at the edges, flickers of light seeming to bloom across her face. 'It was Annina who insisted I design and make the dress. She said that was the only way Maison McIntyre would take the work.'

'And the photoshoot?'

'*Vogue* commissioned Cecil Beaton to shoot it for Mrs M's birthday. He was the one who insisted she wear a Maison McIntyre design. He'd done his research, knew that it was you that launched her into society. He thought it was fitting for her to go back to her roots.'

'She can't have liked any of that.'

'Apparently, according to Jessica Daves, there was an almighty ruckus. But that editor said she wouldn't have her photographed in any other way. It was a Maison McIntyre dress or nothing.' She laughs, leaning over towards me to pick up the magazine. 'Wouldn't you have liked to be a fly on the wall during that conversation?' And then abruptly she bends over and rubs her knee. 'Think I'm getting housemaid's knee. I've done nothing but wash and scrub and clean for the last few days. Feel like I need to get the smell of death and illness and sadness out of that apartment.' Gently she rubs the kneecap in a circular motion, soothing and hypnotic.

'Come and live here,' I repeat.

She stops the circular motion, frowns, thinks, undoes a jacket button, does it up again. She's blinking furiously, looking away from me, trying to hide her emotions.

'We haven't let out the apartment below yet. You could live

there. Now that I've put an elevator in you can come up any time, housemaid's knee or no housemaid's knee.'

She's still blinking, but now starts to flick through the magazine until she finds what she's looking for. 'You seen this?' She holds up a photograph of a young model wearing a tunic dress with a hemline well above the knee. 'You heard of Mary Quant?'

'A little,' I say, distracted by her lack of response.

'You seen these tunic dresses? Seen how short they are? Just like you said all those years ago. I know I'm an old woman, but this is too much.' She bats the picture with the back of her hand, clicking her tongue in disapproval.

I can do nothing but laugh. 'Always a prude, Oti Jackson.'

We're silent, the unanswered question still hanging in the air.

'If I live here, what are two old ladies going to do with themselves? We can't just sit here and reminisce, that's not a good thing to do. I need to be busy, making something, creating something. Can't just sit twiddling my thumbs, I'll be dead before you know it. Not going to waste this time, having been nothing but a nurse for the last year or so, I've got some living to catch up on.'

'I wondered if you'd like to help me with something.' I rub that ache in my jaw again.

'You got toothache?' Oti asks. 'You've been rubbing that jaw the whole time I've been here.'

'Probably. I'll get it seen to,' I say, wanting to dismiss any talk of my health. 'But I've been thinking about trying to recreate those shawls Rosa used to make. I've seen nothing on the market that comes anywhere near them. Annina tried but it wasn't her strength, so I thought I'd give them a go. They're complicated, intricate and full of colour, they remind me of Rosa and also have that connection to Scotland. I'd like to see if we could make them commercially viable.'

'What? Two old ladies sitting here knitting. Are you serious? Sounds like you've gone and lost your mind.' Her eyes are
wide. 'I was thinking about travelling a bit, going to some of
those nightclubs down in Harlem, getting out of these suits and
putting on a colourful dress, not cosying up with a pair of knitting needles and a ball of wool.'

I laugh. How good that feels. 'I was thinking more along the
lines of creating the designs here and when we were happy with
them, we'd send them to Maura in Hawick and get her to make
them up on the machines, using the soft cashmere. So, no, we
wouldn't be sitting here churning out shawls and scarves like
two old women.'

She leans back in her chair. 'Thank goodness.'

'Don't worry, I have every intention of making the most of
the time I have left.'


I wake the next morning after the best night's sleep I've had in
months. Usually I wake in the night, my feet feeling cold and
my legs almost paralysed. But I slept through; maybe all that
reminiscing was good for me. My legs are better than usual. I
know it won't last but I'm going to make the most of it whilst
I can.

Mandy is here to help me get up.

'You got toothache?' she asks.

I press into my jaw, momentarily relieving the dull pain. 'I
think so.'

'I'll make you a dentist appointment,' she says as she puts
my shoes down by my feet.

I look down at my shoes, my hateful shoes. I can no longer
wear anything with a heel, I need to have sensible, stabilising
shoes that help prevent me from falling over. I must concentrate
when I walk now, I can't even talk when I'm taking the stairs in
case I'm distracted and then, no doubt, I'll fall. I long for my

everyday high heels that made my ankles look elegant, made me taller and improved my posture. Now I have these soft, rubber-soled fat flipper-like shoes that make me want to cry at the inelegance of them. I'd rather wear sneakers. How delicious it would be to wear a pair of those Converse basketball boots with an evening dress.

'I'd like to take a walk today,' I say.

Mandy looks at me quizzically. 'You sure your legs are up for that?'

I nod. 'Only a short one, but there's somewhere I'd like to go, somewhere I'd like to walk to whilst I still can.'

# Joseph

The yellow cab drops us close to the Bethesda Fountain, and I ask Mandy if she can give me half an hour by myself. She is always somewhere close by, keeping an eye out for me, making sure I've not fallen, doing her best to let me hide my inabilities. I can see she's nervous about leaving me alone, but I think she realises there's something I must do.

Mandy helps me down the stairs to the fountain and then leaves me to walk along the shore of the Lake until I find the bench. I must look like one of those old widows that I used to watch. I'm hunched over my stick, in my new dark-blue silk suit, a straight, mid-calf skirt and single-breasted, straight-cut jacket with mandarin collar. The Maison McIntyre colour is in the red contrasting double cuffs, collar and the matching bright-red frog buttons.

The bench. It's the bench where I was sitting when I first met Joseph, where I first saw that smile, where my life in Manhattan really began. I sit at one end and look out over the water. It's a warm end-of-summer day. A few boats are out on the Lake, a toddler staggers past me, his mother behind, ready to catch him. I smile at the irony of it; that's me, I've gone full circle, Mandy is the one who now waits behind me whilst I shuffle along, feet going slap, thud, slap, thud, trying my very best not to fall over. I lean back and close my eyes, enjoy the heat of the sun on my face, just like I had then, forty-seven years ago. Now I don't have that excitement, that fizzing in my stomach as I'd looked forward to a whole life ahead, now I have a leaden dread in my legs. Then I felt as if anything could happen, as if I could open all those doors ahead of me. Today those doors are slowing shutting, becoming heavier and heavier, more and more difficult to push open. Still with my eyes closed, I can smell the water so close to me, hear a whisper of the leaves in the tree behind me, an efficient click-click of women's shoes, and then the rustling of a paper bag, the smell of something familiar but I can't place it, it's too far away in my memory bank, I can't quite reach it.

'Here you go. New York's finest soft pretzel.' I recognise the voice, gentle and thoughtful.

Opening my eyes I see Joseph kneeling down in front of me. He's the Joseph I first knew, the beautiful, smooth-skinned Joseph, in a white collarless shirt, with the sleeves rolled up and tucked into a pair of brown woollen trousers and flat cap. There's that little vertical scar that cuts through his left eyebrow, like a chalk mark. The sadness that comes over me when I realise that I never found out how he got that scar almost makes me weep, but I can't do that because he's smiling that overwhelming Jackson smile that makes my heart hurt so hard I have to put my hand to my chest and catch my breath, tears beginning to gather in my eyes.

'This'll help,' he says, handing me the paper bag with a fresh pretzel in it. He does that nervous double blink, before getting up and bringing over the boy, that boy I dream about, those wild black curls framing his slightly chubby face, the youthful soft skin and almost green eyes. He also has a pretzel in his small hand and that Jackson smile that's anticipating the treat to come. They both sit beside me. I look out over towards the Lake, the light catching the ripples on the water, winking at me conspiratorially as I try to understand what's going on, whether I'm dreaming, having fallen asleep on this bench and fantasising about a parallel world that could have been. I turn to the two of them again and Joseph gestures at me to eat my pretzel, the boy already eating, a cheeky grin amongst the chewing. I take a wee bite. I'm dazed by the warm, pillowy, salty, yeasty taste, so evocative of my early years in New York, of my relationship with Joseph, of those long walks we used to take, those yellow daffodils he gave me on my first day in my studio, of the tiny bolts of electricity whenever I brushed his arm, of the softness of his cheek when I'd kissed it, the slight pain in my heart as I'd yearned for more. My whole chest seems to expand with the effect of the pretzel, the memories, the smells, the tastes, the touch. I can hardly breathe, but I don't care, everything about this moment is delicious.

He leans over and takes my hand, putting it gently on his knee and keeps a hold of it, his head nodding unhurriedly. There are none of the usual sounds, just a roaring in my ears as his touch sends a tidal wave of warmth surging through my body, releasing the dread and the fear that's been building in me over the last few years. Suddenly the life ahead of me doesn't seem so horrifying, I feel at ease, as if it's a Sunday afternoon and the three of us are out for a stroll with nowhere we need to be; we can amble at our own pace, we can look down at the beetle in the grass, we can throw a morsel of pretzel to the ducks in the Lake, the boy sits on his haunches in that endearing way children do, picking at a flower in the grass. Joseph puts his arm around me and it feels as if every ache and pain, those dead legs and all that fatigue have just drained away leaving me feeling as if we are floating, arm in arm.

I let out a sigh of long-wished-for contentment.

New York Times, *September 26, 1958*

## *Maisie McIntyre, world-renowned couturier, dies aged 68.*

Maisie McIntyre, who, for more than half a century, led the couture house Maison McIntyre, dressing the likes of Mrs Harriet Bailey Parsons, Mrs Rex Marshall, film star Helen Montrose and more recently the former First Lady Mrs Eleanor Roosevelt and Mrs Jacqueline Kennedy, wife of Senator John F. Kennedy, died suddenly in New York yesterday.

Miss McIntyre was revered for her use of colour and embellishment in her couture creations, rivalling designers such as Schiaparelli and the House of Lanvin. Her work was marked out as extraordinary when she began using the embroidery atelier Joseph Jackson, set up by the brother of Miss McIntyre's Premier, Otella Jackson. Her support of a company that employed wounded veterans was seen as groundbreaking.

Miss McIntyre often courted speculation, her outfits revealing her unfashionable opinions: a dress championing the vote for women during a charity event for the Great War, a black trouser suit with colourful trimmings worn to her long-time lover's funeral.

Born in Edinburgh, Scotland in 1890, she moved to New York when she was nineteen. She was employed by the Triangle Shirtwaist Factory but missed working the day of the infamous fire, which killed many of her friends. She set up her own business soon after, moving into her first studio on MacDougal Street. In 1914 she opened the first Colour Emporium shop on Fifth Avenue, a revolutionary homewares business that was to expand and become a worldwide phenomenon. She ran the costume *department at Samuel Goldwyn Productions for four years before moving to Hawick, Scotland, where she remained for the duration of the Second World War, running a hosiery factory, eventually leading to the set-up of her ready-to-wear business McIntyre Cashmere, well known for its colourful cashmere cardigans, jumpers and jackets.*

*Although the cashmere, couture and homewares businesses have been rapidly expanding since the war, there had been rumours of ill-health and financial troubles.*

*Miss McIntyre never married but is survived by her daughter, Jessica Smyth-Black, whose father was the murdered Senator Torridon Smyth. Miss Smyth-Black will take over as CEO of Maison McIntyre, the Colour Emporium and McIntyre Cashmere.*

*Miss McIntyre's body was found on a park bench in Central Park, three fresh pretzels placed in a neat row beside her. Police believe she died of a heart attack and have ruled out foul play.*

# A Letter from the Author

Dear Reader

Thank you so much for reading *The Rebel of Seventh Avenue*. I hope you enjoyed it. If you'd like to find out about further book releases, you can sign up to my newsletter here:

www.stormpublishing.co/annabelle-marx

I'd appreciate it if you could leave a review and let other readers know about Maisie and her band of unconventional friends.

I'm ashamed to admit that I am no seamstress – I can't knit (I get into terrible knots and drop stitches all over the place), my husband leaves the house when I try to make curtains because the swearing is so bad, I've been known to do a bit of needlepoint, but my last effort is half-finished, not touched for over twenty years. But my mother is a terrific needlewoman – she knits, quilts, embroiders, used to make curtains, children's clothes... the list goes on. Unfortunately, I didn't inherit that gene. But I love the *idea* of making, of being creative with thread or wool or silk. When I'm around high fashion, delicate embroidery or colourful quilts I find that stories are whispering in my ear, there's a little fizz in my stomach, that I need to sit down with my notebook and pen.

When I had the original idea for this book, I took myself off to places where I could be surrounded by the very things that inspired me – needlework and colour. I was lucky enough to be able to see the Chanel exhibition at the V&A in London in 2023, a Kaffe Fassett show of his vibrant quilts in Bath, as well as Candace Bahouth's kaleidoscopic mosaics. The Crown to Couture exhibition at Kensington Palace had me running for the café and sitting for hours, ideas pouring out. Just looking through a book of Christian Dior's designs had me in a creative stupor.

And that's how the story of Maisie McIntyre came about. I enveloped myself in some of the world's most innovative designs and ideas and used their genius to create a narrative full of colour and creativity.

Thank you again for reading my novel, I truly appreciate your readership. If you'd like to follow me on social media where I talk about books, writing, Scotland and a lot about my inspiration, I'd love to hear from you.

facebook.com/annabellemarxwrites

instagram.com/annabellemarx_writes

linkedin.com/in/annabelle-marx-284046200

# Author's Note

For the many historical references and real-life events that I use in this story, I have tried to keep true to their historical timeline and accuracy, such as the Triangle Shirtwaist Factory Fire in 1911, the suffrage parade in 1912, and the Fashion Fête in 1914, but occasionally I have changed the timings to suit my story.

I brought forward the death of Harriet Quimby and the Democratic National Convention in Baltimore from 1 July 1912 to mid-May, to coincide with Maisie's creative surge. The Goodwill charity was founded in 1902 but I struggled to discover whether it had expanded to Los Angeles by the late 1930s, but I liked the idea of Netta using her knitting skills to clothe those children of California affected by the ongoing Depression.

The building at 130 MacDougal Street does have that beautiful cast-iron double-porch, the lacey filigree is there for all to see, but those beautiful ceiling lanterns that created so much light in Maisie's first studio have been stolen from elsewhere. They belong in a former Friends Meeting House in Bath, England, which is now home to the fabulous bookshop, Topping & Co.

# Acknowledgements

A novel is made up of many threads, on which the author is reliant to ensure the novel makes sense, is true to its purpose and is publishable. These are just a few of those threads that I am very grateful for.

The staff in the Brooke Astor Reading Rooms at the New York Public Library where I spent hours poring through the minutes of the meetings of The Fashion Group International. The staff at the British Library, Bath Spa University Library and Bath Central Library. Emily Hart and all the staff at the Hawick Heritage Hub. Caroline Little and all the staff at the Hawick Library. Shona Sinclair and Gordon Macdonald at the Hawick Museum. Allan Godfrey at Teviot Knitwear Ltd. Thank you all for your time and boundless energy.

To Geoff and Barbara Whitten for giving us a bed and hearty welcome whilst we spent time researching in the Borders of Scotland.

Lily Lucas at Ulla Johnson, for giving me an invaluable insight into the fashion world in New York.

The Tenement Museum in Orchard Street, New York.

The online fashion archives from the V&A Museum, London and the Met Museum, New York have been an invaluable resource.

My Creative Writing MA pals who have been nothing but encouraging, enthusiastic and supportive, but never afraid to tell me where I'm going wrong. My heartfelt thanks to everyone who I studied with and for their thoughtful feedback, but most especially to the finest of writers, Sarah Wright, Samantha Stewart and Diana Smith, as well as my tutors at Bath Spa University: Nathan Filer, Richard Kerridge, Philip Hensher and the peerless Celia Brayfield.

Claire Abernethy and all her team at Dexter's Coffee Shop, Bath, for supplying some of the best coffee, as well as everyone at Mother & Wild, Corsham. This book has been built on a sturdy foundation of good strong, black coffee.

Luigi Di Pasquale for checking my Italian. Any mistakes are wholly mine.

My long-standing early readers: Amanda Wylie, for being the bravest of my friends and giving me such a detailed insight into MS; Kassia Scott for the enlightening 'plot walks' and helping me out with some knotty problems; my mother, Rosemary Briggs, for constant encouragement and catching glaring errors.

Of course, none of this would have got anywhere without my agent, Jenny Brown, of Jenny Brown Associates, who loved this story and has championed Maisie and her band of outsiders before I'd hardly even put pen to paper. To have Jenny's support has been the greatest revelation of my writing career.

Huge thanks go to Claire Bord, my editor at Storm, who has nurtured this story and helped me turn it into something with greater resonance and nuance, and for that I am truly grateful. The careful copy-editing of Jane Eastgate, plus the organisation skills of Alexandra Begley, whose other superpower seems to be mindreading. For Becca Allen's precise proofreading. I've loved working with everyone at Storm; they've made the once scary world of publishing seem welcoming and inclusive.

Of course, absolutely none of this would have ever happened without the support and love of my family. To my husband, Andy, for putting up with being dragged around a *freezing* New York and for supplying chauffeuring skills and feeding me during my research trip to Hawick whilst trying to juggle his own work. I am forever in awe of your unwavering support. And to our sons, Harry and Harvey, who have always believed that this is what I should do. This book is for all of three of you.